e kept

ved

THE
WINGS OF
MORNING

Karen Harper

THE
WINGS OF
MORNING

A DUTTON BOOK

DUTTON

Published by the Penguin Group
Penguin Books USA Inc., 375 Hudson Street, New York, New York 10014, U.S.A.
Penguin Books Ltd, 27 Wrights Lane, London W8 5TZ, England
Penguin Books Australia Ltd, Ringwood, Victoria, Australia
Penguin Books Canada Ltd, 10 Alcorn Avenue, Toronto, Ontario, Canada M4V 3B2
Penguin Books (N.Z.) Ltd, 182–190 Wairau Road, Auckland 10, New Zealand

Penguin Books Ltd, Registered Offices:
Harmondsworth, Middlesex, England

First published by Dutton, an imprint of New American Library,
a division of Penguin Books USA Inc.
Distributed in Canada by McClelland & Stewart Inc.

First Printing, June, 1993
1 3 5 7 9 10 8 6 4 2

 REGISTERED TRADEMARK—MARCA REGISTRADA

LIBRARY OF CONGRESS CATALOGING IN PUBLICATION DATA:
Harper, Karen.
    The wings of morning / Karen Harper.
        p.   cm.
    ISBN 0-525-93614-9
    1. Saint Kilda (Scotland)—History—Fiction.   2. Sanibel Island
(Fla.)—History—Fiction.   I. Title.
PS3558.A624792W56   1993
813'.54—dc20   92-39272
                                                                     CIP

Printed in the United States of America
Set in Sabon

Designed by Steven N. Stathakis

*To Don and my "Scotland-loving" friends
in Columbus, especially Beth Ann Daye*

The triumphs and tragedies of the people of St. Kilda—including the treatment of women and the shocking fate of the children— actually happened. With the exception of the minor characters of Lady Grange and John McKay, the people of this novel are fictional, but their story is all too true.

I have been unable to locate another novel that uses the setting of the luring Scottish Island of St. Kilda, although several nonfiction books have been written by rare early visitors. I have endeavored to be as accurate as my research allowed to portray this unique people and its customs.

—KAREN HARPER

PROLOGUE

Long after the silver gloaming had deepened to darkness, Abigail heard her lover's secret signal, nearly swept away by wind: "Yo-ou, you, yo-ou!" Douglas imitated the long-beaked curlew's cry so perfectly, she thought, not even a canny fowler would ken it was a lad calling his lass and not a bird its mate.

Abigail's half-darned stocking tumbled from her hand. She lowered the wick of her lamp, seized her plaid shawl, and peeked out the door to be certain no one was in the street at this end of the village.

She fled on her familiar, fleet-footed way, fretting that there must be more to this summons than the usual invitation. She had bid Douglas goodnight a scant hour ago at their lofty trysting place they called the castle, tucked in the rocky folds of Mullach Sgar. In his calling her again, so soon and so late, she scented danger or disaster. He should be home, helping his father mend the climbing rope for the old man's journey tomorrow. Surely their meetings had not been discovered, else his mother or village folk would have been at her door ere now. For years she and Douglas had been, of necessity, skillful at stealing hidden hours; now, Douglas had said, finally freedom was but a week away!

She left the silent sprawl of village street and took the upland rise easily in stride. She could hear the muted boom of breakers crumpling against cliffs below; her heart boomed as hard. She had forgotten bonnet or kerch, and her waist-length hair whipped free. Crisp air bit deep into her lungs, and soon her muscles heated with the ache of the climb.

Ignoring the meandering path, she scrambled higher. The stalks of new heather under her feet merged with the pebbly slide of rocks from the peaks of Mullach Sgar to make footing more perilous. She knotted her shawl over her breasts to free her hands should she skid or fall. But she was only to the first big boulder when she heard "yo-ou, you, yo-ou" again. She turned toward the sound.

Douglas's broad-shouldered form loomed large against the gray arch of sky. His straw-blond hair glimmered white, but his deep-set eyes and slash of firm mouth hid in black shadow. Balanced on the steep slope, he came closer, clasping her upper arms, then pulling her into his embrace. She held to him, her face pressed against his wool jerkin. He clamped her closer, his chin against her temple, his powerful arms and thick wrists like metal bands around her.

"Abby lass! I'm in a rush, so we shalna go up to the castle."

"My love, what's amiss?"

"All of a sudden, father says I must go to Boreray with the men tomorrow, and for so long without ye! But Parliament decided one young cragsman should go too. Edmund Drummond put my name forward, and they gave approval to a man."

Abigail heard the pride in his voice rise above his disappointment. She heaved a sigh of mingled relief and regret. When St. Kilda climbers went for gannet feathers on the nearby outlier of Boreray, they stayed for several days, as there was no place to land a boat. The fowlers leapt ashore and the crew came back for them later, depending on weather and tides. She was proud her lad had been selected, but grieved he would, no doubt, be gone next week.

"I'm glad for you, my Douglas," she murmured as she drew in

the manly scent of him, mingled with salt air. "At least, your news isna someone saw us, as I feared."

"To tell true, but for leaving ye, I'm glad to try those cliffs. 'Tis a test of even braw climbers' skills to get ashore with waves rising and falling so high at every pitch!" he said, as if he saw it all this very moment. "The gannets must be taken at night, ye ken. Aye, the cragsman's at his best there, and it's no sabbath stroll! But," he lowered his voice and pressed his lips to the wild hair at her temple, "to be there and ye here, the very day we been waiting for so long . . ."

He tugged her above a nearby outcrop of rock so he could lean on it and she, full-length, against him. She reveled in his hunger for her; her own need swelled. The bittersweet lure of their yet unfulfilled passion made her knees go weak, but she wondered if his desire right now was not more for his grand adventure than for her.

"Time will crawl without the hope of seeing you, even for a stolen moment," she told him.

"Ye'll stay busy as I. I couldna just have ye surprised to see me depart tomorrow with everybody standing by. I had to say a right farewell, even if for a wee while."

"But when—" she got out before his lips covered hers, and she opened her mouth willingly to tempt him deeper.

Since their youthful friendship had bloomed to adult love, they had struggled with themselves and each other to be clever, controlled, and careful. They had fought plunging themselves into the familial act for which they so longed. Often they had been only a step from that precipice, but had not fallen completely. They had vowed to await the blessed day next week when Douglas Adair turned twenty-one and when, as a far isles man, all things were then possible.

The reasons their love and union were frowned upon, and thus forbidden, were a twisted skein: his peoples' pride, her parents' past—and Douglas's lofty perch in the islanders' regard from which she feared she could topple him, however much she loved him.

His breath came harsh as he broke the kiss and tipped her back in his arms. "I wanted us to be together on my manhood day. I wanted to decide and share everything then, whatever they do!"

"What can they do when you are a man and sit in the island Parliament? Only, I fear that—"

"Fear naught, lass! Only that we have had to wait so long for the real loving, the one thing that would bind ye even tighter to me!"

"And maybe make a bairn before 'tis proper, my own dearest," she reminded him. She poked him in the ribs but her voice sounded sad and heavy. "I want a child with you more than life itself, Douglas Adair, but not 'til everything is right. Life is hard enough for bairns here even when their parents not be tempting the way of things."

"True enough," he agreed, "but when I ask ye right and proper—well, just ye practice reciting yer 'Aye, my love!' while I be gone then. And, think of this!"

He crushed her to him again, lips and limbs. Though she fought to keep her head for both of them, passion louder than the sea roared in her ears. His beard stubble rasped her chin and upper lip, but it was a thrilling ache. Her mouth felt sweetly swollen when he finally, slowly set her back; she wet her lips to taste him yet again.

"And when I return," he vowed, his voice gone rough, "we'll be done with this blasted burrowing about like puffins to mate! And things shalna ever go wrong for us again! I'll send ye home alone now, and, for the last time, I swear it, Abigail MacQueen. Tomorrow, ye'll get a mere nod and wink when I set off, but there will be much more when I return, no matter if they think we must have tricked them all these years!"

She squeezed his hand as they started back down the slope. She prayed all would be well so they could walk and talk together in daylight as well as darkness. But she still feared, deep down, what she had been terrified to tell him lately, the one thing her braw lad had never fathomed. If St. Kilda folk frowned upon Douglas Adair's bold decision to take Abigail MacQueen to wife, for his sake and that of the islanders, though it would be the very death of her, she must find the strength, the love, to tell him no.

Part 1

St. Kilda
1851–1858

And then I loved thee,
And showed thee all the qualities o' th' isle.
                                    —SHAKESPEARE
                                The Tempest I, ii, 336

Too late, women see the thrust of the storm,
If love for a man be too strong.
Wave walls smash our islands worn by the sea
For all the world's ways that go wrong.
                                    —ABIGAIL ADAIR
                                A St. Kilda hearthsong

1

St. Kilda's far isle,
Bold-browed, spray-swept,
Crags, clefts, winds, waters,
Snared from sky and wild sea.
Old hearthsongs sang thus to me.

Questions questing,
Awestruck astonishment
Snare me and my lad,
Till hand-in-hand we fly free.
My heart-wings sang thus to me.

Tall, red-haired Abigail MacQueen
leapt from slick boulder to boulder above the swirl and shift of
foaming green water. Her long legs were bared to half-thigh; her
toes skillfully gripped the slick surface of the stones. She had removed and knotted her stockings about her hips and caught up her
hems to save her skirts from a sloshing. A wool belt of rainbow
hues cinched her brown gown at her waist. Pushed back from her
oval face by twisted heather, her long hair whipped free. She had
stuck her small, sheathed dirk behind her ear for safekeeping. She
held a cloth sack in her teeth so both arms were free to balance her
bounding progress across the low-tide inlet between St. Kilda and
the rocky ridge of Dun.

Her rich, deep voice hummed her song through the sack as if
to challenge the cacaphony of wind, water, and birds. To set free the
words of her own making, she seized the sack in one hand and let
the song pour forth. Then, she seemed to fly across the boulder

bridge with freedom and exuberance, like a flapping, soaring bird of brown and russet plumage.

Reaching her destination, she propped her bare feet on a boulder and leaned back against the sheltering rock drapery of Dun. She untied her stockings, and wriggled into their knee-high, thick wool warmth. She thrust her dirk into her belt, then pulled a chunk of cheese and a barley bannock from her sack and devoured them.

She tried to tell herself that the day was too lovely and life too wonderful to let her great trial turn her hopes to black stone like this rock against which she rested. She breathed in deeply, then began to sing again. But that drifted to humming, then silence. Her heart was as heavy as the old hearthsongs, and she soon turned to brooding.

Abigail was two months from age twenty-one, but her beloved Douglas reached that venerated age today. Though St. Kildan folk made no great show of birthdays, twenty-one marked the time a lad formally became a man and was allowed to sit in the daily decision-making gathering of island men called Parliament. And a man could marry whatever lass he willed, no matter what his folks, kin, or the other men counseled—and therein lay her dire dilemma.

"Aye, Douglas, my love, wish you were here to turn my head, but 'tis my burden to decide too, and that's the way of it." She glanced in the direction where the steep-sided cliffs of Boreray, which her Douglas climbed, lay, four miles off St. Kilda. But broad granite Oiseval Mountain blocked her view just as she feared the St. Kildans might block her way to Douglas. She shook her head and deftly climbed to rocks above the high-tide line where she would find lichens for her dyes.

She knew she would be alone here today to make her momentous decision, for none of the other women ventured out this far. Still, she always offered to share these lichens which produced the unique rose and crimson dyes the islanders would not use for tradition's sake. But forgoing a life with Douglas would be a thousand times worse than forsaking her dreams and desire for brilliant-colored clothes!

"I ken you St. Kildans fancy the bright hues," she muttered, "so why let the old ways keep you from wearing or selling them, you stubborn Scots!" Her high brow furrowed as her thoughts fled to Douglas again.

Abigail had loved Douglas as long as she had memories, and he loved her in return. They had been reared in neighboring cottages, and though their folks had never kept company—to say the least of it—the children had. As mere bairns, Douglas and Abigail had protested heartily when they found they were expected to act differently because lads and lasses had separate paths to tread.

Like all island lads, Douglas Adair had learned the bold skills of a fowler and climber. At age three, he clung to the rough, rounded cottage stones; as a lad of twelve, he skillfully clambered up clefts to leave other boys far behind; at fourteen, he scaled sky-high cliffs to harvest birds. Now, he was admired as one of the island's youngest of a select group of fowlers called cragsmen, a hero soon worthy of his own hearthsong. But always in his ascent to manhood, though Abigail had heavy, earth-bound woman's work to do, she and Douglas had smiled and shared whispers in the dusk between their cottages at day's end.

Even in lamp-lighted rooms with the others, their eyes had met, eagerly then shyly, in the years of their youths. When his parents subtly then stringently forbade them to keep company, they secretly defied them. Today, Douglas no longer needed his family's nor Parliament's approval for anything. Only, now, nearly too late, Abigail realized that for him to ignore them might mean disaster for his reputation and his future—and endanger the island's welfare too.

Lately, as reality had come home to roost, she saw their union might hurt him more than help him. It would probably cause a rift in the Adair family, and she could not bear that, even if Margaret, his sister and her best friend, sided with her and Douglas. Margaret was Douglas's younger, married sister and Abigail's boon companion. Theirs was a frowned-upon friendship too, for Margaret's mother approved of it only a bit more than she did Abigail's so much as speaking to Douglas. Some villagers, though none said it to her face, evidently still saw the stain of her parents upon her, and would, no doubt, think she was unsuitable to wed him. Then, even if the marriage did take place, she feared she would not be the dutiful and sweetly meek wife Douglas needed as he rose in St. Kildan admiration over the years. If people disapproved of her, Parliament could cut back his duties, though that would endanger the food and other supplies a great cragsman would harvest over the years for the island's profit and very survival. No one had ever been exiled from the island, but they might be ostracized: to be an island on an island as her father had once been—she could not face that for herself nor consign her beloved to such a fate.

And yet, if she told Douglas he should wed another, even the bonny Flora Fergusson, whose green eyes followed him everywhere, Abigail feared the consequence of his fierce anger and bitter agony as well as her own desolation. He might claim she had led him on and betrayed him. She kenned well how hurtful words flowed from a man's wounded pride by listening to her father after he was abandoned, especially after her mother's death. And if Douglas did not understand it was all for his own good and turned against her, she might as well cast herself off the cliff of Oiseval as some folks said her mother had one stormy night.

"Blast, my dearest lad, I fear I wilna have the strength to tell you no!" she fervently admonished the slick rocks, but she saw only Douglas's beloved face before her again.

She heaved flat, gray-green lichens into her sack so hard some bounced back out. Finally, she turned to rest her elbows on an outcrop of rock, frowning in concentration until the beauty of the outer weather again lured her attention from her inner storm.

Though clouds often clustered to blur then blot the scene, today the sky was brilliant blue and the sun warmed her. Its midafternoon heat beat down on the passage from the southwest, illuminating a green-walled cave carpeted by ruffled, sun-gilt sea. To her left, the far end of the passage took the fury of the westering waves; the east end, which emptied into the curved harbor of Village Bay, ebbed with the gentle flow of waters protected by the bold, black breakwater of the Dun, which once had been part of the island. These far isles, called St. Kilda, were comprised of this island, its smaller outliers, Soay and Boreray, and several now stranded stacks of stone. St. Kilda lay forty miles farther west from Scotland than the Outer Hebrides and seemed to those few outsiders who ventured here to be the rocky roof of the world arising from the depths of the north Atlantic.

From this sheltering arm of Dun, the view was spectacular, even to one who was used to it. Above and around her, goldheaded, white-bodied gannets darted and dove for fish. She wondered how many Douglas had gathered on Boreray; it took nigh on two hundred forty of them to provide feathers for one good mattress in Glasgow. From her view here, graceful, gliding fulmars, on which the island greatly depended for its food and other supplies, seemed to drench St. Kilda in a blizzard of bickering bills and wild wings. Feathers floated in the air like strange-shaped snowflakes. On this side of Dun's serrated spine, she admired green grass cropped by sheep and the spongy turf burrowed by puffins, which were just now returning from their winter migrations. For centuries, the arrivals and departures of the many birds that made the isles their home had governed the St. Kildan calendar.

Beyond the sheltered arc of dark blue Village Bay lay the islander's homes in a sweep of a single street overlooking all this God-given wonder. From this distance, the thirty-two stone cottages that comprised the island's only inhabited town of one hundred ten folk seemed a crescent of fairy-size buildings: the church; the minister's gray stone, slate-roofed manse on the far end; then the factor's house before the curve of smaller, lower thatched cottages; hers, called Lady Grange's cottage, one of the oldest, was at this end nearest Dun and lofty Mullach Sgar.

Above the village, the irregular stone sheep pens and the walled cemetery climbed the rocky hillside toward clouds encircling the stony steeps of Carn Mor and Oiseval mountains. Beneath the village lay the strips of fields which, in its windy wrath, sea-savaged Dun doused with spray like rain. Abigail licked her lips and tasted the familiar salty tang. The villagers were used to it, but not the crops, meager and sporadic most years. The seasonal harvesting of birds was for survival as well as feather rent to their landlord, the laird, MacLeod of Harris. The man himself never set foot here, but each June he sent his factor for a month to land his smack on rough rock to collect the woolen cloth and feathers that were his due.

"Abby! Ab-i-gail!" floated to her on the wind. Her head jerked up. She squinted across and up the boulder-strewn gap she had crossed. Margaret Gillies waved to her from the last grassy height before the rocky shore below began.

"Wha-at?" Abigail's strong voice lilted back across the gap. It was those bell-clear tones more than the talent of her heart-wings— her imagination—to create new songs that had made her the only woman hearthsinger at her young age. Quickly, just to be certain Douglas's boat had not appeared, Abigail shaded her brow and squinted across the harbor. No sign of any craft yet, so Margaret had not come to tell that. She scrambled to strip off her socks before leaping back to the mainland.

"Yer waaant-ed . . ." came to Abigail's ears as she made her way across, though she could not discern the rest.

Wanted by whom, she wondered, but her friend's form, heavy with an eight-month burden of an unborn bairn, had now disappeared from view. *You're wanted.* The words echoed in her head and heart as she balanced her way back across the slick stones. Wanted by Douglas, she knew that. Wanted by the villagers to make fine cheese and traditional dyes and to sing the old hearth-songs and not create new ones questioning the way things were. Wanted by the factor's resident accountant here, Edmund Drummond, whom she had refused to wed. And she had been wanted and loved by her parents, for, with her two brothers' infant deaths, she had been an only child. But today she had no time for those thoughts as Margaret, too, wanted her.

Just as with Douglas, Abigail could not recall her childhood without Margaret Adair Gillies prancing through it. They felt as close as sisters in their mutual, abiding affection. Sometimes Abigail was actually surprised to realize the two of them did not look more alike. Though they both had the island women's fine, clear complexions, burnished to a rosy glow by wind and spray, their physical similarities ended there.

Abigail looked more foreign than blond, blue-eyed Margaret. Three-fourths of the islanders, including the Adair brood, had inherited their coloring and big-boned bodies from their Viking and Scottish fore-elders; one-fourth of the folks, like Edmund Drummond, had the darker, more compact Celtic looks. But Abigail did not seem to belong to either of these groups. She was tall for a woman, but small-boned. Her limbs were lithe, not sturdy-looking, though they had a wiry strength. Her hair was not yellow, nor brown, nor black, nor were her eyes of blue-green or hazel hue. Her golden eyes were slightly tilted, and her slashes of cheekbones slanted to corners of a full mouth. Abigail's clear, high brow and lush, red-gold tipped lashes and tresses gave her the look of otherness, even compared to the few other redheads of St. Kilda. She even spoke a bit differently since her mother had been reared and educated on Harris. So here, on a six-square-mile island bound by ties of tradition and unity, even Abigail MacQueen's physical attributes were not a common thing.

"Who wants me?" Abigail asked the moment she scrambled up the stony, zigzag path to where Margaret awaited. "You need to save your strength, lass."

"Och, Edmund Drummond, no less, came by to tell ye the Parliament wants to speak with ye first thing tomorrow. Aye," Margaret added when Abigail rolled her eyes, "and without Douglas here to be sitting in his new, proper place. What have ye done wrong, my dear?"

Abigail shook her head as the two of them perched side-by-side on a boulder. Just as last week when Douglas had called her late at night, she beat down the fear someone had discovered their lovers' trysts. But even Margaret, with whom she shared so much, still did not know. As for other possibilities for the summons, Abigail had not suggested for months that more folk wear brightly colored cloth, more daring than the indigo hues, the only exported dye allowed. Folk had seemed to fancy her latest songs, and even the dear children who filled her cottage to learn them had taken to the lilting tunes.

"I dinna ken," Abigail admitted with a shrug, but her stomach knotted tighter. "Perhaps my idea of exporting the blued cheese so the feather count doesna have to be so high. I dinna ken."

"Och, to be called in and not sent a hint why! But we wilna fret," Margaret declared in her usual perky manner and smacked her palms on her spread knees. "As for my walking out here, it got me away from duties, that it did."

Abigail turned to Margaret and smiled wryly as she waggled her finger at her. "And any lass in a family way who can walk a mountain path twice a day to milk her cows when I told her I'd do it for her, sure can walk to the Dun to fetch a friend when Parliament wilna meet 'til tomorrow morn!"

"Anywhere I walk these days, I have the look of a very fat fulmar or puffy puffin!" Margaret said, patting her belly.

She snorted a little laugh and elbowed Abigail hard enough to nearly knock herself off the rock, and Abigail had to catch her arm and haul her back. That sort of ungainliness, Abigail thought, was exactly why she had turned shrew to convince Margaret she should not walk to Gleann Mor and drag the heavy pails back. But so far her pleas to take on some of Margaret's tasks had fallen on deaf ears.

Abigail shoved her long legs into her socks. As healthy and hardy as she was, she could never quite abide bare feet from March through September as most of the other women. Though she kept ever busy, her feet and hands were often cold. Slowly, they walked back down toward the village, though Abigail sensed there was something else Margaret wanted to say.

"Spit it out, lass," was all she needed.

"A very big favor, Abigail," Margaret said, coming to such a quick stop her skirts swayed.

"Anything, my dear, big, wee, or in between!"

They leaned against another boulder while Abigail squeezed Margaret's hand. "What ails you, Margaret?" she prompted.

" 'Tis the bairn, the birthing of it next month, I mean."

Abigail nodded. The curse of St. Kilda was its great loss of infants barely a week old. Some women had lost more than half their brood to the dreaded eight-day sickness. The two women clasped hands even tighter. This would be Margaret's first bairn in a marriage but a year old, but there was no way to predict about the first child or the tenth. *The hand of God . . . women's righteous punishment for sin . . . we must accept the way of things,* the old hearthsongs and the new minister sent from Glasgow always said. But, through her mother, Abigail knew things were not like this in other places, and sometimes she longed to be in such enlightened lands.

"I want ye—ye and Douglas—to be Neil and my bairn's proper sponsors, no matter what mother says," Margaret blurted, and the rest spilled from her in a torrent. "Neil said I might ask ye myself and we'd both ask Douglas when he returns. I warrant Douglas will be wanting to woo ye when he comes back—aye, I ken ye two are yet dear to each other or else he would have gone to wooing Flora, however busy he be. I'll ever stand by ye and Douglas as I ken ye will by me! Someday soon, all yer waiting will be over, Abby. And when mine is over and the eight days pass, if ye and Douglas just agree to be the bairn's *gosti* at the christening, all will be well!"

"Of course, it will! I accept with joy! Such an honor! But as for Douglas and me—well, we shall see." Watchful of her friend's bulk, Abigail leaned over to hug her. The relationship between a bairn's

parents and godparents was sacred. But what if she had to tell
Douglas no? Or what if he himself in his days with the older men
on Boreray had seen that wedding her might be more of a burden
than parting would be, and that he did not want her to be *gosti* to
his new niece or nephew! She choked back a sob. "And your bairn
and everything will be fine, just as you say!" she whispered fervently to her friend.

But even more than Margaret, she was afraid. She feared for
this unborn child's deliverance and for what the men of Parliament
would say to her tomorrow. Mostly she feared she must refuse
Douglas so he could provide for St. Kilda as an honored cragsman
and protect his family unity. Abigail had no family now but her father's elderly friend, Alistair MacAuley, whom she called "grandfather." But she believed in and treasured any sort of family, even one
patched together from dear friends.

"Let's walk back, then, and I'll give you some cheese for dinner," she told Margaret with a bright smile, not wanting them to
cry. Once either went to sobbing or giggling, the other was soon far
gone too. "And maybe I'd better take a wheel of it to the big, braw
lads sitting there in judgment of one wee woman tomorrow, eh?"
she teased.

Margaret laughed, but the wind whipped the sweet sound
away to mingle with the shrill shrieks of the birds.

Abigail's spirits lifted when children ran toward them in the village.
Young lasses of four or five toting loads of peat or water, a few
young lads with their short scaling ropes or toy bird snares tagged
along.

"Sing us a song, if ye will, Abigail!" plump Ian Lewis wheedled
and took her offered hand to walk beside her.

"Aye, the one about bonny lands," little Fionna Fergusson insisted with a turn of her blond head that nearly toppled the prodi-
gious pile of peat balanced there.

"The wee ones love you," Margaret told her with a proud
smile and a pinch on the arm. "And, 'tisn't for yer fine cheese ye
spoil them with either!"

Abigail nodded. Yes, at least these young children of St. Kilda
did not look at her askance because of the burden of being who she
was. In her now crowded little cottage, Abigail even laughed as she

handed around slices of her blued cheese to the seven children. She cut off a larger hunk for Margaret. The women waved as if they would not see each other for days when Margaret set out down the street for home, three cottages away.

"Now, about that song," Abigail told the children as she turned back to them. "The one Fionna favors is an *auld lang syne* hearthsong, and your mothers could teach it to you too."

"Not as good as ye," round-faced Jamie Lewis mumbled through a mouthful of cheese.

"Well, when you're done with the eating, as 'tis proper manners, we shall sing it together then."

How she loved to have her small cottage crammed with children. How she—just as Margaret—longed for her own. Children were precious on St. Kilda, and though they worked hard, they felt the love and protection of all the islanders. If only, she thought, she could set up a small school here to teach them lettering and numbers as her mother had taught her with recitations and a slab of slate to write on! Her heart leapt, and she pressed her palms together at a thrilling thought. She had suggested to several women on the milking trek that she would be pleased to teach the children. Could that be the reason for the summons to Parliament? Could someone have suggested to her husband or father that Abigail MacQueen would like to start a wee, humble rote school, and she was to be allowed to do so? Oh, if only they thought her worthy, she prayed. Hope swelled with her voice as she led the song:

> *The Lord's first lad and lass*
> *He made wi' His own hands*
> *Named all the flowers and fauna*
> *Of islands and mainlands.*
>
> *Eve loved bonny Eden dear*
> *But she gainsayed God's ways,*
> *So we must now toil day and night*
> *Till the end of all our days.*

The song went on with verses rambling through most of the early Genesis stories, but Abigail always skipped the rest of those about how all mankind's trials were Eve's fault for eating the forbidden fruit. After all, she thought, the Scottish Free Kirk preached that God declared a man must be head of his household, so Adam should have kept a better eye on Eve than to let her chatter with serpents and gobble pilfered apples! Abigail secretly believed the whole burden of sin should be put right in Adam's lap—unless the men around here would allow a woman to have her say about things at least now and again. Then, of course, she supposed men and women should share the blame.

The lively singing muted, then stumbled to a stop when a form blocked the light from the door. Abigail turned to see a stormy-faced Flora Fergusson, hands on shapely hips, standing there.

"Flora, please come in," she invited with a sweep of her hand with which she had directed the little choir.

"I dinna come for a visit, but to fetch Fionna home," she said sharply, glaring at her younger sister. "She isna to be dawdling about and wasting time. Best mend yer ways, my wee lass, or ye'll be sent to Harris where bad bairns go," Flora threatened with the traditional, tongue-in-cheek island warning.

It always amazed Abigail how such a bonny lass as Flora could look so stern and sour. And it annoyed her to no end that the place from which her mother had hailed was the same one about which the St. Kildans made endless jibes, as if the closest inhabited island was a very Sodom and Gomorrah! She used to think it was because Harris was St. Kilda's rival for the Glasgow tweed market. But it was the St. Kildan refusal to dye exported cloth that allowed the multihued Harris tweed to predominate, however unique St. Kilda wool for being plucked instead of sheared. Once Abigail had thought the bitterness existed because the factor and the laird lived on Harris, and islanders were ever suspicious of outlander authority. But surely it was something more she had not yet discovered.

Obediently, under the seventeen-year-old Flora's narrow green stare, little Fionna made for the door to retrieve her abandoned stack of peat. The two other lasses straggled after, one squeezing Abigail's hand as she passed, as if in secret farewell.

Suddenly, before Abigail could bridle her tongue, in the broad St. Kildan brogue she seldom employed, she told Flora, "I am sore sad to hear ye deem the bairns learning Bible songs a waste of time, but I ken each lass must have her own opinions."

"Aye—or so yer new hearthsong did tell, all about questions and questing and flying free with lads I heard on Fionna's lips last week!" Flora opened her pink mouth to say more, but evidently nothing tart enough would come. Instead, she scanned the room as if to silently disparage the shabby interior of Abigail's old cottage. With a shake of blond curls, not quite covered by her proper pale wool kerch, Flora turned her back and flounced away with her sister and the other lasses in tow. As if Flora had scolded them too, the lads bid Abigail goodbye and drifted back to their scaling and snaring games outside.

"Blast it!" Abigail cried as she flopped down on her bench by the door. She should not have been so vexed with Flora. She liked her, she really did, and had to admit Flora had keen taste in lads, if she was holding herself for Douglas. But Flora made her feel she was featherbrained to hope the village would entrust the wee ones to her for learning. Aye, doomed, just as her hope to wed Douglas Adair and her desire not to have her wayward Eve-with-the-apple reputation smudge him! Abigail loved her neighbors as the Good Book said, but sometimes it hurt to keep turning the other cheek. What an unfair burden it was, she fumed, to be blamed for things folks thought a body's parents did, as well as for one's own desire to see some things different!

She sat, knees bent up to her breasts and arms around her shins, staring long into low-burning peat ashes of the hearth, her mind mired in desperate desires again.

Abigail sat there until daylight decayed in her single door and window. She roused herself to stir the ashes and light the twisted heather wick of her iron crusie lamp, fueled by fulmar oil. She broiled a bit of fowl for her supper and washed it down with whey. Though the warm spring winds and late-lingering daylight would soon encourage her moving her dye pot outside until autumn, she hauled it over the central hearth and hooked it on the iron crook which hung by links from the roof ridge. With her work apron, she fanned the flames.

She must gather her wits for the morning, she urged herself. She was stirring her brain and boiling her emotions by so much brooding that she'd be a blithering bairn before the men. Perhaps, if she kept busy and then got some soothing sleep, a way out of her dilemma would descend on her like a heavenly dove. If not, the only thing she knew to do was to try to read Parliament's attitude toward her tomorrow and let that guide her decision about what to tell Douglas when he asked for her hand. After all, if the men had summoned her to inquire about her starting a school, she would dare to wed him and hope his high regard in the islander's eyes could climb even higher through her good works. But even then, she must rein in her discontent and further curb her tongue. As for the questions hinted at in her latest hearthsongs . . .

She could only sigh as she began to hum yet another tune, but she went to work with a will. She chopped her fresh lichen and put them in a jar of rainwater to stand overnight. To the dye pot, she added some of last summer's crottle, a yellow-green lichen that would give her plucked wool yarn a fine crimson to a pale rose hue, depending on how long it steeped. Then, as was tradition, the men would take the yarn from her and other women and, during the winter, weave the island's cloth. But only her adopted grandfather, whose blue-veined hands now trembled at the task, would agree to weave her brightest wool and only for her private use.

She went to kneel beside the brass-bound wood chest that held her meager wardrobe and household yard goods. She burrowed beneath her single change of daily garb, then under the extra crimson blanket for her bed, the bright-banded curtains she dare not hang in her window, her proper blue indigo Sunday gown, and the dark tartan shawl the women wore to church. And there, on the bottom, lay her pride, the form-fitting, brushed woolen gown she had dyed in rosy hues, shell pink at the bodice and gradually darker toward the hem. She fingered the softness of the gown she had oft thought she would dare to wear when she wed Douglas, no matter what tradition said, no matter if the wedding were in winter, the usual proscribed season, no matter—

Startled by a sharp rap on her door, she slammed the top of the trunk. The door stood yet ajar to let in sweet sea wind, for, though all village doors had a wooden lock and key, few thought to secure them. Lamplight was in her eyes until she strode closer. Perhaps Margaret had come to assure her again, she thought, but Margaret would have sung out and come in. Then she saw that the hand which shoved the door farther ajar at her words, "Who is it?" belonged to Edmund Drummond. He held the slate pencil in his right hand that he had at all times, perhaps, she mused, even when he slept.

"Good evening to ye, Abigail. Just wanting to be certain ye received tomorrow's invitation."

"A pretty way of putting it, but yes, that I did," she replied and stood her ground just inside the doorway, hands clasped before her. Edmund smoothly snatched his flat blue Glengarry bonnet off his dark, straight hair.

Though Edmund Drummond had never done her a direct wrong, she felt a natural aversion to him. Not only had she once overheard him telling others that her mother was demented and had killed herself, but he had three times asked for Abigail's hand after his wife Elizabeth died of the boat cold just last year. Three times, when she was trying so hard to keep her fervent feelings for Douglas hidden and when most island girls were wed by sixteen! Three times, when she had told him clearly she did not favor his suit! Yet he always watched her; she could feel his gaze grasping at her, sometimes down the length of street or even in kirk. That hardly bred the same dazzling warmth Douglas's stare did. Then, too, though most important men on St. Kilda were humble and honest, she thought Edmund both proud and sly.

As right now, he often flaunted the MacLeod of Harris tartan scarf about his neck over his jerkin. Yet he was a St. Kildan by birth, who had only visited Harris and was not of the laird's clan. But Edmund worked for the MacLeod factor here by keeping continual accounts and caring for the factor's house the eleven months he was away. He had lost the index finger on one hand in a boyhood accident loading the factor's smack years ago. Abigail's mother had once told her that Edmund was the only man she knew who could turn the tiny tragedy of a lost finger into a huge, fortunate future as "the factor's lord" here. After all, her mother had been another factor's daughter on Harris, and she had never put on Edmund's airs! For one thing, even now, he crackled a piece of parchment on which he kept his running accounts of birds, feathers, wool, and crops in his other hand as if to say, "I'm watching and recording what you do, all of you!"

When Edmund stepped back and indicated she should join him outside, she dutifully followed him. It wouldn't do to ask him in since she lived alone. Reputations here could be as fragile as eggshells, especially for the spinster MacQueen. Abigail was allowed to live alone mostly because no one wanted Lady Grange's small, old place, and the smell of her dye pot bothered some. Then, too, it was also expected she would properly wed, so her husband could move in here without the village men having to build and thatch yet another cottage. Most of all, the outcast reputation she had inherited from her parents' doings made everyone more easily accept she should live separate in the small, tightly woven society.

"Will you tell me the nature of the summons then?" she inquired, forcing herself to gaze up calmly into Edmund's avid face. He was actually a bit shorter than she, but he had stepped onto an old hand millstone she used for a low seat outside her door. He acted as if he merely wanted to glance down to the bay, but she knew his stature bothered him; he often stood uphill when he spoke to people. Edmund's broad nose seemed to push his wide-set eyes even farther apart. Still, his gaze, like his hair, seemed to meld with the darkness while his clean-shaven, round face glowed like a pale moon.

"The nature of the summons will be told at the time," he said formally, but his voice sounded warm. "But yer not to let it nettle ye. I will be there, and harm shalna come to ye, take Edmund Drummond's pledge for that."

She dare not throw that back in his face. After all, she told herself, it was a kindly thing to say, and on St. Kilda, a man's pledge was better than a sworn, sealed document.

"Then I shall rest upon that promise," she said only.

"How I wish ye would trust me even more, Abigail."

"I prefer not to speak of that—of our past now."

His quick smile flashed crooked teeth. "Ooh, bonny lass, how I long for us to have a past. But then," he went on quickly, evidently to cut off her protest, "of course, we have a past of sorts, since your mother, too, knew a laird's factor on Harris."

"I should think the laird would resent his home island of Harris being the place that inspires most St. Kildan jests and threats," she dared. She could have bitten her tongue for that jab; she needed Edmund's protection and goodwill tomorrow. But, if he took offense at her words, he did not show it.

"Aye, yer poor, sad mother didna care for such Harris jests and curses either," he said. "Such a lovely woman, yer mother, bright, educated. A bit of a fish out of water here, just as my reading and ciphering skills set me apart and above most others—but not from ye, Abigail. I think I alone can read yer heart, still grieving for yer mother's loss. And then for ye to lose yer father Coll after, in a way hinting he, too, might have done himself in, och. Ye know, lass, I told him not to go out by himself like that in the boat—ye heard me tell him that."

"I did," she admitted, her ruffled feathers a bit smoothed by his praise of her mother and concern for her father. "But my parents wouldna have taken their own lives. She must have lost her footing in the storm. And Coll MacQueen was stubborn—and terribly changed by losing her."

"And I can sympathize with him! He told me once he fell in love with 'Glorious Glenna' at first sight. Think of the power of that!" he said and leaned a bit closer to her. "And as for being stubborn—well, 'tis a worthy trait we St. Kildans all live up to, eh? Now, sadly, I must not be standing about speaking with ye, or someone will think I be courting ye again, and we dinna want that, do we? I will speak with you after tomorrow, then," he said and started away.

"I—thank you for your kindness and reassurance," she called after him, before stepping into her cottage and closing the door.

She told herself she had misjudged the man. After all, Douglas had said it was Edmund who had put his name forth to be the single young cragsman the veteran fowlers took to Boreray, and Douglas was grateful for that. Perhaps Edmund had promoted her name to set up a small school, which he would help to oversee. She wouldn't mind that, not if it would help the bairns and their mothers too, who could surely learn reading and writing and counting, even if just on the milking treks! Perhaps that was why Edmund had hinted that only the two of them had reading and numbering skills! Surely, he would not come to comfort her if she were facing some dire charge tomorrow. "I will be there, and harm shalna come to ye," he had said. Edmund held sway in Parliament as he did on the entire island. Abigail's hopes soared.

She latched the door behind her and bent to stir her dye pot. The tune she hummed was happy now. The wind whistled in accompaniment, a friendly, familiar sound. She could not imagine in all her heart-wing flights of fancy what a silent, windless night would sound like. In the dim light of the lamp, she stirred the pot and watched the swirl of the forbidden crimson colors.

2

Cragsmen, heroes of highest degree,
Swift, strong, bold they must be,
St. Kilda's survival their only decree.
Yet one of these cragsmen, dearest to me.

In ropes like spiders' webs over the sea,
Walking the cliff face, then swinging free,
Powerful, fearless, humble, happy,
St. Kilda's beloved my cragsman must be.

The next morning at first light, Abigail scrambled out of bed and stirred the smoldering fire before darting back under her coverlet. The flagstone floor was cold, even through her thick stockings. Waiting for the small room to warm, she stared up at the soot-blackened ceiling. Though village thatchers scraped the interior each May and rethatched it in October, it looked dark from winter wear. The walls, too, were smudged from smoke, which always wandered a bit before drifting out the door or small central ceiling hole. No wonder some people called these old cottages black houses, for the manse and factor's house had a hearth and chimney at one gabled end to keep the interior clean.

Someday, Abigail mused, still drowsy despite what the day held in store for her, she would have a fine, braw cottage, one with more than one small, deep-set window to let in the light.

The walls of these black houses were really two walls of unmortared stone set five feet apart and packed with earth to cut the wind. Outside, rounded roof edges did not project but began inside the walls to keep the wind from prying off the thatch, even though it was well secured with gannet beaks and ropes of twisted heather. Someday, she dreamed, she would earn coins from her cheese and dyed wools sent to Harris and hire someone to build her a fancy cottage in bonny Gleann Mor across the island, that she would. It would have warm wool carpets of rainbow hues and walls dyed blue as the sky or gold as the sun, and she would build a dye hut and cheesery too. But, of course, the school for the island's bairns and maybe their mothers, too, would have to be erected here in this village, and its walls would be wondrous with rich colors.

She forced herself up and pulled a shawl over her sleep shirt. Even her dreaming could not hold at bay her worry for this day. In her stocking feet, she padded busily about the room, heating porridge and pulling on her clothes. She ate quickly, then straightened her parents' old bed where she slept alone, hopeful of a husband.

"It will be my Douglas or no man!" she vowed. "And if I wed him, we'll have ourselves a braw bairn to put in my old bed!"

Across the twenty-by-ten-foot living chamber stood the narrow box bed of her childhood. The wooden settle; her trunk of folded clothes; a smaller, driftwood chest holding household utensils; a stool, and small table were the only other furnishings, besides her father's old loom standing silent sentinel in the far corner. Wooden items, even these crude ones, were very valuable on treeless St. Kilda.

On the far side of the only interior stone wall was the second room, the byre, or animals' chamber, with its floor of bare earth. All St. Kildans kept their cows and goats inside for the winter; warm weather had come so early this year they had been driven through the mountain pass to Gleann Mor nearly a month ago. Abigail missed their friendly lowing and snorts through the wall, but she did not mind the two-mile, twice-daily walks for the milking, as she valued the time to talk with the other women and whatever lasses went along.

And she loved Gleann Mor. It had a waterfall, wonderful tumbled-down stone houses of a much earlier, now deserted village, and the spectacular views of Gleann Bay, so much more stunning than Village Bay. No, she didn't mind the walk, but it was hard on pregnant women like Margaret and the older women, who often had more cows and goats to tend. There was no reason, Abigail fretted, why the large portion of milk that was used for cheese could not be worked by herself and other unwed women who could live in Gleann Mor in the summer months. How much time and trouble it would save the others, for village boys could stop their climbing games long enough to help carry it back once in a while instead of the women lugging pails.

She hummed the tune of the old hearthsong "Cragsmen Heroes" as she examined her hemp-wrapped wheels of ripening cheese, now stored in the byre instead of crowded in the corners of the main room. Afterward, she carefully braided her hair, and tied her kerch to hide all the red bounty but her hairline and central part. She planned to leave early to see her grandfather on the way. Parliament began when the men drifted in, as St. Kildans worked hard but never hastily. Today before they were ready for her, the men would no doubt decide on group or individual tasks, debate problems, hear complaints, or, this one day a week when villagers could be called, lecture lads who needed scolding.

Never, since Lady Grange, as far as Abigail knew, had Parliament summoned a woman. After all, it was rare for a female not to be either too old to cause a stir or under the control of her father or husband, and those men responsible for a female's behavior could be dealt with directly. Then, too, since Lady Grange a hundred years ago, perhaps no woman had been enough of a problem to be called.

Rachel Cheisley, the Lady Grange, had been a prisoner, held in forced exile in this cottage early in the last century. Her husband had deeply resented her jealousy of him when he was away on political business in London. She had sent him demanding letters and accused him of infidelity. She even dared to disagree politically with him. Embarrassed by her independent stands, he had her abducted to St. Kilda from their home in Edinburgh, away from her family and their eight children. The lady had protested heartily by tossing into the sea bottles with letters telling how much she still loved her husband. She also petitioned the St. Kilda Parliament and strode into a meeting to speak her mind. But none would heed her unwomanly ways, and she was taken off to die in exile elsewhere.

It is a sad story that Abigail's mother had told her once, "of a woman who loved an important man so much she did not ken she must bridle thinking or speaking for herself." After all, Abigail recalled, the church and men said women should learn in silence and subjection, though women like Abigail's mother obviously often felt the men had read the Good Book a bit wrong. The biblical order "Men, love your wives and be not bitter against them" did not seem to mesh with some of the things that went on in the world, Abigail thought, like the way Lady Grange was treated. "The way of things in this world," Abigail recalled her mother had said, "especially for women, is not as it should be, and can be accepted—or defied—only with suffering."

" 'Tis strange," Abigail murmured as she paused in the doorway, leaning her shoulder there. She recalled her mother's voice, the intensity of her face, her very words clearly now: The way of things for women can be accepted—or defied—only with suffering.

At the time Abigail had thought she meant naught but a tale of the long-dead Lady Grange, but had she been speaking of her own plight too? No time now for that, Abigail scolded herself, else she would become shaky instead of strong. Parliament might not have listened to Lady Grange, but that was years ago, and she was an outsider. She might have seen this cottage and entire island as a prison, but it had never been that to Abigail MacQueen. No, this dear place set her heart-wings free; she loved it and its people, and she was determined to be a useful part of its ways over the years to come, pray God, with Douglas at her side.

Head held high, stretching her strides, Abigail started down the village street toward the factor's house at the far end of the village where Parliament met.

"Abby dear, my heart is with ye!" Margaret called with a jaunty wave out the door of her cottage. "And I hear the wind's so fair that Parliament sent a crew at dawn to fetch the men back from Boreray!"

Abigail smiled as she waved back and walked on. Douglas would return soon, though not in time to sit in Parliament today. She knew that her whole future with her dear lad hinged on what the men would say to her this morning.

For one moment, she had a good notion to just become a Lady Grange, to stride in now to ask the men's help to start a school, but she knew better than to approach them that way. "A cat comes but to sweet milk and not the sour," her mother had told her more than once. Abigail mused that the axiom could be a parable about men. Edmund, for one, oft reminded her of a canny, watchful cat. But today, and perhaps after, she would trust him.

Children on their way to tasks greeted her, but they seemed subdued. Women nodded stiffly or just stared as they swept doorways or washed salt mist from windows. Flora Fergusson's usually narrowed gaze was wide with curiosity. Could the women know something she did not, that she was indeed being summoned to give the village its first school? Could their hopes go with her but they were afraid to say so? Most of them had hardly responded to such hints from her. Or did they all simply want to be certain they saw the culprit for some dread sin on the momentous day she went before the men to answer for it?

She turned into the MacAuley cottage doorway to knock and nearly bumped into Susannah, old Grandfather MacAuley's silver-headed niece, who must have been peeking out. Susannah and her husband, Malcolm, had moved in with Grandfather five years ago when his wife, Euphemia, died. Alistair and Euphemia had lost their children, so Susannah and Malcolm were nearest kin. Grandfather still wove the finest island tweeds, however his eighty years had slowed his hands. His legs had slowed too, for he never went more than a few painful, stiff steps outside the door, hunched over his driftwood walking stick.

Years ago, when Euphemia MacAuley had heard young Abigail's bell-clear voice booming out the catechism in kirk, she had asked Parliament and Abigail's parents if she might teach her the old hearthsongs. But it was Alistair who valued Abigail's wit to compose new songs, for he loved a good tale and had heard all his wife's *auld lang syne* songs for years. It was Alistair who asked Abigail to call him Grandfather and praised her colorful dyes and even more colorful opinions. But he always warned her—just as her mother had—that on St. Kilda "ye must learn to stay to the way of things, but for places yer heart-wings take ye inside yerself."

"Good morning to you, Grandfather!" she called to Alistair after she greeted Susannah. Already he sat at his loom in the back corner where he made room for her on the wood bench beside him. Hardy village men, especially fowlers and cragsmen, only wove in the winter, but Alistair was beyond work other than this.

"An important day for my own lassie," he told her, his voice more raspy than usual. Wise, pale blue eyes peered from a sun- and wind-weathered brown parchment face.

"What is everybody saying about my summons?" she whispered.

"Time to wed, mayhap," he said and took her hand. His touch was rough with thick calluses, tokens of decades of labor with snares or boat ropes as well as the wooden shuttle.

"Mayhap. But I dinna think Parliament summons even spinster lasses to tell them so."

"Hmm. But most lasses wilna be so stubborn—nor so bright—as ye," he added the last words under his breath, and his thin shoulders shook with silent laughter, at what she was not certain.

She smiled back at him but sighed inwardly. She wished, as she did with Margaret, that she could simply unburden her love for Douglas and their dire dilemma, but she did not want him to worry for her. If things went well today, he would be the first to hear of her new school. Still, she did not mention that either to avoid disappointing him later. She only wished that even when he nodded his encouragement and smiled that sage smile of his, concern for her did not lurk so darkly in his eyes.

And she said naught of her worries today with Susannah still in the cottage. Flora Fergusson's family lived on one side of the MacAuleys; the MacCrimmons, Flora's grandparents, resided on the other. Flora, her grandmother, and Susannah were thick as all-night stew, though Susannah had always been kind to Abigail.

"I must be on my way, Grandfather, but I have a new song to sing to you later," she told him as cheerily as she could manage.

"Stop by a wee while on the way back. An old man can use a bit of company when Susannah's out."

She nodded and pecked a kiss on his cheek. He squeezed her hand, then patted it with his other. She had the sudden urge to throw her arms around him and sob out all her fears like a child, but she pulled gently away. After all, she was a woman grown and Douglas would be home today. Still, from the doorway she looked back again and waved. Whatever would she do without the comfort of this fine old man someday? Whatever would she do without him if she could not have Douglas either? As she went out, she stumbled from the dim shelter into sunlight and brisk wind.

She forced herself to a steady stride toward the factor's house. She usually avoided the place; eleven months each year it was Edmund's abode, where he kept the overflow of the laird's due until it could be reckoned, boxed, and bundled, and moved to the stone building called "the store" to await the factor's visit. The store was really a storehouse and was the place Edmund slept the month the factor was on the island.

The factor's house and the minister's manse were grand compared to other buildings. Though the manse alone was two-storied, the house had two separate bed chambers, a dining room, even a library she longed to see but would never ask Edmund for permission to visit. She knew some village folk thought her featherbrained and ungrateful for passing up a chance to live here as Edmund's wife, especially since they thought her the black sheep of the island, still covered with the sullied coat of her parents' shame. But now she prayed all that was past, that her efforts to be a part of life here would be accepted and appreciated. She just knew she could atone for whatever upheaval her parents had caused.

But she stood uncertain before the open door as the buzz of men's voices poured out. Coils of climbing ropes, a pile of oars, and other gear nearly blocked the entrance. Then someone evidently saw her, and Edmund himself stepped out to reassure her with a smile as he escorted her in.

The front room was bare but for a table and two chairs, one of which Edmund had evidently just vacated and took now again, scraping it loudly on the floor as if clearing his throat for silence. Iain Murdoch, leader of Parliament, perched in the other chair. The rest of the men, nearly thirty, sat around the edge of the room on the wooden floor, legs out, backs against the whitewashed wall, some smoking pipes. Hamish Adair, Douglas's father, sat in the far corner, watching her with interest. How she wished Douglas were there in his place. A fire crackled low on the hearth to take the chill off the room, though it could hardly do the same for the chill settling in her heart. She wished Grandfather MacAuley had not given up his place here when he retired from daily outside tasks. Susannah's husband Malcolm was here, but that was not the same. Blast it, she wished this business done and Douglas home and everyone pleased that they would wed!

The hoarfrost-headed Iain began, "Abigail MacQueen, to come

right to it, the gathering has asked ye here today for one thing. For a warning about the hearthsongs—yer newfangled ones."

"The ones I write myself."

"Aye, for instance, the ones praising Gleann Mor to the skies."

Someone muttered; whispers hissed behind her; Edmund cleared his throat but was looking down at his hands folded over his paper and pencil on the table as if waiting to record everything.

"Gleann Mor," she said quietly, "is a bonny place and we women are, of necessity, quite familiar with it, Mr. Murdoch."

"Hmph. Point is, several families who mentioned yer songs have asked to build cottages there—to live there, no less, when the gathering decided long ago the folks live only here now."

"Gleann Mor's a pagan place from the old, dark days," Flora Fergusson's father put in from his place near the hearth. "It might have good grass for cows and goats, but proper, pious St. Kildans live here now, with the holy kirk in our midst."

"But I dinna ever think of Gleann Mor as pagan or dark, only wild and lovely," Abigail protested gently, warming to defend the intent of her hearthsongs and her love for Gleann Mor. Though she had often thought it, she had never said that anyone should actually move there. But now, carefully, she explained her idea that perhaps, just during the peak time for the milk in summer months, the cheesemaking could be moved there.

"But 'tis never been done that way," Iain muttered.

"The cheese would have to be toted back, just as the milk," Edmund Drummond put in. He then reeled off bulk weights of last year's cheese from a black book produced from his coat pocket.

She had a good nerve to remind them how much heavier and sloppier it was to carry milk than cheese made from it, but that argument flew right out of her head when Iain brought up the next point the men had evidently already discussed. Heads began to nod as he went on, "Mayhap the gathering's been in err to have a woman hearthsinger and one so young and—unattached to a source of authority. After all, Euphemia MacAuley was wed as were other lasses who sang the songs o'er the years. Finlay, speak your piece."

Abigail stared down at Finlay MacCrimmon sitting next to Duncan Murray; they were the two male hearthsingers of the isle. Both looked stone-faced up at her. It struck her for the first time like a fist to stomach that she would receive no support from them or perhaps anyone here.

"Ye see, lass," the burly Finlay said with hand gestures as though she could not comprehend just his words, "ye've gone far beyond the pale with yer singing more than the old songs. Ye've added, well—"

"Message songs or some such," Duncan put in. "Our objection is mostly to what the hearthsongs show about yer rebellious nature that we object to."

"Aye, message songs about women," Finlay went on. "Ye've not affirmed the way of the isle, but tried to create and promote new ways. 'Tisn't done, not by a lass, not by anyone but the gathering in total agreement. And especially not by a lass whose teacher in life was a mother who never fit in nor evidently wanted to."

"But I want to—"

"Aye," Duncan interrupted. "Nor by a father who couldna keep his wife on the straight and narrow, nor bridle his own rebellious ways."

"But I am *not* my parents, though I love and honor them yet as the Good Book says," she insisted. "Besides, as to the way of things, changes are often a good idea," Abigail heard herself reply in ringing tones, when she had meant to be canny and calm. "You yourself speak of the good changes from the old pagan days and moving the village here from Gleann Mor. So simple, humble suggestions about dyeing our fine plucked wool yarn brighter or selling more cheese to keep down the high feather count that demands so many birds be harvested, or a village school—"

"How in heaven's name did we get on a village school?" Iain thundered. "Whatever for, lass?"

Abigail's stomach cartwheeled, but she held her ground. Why didn't Edmund Drummond make good his pledge to be certain no harm came to her? He was scrabbling through his book again, evidently looking for records of his precious feather count. Iain's puffy cheeks had gone red as twin setting suns and the men were murmuring louder. Still, she stood straight in the center of the brewing storm, staring down the men, who had to look up at her from their positions on the floor. As she did so, they evidently felt at enough of a disadvantage that, slowly, they began to rise to their feet, a few at a time. Now she felt hemmed in among them. Her blood crashed through her veins, but at least she held their attention now when she might never again.

"Dinna you see, St. Kilda could greatly benefit from a school to teach the bairns to read and write," she implored them. "A body should learn to read the holy book, to keep records, or to get on should he or she ever go to Harris or the Hebrides or beyond. Besides, I've heard other places, even in Scotland, have schools and . . ." Her voice tapered off as several men snorted derisively.

"But this is not other places. Edmund keeps the books for all," Iain insisted. "The minister reads us the holy word, and we dinna need to encourage folks—neither lads nor lasses—to leave St. Kilda, especially for Harris, where yer mother came from and yer unhinged father was rowing back to, looking for her spirit, for all we know, when he was lost. Aye, yer mother kenned to read and write and taught ye things about far off places, no doubt. It has done ye not a bit of earthly good and caused ye to fly free! The island men dinna have the need to read or write. They havena since time began. And learning for womenfolk, who should be busy with their tasks and bairns, be twice as useless as for the men!"

There was a gruff chorus of agreement. For the first time, Abigail's gaze collided with Edmund's, and he spoke at last.

"The lass is not responsible for her parents' doings, Iain. Get on with it."

"Very well, though she be the result of their doings in more ways than one," Iain muttered. He stood and grasped the lapels of his coat as if he would preach a sermon. "Abigail MacQueen, this island's gathering, this Parliament, cares deeply for ye as one of our own lasses. A lass is the weaker vessel made by God from Adam's rib and so subject to him—man as well as God, that is—especially in light of woman leading man to original sin. The way of the isle is that lasses be wed early to give them a strong hand and guide through the temptations of life. 'Tis wrong for a lass to cling to barren spinsterhood when a braw man asks for her hand. Like other lasses, ye need a man to be responsible and accountable for yer proper behavior. Has not a respected islander asked for yer hand three times—three times, a holy number, like Jonah spent three days in the belly of a whale and our blessed Lord in the tomb before he arose to a new life?"

She swayed; she almost fell to her knees in shock. She saw

things clearly now. Disaster. She was caught in Edmund's trap as surely as a fowler caught a fulmar. Douglas had said Edmund suggested he go to Boreray. Had Edmund been watching them so closely he knew of their love? How canny of him to have asked for her hand three times, a holy number! Edmund had lulled her fears, but he had caused her summons here, where she now stood alone, chastised, snared. She saw what was coming before Iain said the rest. She felt indeed like Jonah swallowed by the whale or as if she were trapped in a tomb with Edmund's deadly hands on her, doomed without Douglas, without her school, without the bairns, without her new hearthsongs, without hope.

"Well, lass, yer vow to obey and formally accept Edmund Drummond's proper suit is awaited," Iain's voice prompted. She wondered how long she had been standing here, speechless, staring. Edmund rose and made a little speech of caring deeply for her. She only glared at him while she locked her knees and gripped her hands before her.

"For our duty to oversee all the island folk," Iain tried again, "the gathering of St. Kilda wants yer word ye will wed Edmund Drummond and come under his rightful care and governance. We want your solemn vow to it *now*, Abigail MacQueen."

Edmund dared to smile, a thin, taut twist of his lips. His gaze locked with hers, not beseechingly but triumphantly. She realized there was no way she could have Douglas and not doom him, too, for his defiance of the men. He needed their regard to fulfill his calling as a cragsman. They decided the daily tasks; they could lionize or ostracize a body. And once she gave her solemn word here to wed Edmund, her promise was inviolate, even if Douglas returned the next moment and asked for her hand before them all.

But as for giving her answer now, she could never just spring this on her beloved. He had risked himself to warn and speak with her before they sent him to Boreray; she would risk telling him why she must not wed him. But to lose Douglas and wed Edmund Drummond instead—impossible!

"Shall we take yer proper silence for obedience, lass?" Iain's voice sliced through her agonizing.

"All of you had time to plan this, to think it over," she managed. "I know you would award a weaker vessel time to compose her thoughts, so you shall have my reply in the morning."

"Yer acceptance, ye mean," Edmund put in. But she had already turned her back on them and walked out.

Sunlight staggered her; she felt the weight of the sky pressing against her with the wind. Ahead she saw the street was deserted as the women had begun their busy day. Some had, no doubt, gone down to greet the boat from Boreray as perhaps she should do. But she needed to speak with Douglas in private, though she dreaded what she had to tell him. And she would never make it as far as Margaret's house before she collapsed, and even then she might blurt out how much she loved Douglas and all they had planned. Besides, she had told Grandfather she would see him after. She darted into the MacAuley open door without knocking. When she saw, blessedly, Susannah had gone out and Grandfather already clack-clacking away at his loom, she closed the door and leaned against it and pressed both hands to her face and sobbed. She heard the loom stop; he shuffled over and clasped her shoulders.

"Dearest lass. 'Twas so bad then?"

She could only nod. For the first time vague longings to leave this place and its callous, narrow-minded folk clasped her mind and heart. However much this place was her home, if it weren't for Douglas, Margaret, and her grandfather, she would leave the brain-bound lot of them behind on rock-bound St. Kilda, that she would!

But she did not tell Grandfather of that. Instead, at last, she unburdened herself, telling him of her love for Douglas that she had kept secret for so long. She admitted that they wanted to wed, and what the men had said, and how she would rather take a boat and row into oblivion on the watery deep like her father had done if she must wed Edmund Drummond.

"Ye'll not row out, nor jump off any cliff," the old man insisted, his voice no longer raspy nor weak. "Ye'll not follow yer sire and dam, and ye'll not talk that way!"

She stayed perfectly still, pressed to the wall, his hands on her shoulders, tears streaking her face, staring into his eyes. Her breathing and heartbeat slowly quieted.

"She did not jump," Abigail whispered. "She fell because the rocks were wet and it was dark. And my father meant to come back, or he would have said goodbye. But that storm must have done him in," she added with a hiccough.

"No storm shall do ye in!" the old man told her. "Now, ye listen here. Susannah and some others ran down to meet the boat from Boreray. Aye, word is 'tis ashore. Ye stay here and I'll go down to meet it and have a word with Douglas Adair, that I will."

"But you canna, Grandfather. The path is too steep down and your legs—"

"I been saving them for a calamity, and this be one!" he declared so soundly that she dare not argue. Her tears began again, but this time they were in gratitude for his love and bold determination when he headed out into the blustery March wind, bent over his crooked walking stick. Through the window, she watched him hobble farther than he had in years, slowly, stiffly, down past the factor's house where the men still met, down the pebbly path toward the bay. She was terrified he would fall and hurt himself, but she had seen in his eyes and heard in his voice that her refusal would pain and insult him. And however badly she suffered herself, she could not bear to hurt the old man she loved. Her hands gripping her elbows, she began to pace.

By the time she heard voices and saw villagers streaming by the cottage with their men returned from Boreray, she had decided. She must forfeit Douglas, even if he still wanted her when he heard of today's doings. But she would not submit to wedding that viper Edmund, whose slippery hand she could see behind all of this, however aloof and concerned he acted. If she could not have Douglas and become part of people's lives here, she would leave the island, though the thought terrified her, for she knew no one in the world beyond.

And then, when she could not contain her need to run to the shore any longer, at last she saw them, Douglas and Grandfather, coming up the street together. Douglas had his climbing rope coiled about his shoulders; he held Grandfather's elbow. Her love and pride in both of them swelled until she felt an actual physical pain. She stood back as slowly the door swung open and they entered. She pressed her clasped hands to her breasts. Douglas sat the old man on the stool by the door and closed it firmly, then dropped his rope with a thud. His arms went wide and he said simply, "My own poor lass."

She threw herself against him and his arms clamped her close. "You ken?" she choked out.

"Mr. MacAuley told me. I swear I shall kill Drummond with my bare hands!"

"Only if ye mean to hang before ye wed my Abigail," the old man muttered, though his breath wheezed out between his words.

"Douglas," she cried, "dinna you see, everything is changed now? Your reputation, your family, all threatened if you still want to wed me."

"If? Still? Ye think ye have some pigeon-livered mainlander here? Of course, I want to wed ye! All this makes a wee bit of difference to ye then?" he demanded, his face incredulous as he gave her a little shake.

"I would as soon die as give you up, but I wilna be the cause of your ruin! As the song says, a cragsman must be St. Kilda's beloved before his lass's own!"

He still gaped at her. "I only ken I will be a hollow man over the years without ye and our bairns at my side! Ye mean ye value my reputation enough to give me up, but wilna repair yer own to forgo yer new hearthsongs and yer other ideas that have stirred them all up? Wilna a wedded life with me be enough for ye, as it is for other women here? I only ken I canna be the bold cragsman St. Kilda wants and needs without ye, and if I must, I will tell Parliament that very thing!"

She stood in awe of the simplicity and strength of his reasoning. She knew he would be angry, but had not imagined such defiance. He seemed to thrive on this danger, just as she had during the men's debate today. Under attack, she had reveled in expressing and defending her ideas. In that, as well as other things, perhaps she really was her parents' daughter after all. If only she had gone the next step to demand progress and improvement, but she dare not with all at stake. Yet, if she could have Douglas forever, these things she had wanted paled in comparison, surely they did!

"I love you so much, Douglas," she said. "I loved the bairn and the lad, but I love the man far more!"

"I have done so much thinking about things on Boreray, Abigail. Say aye, and we shall go together to tell them now and not tomorrow."

She stared into his blazing eyes. If Douglas felt so strongly he could rightly defy the gathering, she must trust him. She could subtly work for change with the women if she were wed and not so different from them. She could help the bairns of St. Kilda learn through her own children—hers and Douglas's—whom she would tend and teach some day. Surely, she could do aught she willed with her own brood. Margaret would be happy; with her help, she and Douglas could win his family over. Her life without him would be empty, even if she left St. Kilda and fled to the farthest tropical isle. She felt she had leapt from the darkness of doom to the light of a new day, and all because of these two dear men who awaited her answer. She nodded her agreement of her beloved's wishes.

In exuberant joy, she hugged Douglas, then Grandfather. Douglas rushed her as she splashed water on her face; she hurried him while he washed away salt spray and smoothed his hair. How would it be, she wondered, suddenly shy, to kiss his lips and skin and tousle that golden hair in a sanctified, shared bed at night? How would it be to walk abroad proudly as his wife, to bear his bairns?

They went to the factor's house and Douglas stepped boldly inside. The voices halted, before his voice alone rang out. It was then she was certain that loving and obeying her man would be enough for the rest of her days. She glanced behind her on the street as a smattering of curious women and children gathered. Feeling even closer to them all already, she smiled and waved.

"Ye're back with a Boreray report so soon, Douglas?" Edmund's voice came from inside. He sounded no longer either canny nor controlled, but quite the opposite, she thought.

"Aye, two reports before I join ye here tomorrow," Douglas answered and stepped to the door to motion to her. She joined him inside; she could not wait to speak her piece.

"I must tell ye, men of the gathering," Douglas said, "that Abigail MacQueen and I have favored each other for years, though I knew 'twas best I not court her 'til I could join ye here as a man. I give ye tomorrow's two reports now, Mr. Drummond," his voice rang out as the livid Edmund shifted in his chair. Douglas's father kept his silence, but pride shined in his eyes.

"First," Douglas went on, his fists clenched at his sides, "the cragsmen on Boreray took a great number of gannets to swell the laird's coffers. And the other men thank ye for sending me, Edmund

Drummond, for I harvested near two hundred myself, a lofty reckoning, so they say. And, second, being of manly age now, I have asked Abigail MacQueen for her hand in wedlock the moment I returned to shore."

Abigail started to speak, but, turning to stare down the other men in turn, Douglas went on. "She has accepted, and the proper wooing shall come after, aye, lass? And I have her word that her hearthsongs and behavior will be in the way of the isle instead of wayward," he concluded and shot a possessive look at her.

She could feel Edmund Drummond's outraged fury stab her. "Aye," she said, though she longed to make a speech about hoping that the gathering would consider some of the things she had said earlier. But her speechmaking days, her writing days, her protesting days were over now. She had Douglas to speak and care for her, and she felt the lightening of her load.

"Well, then, th—that's done," Iain Murdoch stammered, obviously balancing the snaring of a record number of gannets and the silencing of one wee woman. If Edmund had not guessed about her and Douglas before, Abigail thought, he did now, as perhaps did Hamish Adair and the rest of them.

"I'm sure we are all agreed," Iain went on. "Edmund will be pleased to get the new numbers of birds and feathers. And Abigail MacQueen shall wed with Douglas Adair—after the proper betrothal, wooing, and such," Iain finished and cleared his throat.

Douglas clenched his fists again and glared at Edmund; Edmund did not meet his eyes but snapped his sturdy slate pencil in his hands.

"Come, Abigail," Douglas said. "And if my father will be so good to join us, we'll give the joyous news to the rest of my family."

She barely felt her feet and legs move as she proudly walked between the two Adair men up the crowded street. Only when Douglas took her hand did she realize that her cragsman hero was shaking nearly as hard as she.

3

Stand before the marriage stool
Hands, cheeks, hearts so warm.
Now live as one in weal and woe,
Whatever be the storm.

Vow to each fidelity.
A sermon, then pipes play.
Dancing, feasting, blessings given,
St. Kilda wedding day.

A crowd always gathered for the public part of a betrothal on St. Kilda, especially if the bridegroom was a cragsman. Tradition dictated that to prove his prowess as a provider, and thus to be worthy of a wedding, a man must scale the sheer, two-hundred-foot cliff called the Lover's Stone. More danger was yet to come, but Abigail felt no fear that anything would go wrong for Douglas. Although spring rains had delayed this ceremony for three weeks while the rocks were wet, today the sun shone. They were to be wed in a mere six days to avoid the unlucky month of May for weddings. This April twentieth Douglas climbed the rock for her, and Abigail's joy flew as fresh and free as the breeze.

She had always known her Douglas was a braw, bold lad; from their youth he had exerted a powerful pull on her actions and emotions. But because her family had trod the edge in the islanders' regard, she had underestimated Douglas's influence over other people.

Many St. Kildans no doubt realized that his sudden decision to wed her suggested they had been secretly, improperly courting. Yet in his new manhood, Douglas's reputation and personality protected both of them. He had faced down Parliament and his parents, so the St. Kildans had evidently decided they must accept.

Yet she had been apprehensive entering the Adair cottage with him and his father to face his mother, Mairi. When Douglas had announced his marital intentions, even when Hamish explained Parliament's agreement, the shocked woman had protested, "And how could this come about so soon, my lad? Ye've never been one to make a hasty, rash decision!"

"I have always admired Abigail from a distance as well as the times we spoke or met over the years, Mother. Many a man here seems to make the decision quickly, but in truth, he's observed and known the lass for years."

"Aye, unless the man's gone to fetch a strange wife on Harris!" Mairi had argued. "But here on St. Kilda, a man needs to go to courting with the blessing of a proper family sponsor!"

"Abigail's guardian, old Alistair MacAuley, was the proper patriarch today when we took the pledge, mother dear. And wilna ye tell yer friends the same, should they ever remark on it? Everyone kens Abigail is skilled with the handgifts and the old, proper hearthsongs. She will make me a bonny wife and be a fine mother to our bairns. I only hope and pray we all get on right well as good neighbors, as we shall be living next door. Come now, lass," he commanded, still facing his mother, "and we shall take a wee walk outside to make some plans."

If the St. Kildans had dared to criticize after word of that speech got about, no one confronted Abigail. The aura of the island's premier young cragsman covered her like a thick wool cloak. True, when Douglas was not at her side there were a few squint-eyed looks, shakes of heads, and Flora Fergusson's snubbing of her each time their paths crossed. But the three readings of the banns in Sunday kirk caused naught but a few sideways glances and a muted mutter. Of course, Margaret and Neil Gillies were ecstatic.

Still, Abigail scolded herself for not trusting Douglas from the first to make all things right. Much of her agony had been for naught. Perhaps, since her parents had departed, she had made too many wee, daily decisions on her own and had begun to believe a

St. Kilda woman could make the big, life-shaping ones too. That was just not the way of things. And she saw now that Douglas was not a bit like her father, who flaunted breaking the rules. Coll MacQueen had caused his own ostracism with his shocking defiance of propriety in kirk, his wild speeches in Parliament, and an occasional rampage through the village to take on someone he imagined had insulted him or his poor, dead wife. But Douglas walked the proper, public path here, and, thanks be to him, she did now too. Delivered from the depths of despair by an influential man to whom she now owed obedience and gave it wholeheartedly, Abigail felt her spirits soar.

But she had never had one moment's fear her Douglas would not handle the ordeal of the Lover's Stone today, even in this spanking wind. Folks cheered him on as he reached the pinnacle above them; he gave them back the shrill victory cry of the cragsman.

"Aye, the folk will never want with my lad upon the cliffs," she heard Hamish Adair tell his friends, their necks craned skyward. Douglas's mother was indisposed with the green sickness again this week, and pregnant Margaret could not take the long walk out. But Hamish had brought Douglas's two youngest brothers, Murdo and Ross, aged four and six. Murdo, who had always liked Abigail's songs from afar but had been forbidden her cottage before the betrothal, now clung proudly to her hand, his coil of boy's rope over his shoulder, his eyes on his beloved elder brother. Ross, though he had thanked her for the wedge of cheese she gave him, thought he was too much a man to cling to a woman.

At least Hamish and these youngsters had joined Margaret in congratulations after Douglas had announced their betrothal to their parents, Abigail recalled. As for Mairi, Abigail shuddered to remember the scene that had passed between them, not so much that first day, but the next when she had called on her future mother-in-law, as was tradition, alone.

"Come in then, lass," Mairi had called from her bed and motioned her in. Now Abigail noted the greenish cast to her skin that accompanied the internal upheaval to the stomach with this bodily complaint; the sickness always came at the end of a long winter. "Wee bit peaked from my ailment and all this rain, that I am. But like most burdens, t'will pass. Prop the door ajar then, for a breath of air."

At first their conversation was light and stilted, but that did not surprise Abigail; she had expected such and was willing to work hard to sway Mairi's opinion of her. For a beginning, Abigail was pleased to have the woman's thanks for her gift of cheese and the dark brown dyed wool she could knit into socks for her lads.

"Sit, then," Mairi had said, as if Abigail had stood in supplication long enough. She pointed to the stool by the bedstead and lowered her voice. "Now that we have time together without the menfolk, we shall have a real talk."

Abigail did not know whether to feel dread or relief, but she launched into the most important points she wished to make before Mairi could turn the talk her way.

"I want to thank you for your kindness, Mrs. Adair. I want to assure you I love and respect Douglas and will strive to make him a good wife and help you all I can too, now that we're truly to be neighbors again as well as family. I ken your friend Isobel MacCrimmon is wrought up that Flora is sad, but I hope they won't hold a grudge as a body canna help love." As well as being a good friend to Mairi, Isobel was Flora's maternal grandmother and, as her mother before her, the island's only knee-woman, or midwife, and thus the most powerful woman on St. Kilda.

"Aye, canna help love," Mairi echoed and frowned so at some thought or memory of her own that Abigail gripped her hands together on her knees. "But just between us, Abigail, I must explain why I kept my lad away from ye these years, though I see it did me not a bit of good."

Abigail felt slapped to silence. The mottled marks on Mairi's once pretty face now gone puffy and slack, seemed to pulse in this dim light. Abigail realized that both Douglas and Margaret looked more like their square-jawed father and the round-faced younger lads resembled Mairi. Mairi stared at Abigail so oddly for a moment that she almost reached for the nearby pot for her, fearing the woman would retch.

"What was ever so hard for me to bear," Mairi said, her voice a strained whisper, "was when my bairns took to ye as some others took to yer mother, God rest her troubled soul."

"I dinna ken what you mean, Mrs. Adair."

"As a young lass, ye didna ken what she was like, of course, yet ye look so much like her, and are like her too."

"I dearly loved my mother and dinna want to hear—"

"But ye must. For Douglas's sake, so ye wilna resent me and turn my lad's heart away from me, ye must."

"But I wouldna do that. I said I want us to be good neighbors and an even better family."

With a shake of her head that shifted her pillow, Mairi plunged on as if Abigail had not spoken. "Ye see, I feared from the first yer mother's stain would be on ye, for the look of her strange beauty was."

Abigail gripped her hands tighter; her fingers went numb. She had to know what had passed between their mothers that she and Douglas had long suffered for. "What stain?" she asked. "I tell you she did not take her own life and just because she hailed from Harris—"

"I mean her sly way with men, how she lured them without seeming to. Before she came here, she defied her folks to follow a lad she fancied clear to Glasgow, a lad far above her station. 'Twas the laird's own son. And when he turned his back, she dared go home to show her face. 'Twas a well-known scandal there. And just after, that was when Coll MacQueen saw her and she snatched his heart, when the men went for Harris brides."

Of all things, it now occurred to Abigail that perhaps St. Kildans made fun of Harris to disparage the "imported" brides men went for when choices were few here. Maybe the islanders derided those from a supposedly more civilized place to be certain the "out-landers" did not put on airs. But her mother had never been vain or prideful nor lured men, she was certain. If she had any fault, she valued her privacy more than was seemly on this island where all should work together. But, perhaps, if Mairi's tale of the young Glenna were true, her mother's sense of sadness and loneliness had come from being humbled by a man, and the laird's son at that. Or perhaps by the way this cold, cruel neighbor had treated her and now treated her daughter, even soon to be her own daughter-in-law.

" 'Tis true," Mairi went on in a rush, her quiet voice rising, "that she was beautiful and not to blame for that, but she was bitter and contrary too. That was her shame. That was another reason yer father fell so hard for her. Coll with rebellion in his very blood, with his defiant love of fishing over fowling!"

"But many a man angles for mackerel from the rocks in the summer."

"Aye, but just for a bit of extra food. They dinna go rowing out as yer sire did and take a wife and wee daughter too!"

Abigail felt crushed by such accusations and implications. Those hours fishing with her father had woven some of the brightest, more beautiful memories of her childhood. She could not help it if the islanders thought eating more fish than fowl would cause skin eruptions, even if her own family had seen that was not true.

"As for Glenna," Mairi went on, "why, she fed his waywardness, since her ways were different too, and she fancied she was high above us. Glorious Glenna, Coll called her when he shouted so loud I could hear him over here. Sometimes others fell under her spell too, and would have rushed to her aid, but . . ."

The door opened wider; fresh air and light swept in when Hamish entered. He frowned at his wife and shook his head as if in warning. "Old tales best buried now," he muttered. Abigail felt so shocked by Mairi's tumbled tirade that Hamish's warning merely jangled in her ears until he said louder, "Mairi needs a bit o' rest, now, lass. Come again wi' Douglas tomorrow, eh?"

Abigail said hasty farewells and fled outside. So much said in so little time! She must tell Douglas and Margaret and see what they thought of it. She leaned her shoulder against the wall of the Adairses' house and pondered this glimpse into her mother's past she had never fathomed. Had there been an incident between Douglas's father and her mother that built a barrier between the families all these years? And if Mairi had guessed that Abigail and Douglas had been meeting secretly, would she not think more than ever that Abigail intentionally lured men as did the mother she resembled?

But it was so unfair! If the story of the laird's son was true, could no one see her mother's side? An innocent misled and then abandoned, at least she had the sense and courage to go home. Did the St. Kildans wish instead she had cast herself into the sea at Glasgow in her shame? Had they let her know their disgust and disapproval for years until she finally felt driven to end her life here?

But no, Abigail told herself as she had a hundred times before: her mother had only made the grave error of walking in a storm that night she died, or was even blameless of that error. She had walked in her sleep more than once; one time Coll found her curled up outside the cottage door, and once she had gone out somewhere and come back to bed after he awoke. He had demanded to know where she had been and woke up wee Abigail to quake in her bed at his raised voice. But then, he realized Glenna was just sleepwalking again and he had begged his wife's forgiveness for his rash words. So on the night Glenna died, perhaps she had sleepwalked to the cliff, then slipped on slick rock and accidently met her end. There had been no hints, no written note, no sudden despair, or did despair not have to be sudden to lead to suicide?

Could her mother have carried the loss of and betrayal by the laird's tricky son inside her like a horrid, cold lump that neither the passionate Coll nor adoring Abigail could melt? If Abigail had lost Douglas, would she not feel that way? Abigail only hoped Glenna did not believe the loss of island children—including her two sons—to the eight day sickness was retribution for a woman's sins. Abigail felt her stomach knot so tight that she wondered for a moment if she had caught the green sickness from Mairi and would vomit right here in her wrenching pain.

"Lass," Hamish's rough voice came from behind her. She turned, wide-eyed, to face him.

"Bad blood between yer mother and my Mairi for no good cause and even sadder purpose," he said. "I dinna know all Mairi told ye, but I heard a bit. Ye ken, there was nothing between me and Glenna MacQueen but my regrets Mairi took on so. I see why ye make Douglas happy, sae dinna ye fret for what's long dead and gone."

Her lower lip caught in her teeth, she nodded. Tears stung her eyes in gratitude for this unexpected outpouring of concern for her. Douglas certainly resembled his sire in more than looks, but it was the woman of the house Abigail knew she would have to get on with.

"I canna thank you enough for—"

"Then just obey yer man, and never punish him for things he dinna do," he said. He scrutinized her face for a moment. Then he touched his fingers to his cap and went back inside the cottage.

" 'Tis easy for Douglas to do!" little Murdo yelled up at Abigail, yanking her back to the present. The memory muted and again she was on the cliff under the Lover's Stone. Murdo tugged at her hand and pointed up toward Douglas. He had taken off his climbing socks and now approached the very edge of the precipice bare-footed.

Despite her confidence in him, Abigail held her breath as he strode to the place where the upward slant of granite slab met air over the slashing sea and rocks below. He planted his left heel on the very edge of the stone, then slowly extended his right leg straight out, balancing skillfully. He grasped his right foot with both hands and tottered there one moment before gaining control, using his natural climbing skills, leaning carefully into the tilt of wind and angle of rock far better than most men who were just fowlers could manage.

"Faint heart never won fair lady!" he shouted the prescribed cry and jumped back from his perilous position. Everyone below cheered and huzzahed. Even those who might have merely nodded to Abigail days ago now patted her back and congratulated her on her coming nuptials. Douglas bounded down the rock and rushed to hug her. Joyously, the bridal pair led the band of folk back toward the village.

"Who's that running toward us, waving and yelling?" Douglas asked Abigail as they rounded their old haunt of Mullach Sgar with the parade of spectators strung out behind them.

"It looks like Annie Fergusson," she replied. She was relieved it wasn't Flora but another pretty Fergusson sister, the middle lass between Flora and little Fionna. Annie had always been friendly to Abigail; sometimes though, Abigail had wondered if it was mostly to spite Flora's flippant ways and tart tongue.

"Margaret!" Annie cried. " 'Tis Margaret, Abigail, gone into her travail—and calling for ye!" she got out between breaths.

"Who's with her?" Abigail asked.

"My mother's too ill yet," Douglas put in as he and Abigail hurried with the girl the way she had come.

"Of course my grandmother, Isobel, is with her," Annie gasped out, "but she's wanting ye."

"I ken next to nothing of birthing, but I can be with her," Abigail told Douglas. "Still, if Isobel MacCrimmon is there, all will be well."

They were running now, the three of them, with the others streaming behind around the stony skirts of the mountain. Abigail's heart beat very hard, not with exertion nor with foreboding about getting on with Douglas's mother, nor even joy at the day. Her dear friend, soon to be even more the sister of her heart, needed her. And, knee-woman in attendance or not, birthing bairns on St. Kilda and the week that followed was something every woman feared.

At the Gillieses' cottage Douglas went off to lend support to his friend Neil while Annie stepped in briefly to wave to her grandmother, then closed the door to leave Abigail alone with Isobel and Margaret. The scene that greeted Abigail surprised her: Margaret was up and walking, though not steadily. The knee-woman seemed to dwarf the laboring woman, though Isobel sat in the chair she had brought, just urging Margaret on. Margaret looked small and helpless; her bare legs looked thin as a bird's where they protruded from the wool shirt she wore over her distended belly. Though this was Margaret's home and she should be the center of attention, Isobel MacCrimmon dominated the room.

"Oh, Abby—yer here!" Margaret got out between panting breaths and leaned for support on the table. "All's well—at the Lover's Stone?" she asked as Abigail hurried to take her hand. Margaret's face was taut with pain and fear, but her eyes softened at the sight of Abigail.

Isobel's deep voice cut off Abigail's reply. "Margaret's mother's feeling poorly and canna come, but I see ye made it straight from yer betrothal to a birthing bed, Abigail MacQueen." Accusingly, Isobel eyed Abigail's stomach.

Abigail stiffened. How dare this woman imply Douglas would wed her because she was in a family way! How hard they had both struggled to be certain that would not happen. But Isobel was the bitter Flora's grandmother, so what did she expect? She must keep calm here; she had come to help Margaret, not take on Isobel MacCrimmon, so she bridled her tongue.

"What may I do to help you?" she asked Margaret. But she realized the battle trenches were dug deeper than she thought when Isobel replied again.

"I shall answer that as yer here only as a favor to this fine lass. If ye stay, ye'll help me and do all I say, for I canna have poking in by someone ignorant of birthing. See the water's kept at the ready to bathe the bairn—warm water, not hot. Warm the anointing oil.

Hold the lass's hand or talk a wee bit to her if ye must, but dinna ye get in my way and for a first birth, oft the worst by far."

Abigail glared at the woman for daring to say such a thing in front of Margaret, even if everyone knew it was true. She would have thought that a knee-woman would bring emotional comfort as well as bodily care.

Abigail helped Margaret walk a bit more, holding one hand, her arm around her shoulders even when Isobel chided her to let her bear the weight herself to bring the bairn faster. Abigail tried to ignore the knee-woman, but she could not escape her narrow-eyed stare.

Isobel looked older than her fifty-two years and acted as if she bore the weight of Mullach Sgar on her broad shoulders, Abigail fumed silently. Isobel had snowy hair woven among the brown with a jag of sleet silver just over her left eye, which her kerch did not hide. Isobel was solid, shapeless, but somehow stately. Of all St. Kilda women, Abigail could not picture anyone ever calling Isobel "lass." If, in the realm of all impossibilities, any St. Kilda woman ever sat in Parliament, it would be Isobel MacCrimmon. But soon Abigail had no time for such speculation. Margaret's pains were coming closer together, and she could no longer stand.

"Help her to the birthing stool, then," Isobel ordered, as if Abigail had been the one forcing the poor woman to walk in her pain.

The birthing stool was really the heavy armchair which Isobel now vacated, one she had toted from place to place with her for births. Perhaps, in olden times, it had really been a stool as had been the marriage stool, a low bench like the one on which Abigail and Douglas would kneel next week to be wed. But island tradition still called things in the old way, even when changes were made. Now Abigail helplessly watched the knee-woman's large hands roll up Margaret's shirt, exposing her belly and thighs. Swiftly, she wrapped then tied Margaret's spread knees to the wide-set arms of the chair. With one plump pillow jammed behind her back, the expectant mother's hips were right on the edge of the wooden seat. Isobel lowered her own bulk onto a low cottage stool so she could watch the birth and, no doubt, catch the bairn in her hands. All the while, when Margaret's eyes were not clamped in pain, she stared at Abigail, who tried to smile and nod and lend her strength for the ordeal.

"All will be well!" she mouthed to Margaret. "All!"

Eventually, as time and the labor wore on, Abigail stood behind the chair to hold her friend's hands and whisper encouragements in her ear. Now Margaret panted for breath; her mounting screams tore at Abigail's forced calm. Darkness descended outside and thickened shadows in the cottage. Abigail lit two crusie lamps and brought Isobel food and drink when she wanted it, though the knee-woman refused to let the thirsty Margaret partake. Sometimes, sitting there on that stool, waiting, watching, Isobel looked to Abigail as if she dozed.

"How much longer?" Abigail finally dared to ask. Isobel jolted awake. "Or is it just in the Lord's time?"

Isobel's narrow eyes gleamed in lampglow; shadows etched her frown lines deeper as she glared up at Abigail. " 'Twill be born in *my* time, and only I can judge when to begin to push."

"What do you mean? Margaret's been pushing for painful hours now, and there's naught yet to show for it!"

"What do ye ken of it? My son Finlay says ye canna even do the hearthsinging proper, but have to add yer own pushy ideas! I am the knee-woman, and I say this bairn will be born at midnight, as ye were, Abigail MacQueen. Ye have heard the old saw, 'A child born at midnight will be different for good or ill,' have ye not? Aye, from yer mother's womb ye fell into my very hands before anyone else's in this life. But had I kenned ye'd be such trouble . . ." Her malevolent voice drifted off, but Abigail feared she would poison the air the newborn bairn must soon surely need to breathe.

Abigail felt sick. This was no place for accusations or arguing. She had not realized the depth of this woman's dislike of her. Was it all because of Flora's losing Douglas or Isobel's son Finlay being a disgruntled hearthsinger? But none of that mattered now. If Isobel was not going to help Margaret, Abigail was.

"All right then, Mrs. MacCrimmon, if you say the bairn will be born at midnight, I shall hold you to it. Then Margaret can have some rest and something to drink!"

As if she had not challenged her, Isobel leaned closer to peer between Margaret's white thighs. She lifted a lamp, then examined Margaret for the first time with probing fingers. Abigail heard Isobel grunt even through Margaret's cries of protest.

"Mm, so I kenned," Isobel muttered.

"Everything is all right?" Abigail asked.

"Time. 'Tis time," Isobel said and stood to lean over Margaret. "Hold her hands tight now or I shall have to tie them too," was the last thing Isobel said as she went to work.

Tears coursed down Abigail's cheeks and mingled with the ones on Margaret's as Abigail leaned close over the back of the chair to embrace her friend's shoulders and hold her arms tight to her chest. She was shocked at what came next. Isobel did not just feel carefully to see how the child lay or prepare to catch the wee body in her hands. She kneaded Margaret's belly as if it were a mound of bread dough. Margaret screamed and bucked and begged. It went on and on, but a tied, held, exhausted woman was no match for Isobel.

"Stop it, stop it!" Abigail cried when she could take no more of her friend's pain. "You are hurting her, not helping her! Wilna you hurt the child that way?"

"Ye dare to question everything!" Isobel spit out as if she cursed her. But she did not stop her ministrations, shoving against the bulges of belly even harder as each powerful contraction racked Margaret so hard they tore Abigail too.

Then, finally, something happened. Isobel stopped and dropped back on her stool, sweating and wheezing. "Push! Push!" she ordered Margaret. Margaret reared back against the chair and bore down with all her might. There was a strange snapping sound, then a plop. Covered with whitish film, a tiny mite slid into Isobel's big hands.

Abigail's legs quaked; her hair prickled on the nape of her neck and shivers shot up her spine. Like Margaret, she shook all over.

"A lass, a sturdy-looking one," the knee-woman pronounced. She wiped the child with wet wool, then cut the throbbing birth cord with the traditional iron knife and anointed the end of the nub attached to the child with heated fulmar oil before she tied it tightly with a double strand of yarn. If it had been a lad, a piece of climbing rope would have sealed the cord after the oil was applied.

"A daughter, Margaret! You and Neil have a daughter!" Abigail told her exhausted friend as she washed her face while Isobel tightly swaddled the squalling child in flannel strips, then caught the gush of afterbirth in a pan. After that, Isobel seemed intent on the child, so Abigail took Margaret's care into her own hands, cleaning her, binding wool packing between her legs. "Here, my dear, I'll get you back to bed and you and your new lass can get some rest," Abigail crooned as she helped the limp woman stagger the few steps to her bed.

Margaret was still crying, but Abigail could tell it was now from relief and joy. Abigail cried herself as Isobel MacCrimmon finally approached the bed to place the wrapped bairn in its mother's trembling arms.

"Thank ye—both," Margaret managed, though her voice was raspy from her screaming. "Fetch Neil . . ." She cradled the child to her but fell immediately asleep.

Abigail MacQueen and Douglas Adair were wed in the parlor of the minister's manse on Friday afternoon, April 26, 1851, a propitious day between the new and the full moon when the tide was in. Duncan Campbell, the solemn, young pastor from Glasgow, preached a sermon about "narrow is the way" and intoned the holy vows they repeated in strong voices. Abigail tried to concentrate on everything, but she was floating in joy.

Though she wore her usual Sunday garb and not her precious pink and rose gown as she had always dreamed, she felt so special. It was if she walked heaven itself, for the parlor's deep blue carpet was soft as featherdown and pliant shoes made from solans' necks shod her feet. Perched on her loosed hair, which fell like sunset-struck clouds around her shoulders, was the village bridal cap, passed from one bride to the next, with its starched ribbons fanned out like angel wings.

How glorious Douglas looked today in his blue kelt coat and white wool trousers. He had become a man indeed—her man. Though his golden hair was wind-winnowed from their walk through the village, everything else about him seemed perfectly in order.

Nearly a third of the islanders were present, including Grandfather MacAuley, Neil Gillies and his folk, and Douglas's family, except Margaret. Even for this event, she would not leave her nursing six-day-old daughter. Abigail had encouraged her for she knew that, despite Margaret's joy with her bairn, she now faced the fear of all new St. Kildan mothers. Blessedly, there were no signs of the infant blight on the child.

But seeing that mingling of sadness and happiness in Margaret's life and in her own, Abigail understood both parts of the Reverend Mr. Campbell's inquiry. "Douglas Adair and Abigail MacQueen, wilt thou vow to live together in both weal and woe?" She was praying for and planning for a life of weal with Douglas, but she had seen enough of woe to know it could lurk around the corner too. Certain people missing the young cragsman's wedding today reminded her further of that: Edmund, Isobel, and the entire influential MacCrimmon-Fergusson clan, except for Annie, who had come at the last minute, maybe to report all she saw to Flora. Abigail thought on such a small island it seemed wrong for folks not to be together to celebrate the good times.

Abigail and Douglas knelt on the marriage stool during the benediction, then were out the door into the sun and wind of their braw new life together.

Ordinarily, the bride's family would give a feast, but the offerings of sorrel soup, mutton, fresh fowl, barley bannocks, and cheese laid out at Abigail's cottage were from the combined larders of the MacAuleys, the Adairs, the Gillieses, and Abigail, as well as Douglas's work on the cliffs. Folks brought their own drinks of whey, milk, or tea. After partaking heartily from the food spread on borrowed tables in the crowded cottage, people spilled out into the street to sing and dance. For several years the Scottish Free Kirk had not allowed bagpipe music at weddings as the old hearthsong described, but this crowd did well enough with mouth music. And through it all, Abigail's heart sang with joy. She joined the young lasses in the old St. Kilda Wedding Lilt, and everyone romped through a reel or two. The minister even clapped and smiled a bit, though of course, he did not join the dancing.

Afterward, with Douglas's blessing, Abigail ducked out to take a plate of food to Margaret and look in on her new niece. Abigail hugged Margaret again; she and Douglas and Neil had all done so earlier, stopping on their procession from the manse. Her friend had purple circles under her eyes yet. It was not fair, Abigail railed again silently, that St. Kilda mothers must face the pain of childbirth only to labor through this agony of watching to see if the child would live or die. In the old days, Abigail had heard, some fathers built a tiny casket outside even as a bairn was being born inside. It was to try to ward off bad luck, but no one in these enlightened times did that anymore. More change for the better that Parliament had denied was needed here, Abigail mused, before she scolded herself for such wayward thoughts.

As she bent over the cradle near the fire, she whispered to her new sister-in-law, "She looks so bonny and peaceful." No one but the parents knew the child's name, and no one spoke it until after the minister said it aloud the first time at the christening, two weeks after the birth. "So, the lass is sleeping well enough with all the noise, but how about her mother?"

"Och, I'm fine, or will be when this dreadful waiting's over," Margaret whispered, wrapping her arms around herself. " 'Til then, I must keep an eye on her for the signs . . ."

Abigail grasped her friend's shoulders and looked into her eyes. "I see only signs of a full life ahead for her and all of us."

"Aye, and I wager ye'll be big with a bairn a scant nine months after tonight!" Margaret teased. She gently pushed Abigail's arm, though she did not smile. Abigail hugged her again and hurried back to their guests. How perfectly everything had turned out for her and Douglas! How foolish she had been to think she would not make him a good wife. She had not even bothered to write down nor sing aloud the new wedding song that had been running through her head all morning. Giving up the inspiration of her heart was a small price to pay for being Douglas Adair's wife and not Abigail MacQueen anymore!

Though Abigail had carefully done everything that was prescribed during her betrothal and on her wedding day, that night, for her beloved alone, she hung her bright-banded curtains at the window, she made their bed with the crimson blanket, and she donned her shell-pink and sunset-rose gown for him. Standing in the wavering light of the glowing hearth and single crusie lamp in his white wool shirt, Douglas stared wide-eyed at the array of color surrounding her.

"My bonny Abby," he said, his usually strong voice a mere whisper.

She smiled at him blissfully. He had made this once lonely cottage a part of himself already: his climbing ropes and oars, his clothes, his fishing pole, his shaving things, and his baskets of yarn

to weave on her father's loom were piled on or around her childhood bed. There, over the years, she had smiled in the dark at
things he had said each day or dreamed of his strong arms around
her in their own home. And now it was true.

"Abby, my wife," he murmured as he came to her and held her
and his lips ravished her wild hair.

She draped her arms around his strong neck and fluttered
kisses up his throat. He murmured and tilted her lower body tighter
to his hips and thighs where she felt the proof of his powerful desire
for her. She could not believe they were safe now, and free, and allowed to love, after the many times they had nearly been swept
away by forbidden passion up in their hidden castle on Mullach
Sgar. Now, the rest of their lives, here in their own castle of Lady
Grange's house, they would share their bodies and their lives in
weal and woe.

He lifted her and, not breaking a deep kiss, put one knee on
their bed to lay her down tenderly. He sprawled beside her; he
seemed to take the entire length and width of bed, but he made
room for them both by cradling her slightly under him. His big
body hovered over her, like a protective roof against the world,
holding out hurt, even if hemming her in. His free hand skimmed
her gown along her curves which fit so perfectly against his angles.
They kissed and caressed until her head spun with the wonder of it.

"I swore to myself, Abigail Adair, I would go slow our first
night wed," his voice rasped in her ear. "But lass, I canna wait after
all our time apart, all the times I stopped myself when I wanted ye
more than life itself!"

He came closer, opening her to him, pressing her down. She
welcomed the gentle, then wild, joining. It felt like nothing else, this
becoming part of him, this moving to his rhythm, then matching it
with her own.

"Abby—och, Ab—" he gasped out as this wonderful new
world she had discovered exploded in a blinding revelation of the
depths of their love.

They swept between exhilaration and exhaustion that too-short
first night as they loved, then loved again. She slept now in his
arms, their flesh and hair silvered by the remnants of fireglow, cradled by the dusky smell of peat smoke wrapping their limbs. But it

suddenly seemed light enough that Abigail could see a woman walking down to their cottage from the cliffs over the sea. Oh, yes, she recognized her now: it was her mother come to give them both best wishes for their wedding. Glorious Glenna MacQueen's arms, open to embrace her daughter, dripped vaporous drapery from her fog-clad form.

Abigail floated from the bed and went to meet her. How good it would be to see her again, to tell her of her great victory with Douglas. But she also must tell her that Coll was gone out to sea and never returned. She unlatched and swung wide the cottage door.

But the woman who stood there had no face, only swirling mist within the frame of hair where skin and features should be.

"Who—are you?" Abigail asked the figure. She tried to call to Douglas; she tried to run, but her feet were leaden and her voice strangled in her throat.

"Lady Grange," the woman declared, her voice wailing like the wind. "This is where my beloved husband imprisoned me, for loving him too much, for protesting wrong and wanting change, for having my own thoughts and dreams. I came to warn your mother, and I've come to warn you before it is too late . . ."

The woman held up a mirror to Abigail, and she peered wide-eyed into it—but there was no face where her own should be. Abigail could only hear the echoing sob from a deep well in the void and mirror and mist.

Abigail screamed to make the specter go away, to call Douglas to save her, Douglas . . .

"Abby! Lass, ye're having a nightmare and calling my name. Abby, wake up!"

Douglas. She clung to his solid warmth. He had a face, a profile in the hint of daylight through the curtained window. It was not night. There had been no woman at the door. She held tighter to him.

"Do ye oft have such fearsome dreams, my lass?" he asked as he rocked her a bit against his bare chest to let cold air under the blanket. "Dinna like the screaming. My folks next door will think ye're ordering me about already, and I wilna have that. Though," he added and cupped one hand, then another under her bare bottom, "ye can call out my name and hold to me anytime at night ye will, and I shall comfort ye."

She still felt a bit dazed as his hands began to wander her flesh again. Slowly, she relaxed and responded. But why, she thought as the memory of the phantom visitation clung coldly to her, had she dreamed such an awful thing when she felt free and so very happy at last?

4

Gleann Mor lives within me,
Moods to match my own,
Beauty wild and free,
My heart-wings' true home.

Gleann Mor, shrine of memories
Of other lives like mine,
Ecstasies and tragedies,
Life daily and divine.

The last day in April, Abigail led the singing of various old hearthsongs as twenty-eight women and eighteen lasses trudged up and through the two-mile mountain pass to tend to the goats and cows. The animals needed to be milked twice daily. On the morning journey, a cap of clouds had garbed the brow of Mullach Sgar and flung down gusty showers to make the passage difficult. But this afternoon, as they descended the twisting path into the green valley called Gleann Mor on the far side of the isle, the sun was warm and bright. The trill of a snow-bunting welcomed them, and little Fionna called out her discovery of an early yellow primrose sheltered in the shadow of a rock.

The path was well worn all the way, dipping and weaving around boulders or the hump-backed stone storehouses called cleits that dotted the island. Built with unmortared stone to shed rain but admit wind, cleits preserved the precious barrels of salted fulmar and other perishable foodstuffs. The domed larders were a bit shorter than a man, and had a small doorway to crawl in. When she was a child, Abigail had called them selkie houses, certain that such fairy spirits that swam from isle to isle in seal skins must have someplace to hide when they came ashore.

"Och, look, Abigail," Annie Fergusson turned back to her and pointed down toward the small loch at the far end of the glen. "Those bonxie birds are making short work of the fulmars again!"

Abigail and several of the others shaded their eyes to see better. Like specks of whirling dust below their view, the dark, hook-beaked bonxies dove after fulmars in flight, seizing the food they were forced to disgorge in midair or attacking the fulmars themselves. They chased them on the cliffs; they even rousted them from cleits where the fulmars, ignorant they were seeking shelter in a man-made gravehouse for their own kind, met their untimely deaths. The noise was so great at times, that the goats and cattle looked up and shied away.

"Let's not be dawdling, lass," Annie's mother, Janet Fergusson, scolded as she puffed her way to Abigail and Annie. She had been walking with Flora, who flounced past without a word. "And no larking about when we start the milking in the glen either. Yer to set a good example to Fionna, just as Flora does for ye," she added as she moved off down the path without so much as a glance at Abigail.

Sighing, Abigail hurried on again to catch up with Mairi. Abigail had learned to expect short shrift from nearly anyone related to Flora or her grandmother Isobel, but it still hurt. Even though she was lugging Margaret's pails as well as her own, Abigail stretched her strides to match Mairi's; from one of Douglas's old ropes and two pieces of driftwood, she had rigged herself a double-yoked harness to tote the extra burden while Margaret was still confined with the child. In just two days' time the Gillieses' bairn would be well past the danger time and her christening would be planned. At least, Abigail thought, both she and Mairi shared the expectation of hearing what the lass's name would be. Whenever Douglas or Hamish were about, Mairi was civil enough to her, but she said little and frowned a great deal when they were not.

"I do thank ye for tending my lass's pails, Abigail," Mairi told her, giving her hope for a better relationship. "With my just getting over that bout of green sickness, the added weight is too much for me right now, though I would do it if I must."

"I'm glad to do it, for you and Margaret too, Mother Adair." Abigail assured her. "And when 'twill be the three of us—with the new child on Margaret's back too—we'll be able to share our daily family doings."

Perhaps to save her breath, Mairi made no other comment. As everyone filed down amid the bogs and rolling meadows embraced by hills, Abigail began the hearthsong of the milking ritual, and the others joined in. As with each journey to Gleann Mor, however burdened bodily or mentally, Abigail's heart sang a silent song of her own making, full of her love for this place.

For unlike tidier, tamer Village Bay, Gleann Mor suited her soul: it had a lively, luring spirit of its own. The face of the glen changed expressions with fitful bursts of sunshine and shadows like a body's moods; it danced with the changeable beauty of the present scene and the voiceless past. The wind ruffled the glen's grassy hair that would soon bedeck itself with butterwort, roseroot, and tiny orchids. The small loch, which this time of year the brazen bonxies thought they owned, reflected the constant change of sky like a giant eye turned to the heavens. The river of the glen tumbled to a waterfall twisting over the cliffside to the sea in a deep rumble of a giant's laughter. No, she thought, there was nothing really pagan about this place as Parliament had said, just something wild and wonderful. And best of all were the tumbled down but enduring stones of old cottages, like memories, of folks long departed who had lived here once and loved this place which so fascinated Abigail.

In what people called the Old Village, some of the beehive houses were rubble, but the one with tunneled halls and sleeping nooks called the Warrior Woman's House still stood. And next to it, where there remained a ruined altar to some unknown Viking god, was the holy well, the Well of Virtue, a spirit which folks in olden times thought must be appeased to give a cure. The few times Abigail had found time to come here alone—especially when it was not the season for the livestock—she had pretended the ancient house and well were hers and she could live here as the queen of this enchanting glen. Then, too, when she was a wee lass and used to make the milking walk with her mother, she had thought the glen must be her mother's own, just from the sound of the words: Glenna's glen, Glenna's golden and green glen, Glorious Glenna's glorious glen . . .

"I said, Abigail, are ye going to sing that same verse of the milking song over again?" young Sarah Nichol said and bounced one of Abigail's empty pails on her yoke. "Not listening to yer own words, are ye lass? Head in the clouds," her voice came louder as more women clustered around. "Not even a week wed, I know where your head really is," she teased. Then, when she saw Mairi's narrow-eyed stare, she added, "Och, sorry Mrs. Adair, but we have been brides, too, eh?"

Abigail laughed with several others and Mairi nodded. But over Sarah's shoulder, Abigail caught a glimpse of Flora's sour face and sobered. How she wished that Flora might forgive her and might smile again to find another lad for herself. But now was not the time to try to make amends with her, for she had Margaret's newborn and Mairi to worry about and a hundred tasks to do.

Having a husband made more work—albeit joyous work—than Abigail had imagined. She no longer ate when she wanted nor what she wanted; she cooked bigger, more elaborate meals. She had rearranged the inside of her house to accommodate and give precedence to Douglas's goods. She cleaned the small area twice as much, picking up and putting back his things. Her evenings, when she used to do the dyeing and make the cheese, were at his bidding. And trying to do Margaret's out-of-doors tasks with her own, as well as helping Mairi and watching Ross and Murdo at times, though she loved them both dearly . . . As the women began to call the cows, she suddenly realized she was exhausted.

That night, her head close to his on the settle as if she whispered some secret to him, Abigail fell asleep while Douglas told her of his day. He carried her to bed. The next morning, after they partook of porridge, he set out with his brother-in-law and best friend Neil for Parliament. Today they would be in a work party to harvest guillemots from the ledges of Conachair. Abigail hurried with tasks and arrived at Margaret's barely in time to hook on the additional four pails for the morning milking trek.

She almost complained to Margaret that Parliament should have heeded her suggestion about turning some of the milk to cheese over in Gleann Mor, but she held her tongue. She had vowed she would neither complain about the way things were nor set forth new ideas anymore; she had promised Douglas as he had Parliament. Anyway, Margaret looked too tired and haggard to listen, or perhaps she had just roused herself from bed. Abigail supposed she looked a fright too, as she had not combed her hair properly, binding it back with yarn under her kerch.

"Just let me take a peek at my niece, and I'll be on my way," she said to Margaret, who blocked the door. "After all, I didna get to see her yesterday."

"Ye'd just wake her with the thumping of those pails," Margaret said with a decisive nod.

"But I hear her fussing inside," Abigail said and began to shrug off her yoke.

"Och. I'll see to her then, and ye stop by later." The words trailed over Margaret's shoulder as she stepped inside and closed the door in Abigail's face.

She stood there, surprised and hurt. But of course having a new bairn was going to change her friend's life, just as having a new husband had changed her own, she tried to tell herself. She and Margaret would be even closer over the years when Abigail bore a bairn or two! She turned away and ran to catch up with the others, her empty pails hitting her legs and clanking against each other.

"Abigail!" Douglas's distant voice jolted her that day near noon where she stood wearily stirring her dye pot.

"Here!" she called and dropped the stick in her haste to get outside. He was nearly running toward the cottage, but when she came out, he motioned for her and started away again.

She hurried after him. "What's amiss? Why are you back already? Nobody went over the rocks?" she asked, referring to the fact that several fowlers died that way every year. Strange, she had never worried about that for her Douglas, but trusted his skills.

"Not that. Andrew Nichol brought word out to the cliffs that Mother sent for me. Have ye not seen Margaret and the bairn today?"

"She told me the lass was sleeping again. It—it canna be!" she cried and tore after Douglas toward the Gillieses' cottage. Had the worst happened? She could not believe it. Her heart thudded in her throat for more than just Margaret's plight. Douglas's mother had sent for him clear up on the cliffs when she had yet to call for her new daughter-in-law in the next cottage! She had still chosen to shut Abigail out from Margaret and her new family in this time when they must all help each other.

"But Douglas, the bairn should be through the wait," she insisted. "Even this morning, Margaret said things were fine, and Neil has been saying the same, so—"

"Neil came back with me," Douglas told her. "He says Margaret's been keeping him away too. He's been gone each day, and she walks the bairn all night while the wee mite whimpers."

Abigail felt as if the ground had dropped from under her. But Mairi had seen the child recently; she had said so. Now which day was that? Abigail had been so busy, so tired, and Margaret had been so protective—that was to be expected, wasn't it? Abigail had been so sure everything was all right! But the scene that greeted them inside the Gillieses' cottage when Hamish opened the door— oh, dear God, Hamish had been sent for too!—terrified her.

Neil and Mairi stood beseeching Margaret to let them look at the child, but she stood, backed into a corner, facing them down. "No, she's fine, just fussy!" she told them, cradling the blanket-wrapped bairn close to her breasts. "And I dinna want the knee-woman here! Yer all fretting for naught! Mrs. MacCrimmon said she is a sturdy child. Didna she say so, Abigail!"

Abigail walked to stand between Neil and Mairi, her hands held out to her friend. Margaret's eyes were wild; her skin stark white. She looked like a cornered fulmar facing down a cluster of bonxies to save her chick. How had she not seen this coming? Abigail scolded herself. Why had she not left her tasks to stay with her friend and sister longer than the birthing night!

"Margaret, no one means to take the bairn from you," Abigail said. Her voice shook, but her tone was soothing. "We just want to see her—"

The door slammed open. Abigail spun to see Hamish grab for it as Isobel MacCrimmon strode in. "Isobel," Mairi said, her voice choked with sobs, "the bairn—the signs."

"No, she is fine!" Margaret screamed. "Ye said she was fine, Mrs. MacCrimmon!" But in the presence of the knee-woman, Margaret edged along the wall and sank upon the bed as if doomed. She bent over the child cradled in the valley of her thighs; her long, lank hair hung down nearly to her ankles like a curtain to hide the bairn. Isobel raised her to a sitting position and bent over to unwrap the child. Abigail gasped at the difference in the appearance of the wee lass: the bluish body seemed already stiff, with almost knotted limbs which quaked.

"The bairn has not been suckling for a day or two," Isobel pronounced. The cottage was silent but for Margaret's racking sobs. Neil went to bend over her, gripping her shoulders; Douglas put his arm around Abigail. "Aye, the wee jaws are locked," Isobel went on, her deep voice like the drone of a bagpipe. "Has she had the fits? Well, has she, lass, and ye been hiding it and not believing it yerself?" she demanded of Margaret.

When Margaret did not answer, Isobel said to Mairi, "Aye, that's the way of it, for I have seen it in six of my eight bairns beside many others. A new mother has the worse time with it."

"I had the worse time with it all three times," Mairi said, and, slump-shouldered, shuffled over to sit on the bed beside her daughter. Standing across the room as if to guard the door, Hamish hung his head and sniffed hard once, twice. Douglas snatched his cap off his head. Abigail walked past the knee-woman to sit on Margaret's other side, so those women closest to her could watch and wait and mourn together.

"I canna—canna lose her," Margaret choked out, seizing both her mother's and Abigail's wrists in a wrenching grip. Then, with her own tears, Margaret Adair Gillies baptized her child, for it was the only christening the bairn would ever have.

On St. Kilda, deceased adults were interred in the afternoon and children in the morning, but for an eight day's child with no name, no cry went out, no formal funeral procession or funeral feast was held. Instead, the bairn's father and his friends took the tiny coffin to the approved spot above the cemetery proper and placed it in the ground amid the numerous other infant no-name graves while the family's women mourned at home. So common were the losses from the sickness that life went quickly on, with prayers another pregnancy and successful christening would ensue next time.

But three days later, when Margaret was still inconsolable, Abigail walked up with her to see the infant's grave. Abigail was touched to see it was not far from her mother's own, for as a possible suicide, Glenna MacQueen had not been buried in the cemetery proper, however much Coll had raged and Abigail had cried.

Margaret's tears had finally stopped. Unspeaking, they sat on a boulder above the oval-walled cemetery, the wind tearing at their hair, memories tearing at their hearts. They planted a few primroses in the newly relaid turf, then sat down on the boulder again.

Finally, Margaret said, "At least the right proper cemetery stones dinna have names either, but 'tis only since everyone knows who lies there."

"You and I wilna forget where your bairn lies," Abigail assured her.

"I—I whispered her name to her before I wrapped her for the coffin, ye ken. My daughter has a name!" Margaret declared and seized Abigail's hands.

Abigail looked deep into her friend's swollen eyes. "And she has her mother's love she took with her," Abigail said. "As tiny as she was, even with the suffering, she had that."

Margaret nodded fiercely. "I am so sorry I didna share the bairn's plight sooner, but there's naught ye could do. Like a dunderhead, I thought if no one kenned she had the signs, she might yet live. But I named her for ye, my dearest friend and comfort, Abigail!"

"For me? You named her Abigail?"

"Are ye sorry since she's gone?"

" 'Tis a great honor, my dear, for I loved her too! And it makes me wonder many things! I am not so sure there's naught we can do, if not for our little Abigail, then for other bairns."

"Ye mean to pray harder and hope the penance is done."

"I mean find a cure. There has to be some earthly reason this happens, despite what the kirk and fore-elders say about God's judgment on all women as eternal Eves. Why would God take innocents to Himself in such great numbers here when he dinna do it elsewhere so sore?"

"Mother says, maybe He wants perfect angels with Him in heaven—little cherubs," Margaret said listlessly.

Abigail shook her head. "Do you think we're worse sinners here with all our kirk-going and the Parliament's stiff rules? We've all heard bairns dinna die in such number in the Hebrides or on the mainland! We should go there to see what they do different!"

"Abigail, I'm angry too, but it dinna do a bit of good to wonder and argue."

Even up here in the whirl of wind, Abigail leaned closer to Margaret and spoke almost in a whisper. "But think, lass," she said. "I guess it canna be the toting heavy pails twice a day right up 'til the birthing, since healthy bairns are born to mothers who do the same. But maybe the cause is the mother not being allowed a wee dram of water during her travail. Or that horrid kneading of the babe from the womb. It seemed Mrs. MacCrimmon was bound to force that bairn from you by midnight, and I pray it wasna because I angered her. The knee-woman—"

Margaret yanked her hands free. She pressed her palms to her ears as if she were a child frightened by a tale of terror. "Stop it, Abigail Adair! I dinna want to live it all again. I dinna want to think of all the pain of having the bairn and losing her! And ye promised Douglas and everybody there would be no more questioning and struggling against the way of things. Ye dinna understand because ye dinna have a bairn of yer own yet, but ye will. No more!" she said and, swiping at the gush of fresh tears, gathered her skirts and hurried down to the village.

Abigail just sat there. Margaret was right to scold; such rebellious ideas and potential accusations would cause nothing but trouble in her marriage and the village. From her own face, she wiped tears of mourning for the infant Abigail, for Margaret, for all the St. Kilda bairns.

She rose and walked slowly to her mother's windswept grave. Despite the stunning view of Village Bay, Abigail did not like it here, for it brought painful thoughts. And on a day so clear as this, she could see her mother's home of Harris, a dark hump on the horizon. When her parents had buried her own two brothers as eight day bairns, had Glenna MacQueen raised her green eyes and seen Harris where her family lived? Had she longed to escape on the wings of morning to the place she had loved the MacLeod laird's own son, the place from which she had followed him and to which she returned to find shame and then Coll MacQueen? Had her mother ever really loved her father, as desperately as he had adored her?

Quickly, Abigail picked more primroses to deck her mother's resting place, then hurried back to her tasks in the village.

In midsummer, when most of the heavy harvesting of birds was done, Abigail convinced Douglas to take her on a midday ramble to Gleann Mor. Holding and swinging hands, they walked the well-worn path the women used. Margaret had been asking her for weeks to let her carry her pails so they could have such a day. Douglas had been on the cliffs so many weeks and was so exhausted at night that they had little time to talk and hardly time for loving before they both fell asleep. Time together was the one thing that could make Abigail yearn for the lengthy winter nights where folks lit the lamps by three in the afternoon and often kept inside before an early bed. There was no sign of a bairn in her womb yet, but they both—despite their fears—hoped for one. At least today, for these brief hours in this lovely place, they had time to treasure each other.

"Let's look inside the Warrior Woman's House before we explore the cave," Abigail coaxed Douglas while tugging at his hand. In his other, he carried a basket with hard-cooked puffin eggs, fresh fowl, and bannocks. " 'Tis right by the well where I'll draw us some water."

"Ye can draw our water from the burn," Douglas told her and pulled her back. "I dinna care if the ancients called it the Well of Virtue, 'tis forbidden. And as for yer fascination with that old ruin of a house, ye can visit it another day when yer done with the milking."

"When I'm done with the milking, my love," she told him as she knelt to fill the pitcher from the swift, clear burn, "I set out straightaway with the others to haul it back."

They carefully made their way down the steep, rocky path toward the sea on the windward side of Gleann Mor's waterfall so the rock would not be slick with blowing mist.

"Here I am, taking time away from my duties, and I have to watch my footing again," Douglas teased, trying to sound gruff.

" 'Tis second nature to you, my love. No wonder you see fulmars and guillemots and gannets in your sleep. Dinna you think Edmund's quotas of those birds wanted just for their feathers is a wee bit high this year?"

"That's for Parliament to discuss, lass," he said, then added, "but the count is higher than last year by far. A hard driving man, Edmund is, but of himself too. And I never told ye, but I had a few words with him over his courting ye, but he argued like a cleric. Said he didna know a cragsman fine as I had my eye on ye, and said I should approve of his taste in lasses." Douglas's voice swelled with pride at recounting all that, but Abigail only shook her head when he was not looking. "Aye, Edmund's only doing his part," Douglas concluded, "and that's the way of it."

Abigail held her peace on that too, especially when Douglas told her, "If ye had been born a lad, my bonny wife, ye'd have been a braw cragsman yerself with all yer graceful climbing!" Abigail flushed with the compliment, but she squealed when they disturbed a fulmar nest and the beady-eyed bird spit its foul-smelling stream of oil at her skirts.

"Oh, the blighter!" she cried, staring at the brown stain while Douglas laughed.

"Dinna touch it with yer hand, lass," he warned and bent to wipe it away with his neck scarf. " 'Tis vile stuff. It always was a wonder to me that fulmar body oil can be so good for things and its spit oil so harsh."

She calmed herself while her proud man tended her skirt like a washer woman. His concern touched her so deeply she thought she would cry. But she mustn't, not on their happy day together.

"Why didna it spit at you?" she teased him. "You're the cragsman!"

"He kens yer the cragsman's cook," he told her, and the breeze lifted their laughter to mingle with the cacophony of birds eternally drifting by these cliffs.

Finally, they descended to a ledge near where the plunging waterfall met the surge of sea. Darting past the roaring crash of green and white foam, they ducked under the veil of mist. Before them lay the cave hidden from land and sea.

They stood hushed in the private beauty of the place few folk visited but once or twice in their lifetimes. Unlike the stolid, stoic St. Kildans, Abigail thought, the cave was changing all the time as the sea kept carving out new alcoves and swallowing stone buttresses and digging deeper floors.

" 'Tis so bonny here," she said above the boom of water as they moved along the shelf of the cave just above the inward wash and outward flow of sea. "It's been years since my parents brought me here . . . here . . . here," her voice echoed.

Douglas nodded, his eyes on the cave wall's dancing flickers of light. "I came once with the other lads who wanted to be cragsmen, just testing our skills," he said, putting the basket down, and turned her to face him. "But, like our castle on Mullach Sgar, this place belongs to us alone, my dearest!"

She nodded as unshed tears prickled her eyes. His words made her miss their old trysting place, however forbidden their actions were then. Still at times, there was something great and grand about forbidden things, she mused—when a body knew that she was right! And then her thoughts scattered as her husband pressed her gently against the damp wall and began to kiss her.

When they touched like this, everything else seemed swept away. Her questions, complaints, and protests all went under in the tidal surge of her desire for him. She held to him, both yielding and enticing, letting her body be molded to his, feeling her emotions pulled by his needs and wishes.

Yet, even when they finally moved apart to sit and eat, the world around them turned as awesome as her inner one. Sleek gray seals swam into the cave to cavort with their pups and sing their haunting, one-note tunes. And sun seeping through the veil of spray made a radiant rainbow to dye the interior iridescent hues.

"We will have a child, Abby," Douglas told her, as if he had read her thoughts as the little seals preened and played. She nodded and turned to become lost in the deep pools of his eyes. And there, she saw the rainbow of his promise too.

Abigail lay drowsy and secure in Douglas's arms on their first New Year's Eve as man and wife. Tonight, returning from his parents' cottage after the traditional feast of mutton, fowl, and oatmeal cake, they had watched the cool colors of the winter lights leap across the sea-black sky that made her recall the rainbow in the cave last summer. And she recalled his promise to her that they would make a child. They had done so, sometime in November, and the birth would be almost a year after that day in the rainbow cave.

She huddled closer to his warmth, as he breathed heavily behind her to stir the tendrils of her hair. She smiled into the darkness as she recalled the happiness tonight on all the Adair and Gillieses' faces—even Mairi's—when Douglas had announced the bairn's impending birth. Abigail had fretted it would hurt Margaret, but she was much her old self now and said almost cheerfully she and her Neil would soon have fine news too.

Abigail sighed and shifted her position to place a hand on her still-flat belly. Douglas warmed her, as she warmed the child. Oh, she had such plans for its birthing! She must keep Isobel MacCrimmon away that day. For her lying in, there would be as much water to drink as she wanted and no bonds tying her down and no knee-woman kneading the child from her womb! Especially not a woman who obviously detested her. She would be certain she began her labor in Gleann Mor where Isobel could not get to her. Abigail knew she could take supplies over there, hidden in her empty milk pails. And she had nearly seven months to convince Margaret to help with her plan.

Her belly radiated heat to her hand through her wool gown. Within, like a far, intriguing, distant, and unknown isle, floated her child, waiting to be discovered. Abigail would give her strength to this tiny isle, nurturing and protecting it until it appeared on the horizon to be known and charted and loved.

If ever a St. Kilda bairn was to escape the eight day sickness, it would be hers! And to be certain, beyond her plans for its birthing, she vowed that she would neither question nor disobey her husband nor Parliament nor the kirk. It was the beginning of a wonderful new year and new life for her and Douglas and the bairn they had created.

April 26, 1852, dawned a happy day for Abigail. The wind was sweet and strong that brought Douglas home from the fowlers' first trip to Boreray this year to harvest newly arrived gannets. Margaret was again with child and so hopeful; the Gillieses' bairn would be born but three months after Abigail and Douglas's. Today, she and her braw love had been wed a year and a day, and a fine supper she would make for him tonight to celebrate. As for the continued making of her own bairn, the future looked bright. She was sleeping well, even with Douglas away this week, and, with his permission, had dyed the small blankets Neil and Douglas had woven this winter a dark rose hue—so dark that it looked almost brown until it met with his approval, she thought, but it was the first real dyeing she liked that she had done this year. She smiled as she hooked her milking pails on the yoke that, surprisingly, several other women had copied, and started out on the morning milk journey.

When they returned, she and Margaret shared some bannocks and cheese in the Adair cottage. They both lay down for a short nap, Abigail on her and Douglas's bed, Margaret on Abigail's old box bed. Abigail did it because she thought it rested the child from being swayed and rocked inside her all the time; it was just one of the myriad theories she silently pursued to care for her unborn bairn. Margaret slept because she could not keep her head up after a noon meal.

Abigail awakened, sure someone was knocking at the door. But it was only the window shutter, banging like a drum.

She jolted alert. The shutter never came loose unless the wind had turned wrong—wrong for boats returning from Boreray to Village Bay.

"Margaret, wake up. The wind's from the southeast," she said. She hurried out behind the cottage to scan the sea. Clots of lead-gray clouds boiled overhead. It was not unusual for a sudden squall to come up in calm waters, but this southerly wind would pound the bay with rolling surf and keep the men from turning back to Boreray if they had set out already. She squinted to see stick figures down by the landing rocks, where the two boats out would have no choice but to put in. Margaret had come to stand beside her; a gust yanked their kerches off and ripped their hair straight back as Abigail turned to her. The wind tore even their words away.

"I dinna see the boats, do ye?" Margaret shouted. "Pray God they will sit it out o'er there!"

Without speaking, Abigail knew they would both head down to the landing place to join the watch. While Margaret went ahead to her cottage, Abigail donned Douglas's outgrown oilskin coat. She coiled one of his old boating ropes over her shoulder and carried his extra grappling hook. She told herself not to strain, not to worry. The child was at her mercy, while Douglas was a trained cragsman and boatman. But she knew, too, that St. Kildans, canny and braw as they might be, were often at the mercy of the weather and the sea.

Walking down the street with Margaret, bent into the wind, Abigail stopped to talk to Grandfather MacAuley. Braced against the wall of his cottage, he gazed seaward, though no one could see the shore from here.

"I hear the birlins have entered the bay," he told her, using the traditional name for the sturdy island boats. Three men rowed and one held the rudder lines; birlins could carry much cargo and up to six other men. They had sails to hoist for open water, but St. Kilda men were skilled rowers, not sailors. She assumed the same eight boatmen had taken the two birlins back to Boreray to fetch the gathering party of six men, including Douglas and Neil.

She squeezed Grandfather's hands and shouted. "I couldna tell from home if they were coming in. I must go down—Margaret too."

"Aye," he said. "Godspeed ye, lasses, but those lads are the best we have, so dinna ye be fretful."

On the shore in the full blast of wind and spraying surf, Abigail felt more frenzied than fretful. Those waiting ashore could barely make out the black lumps of birlins now, tossed by waves and wind and tide. Caught like this, partway in, they had no choice but to try to make the rocky shore. Abigail knew they must be shipping a lot of water, for they seemed upended each time they crested a wave and dipped into the next black, sliding trough. It was taking them forever to make headway in.

"These big landing rocks are slippery!" Mairi scolded as she tugged both Margaret and Abigail back onto the pebbly beach. "I'll not have ye two slip and fall in yer condition." Abigail was grateful to recall that Hamish had not gone out with Douglas at the last minute because Mairi had been ailing with the green sickness this year too; yet Mairi had come clear down here to wait. Abigail saw her father-in-law in the cluster of men with their ropes and long grappling hooks. There was a rescue boat at the ready too, though it would only brave the breakers if the worst happened.

The women huddled together, squinting into the sting of salt spray. The Reverend Mr. Campbell arrived and joined the women with a command couched like a kindly question: "Shall we make worship for the men in dire distress?" Abigail willingly bowed her head, seeking assurance. And yet, deep in her core, she was certain Douglas and Neil would be safe. It might be true that her man's prowess was upon the cliffs, but strong St. Kilda men went to sea as lads to learn the winds and waves en route to Boreray, Soay, or even Harris. If her father had not gone out alone, he would not have disappeared upon the sea!

She squeezed her eyes tight shut in prayer, holding on to Margaret's hand on one side and Mairi's on the other. We are a family now, thank you, Lord, she prayed her own inward words while Mr. Campbell's voice challenged the roar of wind with formal, proper exhortations. And please, she prayed silently, if it be Your will, care for the men as well as the bairns they have made who are going to need their fathers in this St. Kilda life. She felt better then; yet she knew she prayed to a God who, no doubt for His own good reasons, sometimes did not seem to heed weak human pleas.

But when she heard Iain Murdoch's distant shout, "They have to get in before the tide turns against them!" she lifted her head and opened her eyes to stare right over the minister's shoulder to watch the sea again. A turning tide meant the birlins would ship backwash from both sides. She did not flinch when Mr. Campbell ended the prayer and frowned at her for not having her head bowed and eyes closed; she joined in the singing of the familiar Twenty-third Psalm. She loved the tune and sang it fervently, but her thoughts were not by "pastures green or quiet waters." They were out there, tossed and fearful, on the sea.

At last the lead boat made it through the outward surge of surf and headed in a sprint of oars for the rocks. Everyone screamed with hope and shouted encouragement; a cheer went up, then died in their throats. Out beyond the turn of tide, the other boat rose, twisted, and spilled its cargo into the wrathful, shifting sea.

The men on the landing rocks leapt to action. Hands, hooks, ropes grabbed for the rocking crash of the birlin trying to land, while another crew tried to launch the rescue boat. Abigail moved closer to the shore; she saw Hamish lose his grappling hook and nearly go in, trying to hook the prow of the battered birlin. She seized her hook and scrambled out on the rocks to scream his name and thrust it in his hands. She clambered back as sure-footed as when she had leapt the boulders of the Dun to fetch her precious lichens. For the bairn's sake, she let Margaret pull her back. And then, she saw, praise God, that Douglas stood in the landed birlin ready to spring ashore with his precious climbing rope wrapped around his big body.

"Douglas," she screamed and waved. "Douglas!" She searched faces and forms of the men who disembarked for Neil. No—Neil must have been in the capsized boat.

The men's hands and the women's eyes now went to the rescue boat, for the men overboard were too far out to be seen as they desperately rode and fought the waves. The birlin was launched and shoved back. Abigail ran to Douglas; he gripped her to him; his thick coils of rope pressed painfully against her breasts.

"Oh, my dearest, Neil is in the waves!" she cried over shouts and wailing. "But thank God, you are—"

"We have got to go back out to help," he shouted, more to the other men than her. He gripped her upper arms hard through the oilskin coat. His blond hair plastered to his head made his features and his ears look so big; huge eyes drank her in as if he were famished for the mere sight of her. "Get back, care for our bairn," he ordered and pushed her away. He nodded toward the sobbing Margaret. "Take care of yer best friend, while I rescue mine!"

The landed birlin was tipped to dump the sacks of birds and feathers, supplies, and water on the shore; then it was turned prow toward the waves. Abigail felt herself pitched and tossed upon the roaring sea, however solid the shore under her feet. Douglas was safe, but he was leaving her again. Of course, he must save Neil and the others. But still she ran after him and grabbed his arm and shouted, "I love you, my Douglas!"

He spun back, panting hard, his face running water. "And I ye, always, Abby lass," he said with a strange quiet calm before he clambered into the birlin and took the farthest seat to grab the oars.

Three others threw themselves in behind him. Abigail stepped back as the shout of "Hale! Hale!" signaled the shove to launch between the slash of waves. The other rescue boat had not made it out, but this one did.

The men bent and rowed into the gray, sliding, howling mael-strom. They began the rescue, heaving ropes to those adrift. Then, the brutal grip of waves and wind ripped Douglas from her view and from her arms forever.

5

Sleep secure, St. Kilda bairn,
In your mother's arms.
There be nothing now to fear,
Since you have your name.

Sleep secure, St. Kilda bairn,
In your Savior's arms.
There be nothing now to fear,
Cradled in your grave.

The day of the mass funeral all St. Kildans mourned. Each knew well or was related to more than one of the dead. It was the worst island tragedy of memory: in two boats, twelve hale and hardy men drowned, three of them cragsmen, six of them under age twenty-five. The voracious sea had given up only nine bodies, but there were twelve coffins laid across the benches in Christ's Church that day, each adorned with an item to signify the departed soul's foremost earthly handgift. Several coffins bore a fine piece of weaving or thatching; Neil Gillies's coffin had a fowler's snare, and Douglas Adair's was draped with his best climbing rope. He had drowned in its embrace. Its other end was tightly bound under Neil's armpits in a bold rescue attempt that failed. Tied together in life and death, the bodies of the two St. Kilda men were washed up together on the rocks of Dun.

On this dark funeral day, sun dared to spill through the four glass church windows onto mourners and the well-worn earthen floor. Still, as was the custom, sheep tallow candles burned in the three wooden chandeliers. While the Reverend Mr. Campbell made his rounds, families clustered about their kin's coffin to speak low to those who filed by. Women's sobs and occasional outbursts of wailing pierced the buzz of voices. There was really nothing to be said to make things easier; the fact the survivors knew life would go on went unspoken. The Gillies and Adair coffins stood side by side. Garbed in their somber Sunday best, the two young, pregnant widows often spoke and held hands.

Abigail felt empty. She moved. She talked. But she knew she was hiding from this ponderous loss, huddled somewhere black and silent inside her body like her unborn bairn. She was lost in the misty void of a nightmare she experienced once but could hardly recall. Without Douglas, she felt she had no face, no name, no being. Even words of comfort rang hollow in her head and heart.

"Such a loss to us all, Abigail," Iain Murdoch told her while his wife Rebecca nodded at his side. "So braw a cragsman as Douglas Adair comes along but rarely."

"So braw a husband too, Mr. Murdoch," Abigail replied and took Grandfather MacAuley's hand. Ever faithful, the old man had sat on the bench at the foot of the coffin all morning.

"But yer young yet, lass," Iain plunged on, rotating his cap in his hands.

"I feel very old today," Abigail told the Murdochs. Knit-browed, they nodded to her and Alistair MacAuley, then walked back across the aisle to where their nephew's coffin lay.

"I dinna mean to be short with him," Abigail told Grandfather, "but I shalna wed again, if that's what he was working up to. Not after Doug—" she managed before her words snagged in her throat. Grandfather squeezed her hand before she tugged it back to pull her handkerchief from the bosom of her shawl and blow her nose. Though sniffling back the threatening onslaught of tears, she declined Grandfather's offer to step outside. She did not want to leave Douglas until she had to, even for a moment. Grandfather waited until Margaret came over before he hobbled outside.

"I was thinking," Margaret said, dabbing at wet cheeks, "how Douglas told ye to take care of yer best friend while he saved his. Abby, if I didna have ye right now, my folks or not, bairn coming or not, I'd curl up and die too. And just as Douglas died trying to save my Neil, I would die for ye, and gladly."

"I thank you, my dear," Abigail whispered, "but I canna bear more talk of anyone else dying. We'll not have it, will we?" They leaned together, heads close as if to prop each other up. "But to tell true, Margaret, this bairn Douglas left me and your and Grandfather's support are the only reasons I'm bearing up at all. Of course, your parents' concern helps too, though Isobel MacCrimmon keeps so tight to Mother Adair I can scare get near. And I do have a wee favor to ask of you when my time to deliver the bairn comes."

"Anything, Abby, ye ken that! Just tell me then and—"

"Oh, no, dinna look, but here comes Edmund Drummond again!" Abigail muttered, smacking her hands on her skirt. "And where was he that dreadful day? I didna see him helping. Up in the factor's warm, dry house, I warrant, doing his reckoning of how many dead gannets might wash in with the men's bodies!"

"Sh!" Margaret chided but she had nodded at each thing Abigail had said.

Abigail's anger gave her strength as Edmund stopped before them and doffed his cap. He was forced to look slightly up at her, for there was no a high place for him to stand, unless he climbed into the pulpit, Abigail thought bitterly. But her looking down on him in more ways than one had not stopped him before from offering his unctuous condolences to her, when she only wanted him to stay away.

"Such a sad, long wait for the burying this afternoon, especially for lasses far gone with poor, fatherless bairns," Edmund said. "Is there aught I can do, Abigail—for either of ye?"

"Nary a thing, now or later, thank you, Edmund," she replied, trying to keep from flinging herself behind the coffin to avoid those piercing eyes which pretended to be so proper. With Douglas gone, would this man resume his stalking of her, even when she now knew well the depths to which he could stoop? At least he would not dare propose marriage again until the full mourning period of six months passed.

"Ah, here comes the bonny, unwed Flora," she told him with a dip of her head in the lass's direction. Even in her loss, the Fergussons and the Drummonds had been as pointedly cold to her as they had been overly attentive to Margaret and Mairi. "Perhaps

Flora would like some comforting in her cousin Angus's death," she added when Edmund did not so much as glance Flora's way.

"Ah, perhaps," he said, his complexion staining darker, "but the lass has a large family to care for her, and ye—"

"I do too," Abigail declared. "My grandfather, my dear sister-in-law here, and my husband's brothers and his folks."

"Ah, aye, yer beloved mother-in-law, Mairi Adair, yer so close to," Edmund said. His narrow-eyed look hinted more than his words did at what Mother Adair might be saying to her friends about Abigail. Before she could reply, Edmund replaced his cap on his sleek hair and moved on.

"Such brass," Margaret hissed, "but all polished over too."

Abigail nodded. Edmund was a slippery one who needed watching, and she could not bear even to look his way. Yet, later, when they buried St. Kilda's heroes on the hillside overlooking the sea that took their lives, the man Abigail now came to think of as St. Kilda's villain stared so hard at her she felt more than resentment or revulsion boil inside her. It made her so furious, so fiercely protective of her bairn and herself that she began, for the first time since before her betrothal, to recall other losses: her handgift of dyeing wools bright and her hope of exporting cheese to reduce Edmund's demands for more feathers; the hearthsongs of her heart-wings; her speaking out for the women; her desire for a school here. And now, her desire to discover what was killing the bairns of St. Kilda.

She had once willingly given up such dreams to wed Douglas; now she must continue to forsake them to safeguard his unborn child. Without the protection of her husband's personality and place in the community, she knew she must strive even harder to conform. But already she had rebuffed Edmund Drummond. Besides Flora and Isobel and their kin, her own mother-in-law did not like her.

She must be more careful. She must not allow the St. Kildans to turn against her child for her defiance. She would not permit folks to ostracize her bairn as so many had done her own father. And that was why she was going to have to be very keen and canny, she thought. She must bring her child into the world without doing anything apparently against the honor-bound ways of St. Kilda and without infuriating the keepers of those customs.

This new dedication for her life, these powerful emotions raging through her braced her backbone and lifted her chin as she walked from the cemetery without so much as a glance at Edmund Drummond. She might not feel quite so hollow inside now, but she dreaded returning to a cottage and a life eternally empty of her Douglas.

On July sixteenth Abigail knew her time to deliver the bairn had come. For a week, she and Margaret had been discreetly bringing supplies to Gleann Mor and leaving them inside the Warrior Woman's House where they would keep safe and dry. Though ungainly and uncomfortable, with the rest of her things hidden in her pails, Abigail walked to the afternoon milking. When the first racking pains began, Margaret helped her further put into action their secret plan by announcing to the other women that Abigail had begun her travail and she would stay with her. The women promised they would send someone else to help and headed back. But Annie Fergusson insisted she was the one who would return.

"No need, my friend," Abigail told Annie as the lass stood in the doorway. "I dinna want to be the cause of nettling your family."

"I'm coming back anyway, at least 'til dark," she insisted. "I have always admired ye, and ye have been a good friend to me, Abigail. And if mother and Grandmother MacCrimmon scold me, I'll tell them I must be the one to learn about births, for neither mother nor Flora could stomach being the next knee-woman in the family, that's sure. I'll bring some supplies when I return . . ." Her sweet voice floated back to them as she hurried away with her load of milk.

"I guess she dinna notice all the supplies we have here already," Abigail told Margaret and tried to smile. They had brought several of Abigail's bright-colored things like the rose-hued blanket and the curtains to cheer the inside of this stone house. They had vowed to make everything during Abigail's laboring as different from Margaret's as possible, and that included the mood of the mother and the midwife. No frowning, scolding knee-woman, no birthing stool, no restraints, no kneading of the stomach.

"We needna fear Mrs. MacCrimmon's coming, not with the way the long jaunt has been beneath her for years," Margaret told her as they tried to pass the time calmly chatting between Abigail's pains. "Nor mother either, since she's been weak with the green sickness again."

"I'm not so sure Mother Adair would come even if she could," Abigail said and sat up so Margaret could rub her lower back again. Margaret had little to say about that observation. Abigail let it pass, for she never meant to pull Margaret between the two of them. The lass continually risked her family happiness by remaining Abigail's stalwart friend through everything.

As the afternoon wore on, since the knee-woman had forced Margaret to walk and sit up, Abigail lay flat on her back, making no effort at all. Between pangs, she took to gazing up at the clear blue sky through the vent in the roof. This place gave her a strange strength. Despite her own throes and desperate hopes, her heart-wings took her back to when the Warrior Woman of yore lived here. Did she plan her battles here? At night, did she lie with her husband or lover in one of these recessed sleeping shelves? Did she bear a child here too, a strong son or daughter who felt at one with the wild beauty of Gleann Mor and loved life yet wanted to change the way of things?

"Ah!" Abigail cried out as a sharp pain twisted her. "Could you—fetch me another cool drink from the well, Margaret, and maybe—bring back enough water to warm for washing the bairn later too?"

"Of course. Water from the Well of Virtue for the isle's new Warrior Woman—at least yer that as best ye can be," Margaret declared as she went outside.

Warrior Woman . . . as best ye can be, the words echoed in Abigail's brain. She wanted to fight hard and be and do the best she could, to save this bairn, all bairns. But she was the one who needed the help right now, and when Margaret came back, she had Annie with her, come to help with a basket of goods. Carefully, without telling the lass that they were trying to avoid everything that was traditional in St. Kilda birthing, Margaret explained how Abigail wanted her bairn born.

Annie, claiming she had permission to stay to help, remained through the night. Maybe, Abigail thought once as she fought for calm and control of her body, the knee-woman had encouraged the lass to spy. But Abigail did not actually believe that, for Annie had always offered her friendship even when she suffered for it. Margaret was grateful for another pair of hands; Annie, who admitted she had never yet been permitted to observe her grandmother at work, did not protest the way Abigail wanted things done. During the long night, the fifteen-year-old lass proved to be a blessing.

"Ye'll make a braw, kindly knee-woman someday," Abigail heard Margaret tell Annie, and it was true. *If* she did not learn Isobel MacCrimmon's nature as well as methods.

When dawn broke, Abigail held in her arms her slippery, naked, newborn son. No longer an island within her now, he was still attached to her by the birthing cord Margaret was cutting with a sharp new steel knife instead of the usual traditional iron one. As if curious to see his new world, he slitted open his puffy eyes. They shone sky blue even in the dimness before he closed them and wrinkled his reddish face in a healthy wail. Even wet, his hair looked the hue of spun sunbeams curled in tight ringlets to his tiny skull. He had Douglas's nose and chin, she was certain of it, a precious keepsake of his sire for her to treasure. Realizing she could lose the child, she tried not to love him yet, but she did, more than her own life. She was tempted to blurt out that his name was Douglas, but she dared not break every island tradition. Whatever sacrifices she must make, she fully intended to have her son named and christened in the church. He would become a well-respected St. Kilda man, as his father had been.

"Yer so blessed, Abby!" Margaret cried, beaming with joy and pride. " 'Twas a much easier birthing than mine."

"Ooh, such a fine lad!" Annie exulted as she carefully took the lad from Abigail and placed him on the grass-padded pallet they had made for that purpose. She began to clean him under Abigail's watchful eye, then washed and tied the cord with thread, for Abigail had even decided to avoid the custom of tying it off with yarn for a lass or rope hemp for a lad. The child protested heartily and flailed his little legs, and Abigail urged Annie to get him washed and warmed while Margaret was tending to the afterbirth. "Hungry already, that he is!" Annie exclaimed.

"Men," Margaret declared, "always bellowing for dinner!" But Abigail saw the shadow of the grief they yet shared flit across her friend's fine features.

Annie presented the bairn to Abigail much improved in appearance, wrapped in the dark rose blanket his father had woven last winter instead of the usual tight swaddling strips of flannel. Even as she began to nurse the lad for the first time, she soothingly hummed a lullaby, then whispered to the bairn, "So happy your father would have been to see you!"

Love and hope surged through her. Suddenly, she just knew this child would live, but then, she quickly warned herself, she had felt in her very bones that Douglas would survive the storm, and she had been so wrong. He had survived it only until he had challenged it again, trying to help others. And yet, God willing, that was exactly what she wanted to do here on St. Kilda!

"Abigail, I said, didna ye hear the distant voices?" Margaret interrupted her musings. " 'Tis too early for the milkers."

Margaret and Annie both stooped to look out the low doorway. "Ye won't believe it," Margaret called back over her shoulder. " 'Tis my mother, yer Grandfather MacAuley's niece, Annie's mother, and the knee-woman too!"

Abigail's eyes widened. They cared about her, even when she was defying them and their ways! And, even if Janet Fergusson and Isobel MacCrimmon were here out of curiosity and Susannah because Grandfather sent her, Mother Adair was here for more! Warmth and relief flooded her. While Annie ran across the meadow to give them the exciting news, Abigail told Margaret in a choked voice, "We judged wrong to think Isobel MacCrimmon wouldna make it here." She leaned back on her pillow with a huge smile. "But at least she's too late. Neither she nor her old ways are so much as touching my child now!"

When the women entered, glancing nervously about them as if long-dead warriors would leap out in bloody attack, all seemed perfection to Abigail: the baby cooed as Mairi cuddled him, so surely this bairn would patch the tattered fabric binding her to Mairi. And Abigail could not help but think, when she informed the knee-woman all was well and there was no reason for her to tend the bairn, that it was Isobel MacCrimmon who indeed looked a grim Warrior Woman. But the victory, at least this day, was Abigail's.

Three days later, after wonderful, restful hours at Gleann Mor to regain her strength and coddle the bairn, Abigail walked back to Village Bay with him in her arms. But three days after that, her perfectly placid son turned restive, then fussy, then squally. On the eighth day, before his tiny pink gums locked in the dreaded tell-tale sign of the sickness, she knew. She knew, but she could not believe. What had she done that her precious son deserved these muscle spasms, the slow starvation, the agonizing death? When, for the first time in long hours she entrusted the tiny, trembling body to Margaret's arms, she cried and raged.

"This canna be! 'Tis impossible! We did everything different, everything! We changed the place, the people, the methods, the mood! The only thing my labor had in common with yours was that they were both at night, but I ken many an eight day bairn born in broad day!"

"I understand, my dear," Margaret tried to soothe both the mother and the bairn, "but in this place—"

"The devil take this place, for he already has! All of us should leave for Harris or the mainland until we learn the cause of this curse! And I dared—" Abigail choked out, "*I dared to think I could find the answer to something so important, so—huge!*"

"Only God knows about these things," Margaret whispered, her face stiff with despair. She rocked the bairn against her as Abigail had done these last days until she was certain her arms would fall off.

"If only God knows," Abigail insisted, "then we must convince Him to tell us!" She paced, she tore at her wild hair and stomped and beat her fists against the stone walls of this cottage which was nothing to her now but a tomb.

" 'Tis blasphemy yer speaking, Abigail," Margaret said. She stared wide-eyed at her display. "The old ways, even yer precious old hearthsongs say—"

"I dinna care what they say!" Abigail muttered and took her son back in her arms.

Margaret put her trembling hands on Abigail's shoulders, forcing her to meet her tearful eyes. "Believe me, Abby, I ken that there is naught to do but to accept and go on."

"Never, never! In the beginning you did not accept, not until they all talked their weak St. Kilda sense into you!" Abigail declared until she realized her raging was making things worse for the child.

She calmed herself to croon to him, "I care only for this son of mine, named Douglas for his father." She began a sad lullaby of her own making. "I care only for Margaret's lost Abigail, bonny, wee, named for me, and my two eight day brothers. And for the three lost to Mairi, and the countless others. Countless lost others and also lost their mothers . . ."

She gazed down tenderly at her curly-headed son. The tiny brow knit in pain, he looked at her as intently through narrowed eyes as Douglas had that stormy day before he went back out to sea. "Both of you, my beloved, braw lads," she whispered, leaning against the wall for support while Margaret stood there crying, helpless. Abigail began the old St. Kilda hearthsong, "Sleep Secure, St. Kilda Bairn," until her sobs won out and she could only rock the child in shaking silence.

For a week after Hamish buried her bairn, Abigail agonized over how she could have lost him. Tonight, sitting in bed in her lamp-lighted cottage, she could not let her pain go. She fed it and let it tear and claw at her again and again.

She should not have dared to name the bairn Douglas, since his father had just died, she castigated herself. An old hearthsong told of a dying father taking his child to be with him in heaven. But that reasoning was foolishness, of course. The eight day bairns of St. Kilda had seldom just lost a father.

She should not have so smugly and rebelliously reveled in defying the old ways, the pillars of St. Kildan civilization. She had been too prideful, and God was indeed punishing her for that, as He rebuked all St. Kildans who lost their bairns for their own sins. But she could not make herself believe a loving God would punish sinners by taking innocent lives.

She should not have trusted Annie, she scolded herself. But when the lass had brought her flowers yesterday and looked so aggrieved herself, she knew Annie was sincere and not a tool of her grandmother. Besides, Abigail and Margaret had watched Annie every minute during labor and the birth, hadn't they? How wrong to even think of blaming Annie—or Margaret—or yes, blaming herself. Maybe it *was* the curse of Eve's original sin visited somehow upon St. Kilda when the rest of Scotland went—a pitiful, perverse thought—Scot free.

Torn, she felt so very torn. Not about whom to blame now, but about whether or not to dare to fight again for the causes she had once believed in. If she did so, could she not be punished further? And yet, what more could she lose in this life than what she had: mother, father, husband, son—her past and her future. There was no one but herself to protect now if she angered the St. Kildans. But did she even have the strength or daring for a further struggle? Would it not be best to just let life go by now, to treasure her friends and use her handgifts to help others? To become closer to some, and especially, in honor of the only man she would ever love, become closer to his parents? They were shattered by his loss, and little Ross and Murdo's once lively faces had gone still as carved stone. She had Grandfather MacAuley, who had been at her side through both winning and losing Douglas, and then through this new tragedy.

Sitting listlessly in bed this evening, listening to the luring, warm August wind, she jumped when someone knocked on the door. She knew instantly it was a man's knock, and rose to pull on Douglas's coat over her sleeping shirt. This late at night it dare not be that brazen Edmund Drummond. She opened the door a crack and peered out.

"Oh, Father Adair, please, come in," she said and stepped back in a gust of air as Hamish entered.

"Just come to see how ye were doing, lass," he said. "Concerned ye missed Sunday kirk this morning and tonight."

"I'll be there next week," she promised and sat on the stool while he perched on the settle with his cap in his hands dangled down through his spread knees. "I—couldna face it yet today, Father Adair, though I know it's to give a body strength. But to sit there and see all those wee ones lined up, so many with both parents—"

"I ken, lass. I do."

"Thank you. And I'm bitter inside and have to find the way to be more forgiving, before I go back into God's house," she added, twisting a thick strand of hair around her index finger until she realized he was staring and stopped.

"Yer a good lass, Abigail, and Douglas loved ye dearly. Even all those years when his mother and I didna know. Ah, ye look so like yer own mother, I was hoping ye'd be happy, because ye deserved it, lass. I only hope and pray—"

The door swept open, ripping in a gust of night wind. It was Mairi, looking blown and wild.

"I saw ye through the window, Hamish," she said without greeting Abigail. Hamish stood and slowly turned to face her as she shoved the door to slam it and stalked in.

"Just here," he said, "to see if the lass is well. I thought ye were at Isobel's after kirk."

"I'm sure ye did," Mairi said, her usually sallow skin reddening with anger.

"But since yer here to call upon our daughter-in-law now as ye have not the past week, I shall go put Ross and Murdo in and ye may comfort her." Hamish's voice came ever stronger as he made that speech. "And, of course, Abigail, yer welcome at the Adair cottage with or without Margaret any time," he concluded in a tone that sounded to Abigail like a warning he hardly meant for her.

"I am grateful for your concern, Father Adair." He nodded, went out, and closed the door quietly.

"Please sit down, Mother Adair. We havena had a chance to talk since the day we buried Douglas—the bairn, I mean."

Mairi plopped down on the settle Hamish had vacated while Abigail sank in the lower stool again and wrapped the coat closer over her knees. "Were ye in bed when Hamish came calling?" Mairi asked.

"Yes, trying to get my strength back. But if you see Margaret tonight, please tell her I'll be back with the milkers tomorrow."

" 'Tis of Margaret I wish to talk, now that we have a moment alone without my husband here or old Alistair MacAuley ever about this place when his poor legs pain him so to walk clear down here," Mairi said in a rush.

"Anytime you want a word alone with me, I would be so pleased to—"

"But about Margaret. Abigail, I want ye to stay away from her next birthing, and let me and Mrs. MacCrimmon care for it."

"You were ailing last time, you recall, and Margaret wanted me there. Have you asked her about this or only Mrs. MacCrimmon?"

"I surely ken what is good for my own lass, however grown she is! Now, I am not saying ye did anything wrong when ye helped the knee-woman with Margaret's first, but ye always make a disturbance of some sort, and I'll not have it! And yer ideas—like birthing a bairn in Gleann Mor in that old pagan house, and look what happened to my grandson!"

Abigail's pulse pounded. She sat up straighter. "What happened to your grandson was the same thing that happened to your granddaughter that Isobel MacCrimmon cared for! And what happened to three of your own and my mother's two and far too many others with the proper knee-woman in attendance!"

"I'm not here to debate the way of things with ye, lass!" Mairi insisted. "Ye've a temper like yer father and ways like yer mother, and—"

"I'll not have your accusations of them again, Mother Adair, not on top of every—"

"Ye dare to accuse yer betters like the knee-woman and have no respect for things in general!" Mairi was shouting now, leaning forward and bobbing her fist in the air. "Ye ken, just like yer mother, ye recall to me one of those hearthsongs of yers about the selkie folk that live in the seal skins and swim from isle to isle. Under their skins they slip out of when they come ashore is a beautiful, luring woman with enchanting songs who takes men's souls and makes them hers. But even after she might have his bairns, if anyone puts her old skin before her again, she must flee and never return."

"You would like that, wouldna you?" Abigail challenged in a shaking yet stern voice she could not believe was her own. "You'd like me to just dive off a cliff into the sea and never—" she got out before she realized what she said and clapped her hands over her mouth.

"And that's exactly what yer demented mother did, though I dinna really believe a word of that old selkie legend," Mairi declared and stood, brushing at her skirt as if it had been dirtied by sitting there. "Just stay away from the birthing of my next grandchild, whatever Margaret says, and away from my husband too!" she added, her mouth twisted in a thin line. She marched out and left the door open to bang in a wild rush of wind.

Abigail sat hunched over, her elbows on her knees, her face in her hands. Surely, all of *that* could not have been said between her and Mother Adair. Not those bitter words and cruel accusations and worse implications. Oh, Douglas, why are you not here to help? she thought. Her arms felt so empty of him and of their child. Her hopes were wailing with the wind, and life looked so dark, so dark.

She stood and walked to the door. Perhaps she meant to close it, but the wail of the wind and smell of the sea pulled her outside. With Douglas's unbuttoned coat flapping behind her, she walked from the cottage.

She wished she could fly away on the wings of the wind, on her heart-wings that were broken now. Fly with the fulmars who soared and dipped above, launching themselves from the endless cliffs to freedom in the skies. Soar away to Harris or Scotland or England or other isles beyond where babies did not die in flocks of little souls winging away, where people, especially families, must be kinder and wiser . . .

It began to mist, then rain, but she went on, one foot and then the other. The grass and, higher up, the heather felt fine against her bare feet. The rain was washing her, cleansing her thoughts. But for Margaret, Grandfather, Annie too, what did she have? Douglas's father tried to be kind, but that only made Mother Adair worse. Who knew what things she and Isobel and the others whispered like the whining wind. Abigail had no tears left, but rain streamed down her face the way saltwater had on Douglas' that day the waves took him. Her hair, soaked to her head felt so heavy, heavy like each step she took into the darkness. She accidentally disturbed a fulmar nest she didn't see, and the mother bird screamed and flapped its wings. If it spit that bitter oil again, she did not feel it. Nothing else could harm her now.

Lifting her arms straight out from her sides in the stiff battering of wind, she stood on the headland of Oiseval and heard and felt the sea crumple itself on the cliffs below. She almost fancied she heard the selkie spirits or the seals below, singing her their strange, sad songs. It was here her mother had come that time in the rain, sleepwalking or just walking, snared in dreams or nightmares—

Lightning slit the sky above her head. The earth ripped apart under her feet; she twisted and turned and fell. The impact smacked the breath from her. Rocks tore at her skin; her coat yanked away, her shirt rode up; ridges and pebbles tore her belly and dug at her elbows, knees, and thighs. Her chin scraped; she bit her tongue and tasted blood. On her stomach, skidding down feet-first, she waited for the clutch of air and then the sea and rocks below.

But on a steep slant, she held tight to a boulder while the storm cried and clattered all around. She hurt everywhere, outside and in. The pain in her lower belly—was that new or just the agony of remembering the birth that was for naught? She did not know how close she was to the edge of the cliff. Perhaps it did not matter if she let go. Had her mother been exactly here when she went over, far over to swim in the sea like a selkie spirit until they found her body the next day?

But Abigail held on. Despite her pain and grief, she held on. Even in the wash of pebbles and rain, she began to claw her way back up. She dug her fingernails into the ungiving rock and hugged boulders, praying they would not give way. She scraped and crawled. An eternity later, she felt more level ground and slick grass under her body. Sobbing, shaking now in gratitude more than fear, she flopped face up in the rain and dark. And then, when she opened her eyes again, it was light.

She sat up dazed, squinting at a pink dawn trembling on the horizon. She saw she was bruised and cut; her head and belly throbbed, but she had come through. And, as if she had received a boon for survival, she knew two things. She knew for certain now that her mother had not meant to kill herself but, either awake or asleep, had fallen. God had showed her that by what had happened to her last night. But He had saved her, saved her for an earthly calling. And she also knew that somehow God would help her discover a theory and then prove it was the reason the bairns were dying, even if she had to crawl and claw and struggle. That's what she would live for now.

She got to her knees. Vibrant colors pulsated in the sky and in her head. As sore and battered as she felt, she raised both fists, then clasped her hands together and lifted them heavenward before her face.

"Somehow," she vowed, "I shall find the way to keep the bairns from dying! For my own bairn, for them all, no matter what I must do or where I must go!"

She got slowly to her feet and started unsteadily down toward the village. Her insides hurt worse with each step; perhaps she had reinjured her healing from the birth. She stumbled more than once, but stopped when she came across a fulmar nest built defiantly far out from the protection of the rookery—perhaps the same nest she had seen last night. Only now the mother bird lay dead and torn by bonxies, though her three eggs lay newly unguarded and undisturbed.

It was against the rules, but Abigail MacQueen Adair bent to gather tenderly the three eggs into the hem of her shirt. Wrapped in a basket by the fire, perhaps they would hatch. It was suddenly essential to her that she save the chicks. Aching, jarring herself with every step, she made it down to the street and went in her still-open cottage door.

Wind had whipped the rain inside to flood her floor and drown her fire. She blotted the hearth with wool, got some new peat from the byre, and began a new fire. She made the eggs a nest of yarn in a basket and set them near the warmth. Slowly, she lowered herself onto her bed. Then she saw blood on her thighs and collapsed, curled up in pain until Margaret found her.

6

The sea ever changes
Yet never is new.
The new moon begun
Is the ancient one.

Cherished lives lost
Bring pain never new,
Yet my new life begun
Is not the old one.

So many changes took place in Abigail's life in the next five years, many of them because of the young lass, Janie. On this bright June morning in 1857, the child wrapped her arms tightly around her Aunt Abigail's neck while Margaret smiled at both of them from the doorway.

"You help your mother with the milking, our bonnie lass," Abigail told her niece.

"I shall miss you terrible, Aunt Abigail," Janie told her, then skipped out the door past her mother as if there could be nothing terrible in the world at all.

The lass looked as much like her Uncle Douglas as she did her mother. Often Abigail's emotions took a wrenching twist when the child smiled at her. She loved Janie as her own, but still felt deeply the loss of Douglas and her own blond, blue-eyed child. Since she had no intentions ever to wed again—nothing must detract her from her quest to discover why the bairns die—she also mourned the children she would not have. But then, since her fall and injuries on the cliff, she had experienced erratic monthly fluxes or missed them entirely, so perhaps her womb had been damaged. Now, Abigail drifted back to the present to see Margaret still standing at the door.

"Go on then, my dear," Abigail told her. "And I thank you again for taking my pails this morning. Speaking alone to the factor before he goes back to Harris is something I must do, however much 'twill be frowned on if certain folk discover it."

"Aye, the busybodies," Margaret said. "Ye just be certain, Abigail Adair, that devil Drummond has gone up on Conachair to examine the new cleits again." With a little wave, she was gone.

Abigail sighed, but she smiled too. They had heard the most exciting news yesterday: Edmund Drummond, so talk said, would be leaving the island with the factor for good. Promoted, he had been, to doing his precious reckoning for the laird in Glasglow or some such place, and a new accountant would be sent soon. Abigail did not care where Edmund went as long as it was away from here. Until a few years ago, when she had asked Father Adair and Grandfather MacAuley to convince Edmund she wanted no suitors, the man had driven her to distraction.

Yet she had hesitated to anger him further after little Janie was born. There was, Abigail recalled, always someone she loved keeping her from what she would say and do: Douglas, then her own bairn, now Janie. And she did not want to make things worse for Margaret, who had kept her promise to be her friend, whatever befell.

Margaret had defied her mother—even when Isobel MacCrimmon had refused to deliver the child if Abigail was present—to have Abigail help with the birth. Together, as with Abigail's son's birth, they changed many of the traditional birthing practices. Despite Abigail delivering an Adair grandchild who lived and thrived this time, all that had caused a rift between Mairi and Margaret. Even Janie could not heal the tear; it was only patched over as her grandmother doted on her.

Many others also blamed Abigail for the Adair family problems, but Margaret did not. When the laird sent four new workers' families from Harris to help replace the men lost in what St. Kildans referred to as "the tragedy," Margaret and her newborn daughter had moved in with Abigail. Margaret received rent in shillings for her place to give them a nest egg. Anyway, Margaret said she could not bear her old cottage now Neil was gone.

So the three of them—and Abigail's orphaned chicks she hatched from devastated fulmar nests—now filled Lady Grange's old place to overflowing. Little Janie's warm, winning ways attracted other lads and lasses, who might have been forbidden to enter otherwise. For all those she cared for, as well as to be certain she herself was not ostracized or exiled from her important quest, Abigail strove to make friends and placate her enemies. Yet as quietly as she could, she wrote new hearthsongs and carried on her work to save the bairns.

Besides beginning to educate Janie, Abigail had secretly taught Margaret and Annie to read and write. Last year, Annie had wed Gavin Gillies, Neil's younger brother and one of the last few eligible, older men after so many were lost in the tragedy. If the other lads of marriageable age had not been a good bit younger, Annie's kin would not have let her wed one who was friendly with Margaret and Abigail.

It was partly Gavin's support of his sister-in-law, Margaret, that permitted Annie's frequent visits to their cottage when she was not assisting her grandmother with a birth. Also, Isobel hesitated to alienate Annie since she was her grandmother's only hope to pass on the lofty position of village knee-woman to one of her own family. It was on Annie's visits to the cottage that she recorded details of each St. Kilda birth so Abigail could look for patterns in the care and circumstance of bairns who lived and died. Now, with Margaret having firmly taken sides, Annie and Susannah were the only ones who could walk in both feuding camps of the island's women, and Abigail took pains not to endanger that.

Until today. Today, she must visit the factor, however frowned upon it was for a woman to be mixing in men's business. She was getting nowhere trying to solve the puzzle of the disease. She had long been thinking of sending for a doctor, but, until recently, had not struck on a way to pay him, even with the money she and Margaret had hoarded from the rent of Margaret's old place. And once a doctor came, would he even be accepted and allowed to treat the women? Privacy, modesty, and propriety were essential to childbirth here. Island women might not allow an outsider—especially a man—near them when they bore their bairns. Their own husbands were not even permitted in the cottage at such a time. But, blast it, Abigail thought, if such help were here, they would have to at least listen to his advice!

She peered out a crack in her door until she saw Edmund and two workers walk by on their way up to Conachair. She jumped back into the shadows when, as ever, his gaze shot to her cottage window. She counted to a hundred to be sure the way was clear, then was out the door, heading toward the factor's house.

Most women were at the morning milking; the men had set out from Parliament for their varied tasks. Abigail lengthened her strides. She would not even stop to see Grandfather, bedbound now, until on the way home. A bit out of breath, she halted before the closed door of the factor's house, staring at the impressive, painted MacLeod coat-of-arms hung there the month of June he was in residence. It sported the head of a fierce charging bull and the motto HOLD FAST.

"That I will," Abigail declared and rapped firmly on the door with her fist.

The elderly male servant the factor always brought with him from Harris opened the door and looked behind her for other visitors. " 'Tis just I, come to see Mr. MacCallum, if you please," Abigail informed him. She was taken through the room where Parliament met and into the first floor library.

Alexander MacCallum, a short, spare man, had so long been the laird's factor here that the St. Kildans had observed his once sable hair go grizzled, then silver, and his hairline climb nearly out of sight. Now it lifted higher as the servant announced her. Mr. MacCallum's thick-as-thatch eyebrows shot up, evidently in surprise to hear her name and see she was alone. She went directly to her point. She did not want Edmund or any other member of Parliament to find her in private conference with their factor.

"An important request for the laird himself, you say," Mr. MacCallum repeated her words as if to accustom himself to her daring. "Of what nature?" he asked, leaning back in his squeaky leather chair. He had not asked her to sit; as if bemused, he scratched his chin with the feather of his quill as he spoke.

"I feel, sir, we are in dire need of a doctor here to discover why so many of the bairns die of the eight day sickness, which does not afflict Harris or the mainland, so I hear."

His frown lowered his hairline. "There are many infant deaths in all of Scotland, lass."

"Not between seven or eight out of ten as here these last five years alone, sir. 'Twas twenty-four deceased out of the thirty-five live births, four more of the poor bairns being male than female. The laird should be sore concerned, even if just because this means his future workers here will be fewer."

"Adult workers lost on St. Kilda through drowning or falling have been a greater concern. And, I am certain, lass, you dinna mean to question the laird's concern for his people of St. Kilda."

"No, of course not, but—"

"But the infant mortality rate is high. 'Tis no doubt the dampness here or some inherited tendency to disease through long years of intermarriage, even though your lads sometimes fetch Harris brides," he said. "Have you ever heard of the bleeders' disease among Spanish royalty? Ah, no, of course you havena, and 'twas not meet of me to use that comparison," he apologized to make Abigail hope he was softening a bit.

"May I join you, Mr. MacCallum?" The deep voice from behind jolted her. It was not Edmund but the Reverend Mr. Campbell. "Perhaps 'tis best I do so," the minister went on, "as I must admit I overheard the speaker and the topic. Have you met Abigail MacQueen Adair before, sir? She dinna ken of foreign royalty, but she gets notions of her own, since she could read any book on your shelves here."

"Could she now?" the factor asked, obviously surprised. "Then perhaps I should inform the laird if he sends a doctor she will serve as the new factor's accountant here to pay the man's way."

Abigail dared to dream. How perfect an idea! She could do that. Deliverance! But her flash of hope was snuffed out as both men snorted laughs as if he had made the wildest joke. The factor was snickering through his nose and the tight-lipped minister deep in his throat. Her face heated. They were mocking her and her heartfelt, desperate request.

"I thought," her voice rose above the ebbing of their laughter, "that we might begin to export blued cheese or brighter dyed woolen goods to compete in Glasgow so we could pay for a fine doctor to live here if the laird and you, too, Mr. Campbell, could just convince the folk that it was needful. And I have nearly ten pounds saved to contribute!"

For some reason, Mr. MacCallum looked as if he would break into laughter again. "Abigail," Mr. Campbell said, his voice soothing now, as if to a child, "I doubt if any fine doctor would want to live here however many pounds you have saved. And I believe you know the way of it with such radical notions on cheese and dyeing, let alone birthing. If Parliament wanted a doctor, it would ask for one. Though it seems to be your way to challenge things, I would bid you recall what I preached Sunday last: 'God's providence is our inheritance.' You, however, seem to have inherited other things than a trust that God ever does things His way in His own good time."

"But the Lord God puts us here with heads and hearts to solve problems too, so—" Abigail began, but the factor's fist hitting the table cut her off.

"The lass's fine countenance and coloring are her inheritance, Mr. Campbell," he said, hunching over his work as if he were ready to dismiss her. "I recall that little matter with her bonny mother on Harris years ago. No, lass," he said sternly, addressing her now as he glanced up through his bushy brows, "the laird wilna be sending a doctor here at *your* request, for he has much too good a memory when it concerns his son's doings. Then, too, those in authority here on St. Kilda see that things are the best they can be for such a far isle."

"Am I interrupting?" Edmund's voice cut in. Abigail's protest that whatever happened between her mother and the laird's son once had naught to do with bairns dying caught in her throat. She spun to face Edmund, feeling doubly snared and shamed now, for his eyes raked her, accusing, leering. "The cleits, Mr. MacCallum," he went on calmly, "are ready for yer inspection. And what is the lass's business here unannounced and unrequested?"

With a nod from the factor, the minister explained her concerns, casting them in a somewhat favorable light, Abigail thought. At least Mr. Campbell was now glaring at Edmund. The factor looked up long enough to quote what he had called the infant mortality rate she had given him, as if he knew Edmund would revel in hearing any accountings, even of dead bairns.

"I am certain Abigail will be on her way now," Edmund said, "and I shall escort her out and then return to walk up to Conachair with ye, Mr. MacCallum."

Abigail felt so devastated by her defeat that for once she could not even summon up anger at Edmund. She managed a goodbye and started out with him close behind. She was heading for the MacAuley cottage without a look back when Edmund called to her, "I need a word with ye, Abigail, one I think ye will find pleases ye for once."

In the windy warmth of the July day, she stopped and turned slowly to face him. "I doubt that, Edmund. What do you care for dead bairns? You're only interested in the count of dead birds, the more then better!"

"Everyone kens ye've been breaking the rules hatching fulmar chicks for years, but when folks come to me, I say, let her be—so far," he said. He came closer while she held her ground. "Ye see, Edmund Drummond isna such a demon as ye think, lass, and he's about to make ye an offer ye will take if you care so—passionately—to help the bairns. Ye seem to have a keen head for numbers and business, so I shall make you a business proposition, Abigail Adair."

Her mind raced. She knew not to trust him; she knew if he dangled bait, there would be a sharp hook concealed within, but what if it caught her something good in the meanwhile?

"I am listening."

"And I am reveling in that simple fact. Now hear me out. I promise ye that I shall send St. Kilda a doctor from Glasgow when I get there. Once a physician is here perhaps the stubborn souls will heed him. But in exchange ye must come with me yerself and help select the very man."

"A doctor here? But come with you to Glasgow?"

"As my wife, of course. We can be wed on Harris, eh, as Mr. Campbell wouldna even get the banns read here before I leave with the factor next week."

"Edmund, I couldna consider—"

"Not even to select and send a doctor here? Ye could work with him, if ye like, when we come back and forth to St. Kilda, as man and wife."

"I heard you wouldna be coming back."

"Not true," he insisted with a downward slash of his maimed hand holding his slate pencil. "Abigail, ye have built such barriers against me since Douglas died that ye have not given me a chance to tell ye the things I want, things I hope to give this place that bred me and gave me my beginnings up the ladder. Och, we could share such dreams. As yer husband, I could offer ye so much. Ye want to build a cheese export trade here, fine. It would make us and the isle a pretty penny, eh? Ye could make yer dyes wherever we go. I ken a school here has been a hope of yers. Over time we could help to fund one that ye could visit when we come back. I will speak direct to the laird himself for you and get his blessing. Abigail, with these new dealings of mine, I shall be a wealthy, powerful man, and ye are the only St. Kilda woman I would ever consider having on my arm the places I am going! And I am the only one who could handle a strong woman like ye—use and profit yer ideas as well as mine, that is."

She gaped at him through that entire, fervent speech. The perfect answer to her prayers to get a doctor here had the most dreadful solution. Wed Edmund Drummond when she could not abide him and did not trust him?

"I—of course, you would put these things in writing and share them with Parliament, Mr. Campbell, the factor, and the laird before—before we would wed." She could not believe she was trying to call his bluff on this. The whole thought of being Edmund Drummond's wife—his property, as he would no doubt have it— sickened her. But not as much as bairns dying.

"Och, of course, Abigail!"

Leave here to be Edmund Drummond's wife? Leave her work, Margaret and little Janie? She wanted to turn away and flee, but she stood with her feet rooted in the reality of her desperate need, staring at him. She was good as an outcast here, an outright enemy to some. And today, her daring to go to the factor and being refused, would no doubt soon provide more ammunition for her opponents. Still, she had vowed to sacrifice *whatever* it took to save the bairns, to make her own beloved, wee son's death have some meaning, and didn't that include wedding Edmund?

"Well, then, my dear?" he dared.

"I—you will have my answer before sunset, Edmund," she choked out and turned away. She did not stop at Grandfather's cottage as she had planned. Any chance to protect her privacy—her very self—lay in her own hands. And lay in tatters if she did this very thing. But she saw no theories emerging from her studies of Annie's reports, however much she scrutinized them. She saw no parting of the clouds for an angel descending with the answers she prayed to God for. If Edmund could be forced to make public promises, perhaps marriage with him was the quickest way to get a doctor here to make these stiff-necked people stop the bairns' suffering and dying.

She said not a word to Margaret of it, because it was a decision she must make herself. There would be time enough to deal with her friend tonight if she told Edmund she would wed him. Abigail kept her own counsel on the afternoon milking trek, then sent nine-year-old Murdo Adair to ask Edmund to visit her cottage when he could. She intended to interrogate the man more completely about exactly what he would promise to do for St. Kilda if she wed him. She would see it written in his own hand in the cold, hard numbers he lived by. She would get it witnessed before she could bear to even force herself to tell him "aye." And, if she did become his partner for the good of the bairns, it would be strictly business for her. Yet she knew she must brace herself to make him happy. It was only right.

A rapping on her door shot her to her feet. Surely, Edmund could not be here already; had he been lurking outside her cottage for Murdo to find? But when she opened the door, the Reverend Mr. Campbell stood there.

"May I step in a moment, Abigail?" he asked and, with a glance to see she was alone, left the door wide open as he followed her in.

"I must tell you," he began, seated on her settle while she took the stool, "I regret the lack of Christian neighborliness in the way Edmund Drummond has pursued you over the years. After Hamish Adair and Alistair MacAuley spoke with him, I did too, requesting he not court you further. I believe he has been more considerate these last years you have been widowed. He told me, you see, he could bear it as long as you wed no one else, and you obviously had no such inclination. But today, the way he gazed on you so—so

covetously in the factor's house . . ." his voice drifted off as he fidg-
eted in his seat.

She did not know what to say. Had Edmund sent this man to
encourage her to wed Edmund?

"But I would like to request," he went on, "that both of you
make your peace with each other, forgive each other in my presence, before he leaves for Glasgow on his way to London. 'Tis un-
likely he will be back for years if ever with his new post as
MacLeod overseer of the London market for feathers, so—Abigail,
are you unwell?"

"Clear to London? And wilna be back—for years? Maybe
never?" she choked out and stood when Mr. Campbell nodded.
That blackguard Edmund had lied again! Lied again, and she had
nearly given him all she had and lost her dreams to another powerful man, one she did not desire but detested!

Just then, Edmund came to the door. He seemed to her to
block out the air, the light. "You foul, lying, seducing blighter!" she
cried. That brought the minister to his feet, thinking she addressed
him until she pointed at Edmund. "The truth is you would have
done who knows what with me when you got me away from here
and never intended to help anyone but yourself on all of St. Kilda!"

"Abigail, this is hardly the proper forgiveness I suggested . . ."
Mr. Campbell chided as Edmund stood agape.

"Get out of here, out of my sight forever, Edmund Drummond!" she shouted. She bent to lift and heave a pot of dye at him;
it exploded against the door to spatter his trousers and the floor
shiny crimson. "He said if I wed him, we'd come back to bring a
doctor for the bairns and start a school," she tried to explain to the
startled minister.

"Stop it, witch!" Edmund shouted back. "I swear, I will have
ye and break ye one way or the other if it takes the rest of my
days!" He shook his maimed hand in a fist; spittle flecked his face.
"Like this pot, ye will be broken before me, ye will crawl to me and
beg me to take ye—"

"Edmund!" Mr. Campbell protested even as he seized Abigail's
wrists before she could launch another missile.

Abigail could see a crowd growing in the street behind
Edmund. Slack-mouthed, Mother Adair hung on his every word.

"Abigail Adair is a blasphemer," Edmund screamed, "a deceiver, an ungodly woman!"

"A lone woman, one you were glad enough to see become more and more an outcast!" Abigail shouted back. "One you have pursued all these years, though I saw you for the serpent you are, little man! You little, little man!" She turned to the appalled minister and tugged her arms free. "I am sorry for my bitter words, Mr. Campbell, but I thank you for my earthly salvation from this demon. And I thank you for being here so he wouldna kill me as he said."

"Ye sly shrew!" Edmund shouted. "Ye've always led me on! Ye'll be mine one way or the other, someday!" He turned, shoving folks away, and strode off.

"Good riddance to the man," Mr. Campbell whispered as Abigail collapsed onto the stool. "Worse, much worse than I thought. But Abigail, you, too, have a great deal of penance to do."

It was later that day that Abigail tossed her first bottle into the sea with a message, as Lady Grange used to do. Only this note did not beg a husband to forgive her and rescue her from exile. Abigail's missive begged for a doctor to come to rescue the St. Kilda bairns, exiled from life to an early death. She longed, she wrote, for someone to come to change the wretched way of things on this distant island. And though, she vowed, she did not have the proper fee to pay for a doctor's visit yet, she would find it one way or the other, even if she had to follow this bottle far across the sea to more foreign, civilized sites!

The same craft that two weeks before had taken away the factor, Edmund, and several St. Kilda lads wanting Harris brides returned to St. Kilda on July 20, 1858. Abigail stood with Susannah and Malcolm in the cluster of villagers as the boat put in at the rocks and the passengers leapt or were helped ashore.

Folks had gathered to see the new brides. Abigail yearned to welcome them warmly, since she feared it could be as hard for them as it had been for her mother here. But Edmund's public accusations of Abigail's conduct had even further tarnished her in St. Kildans' eyes, so what good could she do these bewildered-looking lasses with everyone staring? Besides Mairi telling folks of her and

Edmund's verbal bout, Edmund had evidently spread the rumor that her continued refusals to wed him after years of leading him on was the real reason he must deprive St. Kilda of his presence—an eligible man, a dedicated worker, and trusted factor's accountant. Young Murdo had told her Edmund had repeatedly bemoaned that the new accountant would not be one of their own but a prideful Harris islander, like her own mother had been. So Abigail remained rooted to her spot on the shingle shore, even more shamed to silence than usual. If something didn't happen here soon to change her mind, she vowed, she would have to take a boat out of here to earn money and find a doctor herself.

And then, in the bright slash of midday sun, with all St. Kilda crowded around, Abigail saw only one person. Her eyes widened, her nostrils flared, her head lifted. For one wild moment, she thought the man might be the doctor she had sent for, but she knew better. It was too soon for that. The man was a stranger, yet she felt she should know him, so attuned was she to him, so . . . compelled. He held a satchel and two heavy canvas packs as he alighted easily from the tilting craft to the rocks as if he had the finest pair of sea legs in the world.

The rest of him looked fine too. Abigail took in his imposing height, his broad shoulders that, unlike most men she knew, tapered to small waist and hips before the strong thighs swelled the straight-legged trousers. No loose, baggy climbing breeks here. He had a well-clipped beard in midsummer, when St. Kilda men wore them only in the colder months. He placed his goods on the rocks and then, after doffing his Harris tweed cap to each alighting woman, helped unload the brides' boxes. Like his beard and eyebrows, his hair was midnight black, but it glinted bluish in the sun with his head uncovered. When he spoke, his deep voice was quiet and controlled, but it still boomed through Abigail's very core, making her want to sprint forward to talk to him and see the color of his eyes.

"Captain Morgan James West, sir, at your service," he told Iain Murdoch, the first of several men who stepped forward to greet him. The St. Kildans slowly, silently, solemnly offered their hands, and Captain West shook each heartily. "I'm captain of a steam and sail vessel currently in a Liverpool dry dock having an engine repaired, but I've come to do a little archeological exploration." His voice floated to Abigail, as if the poor man were trying to fill the silence while he was scrutinized. "The MacLeod laird, whom I met on Harris, was kind enough to offer me the factor's house while I'm here, for I'd never heard of St. Kilda until he mentioned your island, but I'd appreciate it if you could perhaps suggest a family I could reimburse for my daily victuals for a week or two. Such an amazing place you live!" Captain West went on as his eyes skimmed the scene and then returned to scan the crowd.

Brown and rich as loam, his eyes were, Abigail saw, but with glinting gold depths like the loch at Gleann Mor. She was certain he could look right through the folks between them to see her—and probe her very thoughts as she wanted to delve his. A shudder racked her, but not an unpleasant one.

"Never been in these parts before, eh?" Iain Murdoch asked.

"Approaching this sheltered bay, I felt I was sailing toward an Atlantis, a lost island rising on massive pillars from the depths of the eternal sea," Captain West explained.

Iain looked a bit blown over by that answer. Abigail had never heard of an island called Atlantis either, but she would like to hear about that too. She wondered how they birthed their bairns there. Captain West might have come from Harris, but his speech showed he was from far beyond any Scottish lands. Why, he might have spoken with lots of worldly men like himself, perhaps even a doctor or two. She was certain archeological exploration had something to do with digging for old bones. No doubt, no one else had any idea what he had declared himself to be beyond a sea captain with no visible vessel. The brides ignored, the crowd edged forward, all ears and eyes. Abigail, Malcolm, and Susannah stepped closer too.

"Then, welcome to St. Kilda, man," Iain told the visitor. "Yer not Scots nor British, I take it."

"I'm an American, from Baltimore, Maryland."

Such a foreign, exotic sounding place! Abigail marveled. When he spoke, it was easy to believe he sang a song of his own heart. Despite long, windy hours in the boat, next to the other disembarked passengers, he looked fancy and so—orderly. From his high-buttoned tweed coat to dark, toe-capped boots, he was as neatly turned out as his trimmed mustache. The gold watch on a chain he fished from his breastcoat pocket caught the sun as he opened the timepiece and studied it.

"I'd say we made quite good time for a crew that does not like fussing with the sails once they are hoisted!" he announced. The corners of his firm mouth lifted a bit at some private thought; he snapped the watch closed and replaced it while several other men conversed with him. Abigail took Susannah's wrist and moved the three of them even closer.

"What exactly is yer business here, captain?" Iain asked.

"You see," Captain West replied, "I visited the prehistoric monolith called the MacLeod Stone on Harris. From there it was pointed out to me that your little outlier island of Boreray looks like a ship leaning to northward. But the thing is, the ancients used the monolith to site the autumnal equinox on Boreray, so I'd like to hire a crew to take me to see Boreray as well as have a look at any fine old pagan sites hereabouts."

Silence stretched along the shore. Several St. Kildans just gaped at him. Abigail held her breath. Iain Murdoch frowned; Hamish Adair cleared his throat; feet shuffled on loose stones.

"Why would ye be poking aboot old pagan stones and such?" Andrew Nichol asked. "And there wilna be a party heading for Boreray 'til the gannets return again, come spring. I doubt if ye mean to stay long, so . . ."

Abigail scented disaster. She was good at picking up its spoor after all the times she had tried to fight the way of things here. She could not bear it if they were cold to this man, however much of an outlander he was. She must speak with him, yes, about how bairns were born in that Baltimore place he came from, but of other things—everything—too.

"Susannah," she whispered in her ear, "now that your Uncle Alistair's bedbound, wouldna he love to hear the tales this man could tell over yer fine suppers? And you could use the money for the church or what you will."

"Well, if Malcolm thinks so . . ." Susannah whispered back.

Malcolm shrugged. "Could be the man's headed out on the next boat, but I wouldna mind someone to talk with about handling sails 'til he goes."

"Then 'tis decided," Abigail declared with a nod and prodded Susannah to move Malcolm a step forward.

Whatever happened next, Abigail *had* definitely decided. The stranger named Morgan James West—even his name sounded like the sea rippling the shingle shore—was the most fascinating person she had ever seen. He had said coming here was like sailing to a lost island held up by massive pillars. And, since he had stepped ashore, she had felt those very pillars shake.

7

The luring lass from out the sea,
A selkie spirit wandering free,
Puts off her past and comes to me.

Sing to me, love me, stay by my side.
Our different selves cannot we hide
To live together whatever betide?

Wearing his india-rubber boots and toting his paraphernalia including notebooks, telescope, hammer, knives, and picks, Morgan West set out after breakfast the next morning. He climbed the path through the mountain pass to the seaside valley which Alistair MacAuley had called Gleann Mor, the great glen. It was chilly and foggy this early, but he wanted to look at the deserted site of the old pagan village before the women came to milk the cows and goats. Solitude had always suited him, though since his father had died, it brought him too much time to remember and regret. So he forced his thoughts back only as far as last night in the MacAuley cottage.

He had admired Mr. MacAuley's quick mind trapped within an enfeebled body. The food the niece, Susannah, had prepared was rib-sticking if bland, like eating spiceless southern chicken and mashed potatoes in varied guises. Blue blazes, no one here drank ale, whiskey, or coffee, only tea or cheese whey! In short, he had found the St. Kildans as fascinating as their ruins and artifacts. They were literally living in the past and did not want things to change, yet they were suspicious of the ancient pagan prehistoric past he loved.

But his most vivid memory was of that flame-haired beauty who had dropped by the cottage last night, the one named Abigail whom the old man had called his granddaughter, but was evidently no relation. She was a widow who had her young, fond niece and several other youngsters in tow, none of them hers.

Though he could tell the community did not cotton to outsiders, perhaps he would stay here at least a week or two, even if he could not get over to see Boreray since they insisted no one was going back until next spring. He could return to Harris when they sent over the last of the woven goods and feathers, the laird had said, for, after that, who knew when the next boat would allow him to leave?

This trip had been one of the few impetuous risks Morgan West had taken in his well-planned, thirty years of life. He reveled in the adventure of this odyssey, though, like his hero Ulysses, duties at home called. He was now the sole support of his mother and was a loving uncle to his sister Priscilla's two daughters. His partner, Melvin Collins, as well as employees of their shipping firm, Collins and West, depended on him. He would return to his ship *Fidelity* in Liverpool soon enough for the next trip homeward bound. Though he had no wife waiting, Charlotte Collins, his partner's granddaughter, would become his faithful Penelope after their betrothal and wedding between voyages next year. Still, his musings drifted back to this enchanting, other-world escape as he had never known outside of reading—except for those marvelous months he had spent with his father on Florida's tropic barrier island of Sanibel twenty years ago.

He heaved a huge sigh of longing for past times of all sorts and shifted his pack to the other shoulder as he strode across the meadow toward the old stone house and well. The village animals must have sensed he was a stranger, for they shifted away from him. He had tried to be friendly to their owners when he arrived yesterday, but the inherent St. Kildan reticence pleased him for now. Still, he had to admit it had seemed that Abigail had wanted to ask him something she had not been able to. Ah, well, perhaps he would see her again at the MacAuley cottage tonight.

Breathing in the crisp air, watching and listening to the wheeling birds, for a moment he just savored this glen in the cup of mountains. The skies were stunningly seductive out here with their lofty layers of clouds sculpted by the winds. He strolled toward the ancient beehive house which still stood, half-sunken in the soil by the pagan holy well Mr. MacAuley had described. Holding his breath at stepping into the past—how he had dreamed of doing such if he ever got to the Aegean or Greece—Morgan walked around, then stooped to enter the stone house.

Built to last, this place was a well-preserved marvel. He examined every nook and cranny and caressed the interior walls. He took off his heavy coat and removed things from his pack, laying them out neatly in a row on the stone floor. Affectionately he patted his dog-eared, Moroccan-bound copy of the *Odyssey* and placed it on the recessed stone shelf that had no doubt once been a sleeping shelter called a croop. He got out a notebook and pen to make a diagram of the way the stones corbeled up toward the interior vent. He sat on his emptied canvas pack, knees bent, his back to the wall and stared up at the ceiling vent, wondering all that had happened here.

And then, he froze in midmovement. As if his earlier thoughts had conjured her up, the red-haired Abigail stood in the low doorway. The hair on the back of his neck prickled and a chill shot up his spine. Had she dared to follow him out here alone? It almost seemed as if she had materialized from thin air or emerged from the depths of the nearby sea.

"I dinna mean to be disturbing you, Captain West."

Her very presence in this place, her unusual, vibrant beauty and bell-clear voice disturbed him deeply, but he said, "Of course not. Come in, please. Is someone—your niece—with you?" The last thing he needed was to be caught alone with a young, fetching widow, he thought, but when he saw and heard she was alone, he quickly forgot that concern. He scrambled to his feet, paper scattering, pen flying.

"Oh, no need to stand. I shall just sit over here. Do you like the Warrior Woman's House? 'Tis called *Tigh na Banaghaisgich* in Gaelic, and 'tis one of my favorite places, that it is."

She told him a great deal about the house, astutely pointing out some features he had not even noted. He wished he were an artist so he might sketch her, perched on the stone shelf as if this place were hers. She was barefoot, windblown, a mesmerizing Aphrodite stepped from the pages of the book that lay beside her.

"And there is an old altar on Soay," she said, "and one closer on Dun, though the tides are a wee bit high this time of year to reach it hopping boulders. Boreray had a standing circle of stone that might have something to do with your—the equinox you mentioned if you are here next spring," she rushed on, as though she were afraid to have silence between them.

She was bright as well as beautiful, he thought, awed. She evoked a magnetic aura that made him feel he was a compass needle which must tilt toward true north. She seemed unlike most of the St. Kildans he had met: she spoke with a bit less brogue; she seemed to want to please him, not put him off; she emanated emotion, not reserve.

"And on Mullach Geal, there is an altar to Gruagach, pagan god of the seasons, where the old folk used to leave a milk libation, but 'tis generally forbidden to speak of all that now, so I wouldna go asking others about it if you dinna want to nettle them."

She spoke faster and faster, as if she were desperate for something; she almost made him dizzy. "And as a village hearthsinger I ken the old hearthsongs that tell of heroes and the old days too, if that would help you. I would ask just one thing in return, sir," she said, then hesitated, her hands clasped tightly in her lap.

He held his breath. "Yes?"

"Grandfather MacAuley says you are not wed, but do you ken aught about birthing bairns?"

He stared agape at that outrageous request. He did not know whether to laugh or scold. Did she dare to mean how babies were conceived? But no, she was a widow, so that could not be.

"You mean delivering infants?" he floundered, feeling himself flush hot under her riveting gaze. "I am hardly a surgeon, madam!"

She was visibly jolted at his tone or his use of that title for her. Or, could she not know what a surgeon was? Her rosy cheeks paled; he must have cut her to the quick and had to make amends somehow.

"Please forgive my hasty answer," he went on, "but I know so little of intimate—private—women's affairs, or any medical practices. You need to ask a surgeon—a doctor or physician, madam—Mrs. Adair."

"Oh, I thought you cursed at me—you know—said 'I am hardly a surgeon, *damn*!' before," she said, looking much relieved. "Just calling me Abigail will do. You see, Captain West, St. Kildans lose nearly seven out of every ten infants to a disease eight or so days after they are born. Have you heard of such a catastrophe in your Baltimore?"

He felt even more staggered by her news than he had been by her presence. "No, though childbed fever used to take many mothers," he told her. "I regret I cannot be of more help. What are the symptoms of this dread disease?"

He listened carefully to her recital of grief. She did not tell him she had lost a child in this way, but he knew she had. Her face glowed with passion in the telling of the horrendous signs, as she called them. She explained how folks accepted the way things were, how no one wanted a doctor but her. The lass who would be the next midwife was her friend, she said, but the current, unbending "knee-woman" was instructing her. His heart went out to Abigail, but it sounded like nothing he had seen but for one thing.

"The clamped gums you mentioned," he said. "Are some of these newborns ever pricked with a needle? I knew a woman who died of lockjaw once."

"No, nothing like that. Pricked with a needle? Why?"

"Only accidently, as when someone is sewing or someone barefooted steps on a nail. That is a death sentence too."

Frowning, she shook her head. "There isna anything like needles or nails involved." She looked entirely crestfallen.

"I am so sorry I couldn't help, Mrs. Adair—Abigail, but if the folks here, as you say, don't want a doctor, what can one do? You St. Kildans seem to do everything by the book."

"What book?" she asked, perking up again. "The Bible? The minister is always saying we must accept the way the bairns die, for 'In sorrow shalt thou bring forth children.' I believe the Bible, but I think that means only the pain of childbirth and not suffering through the bairn's death. Even after all this time, I canna, I wilna accept their deaths!"

Her determination both shocked him and utterly inspired him.

Imagine a woman here on St. Kilda, let alone anywhere, daring to interpret the Bible contrary to what the church taught. And she had reminded him just now of how his fellow southerners—even his own father—had quoted scripture to him to attempt to justify slavery. But Morgan had no intention of unburdening himself about that or about his father to this woman who should not be here with him alone. Women were to be protected and that sometimes meant the naive ones from their own risking of their reputations too. He assumed she was only untutored in civilized proprieties and not a loose sort of woman. He was both heartily relieved and a bit disappointed.

"I am sorry," he repeated inadequately as he stood, nearly bumping his head on the slanted stone ceiling. "Going by the book just means going by the rules. As a ship's captain and a businessman, I find that a key necessity of life, so I meant no disrespect to the St. Kildans by my remark."

"Oh." She stood, glancing down at his book. In the dimness of the house, she squinted at it as if she could read the embossed title. "I thought," she said, "you might mean going by this book here— *The Odyssey or Homer's Travels of Ulysses.*"

He smiled in surprise and delight at her little joke. "You can read? But I heard people here are illiterate—that no one reads or writes."

"Now that the factor's accountant has gone, no one but the minister and I," she said, sounding fierce but looking forlorn. "And several others I taught myself," she added more quietly. As she started out, he was desperate to keep her here. There were a dozen mysteries about this woman already and he had to know the answers to every one.

"Abigail, I would dare to hope your kind offer still stands— about telling me of the old sites and singing the old songs, especially ones about pagan places. Perhaps at the MacAuley cottage later this evening, for there may be another flock of visitors and you could entertain us all."

" 'Tis a long tale in itself, but I dinna think that is a keen idea if you wish to be welcome on St. Kilda."

Ah, there were thirteen mysteries now. He followed her out into the sunlight of the glen. "You could trust me, if you would come back here tomorrow, Abigail," he said, throwing caution to

Gleann Mor's winds when only moments before he had felt so pompously outraged about her coming here alone. "I would be pleased to pay you for your songs, if you'd write them down for me too."

Her chin quivered. He felt such a tight constriction in his ribcage, he too almost thought he could cry, he who had not shed a tear in years, even through all the loss and pain.

"Though I would appreciate the money to hire a doctor whatever they say," she told him, "some things canna be bought. The songs are priceless, like the bairns' lives, and I canna grasp why no one here kens that. But, if you wilna tell the others or mistake my motives, I could find you about the island for a wee chat, when 'tis possible."

"Yes, of course. And I would be happy to tell you anything I can about the world—beyond St. Kilda, if you'd like, I mean."

"I sing my own songs too," she said, looking shy for the first time. He stood in awe as, with her hair blowing in the breeze, she sang for him a lilting, haunting song about Gleann Mor and its "beauty, wild and free . . . ecstasies and tragedies, life daily and divine." But all he could think was that she, more than this luring glen, evoked all those things.

Then, while he still stared, she lifted one hand in farewell. She stooped in the thick, blowing grass to retrieve some sort of harness. She donned the yoke and started away, pails swaying against the brown skirt that caressed her hips and legs. She turned back once and, though her features were now as indistinct as his must be to her at this distance, they stared long at each other. Later, when he still watched her, she climbed to the crest of the mountain pass and sat on a boulder until the other women appeared.

Only then did he duck back into the Warrior Woman's house, his pulse pounding, his very soul struck through with the piercing presence of this place.

During the next two weeks, Abigail spoke privately with Morgan when and where she could snatch time. She saw he stayed busy at his own occupations, especially after he asked the men if he could help them at their morning tasks and was refused. Even when Morgan was with others and she dared not single him out, she studied him.

He often wrote in what he called his journal; she wondered if he recorded his thoughts of her there. He drew pictures he called diagrams; he excavated the old stone wall between Gleann Mor and Village Bay; he dug for what he explained were artifacts. He said once that he wished he had a photographer with him. She hardly believed him when he told her that men had made a miraculous machine that captured exact images of people or things and printed them in black and white on paper without a pencil or a pen. How wonderful, she had told Morgan, if her dyes could then be used on this photograph to give it color!

But she had not been able to speak with him the last two days, so when she went out alone after lichens this bright early August afternoon, she was disappointed to see he was going way up to her old trysting place on Mullach Sgar. As she climbed closer, she realized he was sitting on the ledge outside the very cave she and Douglas had called their castle. She had not been there since his death and felt a bit guilty even after all this time to be sharing the same area with another person, and a man at that. She could not bear to think it, but it was true: when she was near Morgan West, she experienced the same sweeping feelings she had once had for Douglas and thought she had buried with him forever. Only—no doubt, because he had been gone so long that time had muted her previous emotions—she thought her inner tumult now surged even stronger.

"Abigail!" Morgan called and waved when he saw her below. "I've just found an ancient spearhead after exploring here all week!"

Though the man seemed controlled and calm most of the time, today he looked as excited as a boy with his first snared fowl. She smiled despite herself as he gave her a hand up, then backed off several steps and extended his artifact to her. It was the spearhead she'd seen in the cave many times. To her surprise as well as his, she told him so.

"You've been in the cave way up here?" he asked as he sat down near his pack and pointed his thumb in the direction of the hidden entrance. "I guess I should have known your climbing skills could take you anywhere." She, too, sat, gathering her skirts to keep them from flying free. "I thought the cave looked deserted for years," he added, when she did not answer, "maybe since the earliest civilization here." He sounded as hurt as if she'd tossed the spearhead off the cliff.

"Deserted for six years, I suppose," she admitted. "When my husband and I were courting, we used to meet up here."

"Ah," he said, "you have sad memories of this place then."

She looked out over the vast expanse of sky and sea, both dotted with birds diving, soaring. "No," she managed, "only happy ones, turned to stone now like a treasured artifact."

"I have memories like that too. If the artifact belongs to your cave, I shall put it back."

"If it belongs to my cave, you may keep it. Oh," she said, eager to change the subject before she told him more about how Douglas had once been forbidden her, "what is this leather and glass tube by your pack?"

"A telescope," he told her with a smile. "I shall show you how it works." She knew he delighted in teaching her about the outside world as much as she did in explaining things here. He placed the spearhead in his inner breastcoat pocket where he always carried his watch that so set him apart from the St. Kildans, who told time by their stomachs, tides, or bird migrations. He lifted the telescope, held one end up to her eye, and pointed the other outward.

"Oh!" she cried as the distant birds leapt close to dive right at her. She ducked. She blinked and peeked around the tube before gazing into it again. She smiled. "Another wonder! How close and clear everything becomes! How I wish things could really be that way, when they seem so murky and—impossible!" Another eight-day bairn had been buried yesterday, but her memory of that muted, too, when Morgan's big, warm hand closed over hers on the far end of the telescope.

"See," he said, "you can turn this part to focus it better."

It both annoyed and entranced her how his voice, his mere nearness, now his touch could shake her so deeply. She had to say something before she fell into his arms, and never in this place that had been hers and Douglas's!

"I see a storm coming from way out there," she announced, pointing past the end of the telescope so her finger appeared big and blurred in it. "Have you heard what the factor always says about the weather here? If you can see the bay 'tis going to rain, but if you canna, 'tis already raining!"

She made the mistake of turning to him; he had moved closer than the telescope brought the birds. He was smiling at her jest, his dark brown eyes alight; the wind dared to ruffle his usually tidy hair. She gave him the telescope and moved away to put her back against the cliff wall. "Does it rain much in your home you call the South?" she asked, desperate for talk again.

"Enough to get a whopping crop of cotton this year," he said with a frown as he put the telescope in his pack and leaned back against the rock beside her.

"But that should make you happy if that is what your ships haul."

"Yes, but there's something I haven't told you about the raw cotton or the milled goods made from it that I take back from Liverpool." For one moment, his expression looked so dark, she almost fancied he would confess he was a modern-day Viking, stealing plunder to fill his ships.

"The cotton," he said, watching her intently, "is picked by Negroes—black people—brought in bondage from Africa. That's been illegal for fifty years, but these people are yet bought and sold—slaves of white Americans."

"Slaves? But that is dreadful! You dinna have any, do you?"

"No, but my ship is loaded by them in Baltimore, and I detest myself for allowing that. I believe slavery is unjust and immoral. But when I visit the houses of my suppliers or friends, the house servants are slaves. I protest politely, but I lead no revolts," he said and looked away frowning, as if disgusted with himself.

"Abigail," he continued, "many Americans disagree about slavery, and it looks as if we may even come to blows over it. I'm a loyal southerner, a believer in the rights of states who need the slaves, but accepting the 'economic necessity' of it sticks in my craw! But not my partner's, who was my father's partner and friend for years and is a good deal older than I. He's been to me like your Grandfather MacAuley has been to you, so I hate to go against him. Anyway, I will help to destroy the heritage of my father's and my partner's business and the South if I remain antislavery," he explained, his voice and face growing pained and impassioned. "But I still say abolishing slavery would save the South's soul in the end. If I could only convince my friends and not have to fight them one way or the other!"

She saw such torment in his eyes. "And it's already cost your partner's friendship?" she asked.

He shrugged and did not speak for a moment. "No, I'm still trying to hold on with him. I have ties to him that may even strengthen in the future. I may have inherited my father's company, but my arguing with him cost me his love before he died, maybe even caused his death, and I don't want the same thing to happen with my partner."

She could not stop herself from reaching for his clenched fist on his knee. She wanted to tell him she knew how it hurt to lose a father without a loving farewell. But more than that, what rocked her to her toes was how deeply she felt his grief. He wanted his people to stop slavery, and yet they clung to it at the expense of cruelty and pain to the slaves and the ruination of their own souls. And she wanted her people to change the way things were here, especially to stop accepting the cruelty and pain of dead bairns, which she feared must be endangering her people's souls. Why, *why* did people have to be so narrow-minded and cruel? She wanted to tell him all this, but it was he who spoke first.

"Even the factory system—the mills of northern England—more or less makes slaves of the workers too, but it's nothing like what we have at home. Abigail, America was founded on freedom, so somehow slavery has to be rooted out!" He shook his head as if to cast off his emotion or scold himself for sharing so much. "But I didn't meant to drop all of this on you with your concerns here," he added.

"I'm glad you told me, Morgan, that I am. It shows that even the most new-fledged and wealthy places need change and help."

He held tightly to her hand when she tried to pull it back. They were silent for the longest time, listening to the wailing of the wind.

"Do you want to see the cave again if it's been six years?" he asked.

"No. I can always see it with my heart-wings as it was and that's enough."

"You loved him deeply, your Douglas."

"More than I could explain. Some days I still suffer the loss, but grief no longer screams at me now. Perhaps it will be so with your father's loss."

"Perhaps. But he died at his desk just after we had another terrible row about slavery. I'll regret that forever even if I know I'm right! Before that, I'd always tried to please him, to be worthy of his trust and expectations. He's been gone about as long as your husband, but *my* pain still screams at me. I'm still searching for other cargoes that are not based on slavery, but, other than that, in my father's honor I try hard to fulfill his—and my partner's—wishes for me."

"You shouldna blame yourself for his death. I ken that is worse than others blaming you," she said and tugged her hand away at last.

Tremors from his touch had been creeping up her arm to make her want to move closer. She must not let this happen. What they had between them was precious, but she would not let it go deeper since he surely must be leaving next week when the last boatload of feathers went to Harris. She began to get to her feet.

"Don't go yet, Abigail, please. There is one thing I would ask you—about others blaming you."

She froze, expecting to hear a recitation of warnings from St. Kildans that he stay away from her because she had lured Douglas on. Sometimes, she almost felt she could read this man's thoughts, however different from St. Kilda the places he had come from and was going.

"About Douglas?"

"About a man named Edmund Drummond too. And some superstition about a fairy that swims from isle to isle in sea skins singing her songs and luring men."

She felt her skin heat to the very roots of her hair at what he had said and implied. So Mairi and Isobel and their flock had been at him! Did they know she was meeting him on the sly? Or was it just that she had done that with Douglas once and they still wanted her to suffer for it? It hit her fully for the first time: the only two men who had ever intrigued her she had been forced to meet in secret as if their very presence were forbidden to the likes of her. It made her want to rebel just as her father had, but she knew she must seize her better self and weather it through. So instead, she told Morgan her side of the Edmund Drummond story.

"He's lucky he left or I would take him on for you," he muttered darkly and flexed his big hands. "But I will handle anyone who even talks about him and you in the same breath next time."

"I suppose Mairi Adair told you all this, especially that selkie story," she said.

"No, it was that blonde Flora Nichol, and—"

"Flora, was it!" Flora had wed Gordon Nichol two years ago, but it had hardly sweetened her bitter heart. Even the fact her first bairn had lived did not make her pity other women but rather act more prideful. As much as Isobel and Mairi, Flora reveled in back-biting Abigail every opportunity she had.

"I just thought you ought to know, Abigail."

"Oh, I do know. I just forget sometimes when I become so intent on my own doings! And I understand why you are hinting it is best we not meet like this again, really I do."

As she scrambled to her feet, his long arms reached up to seize her wrists. "I am hinting nothing of the kind, though I admit the furtiveness of it wears on me. I thought it was best at first, but not now. I'll not have us lurking about as if—as if we are slaves to their wrongful opinions of either of us. Sit, sit, please and listen."

She had no choice. His strong arms hauled her back down so she almost tumbled into his lap before he loosed her. The power of the man—his stubborn ways—she had seen it all before and to her own grief. Yet she sat, leaning a bit toward him, listening.

"Two things, Abigail. First, I see no reason why we cannot be friends in the open."

" 'Tisn't done here."

" 'Tisn't done at home in Baltimore, either, unless someone else is along, but why should you not come to the MacAuleys in the evenings or why can't one of your friends go with us if we take an evening stroll? I could visit you when Margaret is in. The only thing I worry about is how they will treat you after I leave. Now, you told me last week some of your happiest memories with your father were when he took you out in a boat fishing. I am skilled with a boat and Malcolm wants me to show him some things with sails. I propose we get Susannah and Malcolm and all go out fishing someday—in full view of everyone here."

"You ken, I have always thought if St. Kildans just ate more fish, it would reduce the number of birds that must be taken. But the folk believe that too much fish cause skin eruptions."

He laughed, then shook his head either at her idea or at that latest revelation of the way of things on St. Kilda. But she was so excited and pleased by his bold invitation that she did not care what had amused him.

"Then you will go?" he asked. When she nodded, he sobered and went on, "Would you still go if you knew that there is a lady— one Charlotte Collins, back in Baltimore with whom I have a certain understanding? She's my partner's granddaughter and the woman my father always hoped I would marry. We're not betrothed, but I suppose we will be."

She stared at him. She felt she was teetering on a pinnacle of rock over the crashing sea, like the Lover's Stone. Not because he had someone he would wed when he went back to his world. Not because he had evidently thought enough of a far isles woman to tell her this. Not even because, God forgive her, in that first moment he had said it, that bit of information had loomed as huge as American slavery and St. Kilda bairns. She balanced precariously on the jagged edge because of her decision to love him or not for whatever scant hours she could have with him.

Then she knew she *had* loved him always—at least at first sight, even as her father had loved her mother so. Despite some deep echo of warning from the past, she could not save herself from her desire to be with this overpowering, persuasive man. And, after all, he would never have to ken how much she loved and wanted him.

"I would love to go fishing," she told him. "And as for the lass, after all, you and I are but friends."

"Then the first good day Malcolm can get the boat, it's settled."

But Abigail's thoughts and emotions were hardly settled. They swirled and bubbled as she dyed the traditional plucked wool an untraditional crimson color, because Morgan told her he would buy it from her and sell it in America. Like so many things here, the fact the St. Kildans plucked their sheep instead of sheared them astounded him. But the important thing was, with that money, she would bring a doctor here!

She watched the colored water seep into the very fiber of the yarn, changing it forever, setting the colors deep, never to escape. She stirred steadily and watched the yarn rotate, even as her thoughts whirled.

It had been nearly a week of rain since Morgan had promised they would go fishing, and she had hardly seen him. During the day when Morgan still went about the island, she had been spending every free moment helping Susannah tend the fragile, fading Alistair MacAuley. Not to disturb the old man, Morgan was temporarily taking his meals with the Murdochs. But last night, Grandfather had seemed to rally a bit and had asked that Morgan visit when she was there. Just as Grandfather had once loved to hear her heart-wing stories, he loved to hear Morgan's real ones.

But last night Morgan had also read to them from his favorite book, which he always seemed to have about his person. One reason he must love to read so much, she mused, is that he had told her he wanted to write a book someday about past civilizations. And she realized how deeply he loved the tales of Ulysses's adventures when, in the dim light, he closed the book, yet went on, reciting the story. His eyes had glowed golden as he gazed across Grandfather's bed at her as he said the words that told of the hero's coming to the island of Calypso, the "sea nymph":

" 'When at last he came to that far-off island, he left the blue sea and passed over the land until he reached the great cave where Calypso lived. There the birds would sail to rest on their outspread wings. But Ulysses was sitting in his usual place by the shore, wearing out his soul with lamentation and tears.' "

And afterwards as Morgan had walked her home at Grandfather's request, he had said to her, "Goodnight from your Ulysses, my St. Kilda Calypso." She could almost hear his deep voice now, echoing in her head, her heart . . .

She jumped as she realized she did hear his voice and in broad daylight. She hurried to the door where he stood, breathless. His gasped words made her feet fly faster, even out into the rainy mist when she discerned their terrible import: "Abigail, your grandfather's taken a turn for the worse and is calling for you!"

Abigail perched on the edge of Grandfather's bed, bending close, holding his hand in hers. His skin felt frost-struck and his legs twitched. Fighting tears, she leaned down to kiss the sunken cheek. Here, she grieved, lay the last loving link to her parents, for he had been kind to them both. He had helped to give her Douglas; he had stood by her side. She needed to thank him for all these things, but Susannah bent close with a folded paper in her hand.

"Here 'tis, uncle," she said, "from yer things just where ye said 'twould be. Malcolm and I—and the captain, since ye wanted him to stay—will be just across the room."

"A letter for my bonny lass," Grandfather told Abigail, clasping the paper in his trembling hand. "Forgive an old man for not getting it to ye sooner, but I was told, not 'til ye were settled in yer life, so ye would forgive."

"From Edmund Drummond?" she gasped out.

"No, not him."

She stared at the paper but was afraid to touch it. She could not believe her eyes, but it was true: a letter from her mother, for she saw now the way "Abigail" was written there in that lost, yet familiar, slanted hand.

"I thought ye would be settled wed to Douglas," Grandfather was saying in such a whispery voice she had to bend closer to hear, "but ye truly werena. Then when ye had the child, well . . ." he choked out and wheezed to catch his breath. "I ken what's written here. I asked the captain to read it to me just a wee bit ago—for I didna want ye to be hurt more than—ye have been."

She leaned closer. "You let Morgan West read this letter?"

"Aye, and prayed ye'd forgive me for that too. I have seen how his eyes follow ye and ye him—not so very different from Douglas—but so grown up ye are with the pain in yer eyes now too . . ." His voice dissolved in a feeble coughing fit that brought Susannah scurrying and made Abigail forgive him anything he ever did amiss.

When she and Susannah had him settled back quietly on his pillow, Abigail stood by the bed. His bluish eyelids flickered open and she leaned down to say, "Thank you, Grandfather, for everything—always."

He barely nodded to her before he nodded in sleep. She wanted to read the letter, but she feared what she would find since her mother had known to write before she—she fell. And she was afraid to lose this beloved old man who always tried to protect and shelter her, even more than he should.

She blinked to clear her threatening tears. His fingers lay limp around the letter; his chest moved slightly when he drew a shallow breath. Carefully, she took the letter, holding it by two fingers as if it would burn her. Near the hearth, oblivious to the others, she opened the crinkly, eleven-year-old missive and read the writing her own so much resembled:

> *8 of Sep't, '45 Y'r of Our Lord*
> *My Beloved Daughter Abigail,*
> *I pray you will live a happy and bless'd life. I would have walk'd this dark path years before, but you have been my brightness. At age fourteen, you are now old enough to keep the cottage for your father. And, mayhap, you will find your way to Douglas best if I am not here to come between you and his people. I see a strength in you, my Abigail, that I lost long ago.*
> *The solution to the great dilemma of my life lies beyond, not on St. Kilda. I strove to return your father's adoration, but 'twas not in me, for my heart was once wed elsewhere and ever since has languish'd in exile. Even when I lost my sons, I felt only dark echoes of that first loss. Then, indeed, I kenn'd I too was lost.*
> *Someday when you are settl'd, with your man and your bairns, singing the hearthsongs, I pray you can love me and say 'twas the only way for one who died long years before she died.*
> *I remain eternally,*
> *Your mother,*
> *Glenna MacLeod MacQueen*

Shocked, she began it again when Susannah said, " 'Tis over. He's gone, God bless him."

Malcolm moved to stand at Grandfather's bedside with Susannah. With a glance Abigail's way, Morgan did too. "I'll go tell the men," Malcolm said, "so the cry can go out."

Abigail's head spun; she heard or saw no more. Doubly shocked by losing Grandfather—and mother, it seemed—in the same moment, she began to shake. Blinded with tears, she opened the door and ran outside.

She cut between the cottages so no one would see her on the street. She had to be alone; even Margaret could not help now. She had to think. She was terrified that the death of feeling her mother had described would corrupt her now, and yet, would it not be easier to feel nothing? She had lost Grandfather in the same moment she had lost her trust that her mother had not left her—had not killed herself. With a tearing sob, Abigail began to run uphill.

How could her mother have taken her own life? She had been weak and selfish! Her husband and daughter had needed her! Her deserting them had ruined Coll and caused all Abigail's early pain. She would never, never be like her mother, she vowed as she stopped to suck in a breath. And yet, as Mairi had long noted, she looked like her—surely, she was like her in the bad ways too, she thought, as she began to climb again.

The drizzle had turned the grass slick; she went down on her hands and knees twice, then scrambled on. Up she went past the cemetery where the lost bairns lay to the place St. Kilda folk had buried Glenna MacQueen outside hallowed ground. Perhaps they kenned what was best in all things: if you chose to stay in this life you could change nothing. You must only suffer, accept, go on. She strode across the grassy upward slant of tableland. High above, tall Conachair reared its head, but she only looked down at her footing as she plunged on through thick, trackless heather.

And Grandfather—how she would miss him, but he had been so wrong to say she was not truly settled wed to Douglas. Alistair MacAuley had tried to protect her too well! He should have given her the letter years ago so she could have learned the truth that her mother was a craven coward and her stupid daughter could be so wrong. So wrong to think Glenna had not been demented as Mairi and Edmund had claimed. So wrong to think that she could rightly solve the dilemma of her mother's death or that of the bairns too.

Panting, with an ache in her side, she stopped and thrust in her bodice the wrinkled, wet letter she had held in her fist all the way up. She would like to throw it off the stony skirts of Conachair, but she would save it so she would not forget what a fool she'd been. Probably about Morgan too. He would soon return to Baltimore and his Charlotte and his own life and she would be here mired in the way of things, alone forever.

But she turned and saw she was not alone. Morgan had run after her; his trousers and the elbows of his coat showed he had fallen more than once; standing nearly knee-deep in shiny purple heather, he looked bedraggled and out of breath.

"Conachair is weeping too," he said. He came up slowly to join her as if he were afraid she would bolt again.

She looked up where he pointed and saw fog streaking, pouring off the summit of the peak. The view was usually clear here, but now mountain mist melded with rolling waves of clouds. They seemed to stretch clear to Harris like an aerial sea just beneath Abigail and Morgan on which they could sail away together. She stared at him, standing so close to her now that she could stretch out her hand and touch him.

"I am sorry to run you ragged chasing me," she said.

"Chasing you—yes. But always, you take my breath away."

He touched her shoulder and, before she knew that she would move, she was in his arms, her face pressed to his chest, her arms hard around his waist.

Slowly, in his sweet, strong embrace, her roiling anger at her mother ebbed, though she could not yet understand nor forgive her for taking her own life, whatever grief beset her. But Abigail's own life seemed more precious now because her mother had thrown hers away. And because Morgan West had simply said she took his breath away. That was hardly a declaration of the sweeping love she felt for him, but in her agony of this new loss, she held to that as she did him.

"So much pain for you all at once," he murmured, tucking the top of her head under his chin. "I'd give anything to help. You know, when old Alistair died, I was thinking that people are like islands too, half hidden from each other, even from themselves. You thought you knew your mother, but you really could not. And when I came here, I had no intention of staying long. But now I see I must to do more exploring of the island, even of myself. I need to do some writing and—other things."

She did not move; she hardly breathed in fierce anticipation. "Today," he went on, his voice catching as if he would cry, "I told the men I would not be going to Harris on the last feather boat. I'm sending letters to my first mate in Liverpool to hire a captain for one run and, through him, to my partner that I will be here until spring."

"And one thing more, Abigail." He sounded controlled now,

but she felt his big body trembling. "It's obvious your mother loved you. That's what you must remember. She said her loving farewell to you in her own way in that letter, just as you did with your grandfather today. I envy you that. I'm only spouting off like a fool because he asked me to take care of you for a few days, and because, God help me, I want more than ever to be near you—like this!"

Even before the kiss began, she drowned in his dark eyes, mesmerized by her awestruck face reflected in their depths. She could see each curled, dark lash fringing his intense gaze before she felt them brush her lids and cheeks. She was not certain who moved first; she lifted her head, he bent to her. His flesh heated hers; his beard and mustache gently rasped her skin as they tilted heads to deepen the kiss. They tasted each other as if starved, then savoring slowly, they breathed as one.

It went on and on, as solid as stone but wild as the wind. Wrapped in rolling mist, they clung together on the heights of Conachair.

8

Life comes close
Through a telescope.
Would I could so probe
Problems which arose.

Colors leap bright
Through a kaleidoscope.
Would I could so know
Beauty of such light.

During formal mourning for Alistair MacAuley, the men did not work. But the first calm, sunny day of the next week, Malcolm obtained one of the smaller birlins so he and Morgan could take Susannah and Abigail sailing in Village Bay. Malcolm had told Parliament he was learning more about sailing. He was a bit surprised when, after his lesson, Morgan lowered the sails and took out four fishing poles so they could troll for mackerel as the sea took them toward shore.

"Dinna ken what the men will say about this," Malcolm told Morgan. "But I see now why ye told me yer Americans dinna get skin disease from eating muckle fish. With the week honoring old Alistair with no harvesting on the cliffs, a wee bit of fresh fish may be welcome on St. Kilda tables tonight, eh?"

"If Susannah would help me," Abigail put in, "we could stew it up and offer some to everyone!"

"Stew it?" Morgan said. "If we get mackerel, we will broil it so we can taste it, Calypso!"

Abigail blushed and turned away to bait her hook. But Malcolm and Susannah evidently did not think a thing of Morgan's telling her how to cook or his calling her by a seductive sea nymph's name. Maybe being at sea had bewitched them today, for all seemed enchantment here. The view of the island's cliffs looked like a kaleidoscope of flying birds, Morgan had said earlier and explained to them about the bright, leaping colors one could see through the tiny telescope he called a popular "parlor amusement."

Abigail saw Malcolm and Susannah were entranced, hanging on Morgan's every word. As for herself, she knew she was quite simply more in love with Morgan West than ever, even though he increasingly, though perhaps unintentionally, dominated her thoughts and actions. She struggled not to resent that fact. It was just that he was a man used to giving orders on his ship, she told herself, an educated man, rich in the world's ways, self-confident in his power and influence. And she was so grateful he was staying for the winter before he went away forever.

Malcolm swung a big mackerel into the boat and the squealing Susannah shoved it off her lap. Abigail raised her voice above their laughter so Morgan could hear her. "Thank you for today. It brings back some happy childhood memories, and I could use a few of those lately."

"But your father just rowed a fishing boat out of this bay and never came back?" he asked.

She nodded. "It was against the rules to row out alone, but he was paying less and less heed to the way of things. Once you get outside the shelter of the bay, the seas turn tricky and mean. I—we all assumed he drowned, maybe that—he meant to or at least didna care what befell him. But today I am thinking of the sunny days he brought me fishing, whatever the islanders thought of him when he was at his most independent and stubborn."

"You are independent and stubborn too," he observed with a wry grin.

"Now, isna that the pot calling the kettle black!" she accused, and they both grinned at each other.

"I'll not comment on that! But I too have happy childhood

memories," he told her, scanning the bay toward the shore, "of being at sea with my father, sailing south to a lovely island."

"In Maryland?" she asked, instantly intrigued by wherever his heart-wings took him.

"No, an isle off the west coast of the state of Florida, almost the farthest south one can go in American waters, a beautiful place called Sanibel."

"Sanibel, far south," she whispered, looking off over the gentle deep blue of shifting water as if she could see it too.

"Sanibel. Only the waters are more blue-green than this, as in the Aegean, and it's almost always warm there. Hot even," he added and turned to lock his gaze with hers.

"It sounds so bonny."

"It is. Palm trees with slender trunks bending in the breeze, but there can be real bad blows there, called hurricanes. There are delicate shells cast up on the shores like tiny treasures, prehistoric Indian mounds, tropical fruit as sweet as ambrosia, sunrises the colors of rainbows, exotic fish, and orchids that grow up trees in thin air. And the birds there would astound even a St. Kildan! Wading birds with long, spindly legs, and even pink birds, Abigail, worthy of your dyes. There's one called a roseate spoonbill with a duck's face but a graceful body. I wish we could sail all the way to Sanibel so I could share it with you this very moment!"

She stared at his transported face, wishing she shared his precious memory and wanted to be as much a part of his thoughts and yearning as he was hers. She wanted so to touch him—to have him hold her and kiss her as he had that day upon the heights of Conachair in the cloaking mists. How she longed to know his body, his life, his very soul.

She startled from her aching reverie and cleared her throat. "So," she said, afraid the ropes of their intimate sharing would fray if she changed the subject, "Sanibel is your Garden of Eden, and you would like to be its Adam."

"If I could have a bright-eyed, wind-blown Eve," he admitted with a wink at her. "But actually," he went on, his voice deadly serious now, "even as a boy, I saw there were half-naked Indians living in the thickets there, hiding from the American Army which was still chasing them during the Seminole—that is the Indian tribe's name—during the Seminole Wars. And desperate, escaped slaves were there as fugitives, hiding on Sanibel from bounty hunters who wanted to drag them back in chains to their owners."

"How dreadful! And you wanted to help both the Indians and slaves find freedom."

"You know me very well." He grabbed for his pole as a tug on his line bent it nearly in half. "You would love the place, Abigail. I know you would!" he added as he began to battle the fish.

She watched him hoist his flopping catch into the boat as she considered his words, "You know me very well." She was coming to, and that was the way of it. But she had blurted out that he wanted to help the Indians and slaves because she kenned that was exactly what she would want to do if she were there. How much alike they were, she thought, and yet so different. But, as he had said that day on Conachair, did she really ken him—or herself?

A great part of the fish feast they prepared for the villagers that evening turned out to be a failure. Margaret, little Janie, Annie, Hamish and Murdo Adair said they enjoyed the broiled—and stewed—offerings the four fisherfolk took from door to door. But most St. Kildans declared they had plenty on their evening tables and refused even a taste. Still, Mr. Campbell, coming back from visiting an ailing soul, stepped forward to try a spoonful from Abigail's kettle and proclaim it "flavorsome," right in front of Isobel MacCrimmon's door that the woman had been about to shut in Susannah and Abigail's faces.

When the minister went on toward the manse, Abigail heard Isobel mutter to her husband, "Even bewitched the holy man, as well as that outlander captain, she has now!" before she glared Morgan's way and slammed the door.

Susannah heard too, but kindly pretended she had not. Fortunately, Morgan and Malcolm walked up a bit late to hear, for although Abigail was moved by how protective Morgan was becoming of her, she saw such possessiveness could have rebounding results.

"It seems just the four of us shall have a feast," Morgan declared defiantly. "We shall toast with tea the hallowed memory of our dear departed friend and relative, Alistair MacAuley, who would have loved hearing about this day we've had. He would have said of the others, 'They didna ken what they were missing, that they didna!' "

Malcolm managed a smile at Morgan's attempt to lift their spirits with his lame St. Kilda brogue. Susannah nodded, teary-eyed. But Abigail just turned away and started toward the MacAuley cottage, toting her kettle of stew. This once she almost regretted the even steeper price she would pay here on St. Kilda for Morgan's influence and rebellions as well as her own.

He, no doubt, could just walk away from here with a few fond memories and go on with his life. She, even if she departed as she had long considered, would carry the double burden of losing him and losing the battle to save the bairns. Parliament and the church's stiff rules aside, there had always been someone she loved whose precarious position here kept her from really attacking the brutalities of this place that was yet her home. First it was her parents, then Douglas and Grandfather, her own child, then Janie. And now, it was Morgan.

But without Morgan here, she would have one less reason to remain in this narrow, backward, hide-bound place which had somehow helped to kill her mother and the bairns. When Morgan leaves, she must too, not to follow him but to pursue her quest in some civilized place. Her renewed anger at the way of things further fired her determination: however much Morgan took her mind off her tasks and sapped her strength, however much some of these St. Kildans hardly deserved her help for their treatment of her and her loved ones, she was still going to risk everything to save their dying infants!

Yet, she could not resist her need to be with Morgan. On a windy day with a storm threatening, she went down to the shore to help him stow away the sails of the birlin they had used. His face lit when he saw her; she felt her insides crash like a breaker on the stony shore.

"Bit of a blow coming," he called to her, his big, capable hands knotting the ropes tighter around the furled sails, even though he was watching her and not his work. "Malcolm said he'd be down to help, but he was assigned to a work party packing fulmar away in cleits on Oiseval. Shall I teach you a sailor's knot or two in case you need to tie someone down, Calypso?"

"You might as well, Ulysses!" she called to him as the stiff breeze buffeted her skirts. "I'd best tie my hems to my ankles in this wind." And, she almost said, you've tied a sailor's knot or two around my heart and my doings already, and here I am to be hobbled for spending more time with you in view of everyone, if they care to come down to the salt spray–swept shore.

Still, they worked companionably as he gave orders. She did not mind his telling her what to do when it was something he had mastered. It was only when he criticized life here and advised her how to do St. Kilda things that she got her feathers ruffled, even though she herself knew many things were wrong and sorely needed changing.

"You know what I've decided?" he asked after he got her to tying something called a reef knot. "I think those long, ancient stone walls I've been excavating between Gleann Mor and Village Bay indicate that two ancient, hostile civilizations existed here at once. After all, there are ruins of old beehive houses in Village Bay contemporary to the Warrior Woman's House, though not in such good shape. The Gleann Mor people must have been wiped out by the ones living on this side of the island. Maybe Village Bay had been Christianized that early and Gleann Mor was still pagan Viking."

"I doubt the Christians would have attacked the pagans. Wouldna it be more likely the other way round? The Gleann Mor group attacked and conquered and then moved over here?"

"I *have* found more spearheads on this side of the island as if some battle had taken place here," he said and fell to brooding. When he was lost in thought like that, she always had to work harder to be included.

"What about the Gleann Mor civilization dying from within because immorality weakened them, like slavery?" she asked. "The old Vikings had slaves, you know, just as you were saying the ancient Romans did."

He had explained to her his belief that ancient Greece and Rome had been weakened from within by such practices, which he feared in modern guise could destroy the moral foundations of the southern states or all of America. That was what he was working on writing about this winter. But now, suddenly standing stock still, he was just staring at her with his mouth open.

"Blue blazes, you continually amaze me," he said. "I doubt I could discuss my ideas on such a level with—with women from home."

"Charlotte, your intended, for example," she said, frowning down at her knots again.

"Well, yes. I mean, I've never exactly tried such discussions, not about archeological theories, and certainly not my antislavery stance."

"Whyever not? Charlotte's grandfather obviously already knows how you feel. Is the woman just to be a housekeeper and—and mother to your children but not a wife to your thoughts? Do you intend to tell her what to do and just—"

"Abigail!" he interrupted, looking past her, his eyes gone wide as saucers despite the increasing smart slap of salty wind. "I can't believe it but—there's a ship out there, and it's breaking up on Dun! It looks like they tried to get in but couldn't negotiate the farthest rocks!"

She whirled to squint in the darkening direction he pointed. Not the old nightmare of Douglas again, not a St. Kilda boat on the rocks! But no, a sleek vessel with a huge, tattered mainsail had gone aground, heeled nearly on its side.

"A yacht," Morgan cried. "A very fine yacht!" He ran back and scrabbled in his pack for the telescope and pointed it outward.

"We'll have to run up and sound the village alarm!" she shouted, untying her skirts so she could run.

"I see men going overboard, trying to get to land! I'm sure I can manage this small vessel to tack out to them. They'll drown or be battered as the storm increases. You go for help!"

Just then she saw Murdo Adair coming down to the shore. She screamed his name and pointed outward. Seeing, understanding, the lad sprinted up toward the village.

Already Morgan was yanking loose his knots around the sails. "Help me shove this out!" he bellowed.

For one moment, staring at the thrashing waves, she saw Douglas's boat tipping, tossing men into the mouth of the greedy sea. But this was now and more men were drowning out there, dying like her own Douglas and she would not allow it.

"I'm coming too!" she shouted, freeing her knots. "You wilna get survivors into this boat alone. I can row when you furl sail!

I know the currents round those rocks from climbing them for lichens!"

"Others will be down to launch rescue boats! It's too danger-ous for a woman!"

She ignored him, helping him turn the prow of the boat out-ward. Holding it with ropes and keeping it off the rocks with the butts of their oars, they clambered out to the slippery landing spot, for the two of them would never launch it amidst breaking waves. Sopping her skirts, she got in and took two oars to row them out until he could hoist the sail. She had never heard him curse before, but he did now, at her or the sea, she was not sure. He shoved the boat and jumped in behind her. At least she had observed the inner workings of this birlin the other day, she thought, as she awkwardly rowed while he fought to control the sail.

"Sit tight and pull those in!" he shouted. "I've got it now!"

With great difficulty, they made for the end of Dun in a zigzag path he called tacking. She could see the ruin of the fine vessel clearly now, broken midships upon the rocks, the fore part of it nearly underwater and the aft section filling. No one could be still aboard or on the steep slant of deck. She tried to count the heads of survivors in the frothing water that smashed them on the rocks at the very tip of Dun. Only one—no two.

"Hidden rocks near here!' she shouted and pointed them out in the twist of whirlpools. Morgan lowered the sails with a huge thump and grabbed his pair of oars.

"I'll keep it steady off the rocks!" he yelled, but she was al-ready lifting a heavy oar to keep them from smashing there. When Morgan's oar steadied them, she thrust hers toward a bobbing, coughing man to give him a handhold.

"I can't help or we'll smash!" Morgan called behind her.

"I have one!"

She had thought the closest man was bald but he was white-haired, fighting for life and limb in the creaming, thrusting foam. He held desperately to her oar while she slowly hauled him closer to the boat. He looked up at her, dazed, gasping, as she looped a rope under his armpits with his help and leaned back to pull him up. She grabbed his sopping shirt and vest, ripped it, grabbed again and got his belt. With his help and Morgan's at the last, she hauled him in slowly like a huge fish.

"All drowned, gone!" the man cried, spitting water. But she spotted another survivor limply clinging to a rock in the crash, crash of each white-capped wave. A whirlpool tried to drag them into the looming jaws of two jagged rocks.

"Scylla and Charybdis!" she thought Morgan cried, but she did not know what he meant and there was no time to ask.

"Here, man! Here!" she shouted as she balanced in the rocking boat and leaned out to get her oar as close to the man as she could. "We canna come closer! Here!"

He turned and stared through the battering of sea, then made a lunging leap for the oar. He went under, sucked away. Morgan maneuvered closer, so dangerously near the rocks of Dun, and stood precariously in their craft to hold them off destruction with his oar again. Abigail froze for one moment, but not from fear. This was the very spot, the very clump of rocks that had snagged Douglas and Neil's bodies so long ago. And now they had a chance to save two men here. They must!

She blinked away salt spray as the survivor's head popped up and she worked him closer with the oar. He was a big man, unlike the old gentleman gasping for breath at her feet; she had to hold the birlin off the rocks while Morgan hauled him in.

They scanned the wreck, the waves, the slick rocks for more heads, even bodies. Two rescue birlins from the village arrived to continue the search so, drenched and exhausted, Morgan and Abigail headed in. The older man was still hacking. When Morgan got the sails up, Abigail bent over to pound his bony back. Finally, the second, stout one looked ashen-face up at her and gasped out, "And I shall live to tell it. Snatched by heaven's angel from the bloody jaws of hell!"

The hired yacht out of Glasgow, the *Good Fortune,* had carried three London passengers and a Scottish crew of three. The crewmen and a valet of the two other gentlemen had drowned in the attempt to cut close around Dun during the rising squall.

Corwin Baxter-Jones was the first man they rescued. He was a handsome, elderly bachelor with snowy white hair and close-cropped mutton-chops, whose interests were traveling and collecting things. "He nearly collected his own death sailing out here this late in the season," Morgan had muttered to Abigail, but he admit-

ted to her he liked the old gentleman's "noble principles and dem-
ocratic demeanor." Mr. Baxter-Jones, who got, as he put it, "into
the spirit of this place" by suggesting they call him by his first name
as St. Kilda friends did, was polite and thoughtful; Abigail, too,
liked him. With tears in his blue eyes, he had thanked them for his
rescue, but did not make them ill-at-ease by continually praising
them in florid speech as the other survivor did.

Parker Rex, in his mid-forties, from a place called Fleet Street
in London, was the owner of the weekly newspaper *Britannia's
Broad Shores*. He had evidently thought it "rather a great lark" to
procure a story about St. Kilda's narrow shores and had talked his
wealthy friend Corwin into coming along. Despite his constant re-
telling of his rescue to St. Kildans in high-blown prose that made it
sound as if he himself were quite the hero, Parker seemed a chair-
bound mainlander to Abigail. He obviously got his noble, hooked
nose out of joint when he also, condescendingly, permitted them to
call him by his first name. Morgan later told her that Parker's family name Rex meant king, and she saw that was the way he preferred to be treated.

But here he was, roughing it with Morgan and Corwin in the
factor's house on St. Kilda. They sat before the hearth in the parlor
there two days after the rescue, the Londoners taking tea with Morgan, Abigail, and Mr. Campbell. Hopefully, the men had said, a
mainland boat would soon come searching for them. Abigail nodded encouragingly. She was not looking forward to Parker's presence this winter even if she did enjoy Corwin's company. However,
when Parker finally got around to mentioning he was the father of
eight children, she was very thankful they had saved him as well as
the kindly Corwin.

"Eight children!" she cried. "How wonderful!"

"You think so, do you, my angel of salvation?" Parker asked,
tugging a wool blanket closer around his shoulders and broad middle. "Poppycock! It often becomes so raucous at the dinner table
one simply cannot hear oneself think. The little rascals absolutely
do one in. I told their mother, 'Let their nanny feed them in the
nursery!' In my day, children were to be seen and not heard. But she
indulges them frightfully, however sternly the queen's Prince Consort sets a fine standard by running the royal roost with discipline

and decorum. Sometimes I deem it a blessing my higher calling and patriotic duties keep me away."

"Your disdain for your own flesh and blood does you no credit, my friend," Corwin scolded gently before the shocked Abigail could remonstrate. "I never had the opportunity to have a child," Corwin admitted with a shake of his head, "not being blessed with the estate of wedlock. And I regret it deeply, whatever other bounty the Lord God has seen fit to bestow on me. But, in deep gratitude for what Morgan and Abigail did, I am thinking of adopting them both," he said with a grin at Morgan and a squint Abigail's way that might have been a wink or might have been his attempt to see her clearly since he had lost his spectacles in the wreck. The poor man coughed again so loudly into the handkerchief Morgan had given him Parker had to nearly shout.

"Best tell them their inheritance will be mostly tied up in that dusty natural history museum of yours, old boy!" Parker declared, brushing back his wispy blond hair on his wide forehead, then snugly replacing the glengarry cap he had been given. "Tableaux of stuffed deer and foxes; dented, dirty old artifacts brought back from world travels; birds under glass . . ."

"Surely you dinna mean live birds!" Abigail put in.

"Oh, no, my dear," Corwin said, quiet now after a soothing sip of tea. He reached over to pat her hand. "But you see, it's all the rage to display mounted wildfowl under glass domes, resplendent in their feathers. And that brings people in to see the other instructional things on display. Morgan and I have been discussing my artifacts from ancient Italy and Greece. Anytime you too would like to visit London, dear girl, I would introduce you to my friends more proudly than I ever did less rare treasures."

At least, Abigail thought, Corwin Baxter-Jones preserved birds for folks to admire, instead of just killing them for their feathers as Parliament decreed here. But her mind was still snagged on the indirect suggestion she visit London. She and Margaret had barely twenty pounds to their name now, but seldom spent a shilling on anything here. Surely London would have fine doctors to consult about St. Kilda's troubles with the bairns.

"Parker," Corwin's voice cut through her musings, "do you think now is the time to broach our idea to these people before we meet with Parliament?"

"May I inquire what idea?" Mr. Campbell asked.

"We shall present to Parliament a grand experiment to modernize St. Kilda," Parker pronounced. "To import Victorian progress! Rather like displaying this island under glass, what say, Corwin, and explaining all about life here through my newspaper with the great goal of bringing civilization to St. Kilda through charitable and educational visits and donations."

"But they have a civilization—*their* civilization," Morgan interjected before Abigail could reply. "Studying it is one thing, but displaying it to change it is something else again. And any Scot I have seen is too proud to take charity however much a few major changes could help around here!"

Corwin looked embarrassed by the way Parker had explained things. Morgan glared, and Mr. Campbell frowned into his teacup. Abigail's mind raced: progress named after the Queen of England could mean a school here, couldn't it? Perhaps a doctor too? But she knew better than to entertain such dreams if the St. Kildans had anything to say on it. Besides, to the depths of her Scottish St. Kilda soul she was affronted by the condescension in Parker's very tone.

"Quite out of the question," Mr. Campbell said. He put his teacup down and grasped his lapels as if warming to a sermon. "I have already discussed the idea of changing several things here with members of Parliament, and they are adamant against it to a man. When I suggested that a doctor could be useful here—an idea, may I say, of Abigail's—they told me the island dinna need one. An outsider wouldna ken their ways and might bring the boat cold or other diseases here, they argued. There isna need for a doctor to deliver the bairns since we have two knee-women for that, and, as if 'twas settled forever, they noted that the laird had never seen the need. No, I tell you, sirs, you will find the idea of either monetary rewards kindly proferred for your rescue or the more radical experiment of bringing what you call Victorian progress to St. Kilda out of the question here, though of course, you are welcome to put it to the men at their daily gathering."

"Abigail, do you think people here would turn us down, if things were put more carefully, in a—a kinder vein?" Corwin asked her, his face so worried now, his blue eyes which sparkled so now muted with concern. "I see St. Kilda as a precious, living museum and I, for one, would want to do nothing to affront anyone."

" 'Tis just that," Abigail replied, "as my mother used to say, 'Cats will only come to cream when 'tis sweet, not sour.' And the St. Kildans think all change—especially from without, but even if suggested by one of their own—is sour. They would have to be convinced or enticed, and I never yet found how, not even when it means the lives of their own bairns being at great risk."

"Ah," Corwin said, looking crestfallen. "Then we shall not insult our hosts further, Parker, no matter what your bloody plans for a series of articles coupled with a donation effort. You know, Abigail, *my* mother used to say, 'If you cannot do what is necessary, then you must simply do your best.' I have the feeling it has been that way for you, dear girl."

She nodded, tears in her eyes. His caring and understanding was almost like having Grandfather back for a moment. And he alone had asked her opinion.

"Rubbish!" Parker declared. "We shall just see about my plans. *My* mother always said money and fame will get one anywhere one wants to go!"

Morgan and the minister began to explain to Parker more about the way things were here. Parker listened intently, she noted, as if an American sea captain and minister from Glasgow would know more about it than she did. Parker evidently did not credit even the words of a rescuing angel of salvation from heaven, as he too often called her, and she fumed. Only Corwin looked her way and patted her hand again as if to appease her.

Her mind spun back to that day Douglas had spoken for her in Parliament. She had been happy to let him, but she had changed now; more was at stake than just her marital happiness or acceptance by the villagers. Yesterday's girlhood dreams were gone; today's nightmare remained. Yet she sat silent now, angry with Morgan for speaking of the problems on St. Kilda, but more angry with herself for loving a man of another realm as desperately as her mother must have loved the laird's son. And she was thinking something else her mother had said once, long ago: "The way of things for a woman can be accepted—or defied—only with suffering." And she, Abigail, who was skilled at suffering from her life here, now bided her time and vowed anew to defy anyone she must for her quest, though it might mean forfeiting or ruining all else she held dear.

❧

As predicted, Parliament turned down the bounteous offer of Victorian progress. A ship from Glasgow came searching for Parker and Corwin and took them away in late autumn. Abigail had been terrified Morgan might go too: Corwin had invited him to London to see his museum, just as he had extended to her, once again, that invitation and promised he would send her money next spring for the journey. She could stay at his house attached to the museum, he said, and would have her own maid for a companion. She missed Corwin's daily conversations however much she had been relieved to see Parker depart. And she was eternally grateful that Morgan had said he would try to visit London on his next voyage instead of now.

As the winter months stretched out ahead of them and daylight ebbed earlier each afternoon, she looked forward more than anything to her evening time with Morgan, properly chaperoned at Grandfather's old cottage. With Susannah, Malcolm, Margaret, Janie, and often Annie and Gavin around, the talk was lively, so Abigail had less time to miss Grandfather and grieve that there was no progress on finding a cure for the eight-day sickness. She had less time to mourn that Morgan would be gone come spring. Less time to admit how she wanted him and how, when he looked at her, narrow-eyed in the fireglow, even across a crowd of chatting, laughing people, his expression and his big, taut body sent invisible sea waves of desire to drown her.

"Ouch!" she cried and jerked her hand up to see how badly she had cut her finger with the cheese knife while she was daydreaming this time. Not much blood, she observed, but she must keep her mind on her task. She wrapped and tied her finger with a scrap of wool and went back to cutting her clotted mixture of cow and goat milk to release the watery whey in preparation for blueing the curds. As if they approved of the care she always took with the cheese, her and Margaret's cows lowed in the byre beyond the wall, and she heard a goat butt its makeshift stall.

At least her dyeing and cheesemaking let her concentrate on something besides Morgan and the bairns, she thought. Annie and Isobel were delivering Flora's second child this very afternoon; how she wished she had the answer to assure the infant's safety, whoever the mother was. But, back to the cheese, she urged herself, and in a low voice sang the old working hearthsong:

Cut the cheese to make it weep,
Add mold to grow blue veins,
Swaddle it so it will keep,
Enjoy it for your pains.

St. Kildans had always blued their cheese naturally in their stone homes, for the moist air combined with mold grown on old bannock bread provided the rich taste. Abigail's secret for her flavorful cheese—a recipe which she had shared with others more than once though they did not change their way—was to put in extra mold so the veins of blue would lend a stronger, richer savor. Strangely, the mold blued the cheese from the inside out, though it was inserted and then skewered in from the outside.

She pressed the clots into a wheel-shape, then shoved mold into the mass with her iron spike. She sealed the skin with fulmar oil and wrapped the entire hunk in a piece of oatmeal-dusted hemp she tied tightly with cord before she cradled it in her arms to carry it—

She gasped and straightened. She dropped the whole thing back down on the work board. Mold entered, she thought, through the skin and was scaled up to make the mold spread. An iron spike . . . fulmar oil . . . tightly tied cord . . . wrapping . . . the cheese had fragile veins like bairns and, when cut, wept whey instead of blood or tears; it was cut and tied like a new bairn's birth cord; both the infant and the cheese were anointed with fulmar oil; both were tightly swaddled. You enjoyed the cheese, like a new child, for "your pains," as the song said.

Her revelation staggered her. She shook with chills but felt flushed. Could the act of anointing a bairn's birth cord with fulmar oil, cutting it with an iron knife, then tying it tight let a—a sort of mold grow in the infant's delicate body, spreading through the veins? Only maybe it took eight days to ripen and not months as for cheese. And fulmar oil—it might be fine to seal cheese skin, but what if on infant's skin it acquired some of the same biting, brutal qualities of fulmar spit? The oil, seeping, then sealed inside the bairn, spread like that disease Morgan mentioned folks got when pricked by a needle or a nail. Lockjaw, that was it! Or could the residue of the iron knife mixed with the oil cause death when it was tied inside and the child's body firmly swaddled for those eight first days of tenuous life?

Still, why did not all of the infants die then? Her son alone, as far as she knew, had not had his birth cord anointed with oil and severed with the knee-woman's old iron knife. Abigail had Annie and Margaret use a new steel knife on wee Douglas and not the older iron one; the stub of his cord had been rubbed only with soft soap. Yet Margaret had wanted the oil for Janie; Abigail had applied it herself. It was Margaret's one concession to Mairi in her vain attempt to placate her. Annie had brought them some fulmar oil she herself had prepared. But Douglas had died and Janie had lived. Beyond that, in Janie's birth Abigail had avoided other customary practices.

This new suspicion proved nothing, but now that she finally had a theory, she must test it further. She must observe closer, warn Annie and, yes, Isobel, and see if she could convince them to stop using the oil and iron knife until more observations—

"And Flora's having a bairn right now!" she cried aloud and seized her coat. She had to tell Annie, to find Morgan, to see what he thought, and tell Mr. Campbell to enlist his help.

She took a lamp as she hurried out into the late afternoon dusk. She tried to hold her kerch around her head in the blast of wind, but she needed to protect the iron lamp more. Her kerch ripped away; her hair streamed free as she ran for Flora's cottage. She pounded on the door. She was grateful it was Annie who opened it and let her in. She put her lamp down on the small table just inside.

"Ye look a fright! Whatever it is?" Annie asked in a whisper, then added louder, "Flora's got a fine daughter."

"Did you cut the birth cord and anoint it yet?"

"Not yet, but Grandmother's just ready to—"

Isobel loomed over Annie's shoulder as the two younger women huddled together. "I should have kenned who let in that blast of air to chill my new grandchild!" Isobel declared. "What is it and at a time like this, Abigail Adair?"

"Mrs. MacCrimmon, I ken you wilna believe this, but I think the eight-day curse could come from the cutting, tying, and anointing of the cord, maybe the swaddling too."

Isobel just shook her head and lumbered back to her work. Abigail noted Fionna was here to make the delivering of Flora's bairn a family affair. She felt a sharp twist of regret and resentment for her own losses, but she dared to follow Isobel. From what she could see from here, fortunately, Flora had fallen asleep already or Abigail knew she'd be tossed out immediately at her ranting. But her friend Annie's presence as the next knee-woman had worked wonders for Abigail more than once.

"Please listen, Mrs. MacCrimmon," Abigail begged. Annie, though she went back to tending Flora, was listening; even Isobel had her head inclined as if to hear. Abigail's heart beat even faster as she tiptoed closer. "About the anointing," she whispered. "We all know how poison that fulmar spit is—"

"This isna fulmar spit," Isobel interrupted, "but fulmar oil."

"I ken, but just as mold works its good wonders in the veins of cheese when 'tis all closed up tight, couldna oil and maybe the cutting knife work bad wonders through the child's veins when the birthing cord's tied tight and the child's swaddled the first eight days?"

Isobel just snorted and kept working. "But," Annie put in, "some live and some die, and all are treated the same, Abigail. And they're only swaddled for eight days because that's how long it takes to ken whether they will live to put them into clothes or not."

"Yes, but now that we have a possibility, we must study it more, working together, and change the cutting and not using the oil until we can tell . . ." Her voice faded away as she watched Isobel cut the birth cord with the iron knife, anoint it with the oil and then, with a flourish, tie the yarn tight around it before she began to wrap her new grandchild in flannel strips.

"And *that* is what the MacCrimmon and Fergusson knee-women think of yer foolish thoughts, Abigail!" Isobel said with a snort.

Annie came over to put her hands on Abigail's shoulders to turn her gently away. "Abby, the idea may be good for the future, but the timing couldna be worse. Best be gone and say naught of it to anyone right now."

Abigail let herself be led to the door. "Annie," she whispered, grasping her hand, "maybe I am wrong because my own bairn had things done so different there in Gleann Mor and he died, but we must follow every lead."

Annie picked up Abigail's lamp and handed it to her with her free hand. Suddenly, the lass's face looked ravaged; Abigail realized what a difficult birthing this must have been. The light cast demonic shadows on Annie's bonny face.

"Abby, please forgive me," she whispered. "I—I did use the oil that day, just wanting to do something special and proper for yer bairn. I took it from grandmother's storage chest on the sly, as I didna want anyone to ken of it. I wanted to help ye so much that day! But I have seen many a bairn born with the oil and the knife cutting and the tight tying and wrapping and no harm came to them, including Flora's first."

Tugging her hand back, Abigail gaped at Annie. Fulmar oil had been used on her own wee son Douglas, and from the best of intentions. But Annie was right about the other bairns who had lived. Abigail's shoulders slumped. This theory too was no doubt a blind end, just as, evidently, her earlier belief that the kneading of the child from the womb caused the deaths. Nothing was consistent, nothing was proven. She wanted to scream and beat her fists on the walls in her frustration.

"Annie, stop dawdling and see to this bairn!" Isobel said so close that both Annie and Abigail jumped. At that tone of voice, Annie hastened to obey. Before Abigail could open the door, the knee-woman pinned her hard against it; the lamp fell from her hands, spilled, and gutted out on the stone floor.

"Best ye consider the blasphemy ye think and preach with this latest evil idea or yers," Isobel intoned. Her eyes were narrowed, her face still with fury. "Do ye dare believe that God Himself would have allowed generations of St. Kilda's knee-women to kill the island bairns, even their own? Aye, that's what yer claiming, ye seducing, sly thing. I tell ye, I have not caused the death of one of the little ones! Keep yer mouth shut for once, if ye want to have any sort of life here!"

"Mrs. MacCrimmon, you ken folks can make mistakes and bring harm, though innocent of that motive!" Abigail protested.

"And ye've made the worst mistake of all now with yer demented accusations. Demented, ye are, like yer mother, and just because ye canna accept that ye lost yer bairn and poor Douglas too.

But God's own justice is clear now, for Flora's husband and first bairn live, and ye are alone but for yer mainlander lover who will leave ye like the laird's son left yer mother when he had his way with her and—"

With a strangled cry, Abigail thrust the heavy woman away. Isobel staggered back but did not fall. Abigail pulled the door open and stumbled out into the bitter bite of wind. She did not run to Morgan, nor to the minister's manse, nor to Margaret who was visiting Susannah with Janie nearby. Nor did Abigail run away to the cliffs as she had before. Tears falling, head down, limbs trembling, jaw clenched, Abigail headed for her cottage to study anew the birthing records Annie had been keeping for her all these years.

9

Outlanders sailing to my isle
Bring all their different ways.
I learn, they leave,
I long, I love,
And will for all my days.

Sitting at the factor's big desk, Morgan was warmed by the bright slant of spring sun. He put down his pen and leaned back from his writing, lost not in thoughts of his work, but of St. Kilda—and, as always, Abigail. During this past winter, despite suffering the throes of passion for her, he had felt strangely at home with himself for the first time he could recall since he had been a boy on Sanibel so long ago and far away. For once here on St. Kilda, he had escaped the continued demands he would make the expected decisions, which in his heart he did not want to make.

Granted, he missed America. For days at a time here the winter weather had been what he thought of as prehistoric: black rain, violent northeast gales, sleet or snow, incessant whining like the wail of wind through the rigging. But the ice stayed seldom thicker than a penny or melted just the way the isle and its people had melted his heart. He had not realized the upheaval of his confused mental and emotional state back in so-called civilization until he stepped away from it all.

The elemental rawness of this place somehow suited him. The knitting of the yarn and of basic human relationships around the fragrant peat fire in the evening; the bland, unvaried food prepared by loving hands of the housewife herself and not a hired cook; the pace of life, slower than the clack, clack, clack of the men's looms; and Abigail, above all, Abigail, who had become an essential part of him. But too soon he must wrench himself away and return to his other life. Had Ulysses felt regret or only relief when he left Calypso on her island of Ogygia and headed home?

And now that he had been to Boreray with the men on their first spring harvest of gannets, what excuse would he have to stay when a ship arrived this spring? He would like to return to Boreray for more excavations, of course, to further study the circle of standing stones that had made him gape in silent awe. But he could not and would not. He had been gone far too long from his family, his ship, his business—and Charlotte. He let her person and personality pale in his mind, fading to a blur so he almost could not recall her at all. He carried an oval photograph of her with a lock of her hair in a tiny velvet case in his things, but he had not looked at it once on St. Kilda and did not want to now.

How cherished his heart's image of Abigail, more vibrant, in flaming colors, amidst all his island dreams. How long he had desired to caress and kiss her again as he had that day old Alistair died, but he had been as cowardly as well as brave this winter. For if he had been alone with her again—if she had responded as she had on Conachair, he would surely have lost whatever shred of control he possessed around her. And then there would be the danger, the shame and pain for her of being deserted, perhaps with his child, who could die of this dread disease that haunted her more than the losses of her family.

And so, Morgan had steeled himself to be with her mostly in the company of others. He had walked her home and, yes, stolen kisses, touched her arm or held her hand when he could, but he had been so careful not to damage her standing further with these people whose actions he both admired and deplored. He had dammed up his rampant desire to possess her . . .

"Though she does possess me, and ever will!" he whispered.

He shoved his papers back and stood, seizing his hat and coat on the way out the door. He had to see her now, not wait until this evening after supper at Malcolm and Susannah's. He would find some excuse—he needed more cheese, he wondered how her new orphaned chicks were faring, something. How like her it was, he thought as he strode the street against the wind, that she had continued to hatch deserted eggs of the very fulmars she theorized might be related to the infant deaths. As soon as he could, he would inquire of American surgeons about her idea, and write to her. But the thought of touching such a vital, bright woman only through black ink on cold pages made him shudder as he hurried on.

Abigail opened the door when he knocked. Her stunning face lit to see him. "Hello, Captain!" rang little Janie's bell-clear voice from the dim cottage. He tore his eyes away from Abigail to see Margaret was there too. He felt deflated not to find Abigail alone, but relieved he would not cause as much of a stir if someone saw. He entered the small, crowded cottage and grinned when they all fussed over him as if he were the President himself come calling: the settle dragged nearer the hearth for him, cheese and fresh bannocks to eat, questions about his day, and three charming faces turned his way.

After Margaret pulled Janie back to her task of practicing her writing on a piece of slate by the window, he observed to Abigail, "I see you've been dyeing."

"While teaching the lass a few songs she has been writing down for practice. Her voice is so good, I shall teach her all the hearthsongs. But do you know what I was thinking? The dye permeates each piece of yarn, changing it forever. Morgan, I ken that is just how the disease works within the bairns' bodies, and I have to find the way to prove it beyond talking of my blasted cheese and dyeing!"

"You will. And as I said, I will do what I can to help when— I've gone home." He frowned but continued to study her face. "How brave you are to go on with this all, Abigail, considering Isobel MacCrimmon's latest lies to discredit you. Perhaps my theory that two hostile civilizations once lived on St. Kilda is proved by the fact that two still do!"

" 'Tis a full-fledged war now," Abigail admitted and swiped at a single tear as she came to sit by his side. They said no more on it, but he watched her nibble her lush lower lip and knew she was recalling how, when Flora's bairn had died last autumn, Isobel had blamed Abigail for bringing a killing draft into the house when the infant was born. Flora's second child would have lived as hearty as her first, Isobel insisted publicly, but for that chill and Abigail's interrupting her and Annie during the delicate birth.

The knee-woman claimed that the factor had told the minister that the cause of the eight-day sickness might be the damp and cold on St. Kilda. She had told any island woman who would listen that Abigail had heard that from the factor on a private visit to him, trying to get her own way with a man, as usual. And so, Isobel said, Abigail Adair had done two cruel and unnatural things to hurt Flora: demented, as her mother before her, Abigail had deliberately endangered Flora's child in jealousy and revenge, and had concocted a wild scheme to blame the island knee-women for the deaths of the infants.

Some had believed Isobel's insidious gossip, some—including Annie—had not. But after the Reverend Mr. Campbell had tried to talk to Isobel and Mairi about "corrupt communications" as the Bible put it, they had even dared to turn some of the islanders against the minister. Now, the families of St. Kilda were even more firmly divided into feuding camps, and Morgan saw how deeply Abigail regretted being at the center of the conflict. To be blamed for that which she strove to cure was the greatest burden of all. But Morgan did not bring all that up again. The more he had defended her last autumn, the worse had been the whispers about them too.

"You know," he told her, "I think St. Kilda has taught me tolerance and patience, among other things."

"Then you are fortunate. Canna say it has taught me that."

"And I've learned so many other things too, which I shall always treasure." He noted the shadows that always settled in her golden eyes when he even alluded to leaving. He knew she cared deeply for him too, but did he dare to hope that she desired—loved—him as he did her? Granted, she had responded fervently to his touch on Conachair, but she had been so in need then. Still, even now, she blushed as he studied her; her breasts rose and fell as she heaved a deep sigh. He felt so drawn to her that he both blessed and cursed Margaret and the child for being here, or he was not certain what he would have done, whatever tattered remnants of reputation Abigail had yet to lose. He would pull her into his lap and hold her, at least. Kiss her, caress her and—

"And," he went on, trying to fill with talk the aching silence between them, "I feel I know this island nearly as well as you do, as much as I've tramped and studied it."

"Do you now?" she replied, her voice taking on that edge it got when he tried to tell her how to do things here. "The side of the island over by Gleann Mor especially, I suppose."

"Of course."

"Then tell me all about the Tunnel, as its western entrance is a stone's throw from there."

"The Tunnel? You know, I vaguely recall old Alistair mentioning that my first night here, but when I saw the Gap, I guess I thought that was the same thing."

"Margaret, would you believe the outlander here thinks the Gap and the Tunnel are the same thing?" Abigail said over her shoulder in her teasing tone that curled his toes. "Shall I show the braw man he is wrong or let him wander on in his delusion?"

"Best bundle ye both up and set him straight, I should say," Margaret replied with a grin.

Morgan knew that he was smiling too as the women shared a little laugh at having bested him. He didn't mind. A new adventure lured him on and with Abigail at his side, away from everyone's accusing stares. With his days so numbered here, the opportunity seemed a gift from heaven he had not the self-control to refuse. And it made it so much easier to tell himself that he could cling to his island dreams a bit longer before they were gone for good.

Abigail was ecstatic at the prospect of a few precious hours with Morgan. They had hardly kept private company since he had insisted they be public with their friendship. Soon his mainland life would win him from her. Each day of mild weather like this meant a supply ship could arrive from Harris or even Glasgow to take the earliest loads of this year's feathers—and him—away.

When she met him in the pass to Gleann Mor, she carried an unlighted lamp and two blankets. In his pack he carried food she and Margaret had prepared.

His eyes widened to see what she had brought. "Why all that?" he asked. "Oh, you mean it's cold and dark in the Tunnel?"

"Yes, and 'tis tradition," she told him, embarrassed that it looked as if she were ready to make and illumine a bed in the depths of the Tunnel. Both suddenly awkward with each other, they walked down through the spring grandeur of Gleann Mor, then followed the cliff path away from the valley. As they wended their way amid nesting fulmars, she warned, "Now, dinna get too close to them, or they will spit their poison at you!" The birds protested the intrusion with their "Ah, ak!" cries but, as if they knew Abigail had been rearing their abandoned eggs for years, they did not spit once.

"The Tunnel is called *Geo na h-Airde* in Gaelic that you never quite got to studying," she told him over her shoulder as they descended toward the sea.

"When I go, I should take you to teach me, as you've taught your other friends to read and write," he said. Her heart thrilled even at that tiny tease, and she silently scolded herself for her foolishness. At least when he left, one good thing would come of it: he would take her letters to be delivered to doctors in Glasgow, Liverpool, and Baltimore. And if Corwin sent for her, as promised, she would talk directly to London's doctors.

She led him down the spray-swept, rocky ramp to the western entrance of the Tunnel. Grasping the old horsehair rope attached with spikes to the cliff face, they entered on a shelf just above the surge of sea, which came in both ends and battled in the middle, scouring the stone deeper and wider. But despite the roar of water, a mere human whisper shivered up and down the walls.

"What an incredible world!" he said, shaking his head in disbelief as he looked around. "But then, all of St. Kilda has been that to me."

He took her arm. She was surprised to feel him trembling, but she understood his feelings about St. Kilda. She missed him already, though he stood so close. She could not bear to let him go and yet she must so that her dream to save the bairns could be furthered. And if she ever really admitted to a man like this his power over her, she feared her strength to fight for her cause would be submerged even more in his needs and desires, as had happened with her beloved Douglas.

They edged along until they reached the central alcove where the footing was better. "There's an old hearthsong about the Tunnel," she said, " 'Like a greedy giant's throat swallowing the sea.' "

"But someday, the giant will regret his appetite," Morgan said, turning her to face him. "Eventually, water will eat away at these walls, and the roof will fall in. . . . I've been the romanticist so long here, it pains me to begin to think realistically again."

He took a step closer as if to pin her against the ungiving rock. He put down the lamp and divested himself of the pack. She still held the folded blankets to her, for it was custom to wrap them around like a cloak inside the heart of the Tunnel. Yet they neither did that, nor lit the lamp. There was no need, for she had never felt hotter, no place had ever glowed brighter.

"When I am with you like this," Morgan was saying, "I am that giant. I bestride the universe, yet I am greedy for more. But the roof of rationality has fallen in on me already to have stayed here so long."

He took the blankets from her and dropped them to the floor of the stone alcove. He tugged her against him and she threw her arms around his neck. She stood on solid rock but felt as if she were sucked away by churning foam.

"I shall miss you so when you leave, that I will, Morgan!"

"Oh, my sweetheart!" he choked out before their lips met in a crushing kiss.

She savored every moment of the mutually fierce embrace, storing up the strength of him to warm and light the long days and nights ahead. She reveled in the exploding power between them. His big hands caressed her back, her waist, her hips. Her head spun, her breathing quickened as she held to him, deepening the kiss. They tilted their heads to let their tongues delve swifter, sweeter. Her knees shook, perhaps his too, for he sat them down upon the tumbled blankets, then slid her onto his lap, staring into her eyes a nosetip away.

"Abigail, I care so deeply for you! I cannot begin to tell you what you—all this—has meant to me." Emotion ravaged his face and roughened his voice. Tears shimmered in the dark brown pool of his eyes. "I have tried so damned hard to put other people between us, sweetheart, to keep things aboveboard so everyone would not sully what we felt—sully you when I left. It's taking every ounce of self-control I have not to seduce you, to take you, Abigail. I would never chance leaving you with a fatherless child to agonize over for eight days or ever after, but I want you so!"

She wanted to tell him how she loved and desired him, but she was afraid. Afraid of her need, her weakness, this overwhelming ache for him to possess her body and protect her forever, whatever the price. She lay her head upon his shoulder, her lips pressed to his warm neck to caress his skin there as she spoke. Her words tumbled out as broken as her thoughts.

"I, too, Morgan! You ken, despite our good intentions, some folks whisper that—we are lovers." She tried to shove away the shrill voice of Isobel MacCrimmon that day she had accused, "Yer mainlander lover will leave ye like the laird's son left yer mother when he had his way with her!" In no way must she let that dreadful woman have spoken the truth!

"I do want us to be lovers," she stumbled on, "but it would be wrong, here on St. Kilda, wrong the way I—both of us have been taught. And I canna abide having those who detest me be right about us, however much I wish for the—the familial act with you. But our friends—like Margaret today trusting us to be honorably alone, and I canna let her down . . ."

Her voice faded as she realized again she partly kept from doing what she desired because of others she cared for. For one selfish moment, she yearned to cast all that aside. Like the greedy giant she would swallow life, rip down the roof of her world, belong only to this man, become part of him. But therein lay the danger of her surrender. And was there not power in denying one's desires for a greater cause, however much the strength of her woman's needs surged through her?

"I suppose," he said, clearing his throat, "in the way of things here, you and Douglas resisted temptation all those times you were alone together in your cave."

She nodded, lifting her head to look into his intense eyes. "We were young and eager, and we were afraid of discovery. Yes, we forced ourselves to wait until we wed—"

"I swear, at least I shall come up to him that way in your mind—by playing the gentleman hero, fondly remembered! We'd best head back—for both our sakes. I turn too impulsive around you," he said gruffly. "Come on, get up before I forgo my damnably honorable intentions!"

As she rose, her hand touched the cold, damp stone to jolt her back to reality. She felt panicked. This alcove was dark and chill, and they were going to flee what could be their last time alone.

"Morgan, I do love you so!"

She was shocked to hear the words she had carried silently inside so long. She wished she had not said them then, but like many things in life, it was too late to take them back.

"I love you too, Abigail. And that's why we have to return to the village now, because all my high-blown sentiments of protecting your best interests are nothing if I could have you one day and leave you the next."

She gathered the blankets and the unlit lamp. He only touched her elbow to steady them both on the way out. One foot ahead of the other, she moved away from what could have been, feeling shattered and yet strangely, painfully whole since he had declared his love. Would it be easier or more awful to lose him now? She was terrified that she would soon ken exactly that.

They said little on their way back across the island. He turned to her in the mountain pass before they began their descent toward Village Bay. "Abigail, I think we both know I have too long shirked my many responsibilities, my family, friends, people who depend on me, my career. I cannot believe I have stayed in this distant place for months when I meant to stay days! Please don't look so downcast, Abigail. I just need a little more time to think things over before I leave, and we will talk again."

"Yes, of course."

"All right then, I will see you later. Now, walk on back down by yourself, and I'll bring the blankets and lamp and follow you shortly."

She stared at him as if to memorize his face forever. His words now hardly penetrated her confusion of emotion; all she knew was that their idyll, their odyssey was over. He looked almost angry with her as she hesitated to accept and obey. She turned and started down from the pass. But as her eyes swept the distant scene of Village Bay below, she gasped and turned back to see him staring too. Not one but two steam and sail yachts much the size of the wrecked *Good Fortune* were anchored in the bay.

"Neither of those are the laird's, I think!" she called to Morgan. She yearned to run to him, but the stony set to his face held

her back. He was looking at those ships—his escape—and not at
her.

She turned and strode down to the village and was barely beyond the cemetery when the onslaught began. She was surprised to
see most of the islanders in the streets now running up toward her
and not down to the ships.

"There she is, that lass there!" Iain Murdoch's voice rang out
above the hubbub as he pointed her out to a cluster of outlander
men.

The strangers—at least ten of them—rushed to greet her, smiling, wide-eyed, while the villagers just stared. Most of the outlanders were dressed as fine as Morgan, and wore their hair and side
whiskers the way Parker Rex and Corwin Baxter-Jones had.

"Queen of Kilda, we salute you!" a red-haired man cried as
several others swept off their hats and bowed. "Every bit as bold
and brave and beautiful as our own Queen Victoria!" he went on
and thrust a large, folded piece of paper at Abigail. "We hear you
can read too, so we'll let you have the honor, though that etching
of her does not do her justice, does it, Nigel?"

"Not a bit. Her likeness on the pottery mugs and plates the paper sold was closer," Nigel, stout and balding, declared.

Abigail gaped at the copy of Parker Rex's newspaper *Britannia's Broad Shores*. "The Heroine of the North, Part the First," it
read at the top of the page. It was solid with small print, a stilted
version of her life here, she thought, horrified as she skimmed it.
And there was a large drawing called "The Wreck of the Good Fortune" smack in the middle of the print. Someone had drawn her
alone in the rescue boat in monstrous seas, rowing for men jumping
off a shattered ship. She glanced up, stunned. Had it not mattered
one wee bit to Parker Rex that an American sea captain was at the
helm of the so-called vessel of salvation?

"Is there a doctor among you?" she asked the men staring at
her, one of whom was now drawing her picture, perhaps the very
artist who had perpetrated this fiction. "Did Parker Rex send a doctor to help the bairns as I asked?"

"No doctor, but several barristers and professors and men
from the paper," the red-haired man explained. "And a few who
just came to see if it was all true, and invite you back to England
to meet your adoring public and serve as a fine example to our

young women. Rather than bring people this far, Mr. Rex thought it would be best if you came and went on some sort of triumphal tour!"

She shook her head and glanced down at the paper again. Ah, yes, here at least was mention about the dying infants on St. Kilda, whom "the Queen of Kilda" was trying to save. But this all made her very angry, no matter how numb she felt after her afternoon with Morgan. She could see a man had set up a huge box on three tall legs with a black drape over his head after lining up wary St. Kildans. Photography, she realized, as she stared at other visitors tossing what looked like small, shiny stones to the curious children and calling, "sweets, sweets" as if they were feeding pet dogs.

"As well as monetary and visitation offers, we've brought some fifty letters from the paper's readership proposing marriage!" another man announced loudly.

She began to feel dizzy. And then she heard fast strides spitting stones and spun to see Morgan approach. He was swinging his arms as he nearly ran downhill; his pack, the blankets, and lamp were nowhere to be seen.

"What in blue blazes is all this?" he demanded of the men surrounding her. "Marriage proposals? Who are you?"

The men closest to her introduced themselves. Their names blurred by. "Abigail," Morgan said with a jerk of his head toward the village, "why don't you get Margaret and Janie away from here for now. And the rest of you, just leave Mrs. Adair alone!"

"Perhaps she does not wish to be left alone, sir!" Nigel stated. "Who in thunderation are you to be ordering us about, her keeper? I am an Oxford scholar come here to observe these 'living fossils of men,' as the newspaper put it. My calculations tell me that over sixty percent of the paper's readers agree that the Queen of Kilda is a 'self-sacrificing paragon of primal British bravery,' so stand aside, sir. Now that I've seen her, I declare I shall ask her to go back to civilization with us!"

"She will not entertain any of those offers!" Morgan yelled. "She's leaving with me for America!"

Abigail gasped. The chaos churned even worse. Two men tried to push Morgan away; he shook them off. Nigel shoved him; Morgan's fist cracked into Nigel's jaw. Flora's husband, Gordon, appeared to slam his fist into Morgan's belly to double him over.

Abigail screamed. Iain Murdoch and Hamish Adair ran over in a futile attempt to separate the men as Morgan leapt at Gordon, pummeling him until Gordon sprawled on the ground. The crowd swelled as both strangers and St. Kildans shoved forward. Squealing, Janie ducked through the press of people to throw her arms around Abigail's hips, spilling two fistsful of sweets on the ground that other children scrambled for. Mr. Campbell arrived and shouted "Shame! Shame, for blessed are the meek and the peacemakers!" until most St. Kildans stopped, then slunk away.

Abigail felt shocked and shamed. Holding Janie tightly to her, she stared into Morgan's furious face as he wiped his bloodied nose on the cuff of his shirtsleeve. Anger swelled in her: to have him protect her was one thing, but his assumption of possession of her—his speaking for her publicly that she would not entertain offers of financial aid or wedlock—or that she would leave with him for America when he had not so much as asked her, stunned her. She was absolutely done with having any man speak for or make decisions for her. He had said he wanted to guard her reputation before, but now he had humiliated her and threatened her dreams. She trembled. Tears tracked down her cheeks as visitors picked up Nigel from the ground and brushed mud from his clothing.

Head held high, pulling Janie behind her, Abigail went over and said to the dirtied man, "I shall read your letters, sir, if you will be so kind as to deliver them to my cottage later, for I decide things for myself." She hoisted Janie into her arms and turned away without another look at any of them.

She was thankful that one of the letters was from Corwin Baxter-Jones. It included twenty pieces of paper money marked five pounds each with Queen Victoria's likeness on every one. She had no doubt the neat little stack was enough for three fares to London, for Corwin urged her again to visit, bringing her sister-in-law and niece with her if she wished. Margaret had already said if Abigail went, she and Janie would go with her.

At least that and Corwin's kindly letter were wee shreds of sanity in the deluge of epistles from strangers who seemed swept away by adoration of a fiction, "the Queen of Kilda, Heroine of the North," a woman Abigail hardly recognized as she read the three parts of her supposed St. Kilda story. The fourth article told how

"Female Virtue Victorious" and her self-sacrificing courage had been the inspiration for numerous sermons, poems, pictures in worsted wool on canvas, and paintings—not to mention the commemorative mugs and plates the paper was selling. Morgan was hardly mentioned. When she thought of how much "Virtue Victorious" still longed for him—Margaret said she heard he would be leaving when the outsiders departed—Abigail hung her head and wept.

Morgan came to see her later that evening after her string of British visitors had departed her cottage to sleep in their yachts. "Would ye like me to stay?" Margaret inquired as her eyes darted between Abigail and Morgan's taut faces.

" 'Tis just a brief farewell we'll be saying," Abigail told her. "You dinna want to miss a chance to fetch Janie from your mother's."

Morgan closed the door behind Margaret and came closer, towering over Abigail, who hugged her knees tighter, not rising from her stool next to the hearth. "I guess I should apologize for exploding like that today," he began, "but I could not help it."

"And just this morning you announced that St. Kilda had taught you tolerance and patience. I dinna see why you jumped in like that, since you can keep yourself from doing other passionate things well enough," she snapped before she could pull back the words.

"Now, wait a minute! You gave me a whole litany of reasons in the Tunnel you wanted me to stop today!"

"I shared my heart with you. Anyway, 'tis all stopped, all over, so let us say no more but farewell and godspeed." She rose to poke at the peat embers with a stick so as not to feel at such a disadvantage sitting at his feet. She knew she was blaming him for something she had been afraid of too, but she could not help the anger that strangled forgiveness in her.

"How can you say that when *I* am the one who unburdened my soul to you today?" he demanded.

"Told me that you have shirked your duties too long, you mean? I quite agree, so we have no argument. But I believe your lengthy list of shirkings did not include poor Charlotte, who is faithfully waiting for you like a good Penelope, Ulysses. So, how dare you cry out for everyone to hear that I was leaving with you, as if we had discussed it and I would do such a thing!"

"You mean you wouldn't?" He seized her shoulders and spun her to face him. "What did you think I meant by telling you I needed more time to think things over and then we would talk again? And don't tell me you weren't angling for marriage this afternoon!"

"I? Certainly not! But then, perhaps the folks are right here. Perhaps I am demented like my mother—to—to so much as care one wee bit for you!"

He gave her a hard shake. "You as good as said you and Douglas had waited to share your bodies in marriage, so I took the hint. And when I heard those bastards Parker Rex sicced on you dare to mention marriage, I just blurted out what you'd been wanting and I'd been agonizing over!"

She gaped at him; she felt suspended in his grip on her shoulders. "I canna believe your sudden, brazen talk of marriage, Captain West. That took agonizing indeed! Imagine taking the wild Queen of Kilda home with you to introduce to your family, your friends, especially your partner and poor Charlotte."

She almost sagged to the floor; she locked her knees to remain standing. She was hurt and angry at his arrogant assumptions and the way he'd put things, but the idea of being his wife was sweet as well as strange.

"But you ken I couldna consider such until the bairns' tragedy is solved," she went on, her voice softening. "Besides, you shouted today that I was leaving with you, not wedding with you. It sounded more as if I was to be your kept woman."

He sat her down on the settle and perched beside her, turned to her, leaning forward. "I can't imagine life without you, Abigail, even back home. I meant to discuss it earlier, but I needed more time to think, then all those men came with letters from strangers pressing around you when I'm so used to having you to myself . . . I didn't just mean you would leave with me for anything untoward. Of course, we must marry then. Haven't I taken great pains to protect you here? I'll take you away from these people who have never appreciated your talents nor understood your needs. It's a sin how the wretches have made you a scapegoat and an outcast. We must leave for Liverpool right away, but you'll have time to speak with a doctor or two there before we sail for home. And then when you're living in Baltimore, you can consult the best surgeons in America and send the results back here. Or if a damned American war doesn't start to trap us there, we can both come back here together someday . . ."

He went on extolling the benefits of Baltimore, as if he were back there now, as if he had already left here forever—as if he were afraid to give her time to think. He spoke of a large brick home he would buy her to replace this little stone cottage of Lady Grange's and Glenna MacQueen's which she and Margaret and Janie now shared—Janie. Had this man understood nothing she had ever said to him about what mattered to her? She could not go that far away and perhaps be trapped by some war while the war for the bairns' lives was being waged here! London was as far as she would risk going to find the "best surgeons." He had considered all these plans for them and never asked her, never consulted her. He wanted to free the slaves, but he was seducing her to be his possession.

Though she told herself she trusted Morgan nearly as much as she loved him, she stared down into a huge, dark chasm of his making which gaped between them. Memories of Edmund Drummond's deceitful promises and even dear Douglas's taking over her life coiled in her heart to strike. And yet, she loved Morgan so, she felt torn asunder.

"Morgan, I would need much longer than you evidently can afford me to consider," she faltered when he finally let her get a word in. "Perhaps someday, after London when—"

"A trip to London to bask in the adoration of an anonymous public is more important to you than our love? Or have the attentions of those dandies turned your head? Maybe you want to include me as little in your life as that damned newspaper included me in the whole rescue story! I know you want to rescue the St. Kilda infants too, Queen of Kilda! But I'm telling you, it would do you good to look forward to a future family of our own instead of being buried in the dead past—"

"Fine words from an archeologist who revels in the past, who fancies himself the new Ulysses taking on new odysseys! Dinna you see I am fighting to save present and future families here? Besides, maybe I canna even bear another child. I fell bad once on the cliffs and—hurt myself."

"Why in blue blazes didn't you tell me before, especially when I was carrying on today?"

"And would it have made such a difference in how 'persuasive' you were if you thought you would not leave me with a child? Besides, I didna ken then we were making lifetime plans—even if you were! Morgan, I have cared for you, but I canna give you an answer on the spot."

"I am leaving with some of the visitors tomorrow, Abigail. I cannot stay longer. I will have your answer now or know you don't love me as you have said, not as much as I do you!"

She shook her head in disbelief at his demands, which he took for denial of his request. She saw him stiffen; his face set hard; he leapt to his feet. It didn't matter now, she thought desolate, for "no" must be the answer if he pushed her amidst such sudden confusion. She jumped up too.

"You're right to remind me I was a Ulysses here!" he shouted, pointing at her. "Calypso seduced him from his duties too, when he needed—he *wanted*—to be home and about his business! She kept him there until he came to his senses!"

"As you have come to yours and bear no blame for any of your decision to stay?" she taunted, hands on her hips. "Besides, *you* were the one speaking of seducing me today. Just leave, Morgan, before we say worse things to ruin all we've had."

"All we had was a delusion if you do not love me and trust me enough to realize I will help you with your cause. I said I'll give you money to consult doctors."

"But it would be your money, and I would be beholden to you then. And I would be far away, unable to return to convince folks here about what needs to be done."

"You think they will listen to you, Parliament and Isobel and her coterie?"

"Coterie? I dinna ken the word but I take the meaning—and your black, pompous view of things here. Dinna you see, perhaps if I visit England, folks would pay a bit to hear about life as it really is here on St. Kilda, so I could earn my own—"

"Most of them would come to gawk at you like some rare, primitive bird in a cage. Do you want that? Let me make it easier for you, protect and guide your entry into the world for your own good."

"Perhaps you dinna have the faintest idea what is for my own good, Morgan! You think I'd let them put me on display like that? And neither would Corwin, and I will take him up on his kindly offer of hospitality, for he trusts me to have my own ideas!"

"Thank God, at least you'll have some sort of chaperone then," he muttered.

"I should have seen you think I need a male watchdog, just as the folks here have believed it of me for years! And I believed you understood me!"

"Obviously not. So, I will leave you to your admiring host of new friends here and in London, the sickening sycophants!"

"I am afraid so primitive and St. Kilda–stupid a lass as I dinna ken what your big words mean, Captain West! Shall I beg you to explain it?" she demanded, then roasted him with a good Gaelic curse to remind him she could speak a language he could not begin to delve.

"Never mind!" he roared. "It's best I do leave for good, for there is one at home who waits and would marry me *now*, without a moment's selfish, stubborn hesitation."

"She's welcome to you, man! But best tell her your high-flying stand on slavery before you propose to the poor lass! No doubt she'll find out about belonging to a harsh master soon enough if she weds with you!"

She tore to the door and banged it open. She could not believe she was acting like this, as wild and loud and unreasonable as her father had at times.

"You are as uncivilized and untamable as I once feared!" he shouted back. He came closer, clenching his fists as if he would strike her or pound the cottage down around her. But he seized her in his arms in the open, lighted door and kissed her so hard the world stopped. One hand clamped in her hair, one like an iron band around her waist, his hips hard against hers, he tipped her back and ravished her lips.

Her self-control stumbled and slipped; she returned his embrace with her arms around his neck, holding his lips to hers, wanting to devour him, opening her mouth under the press of his, then, at last, surrendering limply in his arms.

He lifted his head; his eyes seethed in reflected firelight. Their breathing entwined, then even that seemed to stop. She stared deep into his hot gaze, mesmerized, knowing the rest of her strength could dissolve in his might. Trembling, she reached to embrace him again.

But, looking both triumphant and tormented, he set her back against the wall and strode straight past her so the outer blackness swallowed him.

Her last night on St. Kilda, Abigail had the nightmare of Lady Grange's ghost again. Only this time two spectral women drifted down from the cliffs to her cottage door, her mother coming close with Lady Grange. This time they had clearly defined features, though their midnight eyes were streaming tears like mist. This time, she let them inside the light and warmth of the cottage where they lifted their mirrors for her to see herself. And now, Abigail's face showed tear-streaked—but she had a face! There was no echoing void despite the swirling fog of pain and loss cloaking her. She awoke from the dream feeling stronger and steadier than she had in the four days since Morgan had left.

Wrapping a blanket about herself, she went to stand barefoot in the moonlight washing through the cottage window; she gazed out toward the sea. The wind, as always, was a constant friend, but she also thought how it was blowing Morgan farther away from her, no doubt, forever.

At dawn the day after their argument, she had gone to the factor's house to see Morgan, whatever prying village eyes would encourage whispering mouths to say of her. She had wanted to tell him how much he had given her, how she loved him, despite the cruel words which had passed between them. And, she had wanted to say, if ever you come back again and could give me more time . . .

But he was already gone as suddenly as he had come. The larger London yacht had sailed on the ebbing, predawn tide and would leave him in Liverpool to meet his ship *Fidelity*, which would take him to meet his Charlotte—

She shook her head to rid herself of that thought. She had decided to leave St. Kilda. Tomorrow she, Margaret, and little Janie were sailing with Nigel Fairfax and several others on the other yacht for a place called Southampton in England. It was Nigel's family's boat; he seemed quite wealthy. From Southampton, they would go with him by railway train to London, they who had never even seen so much as a photograph of the huge machine Nigel called "The Iron Civilizer." But that's what she needed, according to Morgan, she thought bitterly, when his true feelings toward her came spilling out: anything to civilize and tame her. And, somehow, whatever it took, when she returned here, even if she did not have the polish of progress and the shine of civilization, she must have the cure for the bairns.

She would not return to this place for any other reason than that, since Margaret and Janie were going with her, she assured herself. She refused to call St. Kilda home anymore, for the St. Kildans had long exiled her even when she lived among them. They had heaped on her head blame and shame for her parents' doings and then her own, when she only wanted to help and belong.

Besides, she would be leaving behind no family or close friends. Susannah and Malcolm had probably been kind only because Grandfather and then Morgan patched things over for her. Annie was merely tied to her through Margaret and wanted to discover the truth about the bairns too. Her own mother-in-law, her worst betrayer, stood firmly in the enemy camp and blamed her now for taking Janie away as she had once "taken" Douglas and Margaret. Even Mr. Campbell's farewell blessing—he told her he was considering a return to his original parish in Glasgow soon—did not make her feel blessed to have lived here. Flora had spit out, "Good riddance!" and Isobel MacCrimmon had hissed, "Be gone, ye sly seducer! Blasphemer! Murderess!"

Blast them all! No, however dedicated she was to helping the bairns here, St. Kilda was not her home! But she agonized, where then was home for Abigail Adair?

The wind began to moan as if to remind her of her inward, bitter tears all these years. She startled when little Janie murmured and flopped over in some childish dream. Margaret and the lass shared the bigger bed while she had returned to her old box bed. Abigail was so grateful at least for Margaret and Janie, like sister and daughter they were to her.

And she was suddenly grateful for all her own mother had given her too, however tormented the poor woman had been. Maybe on this night when so much in her past seemed sour, she could at least begin to understand and forgive her mother's suicide a wee bit. After all, in her farewell letter, Glenna MacQueen had written, "The solution to the great dilemma of my life lies beyond, not on St. Kilda." Good advice for a wayward daughter leaving on a quest this morning, Abigail mused. She said a silent farewell to Grandfather's memory too; she would always carry his love and support with her. He had been so wise to say she was not settled even married to Douglas seven years ago this month, and yet it seemed forever since. And, most assuredly, she mused, she was not settled now.

Abigail was not sure how long she stood, blanket-shrouded, elbows propped on the bottom of the window, staring out into the night until dawn dyed the horizon rosy-hued. She had no tears left. She realized her feet were cold, her fingers, curled under her chin, numb. Her warm breath against the familiar pane of glass made a cloud that swelled, then shrank, an outer heartbeat of her very soul. A hearthsong came to her then, an early one Euphemia MacAuley had taught her and she had taught Janie just last week:

Tears of the faint of heart
Flow on and on.
Black night may be,
But here are we,
Outward bound,
Dry-eyed, and
Ready for the dawn.

Part 2

England
1858–1862

No man is an island, entire of itself; everyman is a piece of the continent, a part of the main.

—JOHN DONNE,
Meditation XVII

❦

Through life in our islands we must reach out,
Not only to ones whom we love.
Launch boats in the blast, face down the storm
For those drowning below and above.

—ABIGAIL ADAIR,
English diary

❦

10

My *heart, glass-domed,*
Scrutinized by passers-by,
Scarlet artifact enshrined
Since he went away.
But in my odyssey
For the little ones,
It yet throbs anyway.

"We're flying as fast as a fulmar!" Janie cried, her pert nose pressed to the window of the first-class saloon of the Southampton to London railway carriage.

"Thirty miles per hour compared to that coach we passed that was only going ten," Nigel Fairfax commented from behind *The London Times.*

Strangely, Nigel's interest in numbers—what he called statistics—set Abigail on edge, for it reminded her of Edmund Drummond. Another thing about Nigel did too. Though he had at first proclaimed himself an Oxford scholar, that had been years ago and in truth he was a wealthy friend of Parker Rex's who dabbled in mathematics and travel to amuse himself. Edmund had been sly like that, implying things not quite true. Only numerical reckoning mattered to such men—not the sad situations behind it—because it gave them power and control over others, Abigail thought. She had learned through five years of studying the accounts of St. Kilda births that, too often, numbers alone, unfortunately, proved nothing and could even be misleading.

She was grateful, however, to hear Nigel recite the huge population numbers for London, for surely Edmund would never find her there. Besides that and the square mileage of the city, Nigel had told her over luncheon that he was starved for "civilized news." So the entire railway journey he'd been behind that paper, occasionally spitting out rates or something called percentages to Reginald.

Reginald Compton, the red-haired gentleman who had first thrust the copy of *Britannia's Broad Shores* at her on St. Kilda that day everything exploded, also kept himself occupied instead of looking out at all there was to see or even bothering to speak with his women companions. Reginald worked for Parker Rex as an essayist and kept scribbling in a notebook, which reminded her all too poignantly of Morgan. She ached for his voice, the very sight of him. She felt a terrible tightness in her chest every time she pictured him so angry at her the night they parted. And that made her feel very alone, even with dear Margaret sitting beside her, staring out the window at the un-Kildan clear blue sky with but one gentle puff of cloud in it like a lost sheep.

Abigail thought of the sacks of wool she had brought along which were stored somewhere aboard with her other precious things: a good supply of lichens, their clothes in the wooden chest— though she saw now they would need new dresses not to be stared at—and her records of the St. Kilda births. So far the two women at the railway station she had asked about birthing practices had been affronted and refused to talk, but, after all, Abigail had not been properly introduced, which seemed to be so important here. Meanwhile, she could only hope that the noisy engine's showers of cinders continually whipping by the windows and the smoke that choked them when they went through a tunnel did not harm her scant possessions. With them she intended to make some sort of living to consult London doctors or she would be lost as well as lonely.

Abigail knew she should not feel lonely: besides her St. Kilda family nearby, she sat knee-to-knee with a woman who had come along "to lend assistance." In Southampton, the men had arranged for this lady of their acquaintance, one Mrs. Georgina Tressler whose sister lived in London, to accompany them to London.

Though Abigail was trying to work her way toward asking Mrs. Tressler many questions, the woman's stiff demeanor did little to encourage any sort of communication.

Abigail knew she and Margaret needed an Englishwoman friend, but she was rather certain it would not be Georgina Tressler. Here it was, a bright day when one longed to feel the sun, but even on the railway platform, Mrs. Tressler had insisted on lending Abigail a flimsy, frilled parasol to keep sun off her already browned face. Now she had to admit the woman's voluminous skirts and curious stare hemmed her in. Still, she was so relieved to be away from the cruel stares by people like Isobel and Mairi that she didn't miss the island of her birth at all. Things would just be different here, that's all, and it was worth any sort of change to be in a more enlightened, civilized country.

Georgina Tressler was a good bit older than Abigail, with silver streaks in her dark hair, worn curled beneath her ribboned bonnet. Whatever it was she wore under her bodice creaked like ropes tugging tight when she moved. But it was the amazing size of her skirt that astounded Abigail and made her keep her distance and wonder if she would ever get close enough to anyone in London to make a real friend and learn what she must.

In grass-green velvet, not so very different from the color of these seats, Mrs. Tressler's skirts bloomed big and bumpy as a St. Kilda boulder. They had bounced into everything when she walked the saloon aisle; now they nearly shoved Nigel over to the window. Even when both he and Reginald excused themselves to go for a cigar, the woman's skirts swelled out to eat up the entire seat. All English women seemed to have large skirts, but this was the most massive Abigail had seen.

"I see by your staring, Mrs. Adair, my crinoline surprises you. I must say, you and Mrs. Gillies will come to master them soon enough. One has no choice, for the cage is all the rage," she informed them with a tight smile and decisive nod.

"The cage?" Margaret echoed, turning from Janie and the window.

"The underpinnings for the petticoats and gown," Mrs. Tressler whispered as furtively as if she had a dreadful tale to tell. With a quick glance to be certain nearby folk were occupied, and with creaking ribs, she lifted the hem of her skirt barely to her ankle to reveal the scalloped hem of a red petticoat, then a wire-mesh sort of thing a body could see right through to her buttoned shoes. Abigail gasped.

"Please don't think I was too forward!" Mrs. Tressler said as her hands fluttered her skirt back down.

"Oh, I dinna," Abigail told her. " 'Twas just the wonderful color of your underskirt there."

"Sh! My petticoat? Do you mean that under those narrow brown day dresses of yours, you don't even wear a petticoat?"

"Only under our blue dresses on Sundays. Besides, one of those cages would blow inside out and sail you away on St. Kilda!" Abigail announced and Margaret nodded.

"Well, I never! And it sounded so picturesque in the paper! Such a place you've been reared, but I am certain Mr. Baxter-Jones will see to it that you are properly attired, especially if he and Mr. Rex intend to introduce you to society." She rolled her eyes as if in warning, then added, "But just one more word about crinolines—be careful of your feet when you walk the stairs and don't get near an open flame. Falls and fires have cost many a life with this new style!"

"But why would someone wear them then if they could cause so much pain?" Abigail demanded so loudly that others turned to stare. But even as Mrs. Tressler rambled on about what the best people did and listed off places like Bond and Regents streets where they could find the best watch-sprung crinolines, Abigail felt more than foreboding. Even here people evidently went with the way of things, whatever destruction it wrought. Had she been foolish to think folks would be wiser here? And it scared her as stiff as Mrs. Tressler's bodice to think of Morgan arriving home where the way of things would be to let slavery slide—and to wed his partner's daughter. She bit her lower lip and glanced out the window at the flying trees.

She knew better now than to question Mrs. Tressler about birthing babies when she had apologized so profusely for showing them a glimpse of ankle. Yet she must try.

But after she had quietly asked her question and explained why, again she felt the scolded child as the woman said in a whisper with darted glances about the saloon, "I grieve for the situation of your infants there, my dear woman. But what you ask is not something a proper Englishwoman would discuss or even know! Why, a lady only desires that—that function—be over quickly, privately, and with as little fuss as possible. And now with even the queen's memory of her last two births being blotted out by her taking that dreadful gas, it's caused such a row. Shocking! The merest mention of it causes arguments. Our dear queen doing such a thing! But don't you see, even fast women who might discuss such things with you are perhaps taking the gas for the function then, and won't recall a thing—blessedly some say, but I think science has gone too far. You may consult doctors, but it's quite improper to question them on such—ah, here come the men back now," she said, looking entirely relieved as she tugged her cage closer so Nigel could sit down again.

"London in ten minutes!" he announced with a smile at Abigail and wink at Janie. "Sing out when you see the big river Thames, my girl," he told the child before resuming his reading.

Abigail sat stiff-backed, staring out, her feet drawn under the seat to avoid Mrs. Tressler's skirts; her emotions flew as fast and hot as the cinders and smoke outside. Some "fast" women here— the queen herself—were taking something called gas to blot out childbirth? And those who didn't take gas wanted to pretend childbirth didn't exist? It was called "the function"? And she would be expected to wear one of those cages encasing her hips and legs that had always been free to climb St. Kildan cliffs?

Noting Mrs. Tressler's gaze no longer met her eyes, Abigail leaned back against her seat. The cliffs here, she realized now, were the ones she would have to climb to convince folks to help her find out what could be killing the bairns of St. Kilda. She stared out at the flat landscape past Margaret's and Janie's heads. London seemed to be enveloped in a haze that sucked their railway carriage right in, a sort of fog floating from the looming buildings. They sailed right over the barrier of the river on a big bridge and into a massive place called Victoria Station, built like a glass cave with so many opaque windows overhead to block out the sky.

Abigail felt dazed and dizzy as they alighted and their things were sent off in one conveyance and Nigel motioned for what he called a hansom cab for them. Amidst rushing, noisy people, the six of them—and Mrs. Tressler's cage—crowded in and clattered away from the station. Margaret gripped Abigail's and Janie's hands. In the wide, busy street, it seemed an entire herd of horses pranced and snorted by, pulling their loads, pleasing their riders. Abigail was anxious to see Corwin, but she had so wanted to like London, and she just wasn't sure about it now.

Until, looking out, she saw the colors of the city: vibrant red, yellow, blue, and white flowers spilling from boxes built under windowsills; store signs lettered in crimson and gold; big, shiny windows displaying a rainbow of goods in rich abundance; people dressed mostly in muted hues who nonetheless flashed a bright scarf or waistcoat or ladies' hat. And grandest of all, a few folk sat on the smooth stone walking path to draw pictures there with pale-colored paints!

"Oh, how bonny!" Abigail said, and Margaret murmured agreement. It was like a sign, Abigail thought, that things would go well here and that London, with dear Corwin's help, could be, at least, a temporary home to her.

"What's bonny?" Nigel said, leaning to the window. "Chalk drawings by those screevers? Thunderation, a dratted nuisance to walk around, and they've always got their hands out, the beggars!"

"And those chatting, busy folks selling things on the street— their clothes are such bright, fine colors, not just a scarf or hat like the shoppers!" Abigail insisted, undaunted.

"Street arabs," Reginald said with a sniff. "Proper people just cut them!"

"Cut them!" she gasped.

"Not literally. You know, snub them, pointedly ignore them to put them in their place."

"I do know," she said, pressing Margaret's hand even harder. Suddenly, she could not wait to be rid of Nigel, Reginald, and Georgina. Corwin would understand her need to explore London and Londoners to further her quest. She must write Morgan to ask him to forgive her rash words and to come to see her here. For, until she solved the dilemma of the bairns, this place must be her home.

In a row of the tallest buildings Abigail had ever seen sat Corwin Baxter-Jones's "Belgravia Natural and Historical Museum" and, next-door, his Number 10 Belgravia Place stone home, called a townhouse. After her first glimpse of it, she always thought of it as his "tallhouse." Four floors high it was, with something called an attic where the servants lived under the lofty roof. Abigail and Margaret were shocked to realize this house had eight servants for one inhabitant: a butler, valet, footman, coachman, cook, skullery maid, and two housemaids, one of whom did nothing but dust the museum's displays. And, for his guests to share, Corwin had hired a "temporary," a ladies' maid named Daisy.

The tallhouse's ground floor, which had rooms burrowed underground like a colony of puffins, contained the kitchen, pantries, and servants' hall. The first floor had a drawing room and dining room, both nearly as crowded as her tiny cottage had been: heavy furniture, fringed and flounced; tasseled draperies; deep-patterned carpets; and what was called bric-a-brac sitting everywhere, as thick as nesting fulmars. On the second floor was a combined morning and breakfast room—imagine one chamber bigger than Lady Grange's cottage just for sitting about mornings!—and Corwin's library with books crowded so close they reminded her of the downstairs bric-a-brac. It seemed to her Corwin's tallhouse was a museum of gathered and saved and displayed things too.

The third floor contained Corwin's bedroom, sitting room, and what he called a "German smoking room." The top floor was to be Abigail and Margaret's abode during their visit. They were so pleased to have a lofty view, and the climb up all the stairs was nothing to them as it was the huffing maids. Paper put right on the walls of the two bedrooms and sitting room bloomed maroon roses. Other wonders included a zinc porcelain bathing tub that the maids filled with cans of water from downstairs and a necessary called a water closet down the hall with two wooden seats, even though there were chamber pots in each room inside a special wooden cupboard with a wash basin, mirror, and towels on top. Behind the house sat a coach house and small garden for growing flowers but not food. The only birds in sight were cooing mourning doves in the eaves and occasionally, small ones in the trees that would not be enough to feed a wee bairn.

"A wee bairn," she whispered aloud as she stood at the window overlooking the garden. "Even here, with so much to see and do, I canna forget the wee bairns."

She sighed and went back to the desk where she had been writing. Though she was eager to visit any London doctors who delivered babies, Corwin had convinced her she'd get further if he could

arrange formal introductions before she went calling. Her inactivity
this morning seemed wrong, almost sinful: no fixing her own breakfast, no sweeping the floor or cleaning windows, no morning milking walk in the silence of this calm, nearly windless weather.
Margaret and Janie had been wise to go with Daisy to the nearby
park for a walk, but Abigail had stayed behind since Corwin had
been so eager to show her the museum display on St. Kilda; she
awaited his summons to accompany him next door now.

She lifted the letter to Morgan she had begun last night. How
to address it? "My dear Morgan"? Or, after their harsh parting and
her calling him Captain West in her anger, should she use that
proper title? And should she send her love as well as ask for his forgiveness for words she did not mean—at least, she did not mean
them now. But he had said hurtful things too, and despite the hungry way he had kissed her, if he had gone home to that woman who
awaited and would "marry him now without a moment's selfish,
stubborn hesitation," would it not be wrong to send her love? But
how desperately she wanted to see him again, to make amends, to
tell him how much he had meant—did mean yet—to her. And to
think this piece of paper would be held in his big, warm hands that
had touched her and tangled in her hair and tipped her back in his
arms for the hottest kisses that made her want to give herself to him
and forget everything else, to go with him anywhere—

She jumped straight out of her chair when the maid knocked
on the door to summon her to Corwin.

"I decided to put the St. Kilda display in the room at the back, as
some long-time objects were just too heavy to move," Corwin explained as they walked through the front entry hall, lined with narrow shelves displaying ancient vases, coins, and jewelry. While he
closed and locked the front door behind them, she wondered if any
of these artifacts had come from areas of Ulysses's travels, but she
did not ask as she followed him in.

In the center of the front room stood what Corwin called a
tableau of mounted deer, foxes, and rabbits; he pointed out each
animal by name when he saw she was unfamiliar with them. At
least the fish in a huge glass box called an aquarium were alive, she
thought, though they had a limited space in which to swim back

and forth compared to their natural home in God's great lochs and seas.

"Oh, my," she exclaimed when she saw rows of boxes with pinned butterflies and glass domes over various birds or birds' nests with their eggs inside, never to hatch. "They look so real for something—dead."

"I prefer to think of them as preserved for aesthetic and educational purposes. If it bothers you, I apologize, but we British find them fascinating. And in the larger back room," he announced and coughed into his handkerchief—he had suffered through what he called pneumonia after returning from St. Kilda—"is my display in honor of you and your far isle!"

She stood stunned in the doorway of the room, well-lighted by three windows. In a central, still-life tableau, two stiff-as-stone puffins sat on real rocks, no longer nodding to each other as they were wont to do on Dun. Fulmar, forever frozen in futile flight appeared to sail over a painted cliff and sea. On the walls were photographs of the village, the harbor, lofty Conachair, and her beloved Gleann Mor. Five oil paintings of the rescue or other St. Kilda scenes looked flat and fixed. Wide-eyed, open-mouthed, she walked closer.

"The photographs are a new addition, brought back on the yacht that Morgan left the island on," Corwin's voice floated to her as if from far away. "Of course, none of this shows the real beauty and majesty of the place, just as this display could never capture your dynamic, vibrant aura. That's one reason I am so elated you have come to visit these Londoners, who think they have seen the exotic wilds when they but visit the Regent's Park Zoo or take a jaunt to the country for a holiday."

Corwin's explanations seemed muted mutterings. She recalled Morgan's accusation that Londoners would put her on display like some exotic, caged bird. She had told him she and Corwin would never allow that. But now she was looking beyond the newspaper articles pressed under glass to the rows of things that bore her likeness. ABIGAIL MACQUEEN ADAIR MEMORABILIA, it was labeled: china plates with images of her painted in a boat alone or striding the cliffs looking for wrecks; bracelets with her face in a small oval; broadsheets with songs of a heroine's bold rescue of lost souls; poems about The Far Isles—one which said St. Kildans, "that primal race," lived in caves upon the cliffs with the birds; a newspaper photograph of a London penny ferry newly named *Queen of Kilda;* and a muted tapestry of her, from head to shoulders, framed by birds with outspread wings. She reached out to touch that worsted wool stitched on canvas, for it was one of the few things not framed or glassed in.

"They call that Berlin Work, and it's very fashionable, like most things German, because of Queen Victoria's German husband Albert, the Prince Consort," Corwin explained. "Both women above and below—social classes, I mean—enjoy such handwork. My dear girl, it is important to me that you understand all this is a compliment—an honor. Victorian curiosity for the distant and different is rampant. But I think the brave deed of salvation by Virtue Victorious, Queen of Kilda, as Parker always puts it, struck some chord in people's hearts here—perhaps an echo of their love of their own Queen Victoria. Abigail?"

She nodded. She felt exposed, displayed, caged. Yet her mind was racing now. This Berlin Work—the yarn was not as fine as that which she had brought with her nor her sacks of wool that could make more. And her lichen dyes would put to shame this rust color woven in her cross-stitched hair and the maroon of the border. Somehow she had to make all this muted, silent, still deadness come to life for people so they would see the beauty of St. Kilda—and then let her speak to them about the ugliness of what went on there.

"There should be something in motion, something lively here when folks come to see," she spoke at last and turned to Corwin. She saw twin reflections of her fervent face in his spectacles. "What would you think if I partly repaid your kindness for taking us in by becoming a part of this—a living tableau when visitors come calling? In my St. Kilda gown, I could make my dyes over by that window we could open to let in some air so it wouldn't smell too strong. I could sing a hearthsong or two, working songs—or ones about the bairns, so people will ask questions. And if ladies come who like to do this Berlin Work, I could even sell them some yarn to—to brighten everything up a wee bit and earn some money for fancy London doctors and not be beholden to you."

"You and Morgan saved my life, Abigail, so you will never be beholden to me—it's rather quite the other way round. But as for putting you on display . . ." his voice trailed off as he frowned. "By Jove, I'm not certain what people would say, as it's not the expected thing, you know. I'm afraid if word got out, we'd be inundated with crowds. Still, to get a sort of approval for it so you are not ostracized when we go out in society, we could do an afternoon by invitation only to test the waters with the proper people after I've consulted a trusted friend or two . . ."

She breathed a deep sigh of relief that at least he meant to protect her from being shunned as she had been on St. Kilda. Corwin had even created this massive display so that she would be admired.

"Then it's decided," she told him. "We shall show Londoners both the good and the bad about St. Kilda so we can find someone who kens a way to cure the bairns' sickness."

Again, she stroked the dyed wool yarns in the handworked piece: she would never tell kindly Corwin, but it was the only thing she really liked in all she had seen of his precious museum.

A week later, as Abigail stood over her dye pot, awaiting the museum's visitors, she felt she had learned a great deal more about London and its people. Corwin had taken the three of them riding daily in a four-in-hand along the Serpentine in Hyde Park since Abigail and Margaret had never ridden a horse and could not partake in that custom on nearby Rotten Row. She and Margaret had learned to play the cardgames Whist and Loo and shopped for new clothing for the three of them on Oxford and Bond streets. Rather than buying those dreadful cages, they had chosen layers of petticoats to fill out the voluminous skirts. They had enjoyed a German brass band in Belgravia Square, eaten cream ice and chocolates during a performance in the Haymarket Theatre, strolled the Royal Botanic Gardens at Kew, and walked among wax figures at Madame Tussaud's.

There they had nearly caused a riot because the waxen image of Abigail standing in a boat was good enough that she was recognized. After that in public, she worried that someone would shout again, "It's her, the Queen of Kilda herself!" to bring others running at her, pressing in, clutching her skirts and hair as if she were some holy idol. It might be just the opposite the way St. Kildans had treated her, but it did not please her nor plump her pride—nor make her feel that this place could be her home. She felt she walked a tightrope with everyone staring, just as they had when the Cremorne Gardens' female rope dancer went all the way across the

Thames on a strand thinner than a St. Kilda fowling rope. Little Janie might claim that a tight rope dancer was what she wanted to be when she grew up, but Abigail knew better. She only made herself the center of attention like this to meet the right people who had the right answers about what Corwin termed infant afflictions.

Today, when folks Georgina Tressler had called "society" and Corwin "the proper people" entered the museum, slowly and staidly, by invitation only, Abigail scrutinized them as thoroughly as they did her. It helped that Margaret sat nearby carding wool in the little scene they had made to represent the interior of a cottage, though the window with its sash up in the background was much too grand to be one on St. Kilda. On a piece of stout canvas, with earth and pebbles on it to safely contain the low coal fire, Abigail stirred her dye pot, longing for peat to waft its musty smell into the air. Corwin stood nearby, giving her confidence as he introduced her to the visitors who stared and smiled and politely asked questions.

Still, too often their names—and most had titles—blurred by her. Georgina Tressler and her elderly sister stopped by. Parker Rex came with his wife, who was as haughty as he, though she not only did not speak grandiosely but hardly made a peep before they departed. Repeatedly, before the observers moved on, Abigail tried in vain to maneuver the brief conversations to something about children. Perhaps they should have brought Janie, but she did not want to subject her to this. Yet, even as she was applauded for her occasional hearthsongs about the bairns dying, she began to feel there was a second glass window separating her from them, without the sash being flung high for fresh air. Looking out, it seemed she stared again at the waxen, unreal figures at Madame Tussaud's, however much these moved and talked. But then there was a stir in the room and everything quickened.

"The Duchess of Man, here with her men," Abigail heard a woman hiss. "I'd know that voice anywhere!"

"She flaunts that foreign accent just to let us all know she's as German as the Prince Consort. I say she's an outsider and ever will be, however long she's lived here!" another woman, Lady something-or-other, said right in front of Abigail as if a St. Kildan could never understand one wee bit of what Englishwomen said.

Heads turned as a throaty peal of laughter rang out in the next room. Margaret stood to see better; Abigail stopped stirring. Necks arched and some stood on their toes. Into the room, on the arms of two men, though Abigail could not fathom how the woman managed her huge crinoline through the door, stepped the most fascinating female Abigail had ever seen. A bonny brunette not much older than Abigail and Margaret, she glowed with life: her rich curls bounced beside blooming cheeks and a rosy smile; arched eyebrows framed sable eyes alight with joy and laughter and avid interest in all about her, especially the bearded man on her left whose gaze on her was as hot as Morgan's had once been on Abigail.

A bell of recognition rang in Abigail's head: how dare others gossip about this woman who loved life and attracted men to her with grace and without guile. They had no right to judge nor treat this appealing woman as an outsider if she lived among them! The three new arrivals approached, the woman still escorted by the older and the younger man.

"Corwin, so this is your dear lady friend from St. Kilda," the woman's low voice rang out in the hushed room. "As lovely as her home island you told me of, so pleased to make your acquaintance, Mrs. Adair. Women rescuing men from their tumbles—it has always been true, but they seldom thank us for it in such grand style!"

With a smile, Abigail shook the extended, white-gloved hand. The woman was exactly her height, but she wore a lovely, rose-hued dress quite unlike Abigail's St. Kilda brown. The lady's teeth when she smiled shown as bright as her eyes. Louisa rolled her r's when she spoke almost as a Scot would, but those women had said she was German.

"Louisa, how kind of you to come," Corwin's voice chimed in as he inclined slightly from the waist. "Your Grace, I have the great honor of introducing to you Abigail Adair and Margaret Gillies of St. Kilda. Ladies, Her Grace, the Duchess of Manchester, her husband, the Duke, and Lord Hartington."

The duke was the older man, and Lord Hartington the hot-eyed one. No matter: it seemed the duchess had both of them firmly in hand, though the duke told Corwin a bit loudly as if he were hard of hearing, "She's as good as dragged me here today, but nothing I wouldn't do for my Louisa. I say, Corwin, care to pick up a few grouse at our Kimbolton come autumn?"

"Now, my dearest," Louisa said and tapped her husband's arm

with a folded fan before Corwin could respond, "it looks to me as if Corwin has enough fowl about this place without having to shoot some with you. Besides, you haven't been hunting lately when you haven't broken a bone, and it takes you forever to mend these days, poor thing, and then you get so testy with the children." Despite being taken to task like a child himself in front of so many people, the duke beamed at his wife and shrugged sheepishly.

"How many children do you have?" Abigail asked as Margaret went back to her carding, still all ears.

"Five, though I declare they seem to be fifty-five some days," Louisa said with a wink at her husband before turning her attention to Abigail. "And you, I believe I read, are a widow and alone, Mrs. Adair."

"I lost my only son as an infant. He died of St. Kilda's eight-day sickness that takes so many of our infants there."

"How dreadful for all of you! I read something of that in one of the papers, I recall, but it was wretchedly downplayed. Don't you agree, Spencer?" the duchess asked Lord Hartington to pull him into the conversation while her husband spoke further with Corwin.

"Shocking in this day and age."

"Indeed. You should go straightaway to Dr. Snow for a solution, Mrs. Adair, as there's nothing he can't do!" Louisa insisted.

"Dr. Snow? Is he your doctor, Mrs. . . . Manchester?"

"Now, you must call me Louisa as Corwin does, and I shall call you Abigail in that free-wheeling way I read you have on St. Kilda. But, as for Dr. Snow, indeed, he is my physician and the queen's herself."

"Is he the one that gave her gas when she had—had the function?"

Lord Hartington rolled his blue eyes, and Louisa pinched back a smile at something she had said. "The gas is chloroform," Louisa whispered and pressed Abigail's hand again. "The wonder of the age, as far as I'm concerned. But we shall speak more of this privately later, you and I, so you simply must ask Corwin to bring you to tea at Manchester House next week when we are receiving."

"Oh, yes, if only Dr. Snow could be there!"

"Now that's a first, Louisa," Lord Hartington said and elbowed her gently. "The Queen of Kilda making up *your* guest list when you are ever trying to get yourself on that of the Queen of England's."

"Oh, I dinna mean to—"

"It's a wonderful suggestion, my dear," Louisa declared, "and—oh bother, what's this?" She stared down at a streak of red on the palm of her right glove.

"Blast it, dye from my hands!" Abigail cried and felt her face heat in embarrassment. How much she wanted to befriend this clever woman who seemed so kind and concerned! "I shall buy you new ones, dinna you worry!"

"But it's nothing. Besides, it's a smashing color, so perhaps you would be so kind as to simply dye the rest of them that hue. St. Kilda scarlet we shall call it and make it all the thing!" She peeled both gloves off with a smile while folks gaped as if she were stripping naked and pressed in closer to see and hear what she would do next. "Reminds you of my scarlet tartan knickerbockers in full view that day I tripped during those silly parlor games, doesn't it, Spencer?" the duchess declared to set everyone agog again. Abigail, awed, watched Spencer blush now, though Louisa did not flick an eyelash as she handed Abigail the gloves.

"You ken, I love scarlet too," Abigail said. "I was thinking of dying yarn I brought from home several bright shades of red and rose for making Berlin Work wallhangings to sell to make some money."

Louisa blinked once, twice at her as if she had not quite comprehended what she had said. "To sell? But, while you're living here as Corwin Baxter-Jones's guest?"

"Yes, if I can only find an artist to draw some bonny designs on the canvas."

"Indeed, it would get attention and fetch you a following, I am sure. But, Abigail, Corwin has fine plans to introduce you to other people—and I do too! And selling goods like that just isn't done when one, ah—does not own a shop."

"Poppycock!" Lord Hartington put in. "Whyever not, Louisa? My mother embroiders reticules, bell pulls, and cushion pads of that Berlin stuff when she's not preaching at me to mend my ways and change my company. I believe your new friend Abigail here is exempt from at least some our tiresome, old rules. You yourself have broken a few in fine fettle you couldn't abide, I dare say."

"Mostly I need money to pay a doctor, like Dr. Snow," Abigail explained, touched at this man's taking her side.

"Of course, and in that instance, I am all for it and shall help you in anyway I can, come what may," the duchess said. "But, my dear Abigail," she whispered, so not even the hovering Lord Hartington could hear her now, "what my friend says about the rules is not quite true. A woman going places must know which ones to break and which ones to merely bend, especially when it comes to advancing oneself in this world men believe they rule, queen on the throne or not. Good day then," she said louder and patted Abigail's hand that held the gloves.

She gave Corwin her hand to bow over and waggled her fingers to summon her husband. "Best be off now, Your Grace, as we've other places to go." A few farewells drifted back to others in the room, including the two gossips who looked as eager to please as puppies now, as Her Grace, Louisa, Duchess of Manchester, with her men in her wake, sailed airily out the door—and anchored herself firmly in Abigail's new life.

11

The anguished cries of city birds,
Snared in want and sorrow,
Must capture us to free them
In a blue-sky tomorrow.

We must teach them how to soar
From their rookery of sadness.
We must show them how to trill
Their rightful song of gladness.

The late July sunshine lay hot and heavy on London as Abigail stepped up into the Baxter Jones carriage and the driver closed the door behind her. She was relieved that, for once, she had interviewed a doctor without Corwin or Margaret at her side, for she was certain she was finally going to cry and didn't want to pull their spirits down too. However good the day's heat felt to her oft-chilled St. Kilda bones, she shivered in frustration and anger.

This was the fourth doctor she had seen and the fourth who had disappointed her, not counting the seven who had declined to meet with her at all. An unwed woman, albeit a widow and "the heroine of the north," wished to discuss childbirth with them! Unthinkable! Now, as the carriage lurched away from the curb in fashionable Mayfair, she felt her natural optimism and determination lurch away too: her friend Louisa's Doctor John Snow, perhaps her best and last hope, had been out of town this spring and summer on a lecture tour. And today's Dr. Willis Wentworth, highly recommended to Corwin, had been actually insulting. She fumbled in her woolwork reticule for a handkerchief as the man's brusque voice echoed through her jumbled thoughts.

"Mrs. Adair, I am a busy man and cannot possibly take my precious time to read through whatever amateurish records you have there, but I don't doubt the malady you describe is caused by the vitiated air in those old, damp cottages and caves on St. Kilda with all those birds roosting everywhere. I read all about it in the articles on your situation."

"Vitiated air?"

"Foul air."

"Fowl air? Because we are so dependent on the birds to exist? But you canna believe the newspaper's claims we live *with* the birds even though I mentioned that fulmar oil, so—"

"*Foul* air, Mrs. Adair! Dirty, spoiled, tainted, et cetera."

"It canna be that. There is always a brisk sea breeze to freshen the air in the cottages, even in the winter when they are more sealed up. Our air is much cleaner than London's with all the sea coal and smells from the factories and the river. If you would but read these accounts, you would see that births in warmer weather when windows are open are not more successful, sir, and there was quite a good sea breeze the day my son was born, and we lost him."

"Pity, but I shall not debate with you my own area of expertise, young woman. Here, you see," he had said and reached behind him to a bookshelf to pull down a musty volume he blew off before he slid it across his dusty desk to her to leave a trail. "*Modern Midwifery* by Dr. William Marvin, 1835."

"Oh, thank you. As I mentioned, I fear when our island midwives, called knee-women, use the oil and then cut—"

"Yes, yes. Well, I don't doubt if it's not dirty air in such an uncivilized place, they have dirty hands, et cetera. Borrow the book if you like and have someone read it to you. But my point is that Dr. Marvin establishes that a thorough cleansing of the midwife and the birthing area reduces deaths in city hospital wards from twenty-one to nine percent."

Abigail's hopes plummeted at his prating those paltry percentages to her: had he not listened when she told him the monstrous numbers of deaths? What had St. Kilda to do with city hospital wards? It had to be more than cleanliness! Workers' hands and the bairns were washed on St. Kilda. She felt her anger rise at this man who dared to have an office thumb-deep in dust, yet preached to her of a foul, filthy St. Kilda. How dare he sit in judgment of a place and people he had never seen!

She did intend to pursue the idea of the fulmar oil being dirty, but not with this man; she saw that his long fingernails, that made it seem he had not worked a day in his life, had dirty half moons under them. Other doctors had told her to wash the child and birth-ing cord—she had discovered it was properly called an umbilical cord—in everything from calomel, isoform, oil of turpentine, to chlorinated lime. But, back on St. Kilda, Annie would never con-vince Parliament or Isobel MacCrimmon to wash the bairns in any of that. And Annie had written that their supporter, the Reverend Mr. Campbell, had been driven back to Glasgow and a new minis-ter would be coming to shepherd St. Kildan souls. Worse, how many more bairns were dying while she floundered about here in this civilized land looking for answers where no one—not even the doctors—wished to speak of the unspeakable.

"So, if you'd like," Dr. Wentworth's voice had interrupted her agonizing, "I could dash off a letter warning those midwives and anyone else in the birthing area to cleanse everything." He plucked a pen from a sooty onyx pen-and-inkwell set.

"I fear we need a more convincing, definitive answer," she had said. "And you should know, sir, that I and several other St. Kildans can read. I could write that letter myself if it would do one wee bit of good. One of the knee-women herself wrote for me these records you are too busy to read. Our inhabitants are civilized too, though, thank God, in a different way from some here." She dramatically dusted off his book just above the piece of paper he was still poised over to write on. Taking the book to read, head high, she took her leave.

But now, in the carriage, she looked down at her dirtied red gloves, remembering the day she had stained Louisa's white ones and then dyed them scarlet for her. Thanks to the appeal and aplomb of the charming Duchess of Manchester, scarlet gloves were all the thing in London this summer social season—all the thing, just as was the Queen of Kilda. But Abigail had no illusions her fame would last. Besides, it wasn't worth one farthing to her since it could not beg nor buy the help she needed.

Yet, there were spots in her London life as bright as this crimson color. Under the aegis of the Duchess of Manchester, Abigail had made popular the brilliantly dyed, plucked St. Kilda yarns on canvases designed by a portrait artist Louisa patronized. They called it not Berlin Work, but Kilda Work. Abigail had sent home for more wool and now had a small, but steady income. Vibrant island birds, flowers, and milkmaids brightened British lives in muted, cluttered parlors or drawing rooms. And this contrast made her miss St. Kilda when she never thought she would.

But still, even that success, even being invited out to meet fascinating people at palatial Manchester House and other grand London homes, Abigail felt so sheltered here. She must always take the carriage or be accompanied, Corwin said. She was usually surrounded by folks going to elaborately planned events, never striking off on her own to wander where she would. She could not wait to get out in the country to see the duke and duchess's Kimbolton Castle and gardens for a weekend this autumn. She would love a day or two of vast open skies and meadows stretching wider than a city square or park. In this hot weather, she longed to take her shoes off and let at least her feet fly free. She felt as if she were a bird in a cage here, just as Morgan had predicted the night they parted. Even her heart-wings felt fettered.

She lifted her head, sniffed, and blotted tears at the memory of Morgan. From her reticule she fished out his letter, over two months old now. It was wrinkled and worn from numberless rereadings and refoldings; its heaviest creases were worn clear through. She had long ago learned it by heart and knew she should leave it behind, but it went everywhere with her:

June 17, 1858
My dearest Abigail,
*   This epistle brings my continued devotion and heart-felt offer to repair our friendship I fear we battered my last night on St. Kilda. I deeply regret how we parted. And I am sorry I was so thoughtless that I left behind your dyed yarn I had promised to sell here; I vow anew, if you will allow it, I shall come in person for it when I am able.*

*Such a journey to find you either in London or St.
Kilda will, alas, take me longer than I would wish. Times
are tense here with war talk and dangerous feelings building: for the sake of my business, I must make several voyages to the British island of Bermuda to establish and fill
warehouses there we may need if worse comes to worse.
Again, I can only pray that it will not—and that we shall
have no more war between us.*

*Please do not take offense at the banknote I enclose
for you to be drawn upon in the Bank of England. Consider it a loan if your St. Kilda pride is yet as staunch. Use
it as you will in London, perhaps to hire a surgeon who
will return with you to St. Kilda to help the bairns. I do
realize and value the absolutely essential nature of your
quest, whatever rash words I said which might, I fear, convince you otherwise.*

*The surgeons I have consulted in the short time I have
been home said, in brief, that the too-tight swaddling
clothes you once suspected might be at fault. One learned,
old surgeon in Boston suggested it might be the mother's
diet being high in oil from fulmar meat that clogs many infants' delicate veins over the first week or so of nursing. I
shall continue my investigations from here as best I can
and hope that you already have discovered the cause of
that dread disease.*

*I will find you someday, as soon as I am able, so that
we might renew our friendship and never part that way
again.*

*I remain your admirer in all things,
Morgan James West*

Morgan still cared for her as she did him. Yet it was a letter as cruel
as it was kind. "My dearest Abigail," he began—did that mean
dearer to him than his Charlotte? He could have wed the woman
and still written this letter of their friendship, could he not? Why
must he torment her this way? He mentioned he had spoken to a
Boston doctor: she could read between the lines. That was where
Charlotte lived. He had evidently rushed there within the "short
time" he was home!

"My continued devotion," he vowed, but he remained merely her "admirer." At least there was to be another meeting between them if only so he could make good his promise to sell her yarn. How tantalizing his comment that they would "never part that way again." Did that mean they must simply not part angry next time? Did he only regret *how* they parted and not *that* they parted? Coward that she was, her second letter to him in answer to this had been as mild and noncommittal as her first.

And as for his meeting with American doctors, whom he called surgeons, she was ever grateful, however meager the results: her own son had not been swaddled and he had died. Swaddling had a long and proven past, for even the Lord Jesus himself was laid in swaddling clothes in a manger, and with all the animals and dirty-handed shepherds about, surely the illustrious Dr. Wentworth would not think it a clean place! As for the mother's milk being full of fulmar oil, both the Lewis sisters on St. Kilda had been unable to abide fulmar meat during the nursing of their infants and had lived on mutton—and both their wee ones had died. The answers to her quest for the bairns remained as murky as did her quest to know how much Morgan really cared—and if he had married his faithful American Penelope, his Charlotte.

Her teary gaze drifted out the window as the carriage swept down Grosvenor Place past a parade of gray-gowned nannies wheeling their charges in wicker perambulators toward Hyde Park for an airing. Abigail caught sight of a blue-eyed, blond bairn in a ruffled bonnet; lad or lass, she could not tell, but so chubby and content. The thought of her own son lost six years ago wracked her: how would he look now? With his boy's coil of rope, he would be scrambling barefoot among the low rocks of the rookeries, practicing his skills by fetching eggs, his blond curls buffeted by the wind. What a comfort he would be to her. If she had not lost him, would she be on this desperate mission?

But when she feared she would cry again, she seized hold of herself. Feeling frustrated and defeated was not helping. She must be strong, she must go on. Somehow she would find the killer of the bairns so her son's suffering and loss would have some meaning. Morgan was working to discover the cause too, and he would visit her someday and then . . .

Even as, composed, she climbed down from the carriage and

thanked the driver, she was suddenly very grateful that Corwin had taken Janie, Margaret, and Daisy to Astley's Circus this afternoon to give her a wee bit of time alone.

Abigail dashed off a note to Louisa of her defeat today and sent it around by Corwin's footman, then decided she needed some tea and toast to pick herself up. It was Cook's afternoon off with everyone away, but Abigail loved to fetch her own food. How wonderful the meals were here—much better than on St. Kilda, however much she missed some things like her cheese and whey. The rich, vibrant colors and flavors of vegetables and fruits, the variety of meat and drink, especially the sweets, thrilled her, even when Corwin said something was underseasoned or Louisa was furious with her cooks or pastry chefs for some small flaw in what they called a trifle. Abigail liked to eat at the kitchen's bare wooden table before the hearth when Cook was not here; she'd made Sally, the skullery maid, promise not to tell. But today, even Sally was not in sight.

Abigail had only started to eat her toast with strawberry jam when the bell sounded at the service entry. When it rang again and no one came, she went to answer it herself. Her eyes widened when she saw who stood there: a barefooted, ragged-looking boy in a dirty smock with a coil of rope over his shoulder and a basket of bird nests with eggs. His face was smudged, but such an angel's face with sky-blue eyes and framed by curly, blond hair.

"Cat got your tongue?" he asked with a jaunty tilt of his head and a lopsided grin. "You a new maid, missy? Bet they call you Carrots with that flaming hair. Curly Natter, the bird nest boy, come to see if the gent'man fancies a fine plovers' nest with five eggs to put under a bell jar in his museum. Had to climb sky-high to get it, so it'll cost him dear, tell him."

"Mr. Baxter-Jones, you mean. He isna here right now. But—you dinna climb trees and take those nests away from the parent birds, do you?"

He shrugged. "Got to pick up a crust somehow. Mostly nabs 'em for the tables of fine folk, but the gent'man here's a kind old codger, gives dev'lish good grub and coppers for the odd nest for folks to see. Selling door to door in this here bailiwick's a far sight better'n walking streets all day with 'em or bone grubbing like me friend Quick Jack."

"Oh, yes, of course it is. I was just having a bit of tea and toast if you'd like some and perhaps Mr. Baxter-Jones will be in soon."

The lad's smile could have lit the darkest room. He stepped in, glancing all about, put his basket down, and walked to the table. When she nodded, meaning he could sit, still standing, shoving hunks of bread in his mouth, he crunched down the short stack of toast. Her heart went out to him; the lad was ravenous. He looked to be nine or ten, small and spindly for his age. She poured him some tea and toasted more bread, spreading the pieces thick with butter and jam. When his gobbling slowed a bit, she carefully questioned him about his life and some of his strange words she could not decipher.

Like all street folks, he said, he was named for his looks or a habit: besides being curly-haired, he liked to natter or chatter. He did not know his age and was a parish foundling. Someone he called Uncle Trotter "took him off the parish" because his high-pitched child's voice made him useful as a shrill—a caller of goods above the noise on the streets. But when Uncle Trotter got a louder lad to scream "pig trotters, hot and good!" all day, Curly fell in with a band of thieves who wanted to make him a "jumper," a boy who was boosted in or climbed a tree to get in an upstairs window of a house to let the robbers in the front door.

"But knew that weren't proper and got knocked round dev'lish bad by 'em. Never wanted to cool my heels in the Fleet like some of 'em had. The Fleet—the clink, see," he explained when she frowned, "you know, boarding school, prison." She was horrified to realize they would lock up a mere lad, but he plunged on, "So used me talents to fetch down nests from country trees, and when eating little eggs went all the thing with London nobs, I was sitting fine. 'Sides, fancy the country with its pretty places, I do. Farm folks more like to give a bloke belly timber than the nobs, though you sure been kind to feed me, missy."

"Your visit has been very enlightening, Curly. And I'm not really a maid here, but a friend of Mr. Baxter-Jones visiting from Scotland. So it would be best if you called me just Abigail instead of Carrots or missy."

"Scotland, eh? Got a chum from there plays the bagpipes up near the rook'ry where I got me a swell place, Abigail!"

"Really? 'Tis a bird rookery?"

"Naw, just the swell place I live."

"But whom do you live with? I mean, I know you're an orphan, but do you have friends who took you in after Uncle Trotter?"

"Eh, that's it. We all live together, see, Moll, Quick Jack, the lot of us. Moll's been kinda poorly, but she's a real dev'lish good child-skinner as well as—"

"A child-skinner?" she cried. That revelation was the worst of the horrors yet the lad had innocently recited.

"You know, lures rich folks' brats off a bit and strips the duds off 'em to sell. Don't hurt 'em, and folks just replace the duds," he said hastily, " 'cause she don't keep the brats and sure don't want her own." His expression was so earnest, she sensed he was desperate to have her believe he was a good person. That and so much more about him touched her deeply.

"Curly, can you read and write?"

"Naw! What for?"

She had heard that answer before from grown St. Kilda men who sat in Parliament to govern others and should know better. But here, with Curly, she had a chance to change things.

"But most of me chums is upstanding street folks," he plunged on, "that's what I was going to say, like piemen, crossing-sweepers, a fire-eater, singers and reciters, and one even owns a coffee stall and gives me ginger beer, but sells lemonade and peppermint water, and curds and whey too."

"What wonders you have seen, Curly Natter. You ken," she went on before she could halt the words, "I would love to hear your singer and reciter friends, for that was a pursuit of mine back in Scotland. And I havena been able to hear bagpipes for years, for the church doesna allow them at home, and I'm yearning to have a drink of that curds and whey, that I am."

"Eh? Would you now? If you got two coppers to rub together, guess I could show you then."

Despite her realization that Curly Natter was not a person Corwin or Louisa would approve of, Abigail left a note saying she had just stepped out for air and went with him. Corwin had stressed she must not go unaccompanied, but she was with one who appeared to be the wiliest and most charming of companions. And it was such a bonny day for a walk. Besides, she wanted to buy him a pair of stout shoes and did so at the first clothing emporium they passed. He walked with less swagger now, his feet hurting a bit, the stiff leather squeaking, but he was inordinately proud of them. And she had not felt so free and happy since that day she had been with Morgan heading for their jaunt to the Tunnel before everything fell apart.

They walked north out of the staid environs of Belgravia, cut through Hyde Park—where she hoped no one who knew Corwin or Louisa or recognized the Queen of Kilda saw them—then cut through a web of alleys near busy St. James's Square. The lad knew every back way to take them around the bustle of Piccadilly Circus. On Shaftesbury Avenue she heard the bagpiper wailing away on the corner before she saw him, a seedy-looking old man, with hardly enough wind to fill the bag and his glengarry cap on the street for money. Further on, she listened and contributed also to an organ grinder with a monkey and those the boy called singers and reciters, though their words were far too bawdy for her ears or a lad's. She smiled and clapped with the crowd anyway. It was as if she were with her child at a circus, just as Margaret was today.

"Best keep a hand on your wiper round here," Curly told her, adeptly snatching out the handkerchief barely protruding from her reticule, then handing it to her with a flourish. "And keep your coppers close if you don't want to lose 'em."

"All right. Thank you for the warning," she said, clutching things closer. Imagine, she thought, a lad like this teaching her the ways of the world. But, despite the dangers he hinted at, for a change it was an alluring, bonny world from where she stood right now.

"Everyone wears such bright clothes here," she observed as she surveyed the surrounding exotic people in a riot of rainbow hues of skirts, shawls, frockcoats, old livery, and even plaids!

"Duds from the second-shops run by Hebrews in Petticoat Lane, if you fancy some yourself," he told her sagely. Swinging his empty birdnest basket—for she had bought all eight of his nests for Corwin to choose from—the lad led her on.

He showed her the man who sold curds and whey, among other, stronger drinks, and she drank down a cup of her favorite beverage with relish while Curly had some ginger beer. The lad introduced her simply and proudly as "me chum Abigail" to most of the sellers of numerous things along the streets.

They walked into older neighborhoods with more ramshackle, smaller, dingier buildings. Stale smells assailed her now, fish, onions, privies or just foul puddles; raucous noises of dogs barking, a screaming argument, the cries of distant babies surrounded them. Suddenly, Curly turned into a narrow, dim alley, lined with dirty, unattended children. They scattered at the sight of a stranger. She nearly gagged at the rank smell as they passed between two more buildings; she pressed her "wiper" to her nose and mouth.

"Where are we?" she asked as he turned back to look at her lagging behind.

"The rook'ry, St. Giles High Street, where I got me a swell room with me chums."

She knew she must go no farther, yet something drew her: the trusting look on the lad's face, her torrent of feelings for him she could not name or explain. But she didn't want to get into some terrible scrape here. She didn't want to meet a woman-skinner or worse; she should have thought to dress in her St. Kilda garb, for folks stared at what they surely thought was her finery. She must turn back and come another day with the coachman or even Corwin, if he would not be shocked.

But then, stumbling toward them came a slender, brown-haired girl in a worn, thin dress. No fine fabrics, no stylish red gloves, no crinoline here. "Moll!" Curly shouted and darted to help her stand. She leaned heavily on him, but the boy could not hold her weight and they both slid slowly against a rotting wood wall into a muddy puddle. Abigail rushed to help.

"Whatever is the matter with her?"

"Dunno," the boy said, " 'less she got rid of the chit, like she said she would."

"What's a chit?" Abigail demanded as the lass's pale green eyes flickered open beneath her frown of pain. Her face looked white as bleached linen; she pinched her eyes tight shut again.

" 'Sides skinning brats in the day, Moll's a lady of easy virtue at night," Curly told her matter-of-factly. "You know—a trollop. Caught a chit and if she had it, it would of just starved and Moll too, 'cause she couldn't work then. Scared to try it before, but now I think she's gone and done it."

Abigail stared aghast as what he was saying sank in. This mere girl had become pregnant by a stranger who paid her for her services. Worse, when she was with child, she somehow took the unborn bairn's life and now she was bleeding; Abigail could see the stains seeping through her skirt. She had no notion such a horror as this existed. Oh, yes, as Louisa had said, she had much to learn of the civilized world. Maybe she had been wrong to judge St. Kildans so harshly. But how could such a thing happen here when St. Kildans to the last woman longed for and cherished bairns that were taken from them? She prayed again that, unknowingly, St. Kildan women were not doing something to kill theirs.

"Curly, run for the nearest doctor and tell him I will pay him to come here."

"Naw, he'd never listen to the likes a me," the boy protested.

Abigail dug in her reticule and pulled out a five pound note. The boy stared agape at it as if it were the royal fortune. "I am trusting you, Curly. I am trusting that you told me the truth today and I can rely on you to do what's right, just as you knew it wasn't right to be a jumper for a band of thieves. I want to help you and your friend Moll here, but you have to run now for a doctor. Go on!"

His blue eyes locked with hers. He snatched the bill and was off like a shot, skidding cinders from beneath the slippery soles of his new shoes. And Abigail knelt in a puddle, cradling the girl in her arms as people went past, peering down or ignoring them, toward the sordid snarl of buildings up ahead that Curly had proudly called his swell place. She tried futilely to stem the lass's bleeding with strips of her torn petticoat, but to no avail.

At last a portly, red-faced doctor came. He took his time climbing from his carriage and announced himself to Abigail as "the Doctor Featherstone of Leicester Square." But he did no more than open his black leather bag and shake his head over Moll, tut-tutting at her sad state, the surroundings, or something in the depths of his bag. He bent over a bit but did not kneel, did not even put his bag down.

"Do something!" Abigail demanded.

"Too far gone," he mouthed.

He was perspiring profusely. He sprinkled what smelled like

peppermint water on his clean linen handkerchief, but held it to his own nose. Moll did not move again but to go limp with her head still on Abigail's lap. Finally, the doctor leaned over to touch two fingertips to Moll's right wrist before he shrugged and shook his head. Next to Curly's empty egg basket in the mud and cinders, Abigail drooped stunned over the dead girl.

The doctor put his bag back in the carriage, then returned to move Moll's head from Abigail's lap and extend a hand to Abigail. Seeing he would just let Moll lie there, she scrambled up herself and pointedly covered the slack face with her own handkerchief. She put her hands to Curly's shaking shoulders, but the doctor pulled her away by her elbow, muttering about "this putrified den of iniquity where no nice woman would ever set foot!"

"We must see she has a proper burial," Abigail insisted.

"Prop—indeed, I'll see the poor thing's taken care of, but you mustn't stay here, for I can tell by your garments you don't belong."

His strident, scolding tone did not pierce Abigail's pain. Somehow, it only echoed voices she had heard long ago. When she haltingly explained how she came to be here, Dr. Featherstone evidently recognized who she was. Shooing Curly away over her protests, he put Abigail in his one-horse conveyance to take her home, assuring her she just didn't know what she was doing. Being "virtue personified from a simple-minded, primal place," he murmured, "you have been led astray by that ruffian rascal there." When Abigail glanced down the pointed length of the man's arm and stiff finger at Curly, the boy fled like a whipped, scowling dog. She called after him, but the lad did not turn back. Now her insides wrenched again, and she thought she might be sick enough to need a doctor.

"Dregs of the earth, you know, this sort of riffraff in this stewpot of sin down here," the man muttered and blotted sweat from the back of his neck while Moll lay at his feet. "It simply doesn't do to really get involved with their like, you see, but fortunately, as often as not, the wretches just do themselves in."

"Dinna you mean to put her in the carriage too?" Abigail asked, feeling suddenly exhausted. Her mind spun to encompass what he had just said. Surely, she had not heard him correctly.

"It's hardly a hearse. I'll send round some—ah, medical students to take care of it. This sort of unpleasantness happens all the time, so it won't take much to clear it up."

Suddenly, Abigail snapped to. Unpleasantness? Clear *it* up? This poor, lost girl was no "it," but a human being! She was so angry she couldn't even begin to question the only physician who had apparently been willing to talk to her since she had been in London. Evidently doctors in this blasted scientific, enlightened, modern town did not really care about how hard things were for street women, children, or infants here, let alone those on St. Kilda! All this man wanted to do was bury the girl like an inanimate object with all the atrocities she represented. He did not want to so much as dampen his starched collar with sweat or have to disturb his schedule by concerning himself with Moll or any woman who stepped over the line of propriety—herself included. And Curly might be just a ruffian rascal to this man and his ilk, but not to Abigail Adair!

Despite the doctor's flustered protests, Abigail clambered out of his carriage and started away. She spotted Curly in the next doorway, huddled there, not crying but white-faced and wide-eyed. The doctor chased her and tried to pull her back. "I have some *sal volatile* salts here," he was saying. "I see you must be in shock, so—"

"I am in shock!" she shouted, turning back as she shook off his hand. "Shocked that you and your like, you—you riffraff of humanity, you dregs of this earth—dinna care a rotten egg for this dead girl, her lost infant, or that poor lad! Curly," she called and gestured to him, "will you walk me home? My friend there will bring us back directly and see to it that Moll has a decent resting place. I'd rather walk with you than ride with this uncaring, this—*it!*"

Doctor Featherstone stood wide-eyed, wheezing through his mouth, holding his nose at the stench of the area—or at her, she was not sure which. She only knew that she had to help not only the lost St. Kilda bairns, but their mothers too. However harshly some St. Kilda women had treated her, they could well be doing something to kill their own infants. Poor Moll had meant to harm her bairn, but what if—

She gasped to realize too late this doctor might know some of Corwin's friends and tell them of her actions. He would, no doubt, be acquainted with other doctors and tell them not to speak to the fallen "Virtue Victorious." Perhaps he even knew the queen's vaunted Dr. Snow she so wanted to interview. But if she had to become a blasted doctor herself to keep infants from dying, she would do it before she'd stoop to ask this man for help.

Curly shuffled over to join her. She seized his arm and marched him briskly away. She hustled the boy along so fast the scuff and squeak of his boots drowned out the doctor's righteous ranting behind them.

Curly Natter's swell place turned out to be a six storey rabbit warren of sordid, stinking, interconnected chambers with as many as a dozen street people crammed in one tiny room at night. Abigail, with her formidable escort of Corwin, his valet, footman, and coachman, visited it two days after they buried Moll and after she had weathered both Corwin and Louisa's protests about going back for Curly to tell him she wanted him to visit Corwin's house every day so she could teach him to read and write.

"Touching, but it just isn't done!" Louisa had insisted at first. "Donate money to the Christian Women's Charity Society who run a few ragged schools if you must, but do not actually get involved with that little rapscallion yourself! Or, I could give the boy a respectable job at Kimbolton if you'd like, stable boy or whatever to get him out of town, away from undue influences."

"By Jove, it's not the expected thing," Corwin remonstrated more quietly.

" 'Tis what I must do, whether or not I am permitted to stay here to live with you, Corwin, and whether or not our friendship, Louisa, precious to me as it is, is at risk or not."

"Well, I suppose I have done a thing or two that set people back . . ." Louisa had admitted.

"But I won't hear of you moving out," Corwin had said. "Of course you may have the lad here to teach if you would like."

Once Curly was convinced to try, he became a quick study and even a more avid student when he met Janie Gillies and realized the younger girl could read and write already. However, one difficult week, when Curly tried to come only for the meals she always fed him before they began so he could concentrate, she made the rule that he would not be fed unless he sat an hour in class first. He protested and disappeared for two days; she thought her heart would break, but she held firm. Soon he was back, more eager to please than ever. Janie taught him to add numbers. Louisa sometimes sent a sack of sweets around, though the rule was that the lesson must be recited before he could partake. Once again, when his attendance turned spotty, she got him to admit he'd been out on the streets earning "a dev'lish bully" livelihood. So, she paid him a whole penny a day to attend but insisted he save half of it for when he had learned his lessons and went out on his own. Still, she could not bear the idea of ever losing him. From mid-September to mid-October, sometimes glaring at her, sometimes with a winsome smile that melted her insides, Curly Natter, like Janie before him, became the St. Kilda students she had never been allowed to have.

Abigail saw less of Louisa now; she had little time for teas or soirees. She began to resent taking part in the living tableaux at Corwin's museum two afternoons a week, but she would never let him down and it did help her save money to pay doctors for their time. Still she was going to Kimbolton the last weekend in October with Corwin and tried to tell herself she would enjoy and indeed needed the escape from the city. But if it had not been for all she owed Louisa and the possibility that Dr. John Snow would be there, she might have declined the gilt-edged invitation. At least Margaret would be staying in London to oversee Curly's lessons each day.

The day before Corwin and Abigail left for Kimbolton, she was upset that Curly was late. She just hoped he had no intention of starting to miss classes again. Had she been too lenient to pay him and feed him too? She did not want to coddle him, but she wanted so to care for him. Today, though, she had a hundred last-minute things to do before she left town, so where was the lad?

She peered out the kitchen door through which he had first walked into her life. They always held their lessons in the servants' dining hall just off the pantry, and ate a noon meal together there. If he didn't come on time today, she'd worry about him every minute she was at Kimbolton. But no, there he came down the steps, half running, half skipping. She opened the door.

"Today I got a good excuse, so don't you give me a basting. Got a capital surprise for you! There's a gent'man friend of yours come calling. A dark-haired fellow knew you on St. Kilda, he says, so he's waiting for you just across the street, and . . ."

Curly's voice went on, but Abigail heard nothing else. She pressed her clasped hands to her breasts. Morgan, here? Morgan had found her as he said he would—Morgan!

She ran past Curly at the door, patting her curls in place with trembling hands. Lifting her skirts, she hurried up the steps, her heart in her throat, crying, calling, "My dearest . . ."

In the noon sun of the street, she gasped and blinked back tears.

"Ed—mund."

"I take it ye expected someone else, though I told the lad I knew ye on St. Kilda. No matter, I shall take yer warm greeting, my bonny, long-lost Abigail."

He strode quickly toward her. Disappointed and furious, she stumbled back, leaning for support on the iron grate above the stairs. She jerked a hand up. "Edmund!" was all she could manage again.

She noted how prosperous he looked. With clothes of finest fabric and cut, he could have stepped into one of Louisa's gatherings and looked at home. His lean body had filled out to make him almost stocky. And, she realized with a start, he was taller; he must be wearing specially made shoes with high soles. But his dark eyes still bored into her as if he possessed and would devour her.

"I—I left my student in the house. I'm teaching the lad you met to read, so I must return," she floundered even as Curly came up the steps to stand behind her.

"Of course, a public street 'tis hardly the place for a proper reunion of such old friends as we. But I have read about the heroine of St. Kilda and wanted to see you. And, as I vowed before we exchanged a few harsh words once, I came to give you a donation for your cause with the poor St. Kilda bairns. Here 'tis, two hundred pounds for a start," he said and extended a thick envelope to her.

She stared at his kind gesture as if he pointed a pistol at her. Such a donation was an answer to prayer to send a doctor to St. Kilda. But not from Edmund Drummond. Not if he thought she would have another sort of reunion with him later, or if he believed he could bribe or buy her, as he had tried before.

"I canna accept, Edmund," she declared. "I have a new life now. I wish you well in your endeavors, but I dinna want to see you again."

"Nor did ye in yer old life," he said. His arm holding the envelope slowly wilted to his side; he forced a smile that revealed his crooked teeth. "As to my endeavors, they have gone well. I am a wealthy man, Abigail, though not of the step on the stair as those ye hobnob with here."

"The feather business—'tis still your calling?"

"Thriving. Percentages of profits way up, not only for bed stuffings, but for the future of ladies' fashion. Feathers on capes and hats will be sweeping in from France soon, ye'll see, ye and yer fancy friends."

It worried her how much he seemed to know of her life here. "Those pillow-stuffing gannet feathers on ladies clothes?" she asked, hoping to keep the conversation away from her friends.

"Better feathers, hundreds of grosses of every kind from far, exotic places. Pink ones, long graceful ones! Plumes, Abigail, fancy fringed ones they call aigrettes that sell for a pretty penny. I have been traveling to set up the importing of them, or I would have called on ye sooner. I've gone far beyond being the Laird of MacLeod's accountant or feather broker, I tell ye."

"More bonny birds killed just for their feathers."

"The point is, ye could help me, get in on the take. If ye and that high-up duchess friend of yers would wear feathers I'd give ye, talk them up—why even if ye wilna let me court ye when I could give ye anything ye wanted—then take this money for yer cause and let me use a drawing of ye in a feather cape and hat in that newspaper that printed all the things about ye when I was away. I could—"

"Then that money is a downpayment of a bribe and not a donation. No, Edmund, and I wilna even say I'm sorry. I never wanted to be a part of your life and certainly want no part of your—your slaughtering birds for your profit and women's pride. Now please leave."

"Never change, do ye, more proud and stubborn than ever, thinking yer better than Edmund Drummond. Eh, but I ken the real woman inside that alluring package, Abigail MacQueen Adair! I heard tell of the American sea captain, and how ye carried on with

him on St. Kilda. Whoring for him, 'til he left ye, now no doubt
here angling for a high-born man. Looking high and low for a doctor who will help the wretched bairns. And teaching ragged ignora-
muses like that lad there, all the while trying to ease yer guilt of
failure at home!"

His voice dripped contempt; his face contorted in a sneer. Abigail had to hold Curly back from rushing to her defense.

"No wonder an upstanding St. Kilda man like myself is sewage
beneath your step, but we shall see, och, we shall see!"

"Edmund, just take your leave, or—"

"Or what? I tell ye, Yer Majesty Abigail, Queen of Kilda, ye
will play things my way sooner or later, or not play at all! And if
ye ever dare wed elsewhere above yer station, when ye belong to
me, ye uppity, seducing, man-haunting witch—"

"Edmund Drummond!" Margaret screamed from the front
door of the house, "Get yer carcass clear of here!"

Though Margaret tore down the front steps, wielding a candlestick like a sword, Edmund kept his eyes on Abigail. Drawn by the
shouting, several tradesmen and carters passing by as well as a
group of ragged children Abigail thought had probably followed
Curly here edged closer to the quarrel.

"Here's a wee downpayment on all ye will do for me, at my
bidding, my bonny whore—" Edmund shouted in a sing-song voice.
He ripped the envelope open and threw a shower of bills into the
air. Strangers shrieked and ran to catch them. Margaret charged
with her candlestick. But it was Curly who exploded past Abigail to
thud hard into Edmund and send him sprawling on the bricks of
the street. A carter's horse shied back, its hoofs just missing
Edmund.

Shouting for calm, Abigail waded through the mess to pull the
lad off Edmund, who scuttled backward. Margaret landed a good
blow across his knees; Curly kicked him; Abigail dragged the boy
back by his collar. A few folks cheered at the fray, but most scrambled for blowing bills. Edmund got to his knees and stood, wavering, disheveled, shamed, and bloody-mouthed where he evidently
had bitten his lip. He bent to scoop up what notes were within easy
reach and shook a crumpled handful of them at Abigail, who held
Curly back.

"I'll pay now and ye, I swear, will pay later!" he roared at her as if there were no one else on the crowded street. He threw the money at her again. Now Corwin heard and came out from his museum, waving a long-empty Napoleonic rifle over his head like a club.

Edmund raised his maimed hand to point at her as if he could strike her dead. Then he turned and hurried away, but not, she feared, for good.

12

Her heart's desire she calls him,
That man who is not hers.
Yet, glittering, she keeps him near,
While gossip round her swirls.

So golden in my eyes was she,
Bright ways polishing the bold.
With pain my heart has come to see
Glitter tarnishes true gold.

"Such a braw, bonny sight!" Abigail proclaimed to Lady Salisbury and Lady Talbert as the three of them halted at the top of the grand staircase of Kimbolton Castle to take in the scene below. Abigail stepped quickly back from the balustrade when air whooshed up from below to bounce out the back of her skirts.

In the hall beneath the women, the forty weekend guests who had worn riding or shooting garb earlier had been transformed into graceful, glittering beings, resplendent in silks, satins, and winking jewels for dinner and dancing.

But as the three started downstairs, Abigail felt like a small ship under full sail. Her huge skirts over her new crinoline, swagged with pink flounces and festoons, looked as if they made waves. Louisa had loaned her a small pearl tiara and earrings which rattled in her rigging of curled, coiled hair and bobbed on her earlobes with each rocking step she took on tiny-heeled shoes.

"Mmm," the elderly Lady Talbert murmured. "The men may have been bagging grouse all day, but Louisa's bagged this new royal appointment of hers—not to mention bagging Harty-Tarty."

"Lord Hartington, you mean," Abigail put in, holding tightly to the curved banister. She had come to know quite well Spencer Hartington, the heir to the powerful and wealthy dukedom of Devonshire, at some of Louisa's gatherings. She knew that his parents were quite dismayed that their eligible, young son preferred the company of the fast "Duchess of Man" to more "suitable" young women he might court and wed.

"He and the duchess are just good friends," Abigail explained. "Spencer Hartington is a chum of her husband too."

"A chum, is he?" Lady Salisbury's pink feather fan flipped faster as if she could blow away Abigail's use of Curly's Soho slang—or maybe blow Abigail herself away. And the feathers themselves seemed an unspoken insult to Abigail after the row with Edmund.

She had been surprised to see that these women Louisa had entrusted her to were the same ones who had gossiped about the "Duchess of Man with her men in tow" that day at Corwin's museum. And here they turned out to be Louisa's friends, more or less; they knew she had recognized them. But why should it surprise her that so-called friends could be cruel? She recalled all too well that some who should have been closest to her on St. Kilda—her own mother-in-law, for example—were among the most critical and unkind.

"You do know, I take it, Mrs. Adair," Lady Talbert explained, "that they say that our dear duchess absolutely beguiled Lord Derby to get her new appointment as Her Majesty's Mistress of the Robes. Just in time, too, as my husband says Lord Derby will soon be out on his ear and Palmerston back in as P.M."

"No doubt," Lady Salisbury put in as they slowly descended the stairs, "Louisa had Lord Derby intrigued, entranced, and entangled before he knew what hit him. That's our Louisa." Her fan shuddered as if its owner would like to. "And then she as good as blackmailed him into pushing the position for her to the queen, when Her Majesty, I am sure, thinks Louisa is the pushy one. Perhaps she fears if Louisa is about the court too much she will ensnare Prince Albert as she has countless others."

"But no one can deny her charm," Abigail insisted. "I dinna know why the queen wouldna like having someone so lively and clever about!" At that the two older women just rolled their eyes.

"And those of us here on her bounty should not say ill of her," Abigail plunged on. "Today I would have protested the shooting of so many birds for pure sport, but I hear we will be eating dozens of them tonight, just like at home. And where I hail from, even though 'tis done, 'tis just not right to criticize a host or friend to others." Blast, she thought, if she could only breathe better she'd tell these women a thing or two. The ladies' maid she shared with several others had laced this corset too blasted tight.

"My dear, island-innocent Mrs. Adair," Lady Salisbury said as they edged their way into the ballroom where people were gathering, "no doubt you would not so passionately defend the woman if a man you favored were ensnared by your terribly 'lively and clever' Louisa."

"Who is this Lord Derby anyway?"

"The Prime Minister of Parliament, of course, a conservative," Lady Talbert explained.

"The man doesna sound conservative to me if he lets a bonny lass sway him. All that makes him sound like he's from the liberal party Corwin talked about," Abigail insisted.

After a shake of her head that rattled her earbobs, Lady Salisbury whispered, "Mrs. Adair, since you seem to have the duchess's fickle ear this season and know *all* about our queen and British politics, you'd best advise Louisa not to disregard the political heritage of this place." She swept her fan in a graceful arc as if to encompass all that was castle, grounds, and little brick village of Kimbolton. "After all, this is the place," she whispered, "King Henry the Eighth sent his divorced Queen Katherine of Aragon to die in exile when she displeased him!"

The St. Kilda tale of the exiled Lady Grange flitted through Abigail's mind to put her even more on edge. One of the things she admired most about Louisa was that she guided the men about her, not the other way around—and they seemed happy that way too.

"If King Henry's queen had been able to please people like the duchess does," Abigail insisted, "it wouldna have happened. Louisa makes her husband very happy. I suppose some envy her that gift."

"Well, if you mean to imply—well, I never—come along then,

Emmalyn, until the duchess can do a better job teaching her—her latest charity endeavor—what to say and what not to say in polite company!" Lady Talbert huffed away like a steam engine with Lady Salisbury rolling right behind. They began to chat with others and disappeared around the curve of the crowd.

Abigail stood half hidden by the huge, open door, embarrassed and fuming, but soon calmed herself. Why would she want to spend her time with back-stabbing folks like those, anyway? Still, she did not want to do anything to reflect badly on Louisa. She had been more at ease today ducking out alone to walk in the forest beyond the orchards, although Louisa had exploded—sitting perfectly still, glaring at Abigail in the mirror while her maid did her hair—when she heard where Abigail had been unaccompanied.

"In the forest—alone—all afternoon? Indeed, you must never do that again!"

"I loved the huge trees, and nothing happened."

"My dear Abigail, that is not the point. When a woman wanders off by herself alone, unless she is snow-haired, stooped, and in her dotage, people think something *might* have happened!"

"Actually, something did happen. I was out, free as the wind for the first time in months."

"I envy you that, indeed I do. But appearances matter here more than on St. Kilda, I'm afraid. You see, Englishmen tend to see women as either housewives or harlots, madonnas or magdalenes, if you take my drift. And so we must guard our appearances and then play our cards cleverly under the table. I—I see you do not follow me."

"I do," Abigail had replied, "but I dinna agree. I told you about Morgan West—he saw me as an equal, a companion and friend to speak his mind with about his love of archeology and hatred of slavery, and he is doing what he can to help discover what causes the bairns' deaths."

"Ah, yes, the illustrious Captain West," Louisa had said while the diamond coronet was fastened in her upswept hair. "Indeed, I must meet this paragon when he arrives. But the thing is, dear Abigail, whatever disagreements you and I have, we admire each other for our own ideas of independence and freedom, don't you agree? Now, May, stop fussing over me and fasten this charming little pearl tiara in Mrs. Adair's lovely red-gold hair—this was once my grandmother's, Abigail . . ."

Yes, Abigail thought now, even when they disagreed, she and Louisa remained staunch friends, unlike these other women.

Rather than trailing after her two former companions into the ballroom, Abigail stopped just inside the door and scanned the room for Corwin. When she did not see him, she studied the faces of the men, wondering if one of them was the eminent Dr. Snow she had long yearned to meet. He had been invited for the shoot today, but had only accepted for this evening and breakfast tomorrow before returning to his busy schedule in London. Abigail caught the avid eyes of several men who saw her staring; too late she remembered more of Louisa's numerous dos and don'ts: "Do not show too bold an eye. And don't sit with your ankles crossed; cultivate a gentle, low, silvery voice; don't do anything in a sudden, slapdash manner, always be graceful, above the fray and in control." Why, Louisa had been as dedicated to pulling her up a step in society as Abigail had been to helping Curly.

She sighed. She missed the lad as well as Margaret and Janie after just one day here. At least she would not worry for their safety, as they had used some of the money Edmund Drummond had scattered on his demented departure to hire several guards to secure the museum and tallhouse against his possible return.

Instead of staring at the people, she gazed up at the vast sweep of ceiling done by an artist named Pelligrini, whom the duke had brought all the way from Italy. Full-fleshed, naked women Louisa had told her were Greek goddesses soared and smiled down from a painted heaven: how Morgan would have loved this ceiling, perhaps for more than one reason. She studied the twin doors into the ballroom, much taller than people needed, so perhaps they were built for these massive deities, she thought wryly. Marble columns helped hold up the ceiling; narrow caves were carved right in the walls, the perfect size for the great marble vases on pedestals there that the deities probably drank from; mirrors as big as puddles multiplied the dancers who had come to entertain the heavenly beings. Kimbolton suddenly seemed a huge house for unearthly giants and so strange to her St. Kilda eyes.

"I take it our mutual friend is going to make a grand entrance with the duke," a man spoke so close behind her that his breath, laced with whiskey, heated her neck. She spun to face Spencer Hartington, looking grim but sleekly handsome.

"So I hear, sir, and she sent me on ahead."

"You're to call me Spencer, remember. I was just thinking that so lovely a lady as yourself should not be unattended. Ah, I see your host Corwin has just come in and is speaking to Dr. Snow."

"Dr. Snow! Then he is here!"

"Alas, had I garnered such emotion from you as that, I would die fulfilled on the spot," Spencer told her with a lopsided grin that lifted his mustache.

No wonder, Abigail thought, folks believed Louisa flirted with this man they snidely called Harty-Tarty, but he was the one flirting. Did men never catch the blame for anything? Still, she smiled at his teasing, then headed for Corwin with Spencer right behind her. Let the gossips link her name with his to save Louisa's, she thought. But as Abigail accepted his arm, the duchess entered on her husband's good arm, for the duke had broken a wrist bone in his other earlier today.

"That will slow the old boy down even more," she heard Spencer mutter as he brought them to a halt. The guests began to applaud the Manchesters' entrance; Spencer and Abigail joined in. Louisa glowed golden in yellow satin with diamonds flashing in her hair and at her throat above the low-cut gown.

It was then Abigail caught Spencer's expression and knew he indeed loved Louisa more than he should: his lower lip dropped, then tightened; his eyes widened; his nostrils flared; he gulped audibly, all while staring heatedly at the duchess. Poor Louisa, if she loved him like that, Abigail mourned. Though she had seen earlier today that the duke and duchess did not share a bedroom let alone a bed when there was not what Louisa called "The Marital Duty to be seen to," the couple was obviously companionable and content.

The ducal pair advanced toward them, nodding, greeting their guests by name. As they neared, Louisa's gaze jumped to Spencer's, then to Abigail, then back again.

"Did you get your fill of hunting yet today, my lord?" Louisa asked Spencer. Without waiting for an answer, she dropped her husband's arm and took Abigail by a kid-gloved hand. "Come, my dear, for I've arranged for you to be seated at table with Dr. Snow, and I want to introduce you properly."

During dinner, Abigail felt heaven-blessed. As she spoke with Dr. Snow, the elaborate, lengthy meal flew by: soup, fish, side dishes, entrees and roasts, savouries, fruits, nuts, and sweets accompanied by wines and champagne. For once, she did not care what she ate or drank.

John Snow was about Corwin's age and a bachelor too, evidently wedded to his important work. She felt so much more at ease when he told her he was a farmer's son who treated working people as often as he had the upper classes until his application of gas during the delivery of the queen's last two children had brought him fame.

He was very proud of his earlier discovery of an air pump to resuscitate newborn asphyxiated infants; he kindly explained all the strange terms to her. He defended his use of chloroform to control pain in childbirth, as if she would argue with anything he said. And he listened carefully to her tale of St. Kilda: he was appalled; he said he thought her fighting the cruel tradition of pain in the loss of infants *after* childbirth was akin to his battle to halt pain *during* childbirth.

"I don't believe," he told her, "that the Great Spirit would have given mankind the scientific wherewithal to fight pain and loss if He did not want it stopped! It's one of His many gifts to us through knowledge that we must use wisely and humanely!" His pale face became so passionate that his gaunt cheeks blushed the color of her gown.

"Abigail Adair, you've been wise and brave through your battle," he went on and took her hand. "Such devastating loss of infants strikes at the very heart of the family, at the very future of your island! It strikes at all of us, even the most enlightened. Something must be done to help your people, to convince them to embrace change! Though I can hardly desert my pressing duties here in London after all the time I've spent away, I shall send a formal letter when we discover exactly what is the cause of the St. Kildan infant tragedy."

Despite happy toasts to the queen and to Louisa's new appointment at court, Abigail almost wept with joy into her champagne. At last, at last, St. Kilda bairns had a champion and a chance.

❦

Dr. Snow sought out Abigail again after the gentlemen had stayed behind at table for their port and cigars. "Would you care to stroll the long gallery and continue our discussion?" he asked.

They walked and talked to the distant strains of waltz and polka music. He told her he had just recalled that there was a rural county in Ireland where many infants died of what was called "the nine-day fits." Noting the similar time frame in which that disease ran its fatal course, he said he would discover more about birth practices there. He had an assistant, an Irishman, Dr. Patrick O'Neil, who could inquire about this through correspondence with friends in Dublin.

Dr. Snow agreed with the absolute necessity of cleanliness in the birthing room, but thought the St. Kilda killer must be much more or the mothers would be dying, too, of what he called puerperal fever. As for the fulmar oil and the cutting of the umbilical cord, he was eager to read her records.

"I'll consult my acquaintance, Dr. Joseph Lister, though he's been working mostly with surgical sepsis, or infection," he told her. "Perhaps the St. Kilda killer is something like infant tetanus, commonly called lockjaw, with those signs you describe."

Lockjaw! What Morgan had suggested their first day in Gleann Mor, she thought. She could not wait to write him, tell him his instincts had been correct and now they were going to prove it.

As the evening wore on, Abigail fully expected Corwin or Louisa to fetch them back to the celebration, but perhaps they understood—or perhaps they felt that Dr. Snow, at least, was in his dotage, and no one would gossip. It didn't matter to her; when she parted from the brilliant man, she floated to her bedchamber on a cloud of gratitude and relief. The maid sat nodding in a chair, waiting to unlace and free her from the dreadful corset and cage. But all night, able to breathe and move at last, she hardly slept. She could not wait to tell Margaret, Corwin, and most especially Louisa, who had arranged all this. She rose and paced, then watched from her window as dawn stained the sky. And then she knew she could wait no longer to thank Louisa.

The duchess always rose early and drank hot chocolate while May did her hair. Especially today, entertaining forty for breakfast at nine, she would be up. At Manchester House in London, Abigail had visited her more than once before her other callers. And she must return this jewelry of her grandmother and tell her all Dr. Snow had said!

Without summoning the poor maid, Abigail pinned her hair up and managed to get into her petticoats and day dress and threw a cashmere shawl over the back buttons she could not reach herself. Louisa's May could do them. She peeked out in the long, dim corridor lined with somber portraits and hurried to Louisa's suite just as she had last evening before dinner. She heard Louisa's low laugh through the door; good, she was awake and in fine fettle. She knocked once lightly.

"Enter."

She opened it and stepped in. "Louisa, 'tis Abigail and I couldna wait to—"

She stopped, flushed at what she saw here—and in her imagination. Spencer Hartington, leaning over the mussed bed, lifted his head to stare, narrow-eyed, at her. He was completely, if haphazardly, dressed. But his hand was tangled in the sheet over his lover's breasts. And Louisa, Duchess of Manchester, lay all too obviously naked and disheveled from his kisses in a bed he had recently left.

"Bloody hell!"

"Abigail!"

"I—I dinna ken. You said enter."

"Oh bother! I thought you were May here to say the coast was clear!" Louisa muttered, then laughed throatily and shoved Spencer away. "Be off, you greedy man, and I shall speak with Abigail."

Abigail had frozen to her tiny spot of carpet, but she wanted to flee. What an innocent she was, how foolish, how—stupidly adoring. But just as when she heard folks gossip, when she saw the way Curly lived, just as when poor, young Moll died in her arms from taking her own unborn bairn's life, she felt dirtied and diminished by this most civilized of places. The way of things on St. Kilda was not the way of things here, but both were wrong at times. And, she feared, however hard one struggled, there might be no way to change them.

Spencer dared to wink at her as he went out. May knocked and darted in to say the way was clear and gasped to see Abigail, then scurried to help her mistress into her wrapper.

"I'm sorry," Abigail said, meaning more than Louisa would ever know.

"A mishap. Come over here, sit in this chair by the bed, won't you, and May can ring for chocolate for us both."

Slowly, Abigail complied. "I came to return these pearls you so kindly lent me and tell you my talks with Dr. Snow were a great success. I'm to call on him Tuesday in his Firth Street office."

"How wonderful," Louisa said, smoothing the sheets around her as May darted off to pull the bellcord. "Abigail, it would grieve me greatly if I thought we would lose our friendship. Not many women can abide me, you know—now just listen, and do not protest. Oh, indeed young ones admire me a bit, but I have made my life in this society where men rule, you see, by ruling men. Women might envy that, but because they can't manage it, they hate me for it. And I'm mad for Spencer. He's worth any risk. He's my heart's desire!"

"But—but folks are whispering about you and Lord Derby."

"Nonsense, a political friendship. I mean it, Abigail, about Spencer. And somehow, someday, I shall really have him. Meanwhile, as is proper, I am the duke's wife, I have given him his heir and his spare and three to boot, and up to now I have adhered to society's Eleventh Commandment, 'Thou shalt not be found out.' Oh, Abigail, everyone does it! No laundering of dirty linen in public, in other words, it's the thing here, so do not look at me that way, I will not have it! I aid and abet you pursuing your heart's desire to help the babies of St. Kilda—and to get that American sea captain of yours back—and you keep my secret and remain my friend. That's our bargain, our trust, Abigail. We're outsiders, both of us, I from Germany, you from St. Kilda. We both speak a bit foreign, think a bit foreign. But we are making our way here with our strength and stubbornness. I indeed admire you for that!"

"That—yes, we share that." And, Abigail thought sadly, they shared that others gossiped about them for luring men, about her on St. Kilda, about Louisa here. But Louisa had done it intentionally; Abigail saw that now. Yet she herself had never tried to manage and control men—had she?

"And," Louisa said, "we share the fact that the men we love cannot, right now, be really, fully ours."

"Morgan aside, I—" Abigail floundered, "well, my husband

and I hid our love for years before we were able to wed at home, but I was not mar—"

"There, you see! Sisters under the skin!"

Louisa chattered on over cups of steaming chocolate. About the day's events; the influence of her new ceremonial position serving the queen, which she would use to help her friends; about Kim's broken wrist bone that would have to be reset in London since they simply could not ask Dr. Snow to do it on his brief holiday here because it was more important that Abigail have time with him. More about Morgan, how she would entertain him when he came to visit, how he and Abigail could use Kimbolton or the river house in Chelsea to get away if they wished. For the first time, Abigail was achingly aware that she—like the Duchess of Man's men—was being manipulated. Especially now with Dr. Snow's promised help, she was greatly beholden to Louisa. The glitter and the glow from her once-golden friend seemed sadly tarnished now.

Abigail and Margaret returned from their third visit to Dr. Snow's office in a brisk, late October wind that reminded them so of St. Kilda's. Soon, Abigail hoped, they would finally be helping the misguided folks at home. Home—well, it was not really that to her, but she had missed the isle and its inhabitants in a way she had never thought she would when she had escaped. Seeing the ponderous problems here had made her realize St. Kilda was, by comparison, perhaps only narrow-minded and cruel in its own small-island way, for despite some dear Londoners she'd met, the big island of England was narrow-minded and cruel too.

Many of the people in power in England did not care about those "beneath" them, and the gap between those above and below was much greater than on St. Kilda. Terrible things here were covered over, prettied up, or just plain ignored: betrayals, infidelities, wastefulness, crassness, callousness, and outright brutality. But at least now she had Dr. Snow who was willing to help both here and on St. Kilda. But would the rock-bound, brain-bound Scots there listen to a worldly doctor and their own shamed, brazen outcast Abigail Adair?

In a week or two, Dr. O'Neil should have word from Dublin about the nine-day fits. And then they would have letters to send making stringent recommendations from both Dr. Snow and Dr. Joseph Lister. They would insist that the knee-women no longer use fulmar oil or traditional old iron knives to prepare infants' umbilical cords for binding. Something unclean in the oil or nearly invisible flecks of iron from the knife were apparently becoming trapped in the wound to foul the infant's tender system and cause *tetanus infantus*. The very words sounded ugly to Abigail.

She would send these letters to Annie, Parliament, and the new minister, the Reverend Mr. John MacKay. She hoped Annie would be able to record results for Dr. Snow. If not, she and Margaret must return to care for all that themselves.

"Oh, Abby, I ken ye and Dr. Snow have done it at last!" Margaret cried as if she could read her mind.

"Not until there isna one more bairn dying!" Abigail said, but she was so excited she was shaking as they disembarked from the carriage and went into Corwin's house, bent against the wind.

Abigail heard the distant rumble of men's voices from the drawing room; another of Corwin's suppliers or fellow collectors must be visiting. She would say hello to them and give Corwin the hopeful news before she went downstairs to teach Curly, who was living and working in the mews out back now. She was always a bit uncomfortable when neither she nor Margaret were there to oversee him, however much progress he was making. At least she was not worried that Edmund might try to harm the boy or follow through with his other threats right now: the man Corwin had hired to investigate the rotter's whereabouts had discovered he was away on one of his lengthy business journeys to South America. Though it was not known when he would return, she thrust that worry from her mind for now.

She untied her bonnet before the mirror in the hall and patted her windblown curls into place as Margaret went upstairs to Janie at her lessons. And then, the voice of Corwin's companion, deep, low, resonant—not British—permeated her busy thoughts.

She froze, staring at herself in the mirror. Her mouth opened; her eyes widened. It couldn't be, but at last, it had to be! She had heard Morgan's voice so many times in her thoughts and dreams, but this—this had to be real. Tears blurred her view to make two Abigail's staring in the mirror, trembling uncontrollably.

She ran down the hall, ignoring the memory of the shock that had greeted her last time she knocked on someone's door. What if

Morgan were wed and had brought Charlotte here with him? A woman's voice would not carry as the men's did. What if he came only for her yarn and to say farewell forever? What if—

Corwin opened the door at her knock. "By Jove, I did not hear you return, my dear, or I'd have come to fetch you," he said. "Wait until you see who's here!"

But she was looking beyond Corwin. Morgan rose to his feet, not smiling, his eyes wide. He looked bronzed from the sun, so broad-shouldered and solid—so real, stepping at last from the fictions of her desires. And he had come alone.

"Abigail. You're looking as bonny as ever. I managed to get two months in London between hauls and so—"

"Oh, Morgan!"

No matter how properly things were done here, or how restrained she should be, she ran straight and hard into his arms.

Her eyes devoured only him at dinner. She had forgotten how tall he really was; how his big, strong hands could be so graceful; how trim he kept his mustache and beard; how deep brown his eyes were, like the cliffs of Conachair. She drank in everything he said, the way his mouth moved, the resonant tone of his voice and drawl to his words compared to the lilt of the Scots or quick clip of the British.

Because, he said, he and his partner feared a civil war in America could be triggered by any mishap at home, they had decided to keep warehouses not only in Bermuda and Liverpool but here in London as well. He had come to lease storage space; he would be sailing back and forth between southern U.S. ports and London to stock the warehouse, in case war began and there was a naval blockade.

"Even then," he told them, his eyes on Abigail, "I would try to run the blockade to be here and for more than just cotton."

She thrilled; she curled her toes so tight under the table that her leg muscles cramped. He had mentioned he had not married "in these tense times," though nothing specific about Charlotte; he had not said he would never wed her. But if he were here for "more than just cotton," Abigail dared to dream.

"You mean, besides your business, you're here for political reasons, I take it," Corwin put in.

Abigail's soaring hopes plummeted. Why didn't Corwin ask if Morgan were here to court her? After all, Corwin thought of himself as her guardian, even if she didn't. Political reasons? Of all things British, politics was not something Abigail heeded nor needed. All those debates in Parliament people spoke of and read about in the *Times* were as endless as the ones she'd heard about in Parliament at home—or the one meeting she had personally experienced. She believed in immediate, personal results like helping Curly, whom she had told Morgan about over dinner, or like the changes that must soon be made on St. Kilda when the eminent British doctors' letters arrived there. Now she realized that Morgan had encouraged her to talk more about her doings than he had spoken of his tonight. What were these political reasons Corwin mentioned? She felt doubly worried: perhaps Morgan was not in London to see her but had come calling to apprise Corwin of his plans. And here she had told Louisa that Morgan discussed heartfelt things with her!

She began to fret that she had been too forward to rush to his arms, to forgive him everything of their harsh parting. She had tended her love for him like one of the hothouse plants in the glass conservatory at Manchester House; it had grown wild, while he, although glad to see all of them, cultivated no such passions. Taking a cue from Louisa's warnings, she forced herself not to look at him with such a bold eye over the sweets course. Always be above the fray and in control, Louisa had said. When Margaret took Janie up to bed and Corwin finally left the two of them alone, for one moment she wanted to flee too. She tried not to feel nervous and hurt in his presence as they went into the drawing room, at last alone, together.

They sat in matching, facing upholstered velvet chairs before the low-burning fire in the grate, regarding each other intently, then looking away or suddenly down at their hands as if each would reveal something best unsaid. Abigail sat stiffly, feet together, despite the easy way he crossed his muscular legs.

"It was very kind of Corwin to insist I stay in the suite of rooms above the museum until I let a place here," Morgan said. "I am ready to sleep elsewhere than my cabin on the ship."

"He is always kind, still so grateful to us both."

"He is anxious to show me his displays tomorrow, especially the St. Kilda one you have made so popular as a living tableau."

"You will like his artifacts from Greece, of course. But since you've seen the real St. Kilda, perhaps you wilna enjoy the tableau."

"I think I shall, even if I become a part of the Queen of Kilda's living display."

She glanced at him, then toward the fire. Had she caught a taunting tone, shades of the argument when they parted? "Never, Captain West, will you be under glass like those dead things, aesthetically preserved as Corwin puts it."

"I must say I feel very much alive, Abigail, especially since I arrived in London this morning. I've been here several times before, but this time the place has a new aura."

"Does it then?" She dare not meet his eyes. "Because of your political needs you spoke of?"

"Yes, and another burning need too. I swear, despite this fire, is there a sudden chill in the room? London is always milder than St. Kilda, but I feel a distinct draft."

She studied him through her lashes as he took the brass poker, opened the grate, and stirred the coals. Her heart pounded so hard it reverberated through her. He referred to her caution with him, didn't he? He wasn't smiling; she wasn't sure. She suddenly was not sure of anything about him.

"As I said, Morgan, I am ever grateful to you too, just as Corwin is, but for your continued correspondence about the bairns."

He replaced the poker and straightened; his eyes glowed golden in reflected flame as the heat from the open grate poured out between them.

"And did you read between my tortured lines? Abigail, I am here as a suitor for your help."

A suitor, yes, but only for her help, she thought, and not her hand. Staring at him, she gripped the carved arms of her chair.

"The political need Corwin alluded to," he went on, "I had planned to explain to you as soon as possible. Although I have told my partner that I will give all I have to see our cotton business through the war—and, if worse comes to worse, I will be loyal to the South in battle—"

"Surely, it canna come to that!"

"I am afraid so. President Buchanan is too weak to stem the torrent of southern protest. I have told my partner that though I will be loyal to my father's heritage in the business and to my birthplace, the South, I will not be loyal to the damned institution of slavery. From here on out, I will only haul cotton already picked, cotton loaded by paid workers, not slaves. And I have told him I must stay here in London at least until the new year to make what political contacts I can to urge Her Majesty's government to remain neutral if war begins, despite the English need for cotton that may sway them toward the South's side. English neutrality will make what will no doubt be a quick war over even quicker, and though I have not said so to my friends at home, I believe English neutrality will mean a northern victory—and the end of slavery! If that turns out to be, my partner has agreed that Collins and West vessels will only carry cotton picked by paid, free workers."

She stared at him through that impassioned speech. "But you would throw in your lot with the losing side? And act here to keep your side from winning?"

"When have you ever feared to throw in your lot with the losing side for love or loyalty's sake, Abigail? Though my state of Maryland is geographically caught between the North and South, southern sympathy is rampant there—and I am southern born and bred. My mother and sister are southern in sympathies, and I shall not cause their distress and be alienated from them as I was my father. So my body shall be for the South for the cause of states' rights, but my heart and soul shall fight here in England for slaves who have no rights."

"But how can I help? I ken naught of English politics."

"Corwin says he knows quite a few influential people. I must make inroads with them to seek interviews with the top men—Lord Derby, I suppose, though I hear he may be replaced as Prime Minister by the man who was in previously, Viscount Palmerston, so I had best speak with them both."

"I see. Well, I do ken someone who has—influence with Lord Derby, no doubt other influential men too."

"Your duchess friend, you mean. Corwin told me. I would like to meet her, Abigail. Perhaps, together, we can convince her to help."

Oh, yes, Abigail thought. Louisa would love such a chance, mingling in the world of men, manipulating things her way—perhaps manipulating Morgan too. And what a challenge for Louisa even to get to Palmerston if her friend Lord Derby was going down and his liberal enemy was to lead the queen's government in the future. It would be fascinating to see Louisa do it—if Morgan were not involved. Abigail would be happy to help him too, but she had dared to dream he had come back to see her, perhaps to propose again, that he had missed her as much as she had him. Now she saw he had come only for his business and his cause. She, who was ruled by a cause herself, must accept and abet that as he had her struggle to save the bairns. And she did believe in helping to stamp out slavery, at any cost, any sacrifice.

"Abigail?"

"Of course, I will do anything I can to help you."

"Then stand up."

"What?"

"Stand up. Blue blazes, I am sick of all this political talk, this polite posturing between us when I only want to touch you. When you ran to hug me today in front of Corwin, I could hardly respond as I wanted, but now I shall dare."

When she hesitated, he reached down to pull her to her feet and directly into his arms. She went against him full length, petticoats and skirts crushed between them. He lifted her chin and lowered his mouth to cover hers. Did she open her mouth to protest or to gasp in surprise? It didn't matter: she responded wordlessly to kiss after searing, invading kiss, clinging to him, bent back and cradled in his iron embrace until they both gasped for breath.

"Well," he said and cleared his throat as he stood her shakily back on her feet, "I suppose—if you've learned a thing or two from your society friends here—you will now slap my face for that affront."

"I shall slap it only if you do not hold me again. Oh, Morgan, I feared you came back for the yarn, and then to see Corwin, or just to patch things over before you left for good, and now for politics and—"

"And a free meal and place to stay."

"Yes, blast you! Something like that."

"Abigail, you've always been so sure of things, and I'm the one who's wavered. But now we'll have some time to decide how it will be between us—besides this sort of thing, I mean."

He sat in the chair and tugged her onto his lap and began to kiss her again. His heavy hand cupped her knee right through her skirts, then slid up her thigh to skim her hip and grasp her waist. He nibbled kisses down her throat. She could have flowed sweetly into him, politics and causes and the whole gossiping, warring world aside. She loved this man. For whatever reasons he had really returned to her, she loved and wanted this man.

13

In the hothouse of my thoughts,
Weeds tangle with the flowers.
Thorns embrace the bonny blooms
Far too many hours.

I try to garden in the heat,
To cut back, pluck, and prune,
And take the sweetness threatened here
Far outside this room.

Morgan finally moved away from the cluster of men to whom he had been speaking about the need for English neutrality in the face of the possible probable American war. It was the first moment he had been alone this evening; his voice was hoarse from so much talking above the buzz of the crowd. He saw clearly now that the fact he was a private citizen acting alone was making his efforts suspect and difficult. The duchess had finagled a brief meeting with Lord Derby, but it looked as if Palmerston could sweep back in power and he had to get to him. He had no intention of giving up, any more than Abigail had given up when the entire leadership of St. Kilda had turned against her desperate efforts.

From his vantage point between two potted palms in the Manchester House salon, he watched Louisa and Abigail make their way toward him. For once, he mused, there were no men dancing attendance on the duchess, not even the ever-attentive Spencer

Hartington. Then it occurred to him that she had probably gone in search of the man, for he had disappeared a good hour ago and it was all too obvious she liked to keep him close. Having introduced Morgan to some key people, Louisa had declared she needed a moment alone and had snared Abigail to accompany her, though Morgan could tell Abigail had not wanted to leave him. His St. Kilda Calypso might not feel at home in the crush of these soirees, but she obviously did feel at home with him. Amidst it all, that thought made him want to soar.

"I am afraid, Captain," Louisa began, "it looks as if Viscount Palmerston's people aren't going to put in a showing as promised. That ogre Lord Devonshire seems to be twisting their arms to stay away from here."

"I appreciate your efforts in my behalf, Your Grace," he told her. "Bad timing since your ties are to his political rival Lord Derby."

"I tell you, there is a way and I shall find it. Anything for a friend of my dear Abigail, of course."

Morgan assured her of his faith in her, but today was November twentieth and after more than three weeks here, even with the duchess's help, he felt he was trying to swim through molasses to get to any of Palmerston's cohorts. If he hadn't seen Lord Derby, bought and begun to fill the Thames warehouse—and been courting Abigail—he would have felt a failure here so far.

" 'Tis hard to be continually rebuffed," Abigail put in. "I went through months of searching for a doctor to help before Louisa introduced me to John Snow."

"Indeed," Louisa muttered, twisting her bracelet around her wrist, "we needn't wonder at the Duke of Devonshire's motives in thwarting my approach to Palmerston! The man treats his heir Spencer like one of those slaves you are championing, Captain, not even able to choose his own friends! Speaking of Spencer, have you seen him?" She steadied herself on Morgan's arm to stand on tiptoe and scan the room.

"Not for a while, Your Grace."

"Indeed, I must mingle. You two take a stroll through the conservatory, why don't you?" she urged and smiled at Abigail without releasing his arm. "My dear, I know you still can't abide these gatherings, so the quiet in there with all the pretty plants will do you a world of good, as you've been looking a bit edgy lately, hasn't she, Captain?" And she was off into the crowd.

"That woman absolutely bowls me over," he told Abigail.

" 'Tis obvious enough."

"You said she did you too, from the first time you met," he said, feeling for some reason he must defend himself.

"I did. And now I know the woman quite well."

"The thing is, she's mad for Spencer Hartington, and she's gotten herself in trouble taking on his father's forces on my behalf, not to mention that her ties to Derby make Palmerston angry when she tries to get to him."

"I ken the Duchess of Manchester can take care of herself."

"She's right about you, Abigail. You're not enjoying yourself tonight, and I am going to see to it that you do. Come with me into the conservatory, as our hostess suggested."

"We dinna need to do everything she suggests."

"Ah, my sweetheart, you seem to have a rather large burr under your very attractive saddle tonight, which, gentleman that I am, I shall do my best to remove for you."

"Morgan West!" she remonstrated, but she smiled at him at last.

He, too, was on edge tonight, for he had come to a momentous decision. From that first day he met her, he had tried to battle the inevitability of Abigail Adair in his life, but she had stormed every barricade: he had tried to keep her away, to avoid being alone with her, to leave her, to forget her, and to wed another. In each of these forays, he had been defeated. So now he would try something else: he would surrender. If he could just get her off alone tonight, he would not wait a moment longer.

As they entered the large, glassed-in conservatory at the rear of Manchester House, moist warmth and rich-loam smells enveloped them. "Ah," he said as he took her arm above the top of her long glove to feel her silken skin there, "but for the stillness, it smells like the tropical isle of Sanibel, where I am going to take you someday. After the Seminole Wars ended in Florida, my father was able to use some shipping contacts to get special government permission to buy some land there, and someday I shall share all that beauty with you—an exotic world to make this place pale by comparison."

He steered her toward a wrought iron bench back in a leafy

grotto lit by lantern light. He had carefully examined this place on an earlier visit when the duchess had laughingly told him it was perfect for liaisons or propositions. For a moment they were both silent amidst the lush beauty of deep blue tree violets and a jungle of ferns. Abigail fluffed out her ice blue satin skirt; he crushed it back with his hip and leg to get as close as he dared. His heart was in his throat to stop his voice. Should he get right to it? Perhaps he must literally clear the thick air between them first.

"Something is bothering you tonight," he began, turning to her to take one gloved hand in both of his. "I thought, with the way things are going, you would be happy."

"I am, since the doctors' letters have been sent to St. Kilda. 'Tis just I feel I am a burden to you at this sort of affair, which you enjoy and I detest. But I ken you need to be accommodating and engaging here to further your goals, and I shall never criticize you for that."

"You are never a burden, but quite the opposite, however much, thank heavens, the Queen of Kilda mania now seems to have run its course. And you have made acquaintances at such gatherings who have given you donations to help send a doctor to St. Kilda and support him there." He himself, facing possible financial disaster if there was a war, had given her a large sum he could scarcely afford.

"Yes, but sometimes it doesna seem quite honest to cuddle up to folks with an ulterior motive. If they canna give from the heart when they hear of it, I canna see hanging all over them."

"Cuddle up and hang all over? You're angry with Louisa."

"I am just different from her, and I dinna mean only in background and goals. She doesna see a thing wrong with carrying on with Spencer while wed to the duke. 'Tis fine as long as she doesna get caught, she says. Yet I admit we have a great deal in common at times. And I am grateful to her. As for not feeling at ease in a place like this, 'tis just I dinna want to hold you back from mingling with these fancy nobs, as Curly would call them, when I am still more at home with him."

"I understand, but why can't we feel at home with all sorts of people? Curly and I, as different as we are, had a fine time that day I took him to the ship and the other days we've been out together."

"That he did! The lad adores you."

"Now, if only I can get such adoration from a certain lass I desire. Abigail, I hear it is the done thing here to make certain propositions, or should I say, proposals, to ladies in conservatories. I wish you and I had come to this point on St. Kilda with a stiff wind and wild cliffs and the smell of sea and heather, but this musky, still hothouse will have to do."

As if what he was intending had dawned on her for the first time, she stared at him, her golden eyes luminous with unshed tears, her moist lips slightly parted.

"Don't cry, please."

" 'Tis just that—so bonny as you put that—I ken I will ever be a St. Kilda lass and not a hothouse lady, and not perhaps, one that would be best for you. As for the done thing here—oh, Morgan, I just dinna want our different pasts and causes to pull us apart again!"

He made another decision then. He stood and raised her gently to her feet. He bent to kiss her, constrained, not sweeping her off those feet as he would have liked. "Come with me, my Abigail. We're leaving."

"Leaving?" she asked as he propelled her toward the door. "But what if Lord Palmerston's people should arrive after all, and you would not be here, and—"

"I've something much more important to do tonight and that's that!"

He hurried her through the corridor, not even going back into the salon to bid the duke and duchess goodnight. The duchess would have to understand, he thought. The way she fussed and pouted over that handsome devil Lord Hartington, she would surely understand a once rational man turning hopelessly passionate. Morgan sent for their coats, asked the footman at the door to fetch him a hack, and helped Abigail in when it pulled around.

"Are we going back to Corwin's?"

"I have the sudden urge that you should see the new Collins and West warehouse on the river." He shouted to the driver, "St. Katherine's Dock off East Smithfield," and they clattered off.

When they arrived, he paid the driver to wait and knocked for the night watchman to let them in. He had the surprised man light a second lantern he carried as he escorted Abigail through the vast wooden cavern of the building, stocked now only with the single cargo of bales he had brought with him. But he would make other voyages soon, as many as he could until war exploded—if he was certain each cargo was already stored and not newly picked by slaves. He no longer prayed that war would not erupt, only that it would bring a quick end to slavery. Fighting for the South and yet against it, he would survive as best he could, but war was war, and, as in ancient Greece and Rome, civil war was the worst.

Being such a realist about that had brought him to this decision tonight. After all, life was precious and short. And this woman who had possessed his heart and mind and soul since that first moment in Gleann Mor must be his, problems and perils be damned!

As he hurried her up the narrow board steps to the door in the roof, she drew back. "Morgan, wherever are—"

"Trust me. I want a lofty, windy place for this, for my St. Kilda lass. Trust me."

Her fingers curled tighter in his hand and her sure steps quickened to twist his heart.

It was even colder and windier on the warehouse roof than he had expected. "Oh, what a view!" she exclaimed, apparently reveling in the weather. Her skirts billowed, her bonnet clung by its ribbons, and tendrils of her upswept coiffure tumbled loose and whipped around her stunning, expectant face. "I havena been on a high place but the attic at the tallhouse for months!"

The moon skittered behind fast-flying clouds; he set the lantern at their feet. But it was neither of those reflected sources of light that made her eyes and smile beam when he gazed at her. His Abigail glowed from within.

"You see," he said, putting one arm around her waist and sweeping outward with the other, "here we are on our own Mount Conachair on St. Kilda tonight with the sea far below, and ships waiting on the shingle shore of Village Bay."

"And the cry of the gulls and those pigeons on the roof," Abigail added, "they are really fulmars and gannets. And those little buildings below are the cottages, and we could sail on those clouds above the sea to the distant isle of Harris or swim like a selkie spirit clear to . . . Oh, Morgan, with the way of things on St. Kilda, I never knew I could yearn for it so! 'Tis my home no more but I love it yet!"

When her voice broke, he tugged her closer. "And I love and

want you more, my lass, than I ever could have imagined when we were on St. Kilda. I knew I loved you that night I chased you up the side of Conachair and first kissed you. I wanted you in my life forever, but then—I was—afraid."

He was shaking now; he knew his voice was raspy. He turned her to him and fumbled in his inside frockcoat pocket for the tiny ring box. "Whether we live here or in America or on some far isle, Abigail, I would ask—entreat—you to be my wife. I am certain we can blend our lives and our loyalties. You could live in London when I go back and forth these next few years, as I plan to be here as much as home. That would give you time to continue to work with Dr. Snow and build a fund to send medical help there. Someday, we can even visit there if you think they'll allow you back. If and when the time comes that there is war, you would be safer here if Baltimore is sucked into the heart of it. Afterward, we would need to live in America, but that doesn't mean you couldn't sometimes go back and forth with me. And when we have a child—"

"I told you once, I dinna ken if I can, Morgan. Every man wants children."

"We will have a child, I know it! As long as I have been waiting to really love you, I swear to you we will have a child!"

"What lass could turn down a lad so determined?" she said, her voice a mere whisper. "What woman could say no to a man she has loved and desired for so long since she first saw him climbing out of that boat with the brides that had been brought in? Only I dinna ken that day that the same ship brought me a groom. 'Twas for me on that day, Morgan, as when my father saw my mother. Love at first sight, all hidden away in the dark places in my thoughts, oh, my love . . ."

He crushed her to him before he could even show her the betrothal ring in the satin slit in the velvet box. They clung together, melded in an endless kiss. She was his now. Whatever befell, she would always be his!

Abigail MacQueen Adair was determined to let nothing dim the glory of her wedding day, this Saturday, December 18, 1858. Not the fact that the night before she and Margaret had been up for hours nursing Janie through a cold and a dreadful cough, nor the fact that when Abigail finally slept, for the first time in over a year she dreamed of Lady Grange.

Nor, they vowed, would this special day be ruined by the terrible news Annie had written from St. Kilda. Parliament and the new minister had rejected Dr. Snow and Dr. Lister's letters, even though Dr. O'Neil's findings about the nine-day fits revealed that Irish babies had probably died from rancid butter being used as salve on their newly cut umbilical cords. It was proof to the doctors and Abigail too that the fulmar oil was at fault. But the attempt to educate and warn St. Kildans, according to Annie, was deemed "unlawful, unholy meddling by outlanders, including Abigail Adair," who was judged "justly, permanently exiled."

And, for the first time, Annie wrote, her grandmother Isobel had boxed her ears and called her evil, "corrupted by that Jezebel." Annie was forbidden to deliver so much as one more bairn if she continued to correspond with Abigail. So, Annie hoped Abigail understood why there must be no more letters. How Abigail grieved for her dear, loyal friend as well as the bairns now—and for the blinded, blighted folk at home who let their own innocent flesh and blood die so cruelly.

At least Dr. Snow had vowed he would go to St. Kilda himself next summer if Abigail would accompany him. Morgan planned to be here to escort them. Sadly, Dr. Snow and Dr. O'Neil had not made the wedding or celebration today, though they were invited and expected. But everyone understood how men who delivered babies could not rule their own lives even in this so-called civilized and scientific society.

And she and Morgan had decided that even continued refusals that he be allowed to meet with the powerful Palmerston's coterie not darken this day. Then, too, the weather had tried to get them down, for it dared to dawn gray with spitting snow. But nothing could deter them from their joy during the service in Corwin's church near the house. Morgan could not stop smiling, Janie jumped up and down, Margaret grinned, and Corwin beamed when he gave the radiant bride away.

The Duke and Duchess of Manchester hosted a wedding luncheon at their London house; the gathering was small and private at the bridal couple's request. None of Louisa's friends had been invited, for Abigail had wanted Curly to attend. But however hard

Abigail had worked with Curly, his excitement at seeing the wedding and the mansion made him rather unruly today. His colorful banter and teasing Janie at the table would probably have kept Morgan and Abigail from ever setting foot in the presence of polite society again had any but the Manchesters attended. The lively lad both amused and amazed Louisa; the duke, blessedly, sat at the far end of the table and did not hear too well.

Finally in the premature, snowy dusk, the bride and groom headed home to the small house they had let on Cheyne Walk in Chelsea. After a month's honeymoon, Margaret and Janie would be joining Abigail, and Morgan would be sailing to America for another load of cotton, whether or not his desperate political quest had been fulfilled in London. But today, perhaps just this one day, they were not letting any of that intrude.

"Everything was absolutely perfect," she told him, cuddled up to his bulky, bundled-up warmth in the cavernous Manchester carriage.

"You have not even begun to experience absolute perfection," he said, his voice so low and rough it sent shivers up her spine that had nothing to do with the weather. He leaned closer to kiss her. Despite the fact that she had been wed before and had now reached the lofty age of twenty-seven, she felt her cheeks flush in the chill carriage.

"But you said our second honeymoon on Sanibel will be warmer than this," she said with a provocative pout, then giggled like a lass.

He kissed her again, darting his tongue in her mouth, tasting, teasing. "You will not be cold once we get inside, I swear it on my life!"

They thanked the driver and hurried up the slick walk toward the lighted windows of their first home. Their staff had seemed enormous to Abigail, but Morgan had insisted: a lady's maid, a housemaid, a cook, a temporary valet; the valet, Jasper, and maid, Sarah, greeted them and helped them out of their snow-speckled coats. Sarah seemed as blushingly happy to see them wed as Abigail was. They soon dismissed both of them, saying they would need nothing until a late breakfast tomorrow. Hand in hand, they climbed the carpeted stairs from the front tiled hall to their second floor suite.

"I really should summon Sarah to unhook these tiny buttons," she whispered, as if someone stern were there to overhear.

"We will manage. We will manage everything together from now on!"

In their bedroom, he turned up the wick and sat before her in a chair to help her unhook the buttons of her sky blue velvet bodice. His hands were too big, unskilled at this, too hurried. Soon, she took over, using the button hook with more success, annoyed at how the soft bodice was so stiffened by the corset beneath that made it hard to look down. But she had only worn petticoats and not a crinoline today or Morgan would not have been able to get as close to her as he did, watching intently.

"Am I the only one undressing here?"

"I have waited so long for this. I have always found watching you fascinating, but now I find it—hypnotizing."

"Will you go into a sleepy state then, and I shall have to wake you up, Captain West?"

"Temptress, Mrs. West!" He reached up to help peel the gown from her shoulders. "Calypso, your Ulysses adores you!"

He kissed each smooth stretch of skin he uncovered as the gown whispered to a pool around her feet. She helped divest him of his frockcoat and waistcoat; he had the studs out of his cuffs and shirtfront in the flurry of hands and kisses. She almost tripped in the growing puddle of their clothing as she turned away to unhook the constricting corset while he unbuttoned his trousers and removed them, still sitting in the chair. Wearing only his underdrawers, he pulled her back to stand before him and skimmed off her chemise—and gasped.

"Look what that damned thing did to your soft flesh!" he muttered and turned her back toward the light, completely nude but for her stockings and garters. "You are perfection, but even with cloth between the corset and your skin, there are marks where those stays were here and here!"

"I canna abide them, but in England, I must."

"But not this month when we're here at home together. You are slender enough—perhaps I shall not let you wear them—or anything for me—ever again!"

She reveled in his touch and his possessiveness, even though he was joking. Yet she fought down rising rebellion in her at being mastered now, being taken over—and wanting to be so.

He began to caress, then to kiss the lines the stays had made along her rib cage. Her lungs filled now with more rapid breaths; she felt her pulse pound harder. His ministrations moved up to where the stays and wires had thrust the weight of her breasts up. And then he moved even higher to touch and taste.

"Oh, Morgan!"

"May I not kiss my wife anywhere?"

"Yes! In the carriage, in the parlor, in our bed."

"Tease me, tempt me, but know tonight you pay the full price of that, my sweetheart. No more waiting, putting off, doing what is right for others . . . and here, the marks your garters have made along your hips and thighs," he went on as he skimmed down her stockings, lingering on the satin flesh, lips following where fingers went. Then, just when she thought her legs would buckle at the wonder of his touch, he murmured, "Enough of this delicious torment and on to another!"

He stood, lifted her in his arms and strode to the bed to lay her down gently. He turned away just one more moment, then returned with the double-globed lamp to place it by the bed.

"I don't want the light in our eyes, my sweetheart, but I hope you will allow me to keep it here. I have long yearned to love you under the sun in broad daylight, so this will have to do for now. And I will try to keep things warm enough that we will not need those covers nor nightshirts and flannels and nightcaps that would be so proper—"

"Blast proper things!"

Everything began to blur by for her. She wasn't certain where his big body ended and hers began. Her heart beat tight against his, thudded like thunder as he moved closer to kneel between her thighs to make them one perfect whole at last.

But just before they joined, he lifted his touseled head. Passion stretched his features taut. He breathed hard. She thought he meant to ravish her lips again before he entered her, yet he froze as if listening. "Damn!" he muttered. "That rapping can't be at our door. Has our new staff gone mad?"

Abigail lay still to listen. The knocks were indeed at their door, tentative at first, now louder. Her head cleared just a wee bit. "Either so or something's wrong!"

With a groan, Morgan rolled off her, arose and threw the covers up over Abigail; he dragged the counterpane off the bed and wrapped it around his nakedness. He padded to the door.

"What is it?"

"So sorry, Captain, but the Duchess of Manchester waits below and says it's most urgent about seeing Lord Palmerston. And she has a letter for Mrs. West too."

Morgan shook his head, then slapped his palm to it. He seemed to waver a moment; his eyes met Abigail's as she sat up, clutching the bedclothes to her chin. "I can't believe it," he whispered. "Now? I suppose Louisa probably thought she caught us before . . ."

"Who kens what she thinks sometimes," Abigail said more bitterly than she intended, "but you must go down to see her."

"Must I? Must we do anything anyone wants of us today?"

"Captain?" came in shaky tones from outside the door. "Her ladyship's most determined."

"And so," Abigail whispered, her head in her hands, "are we determined for you to see Viscount Palmerston. My darling, I regret to say you must go down."

But in the moments it took her scrambling to help him redon his clothes and smooth his hair, she silently cursed Louisa, Duchess of Man, for her timing and her tenacity. With a groan and a quick kiss, he went down.

He was back upstairs in five minutes, his face lit by another passion besides that for his new wife. "You will not believe this! Palmerston will see me this evening at his home in Mayfair, but secretly."

"This evening? Now?"

"Louisa fears if we turn it down after all her going out on a limb for me, the precious opportunity will slip away. Perhaps when he hears I have come from my new bride on our wedding night, it will be impressed on him how important my message is."

She wanted to be happy for him; she *was* happy for him. The culmination of weeks of work on his part and Louisa's! And yet, she wanted to cry and scream and break things that he was obviously thrilled to be going—that he had not really given her any say in the matter. That he would go off with the Duchess of Man—oh, of course, she trusted Louisa with him, and yet she had seen how men who owed Louisa no such debt as this worshiped her. She was eternally beholden to Louisa, she loved and trusted this man; yet they had vowed nothing would intrude on their special day.

"Shall I dress and go with you, Morgan?"

"That would take too long," he said as he turned away. "Besides, I want you here, like that, waiting for me when I return." He pulled some papers from the bureau across the room. Although they had selected this furnished house together, he had been living here for two weeks: suddenly she felt a stranger in this place. She had no idea what those precious papers were.

He strode back and kissed her hard on the lips as she sat on the edge of the bed. "Oh, blue blazes, almost forgot," he said and pulled a letter from the inside pocket of his frockcoat. "This came for you from Dr. Snow to Manchester House just after we left today. Kind of Louisa to bring it right over with so much on her mind. I will be back as soon as I can, Palmerston and snow notwithstanding! And we shall begin exactly where we left off, my sweetheart."

And he was gone.

She sat there, stunned, listening to him pound down the stairs, the closing of the front door, the snow-muffled creak of the departing carriage they had not heard arrive. She sat there, yanked from the midst of beautiful dreams of a secure future. She was thrilled for this chance for him, she told herself. But why, *why* did his dedication, which she so greatly admired in him, have to pull them apart tonight of all nights? She gripped her hands tightly together; it was only then she saw that she held the letter. She opened it quickly, leaning closer to the lamp—meant to illumine their loving—to read it:

Dear Mrs. Adair, or Mrs. West now—

Dr. Snow has suffered a grievous stroke at home and appears to be greatly paralyzed. His speech is slurred, but I believe he is calling for you and is most agitated. I realize this is your wedding day, but I trust you will come as soon as you can.

In haste,
Patrick O'Neil

"Sarah!" Abigail ran into the dim hall, wrapping the voluminous skirts of her discarded wedding gown around her like a huge cape. "Sarah, rouse the captain's valet and send him out for a hack, then come up to help me dress! I've a predicament too!"

She must not blame Morgan, she scolded herself, for what happened tonight. She had people and a cause that demanded her immediate care. What would she have done if this summons had come and not his? Yet, how could this be, this separation on their wedding night? As she scribbled him a note, she prayed it was not a harbinger for their future.

Within a quarter hour of when Morgan departed his marriage bed, she was being driven through the snow-shrouded streets of London.

Dr. Snow's living chambers above his office were full of somberly garbed, whispering doctors shepherded here and there by his younger, obviously distressed associate, Dr. Patrick O'Neil.

"Step aside, if you will, gentlemen. This is the lady he has been calling for."

She heard buzzing behind her as Dr. O'Neil took her into the sick room. "Didn't know he had a young relative. Niece? Former patient? I say, but wait 'til Her Majesty is informed the old boy's dying . . ."

Dear Dr. Snow looked waxen, lying unmoving on stark white sheets, his eyes closed, his mouth drooped. Her grandfather's face flashed before her and his voice rasped from the depths of memory: "I thought ye would be settled wed to Douglas, but ye truly werena. Then when ye had the child—well. I didna want ye to be hurt more than ye have been . . . so grown up ye are with the pain in yer eyes now . . ."

"Dr. Snow," Patrick O'Neil began, "Abigail Adair—I mean, West—is here."

Yes, she still felt like Abigail Adair, not Abigail West, she thought.

"G-gail . . . Ab . . . Ab," the old man managed.

"That's all he says," Dr. O'Neil whispered, bending over him to cover the thin hand with his. "But just yesterday he was saying again that the letter you received from St. Kilda was barbaric in its cruelty to the infants and to you, and that he would go there with you. But now—now, I think he means to say he can't and he's so sorry the bairns will go on dying."

"They wilna," she said, amazed her voice came out so strong. She leaned down close to the stricken man to be sure he heard her. "I will yet find a way, dear Dr. Snow, to help the bairns of St. Kilda, that I shall. But you must rest and get well now. Dinna you fret for a thing, for you have done so much for me as well as all those mothers in pain and their bairns you saved on your own island all these years."

That seemed to calm him; he slept at once. Dr. O'Neil took her out. In the parlor downstairs, he still clasped her hand as if to say farewell, but clung to it.

" 'Tis so difficult for you to have him like this," she said.

"They say he will never recover." He shook his head as if he could not believe it. "I shall try to carry on his work, of course, but I am not worthy even to open the doors through which he walks— walked." He loosed her hands and turned away to gain control of himself, wiping his spectacles on his handkerchief. "I can't thank you enough for coming on your wedding night," he said at last, turning back to her. "What must your husband think?"

"My husband will understand."

That was all she said aloud. But she added to herself, he *must* understand, for he is out seeing important people too. But how frightened she was then, not only that Dr. Snow might die, but that she and Morgan would always have things pulling them apart, even when they needed each other the most. And that she had wed a powerful man for the second time, one who could leave a marriage bed and a wife in England, even if for his own—as well as her— compelling reasons.

When she climbed from the hack before their house, Morgan yanked open the front door and ran out without a coat, nearly skidding on the walk.

"How is Dr. Snow?"

"Paralyzed with a stroke. 'Tis fatal, they say."

"I am so sorry, but you should not have gone out at night alone in this snow!"

"I didna have a duchess and a four-in-hand to take me."

"I would have come after you, but your note didn't say where you went!"

He looked more than worried, even angry, as if she should not have gone out when he did the very same.

"And your news?" she asked.

"Better than that, thank God." He paid the driver and hurried her up the walk. "Palmerston said he believes it will be in England's best national interests to remain neutral if there is an American civil war. Peace yoked with building up defenses will be cornerstones of his Liberal party's policies if he gets back in office as he hopes and plans! But we are not to broadcast that I've seen him, and we will talk again later, when I bring him more information—oh, sweetheart, I didn't mean to rattle on with all this after—after the day you've had."

"The day we've *both* had," she told him as he led her into the parlor where steaming cups of fragrant coffee awaited them on the tea table. The staff was nowhere in sight; Morgan helped her take her coat off.

"It's getting so late, Morgan. That coffee will keep us awake."

"Something else will too," he said, but she did not respond to his forced, light tone.

"Morgan, I canna believe that on our wedding night, the most sacred of times we should share, you were out doing your duty with the duchess and I was comforting poor Dr. Snow. If it is true on our wedding night that we cannot find time to be man and wife without the needs of others—"

"You have always wanted to help others," he countered, taking her hands in his. "Other people's bairns, orphaned fulmar eggs, Curly, even the poor, misguided St. Kildans. And, I hope and pray, an American sea captain whom you have taught to love and not to be afraid to take risks by reaching out."

He reached for her and lifted her into his arms, a lovely, lofty perch. The coffee went untouched as he carried her upstairs, as he repeated his earlier ministrations of undressing her.

"There will be no other interference or intrusion tonight, Abigail, not even our own thoughts of people or things we are fretting over or what we must do—individually and together. All that will come later, Abigail West, much later," his voice crooned as if to mesmerize her. "Right now, you will think only of the man you love, the man you wed today, and the love and pleasure he gives you. Say it."

"I will think only of you, love only you," she murmured as he laid her down again on their soft bed and lay, as naked as she, beside her.

"And the love and pleasure he gives you," he repeated, caressing, stroking her skin.

"And the love and pleasure he gives me."

"And the child he intends to give you."

"Oh, Morgan, if it could only be true!"

"We shall make it come true, you see, beginning like this . . ."

And for all that long, dark, snowy night there was room in her body, head, and heart for no one but her beloved husband and the love and pleasure he gave her.

14

Torn in two, my other self at sea
With my captain, commanded I shall be.
The close self tempest-tossed,
Commanded just by me.

A woman's scream, very close, jolted Abigail awake. She reached out for Morgan, then remembered he was gone. Slowly, reality flooded back: two days ago had been their sixth parting, but it never became easier. Now, she realized the scream had been her own.

She heard fast footsteps in the hall. Margaret hurried in, lamp in hand, nightgown billowing, feet bare. When Morgan was away, she and Margaret almost always left their doors across the hall ajar at night. Abigail just hoped she had not awakened Janie.

"What is it, lass?" Margaret whispered.

"Sorry. A silly dream," she admitted sheepishly.

"Not the one of Lady Grange?" Margaret asked. She left the lamp on the table inside the door, then hurried over to perch on the edge of the bed. Outside, the February wind howled its British best, though it was nothing next to a St. Kilda blow.

Abigail moved over to make room for her friend. "No," she

told Margaret, "I havena dreamed of poor Lady Grange for a good while. But I see I've churned these sheets to waves."

"Like the sea yer man's sailing on. 'Tis easy to understand why ye would fret, 'til ye receive the first letter from him."

Abigail nodded as Margaret climbed in on Morgan's side of the bed. The two of them need say no more, for their common memories included those of dear ones lost at sea. "The dream," Abigail said slowly, as it came back to her, "began with two women trying to pull Morgan apart." She shuddered and hugged herself. "One woman had one arm, the other—"

"Aye, as ye said, 'tis a silly dream."

"But then, when I tried to defend him, they turned on me like two furies, yanking at my arms, pulling me nearly asunder, while I screamed for them to stop."

Margaret patted her hand. "Ye're torn over him going back and forth without ye, but 'twill soon be past. This summer, after St. Kilda, ye two lovebirds will be so happy in Baltimore—oh, Abigail, Janie and I shall miss ye terrible when we part!"

"And I you! Wilna you reconsider coming with us? We're a family now, all of us together. I canna believe we've been away for nearly three years from St. Kilda when we told your family that you and Janie, at least, would be back sooner—something else for your mother to hold against me."

They sat silent over that, for there was nothing good to say. In the two years and two months Abigail had been Mrs. Morgan West, everything they had heard from St. Kilda was bad. The new minister and the forces of Isobel MacCrimmon held sway: traditions ruled, and the Reverend Mr. MacKay evidently added some of his own. Bairns still died, though Annie could no longer write to say so. Corwin had found it out through acquaintances he called "channels," whom Abigail had learned included the new MacLeod laird—the man her mother had loved years ago. Perhaps he felt a wee bit of guilt about seducing and deserting her and so told Corwin's friends what they asked of St. Kilda; perhaps the new laird felt only resentment as his father had and passed on the bad news eagerly, knowing how it would hurt the daughter of Glenna MacLeod MacQueen.

"Abigail, dinna ye think that's what the nightmare meant, just being torn in two over separations?" Margaret's quiet voice tugged at her frenzied thoughts.

"Oh, no doubt," she said, but somehow she knew that was not quite all of it.

Margaret soon headed back to her room, leaving the lamp. Still feeling unsettled, Abigail decided to get up to write a hearthsong. She had kept them in a sort of diary all this time in England; she thought of them more as musings, not songs here, for she had set to melody only the one about city birds for Janie's lovely voice. Now the thought of Janie returning to St. Kilda, perhaps to become the next woman hearthsinger, did not fill her with joy and pride as it had at first. The place was sullied in her heart even more with these latest tidings. She longed for the bedrock beauty of the isle itself, but while the bairns still died, while folk shut out their cure— and her—she thought of that place as dirtied with a fearful fog. Yet she knew now England was cloaked in different, but dark clouds too.

She shoved her feet into warm slippers decorated with Kilda Work. It had not yet become passé as had the rage for the Queen of Kilda herself—and bent back to straighten the bedsheets. And then she saw the telltale sign of her erratic and unwanted menstrual blood. Her maid Sarah always referred to it as the curse, and, for her and Morgan, that it was.

"Blast it!"

She leaned over the bed on stiff arms, trying to dull the stab of keen disappointment. How she had dared to hope for a child after all of her and Morgan's fervent loving the months he was here! This time the flux had been later than usual. They had spoken of the possibility of a pregnancy when he had sailed; he had been so excited. Before he arrived last time, she had been examined by Dr. O'Neil to see if there was some reason she could not conceive. She told him of giving birth years ago; she explained her fall upon the cliffs and how irregular her menses had been.

"There is a bit of scar tissue near the neck of the womb, but it's not blocking it," he had told her when she faced him across the desk in the deceased Dr. Snow's office. Dr. O'Neil had been advising her now about sending help to the bairns. He cared deeply, but did not have the influence nor experience to interest other physicians in her cause as Dr. Snow had done. "As for your irregular menses," he had explained to her, "the best medical wisdom cannot say what if any part they have in conception, other than their cessation being a sign of pregnancy. Menses are caused by the pull of the moon, though, and like some unusual tides, yours are a bit off. Still, I see no reason why you and Captain West should not have a child. Sometimes, even modern medical science has no reason to give," he had admitted and shrugged as helplessly as he had when their continued efforts to convince doctors to visit St. Kilda had gone for naught.

Yet his diagnosis had given her such hope. Until now.

"Blast!" she cracked out again.

She did not summon Sarah, though Louisa had lectured her about using the girl more and not "doing for yourself if you have a glimmer of keeping that skeletal staff of yours in line." She wrung out a flannel square from the basin and scrubbed at the stain, threw a towel over it, then tended to herself by donning pantaloons under her nightgown and pinning folded flannel to them.

Determined not to cry, she took her diary from her desk. In the bottom of the drawer, she glimpsed the newspaper drawing that had been a nightmare in itself.

She picked up the piece of newsprint with two fingers as if it would burn her. She studied the elaborate, flattering drawing of her head, bedecked in a bonnet with long, gracefully arched, fringed feathers from some exotic bird she could not name. The drawing had not been done from life, but the likeness was quite good, unlike in earlier papers. Perhaps *he* had told the artist each detail.

"The Queen of Kilda Adores Drummond Imported Feathers" the headline read. " 'Feather Fashions Are All the Rage Whether on St. Kilda, in Paris, New York, or London,' Says the Heroine of the North."

"Bastard!" she spit out and stuffed the picture in the drawer. Then, seeing she had folded it so that it read "The Queen of Kilda Adores Drummond," she tore the page in two and dropped in it her rubbish basket.

The drawing had appeared last year in Edinburgh, Glasgow, Liverpool, Bath, and York papers, but not London as far as Corwin's solicitors had been able to ascertain. Corwin had counseled her and Morgan that the best way to stop such exploitation and—in this case—harrassment was to summon the blackguard to a meeting in Corwin's solicitors' office and present him with a lawsuit. He must never again use her likeness and reputation to promote something without her approval. Corwin's lawyers had tracked down the Lincoln's Inn solicitor who represented Edmund, but his client, he claimed, was abroad and would not be back for months. And so, justice for this outrage had been held in abeyance until Edmund's uncertain return. Anyway, if it took much longer, she thought, she would be living in America.

Angry now, as well as sad, Abigail got back in bed on Morgan's side and tugged the covers up to her chin. She curled into a warm ball. Why did it always seem that everything crashed in on her when Morgan left? Louisa had been impossible today, fussing and fuming, since she was certain Spencer had the wayward eye for someone else—perhaps someone younger, someone prettier, or horror of horrors, someone unmarried.

"For all I know, Harty-Tarty could have a woman in every port!" Louisa had exploded. "Oh, sorry, dear Abigail. Indeed, I didn't mean to put it quite that way, with Morgan being a sea captain gone so much and all."

It hurt Abigail to see again that the golden goddess had feet of clay, and all for a man. Yet, Abigail agonized, who was she to talk? She adored Morgan; she had promised to leave all her concerns to move across the sea. At least Curly was maturing and learning; he would be able find a good trade to keep him off the streets. She felt so torn to leave him and Corwin here—to leave her work yet torn without Morgan, just as he had been torn to leave his family and those he loved—

Her limbs jerked; her body went rigid. Perhaps that was it, the meaning of the dream tonight! The two women pulling at Morgan: he had admitted he had "run into" Charlotte at his partner's house when he was home; he said she had not married. Abigail had tried to forget the comment, but it had evidently preyed on her mind. The two women pulling at him could be her and Charlotte. Could Charlotte still hold a certain allure of daintiness, even helplessness, for him that Abigail could never offer? Probably anything Morgan said would be fine with Charlotte; he would need to make no compromises, share no large decisions. Charlotte would have wed him at once, not turned him down the first time, nor would she have had what amounted to a consuming cause of her own. Charlotte

had so much in common with Morgan: she was American, probably adept in social skills, no doubt able to have a child. And if the
woman had not wed, was she still carrying a torch, as they said, for
Morgan, and he of course felt regretful and protective and
responded—

No! Such thoughts were unworthy of her and of Morgan. She
trusted him, they were very happy together, and she had agreed to
go to Baltimore to live. There were no two women pulling at him!

Perhaps the two women—even the two women of her earlier
nightmares—were aspects of Abigail herself, pulled this way and
that between controlling her own destiny and letting a strong man
take over. Between commanding herself to love only enough or letting oneself love so desperately that the man held sway no matter
what. Maybe she was both women with Morgan, both parts of that
dilemma, tearing at herself.

To be whole, must she decide to be one way or the other, to
sacrifice her independent self or her surrendered self? She had once
admired Louisa's control of her life, but now she, too, was tottering
on the jagged rocks of her passion for Spencer Hartington. And she,
Abigail Adair West, was perhaps fighting so hard to keep both her
powerful man and the powerful part of herself that she was unable
to conceive his child!

"Nonsense!" she whispered deep in the sheets. "Too much
thinking has always been your problem, lass, so let it be."

She tried to comfort herself, to lull herself to sleep. But the
thoughts would not let her go, so she got up to write in her diary
a verse of just four lines about feeling torn in two. That helped
some, but back in the lonely bed again, night stretched on and on.

April 26, 1861, blossomed a beautiful day in London, though it
was, Abigail recalled, exactly nine years ago today she had lost
Douglas and Margaret had lost her Neil. Since then, how far they
had come in many ways. She was sad her dear friend had no one
but a daughter to hold dear. Yet, Abigail thought, tying the ribbons
of her featherless bonnet, she herself might have a husband, but he
was not here and she had no child to love.

Since Abigail never allowed this sad anniversary to be quiet
with too much time to think of the old days on St. Kilda, she and

Curly were going for a walk. With Curly at her side, surely this day would be anything but quiet!

"Off we are, then!" the boy said with a jaunty doff of his cap. When he smiled at her like that, her heart always swelled with special love for him. Even the shine of education and a softening of his harsh world had not muted the boisterous boy within, and she was grateful. She only prayed that without her to keep an eye on him after this summer, the twelve-year-old would continue on the right path in life. She had thought to ask Morgan to take the lad for his cabin boy, but she could not imagine Curly Natter ever being hemmed in by the confines of a ship.

"Off we are indeed, my lad!" she replied and mussed his blond curls before he could get his cap back on.

But as Sarah draped a shawl around Abigail's shoulders and opened the door for them, the massive Manchester carriage rolled up in front, unannounced. Louisa spilled out in a gush of skirts before her footman could even leap down to assist her. She swept up the walk at them, looking neither right nor left, her face a storm cloud ready to burst. She darted into the house and turned into the parlor where she slammed the door.

"Her Grace don't look real happy," Curly announced.

"*Doesn't* look real happy," Abigail said, and left Sarah and Curly on the step to go in to Louisa.

She opened the parlor door slowly and peeked around it. She had never seen Louisa in such a state. "Am I to stay out of my own parlor?" she asked quietly.

"Hardly! Come in and close that door! I just didn't want to make a scene before the servants."

Abigail perched on the settee beside the distraught woman, who stared down at her hands clenched in her lap.

"Is it something I have done, my friend?"

"It's him. *Him!*"

"Spencer?"

"Of course, Spencer!" She sprang up to pace in a rock and swirl of satin skirt. "I've known for months he had the wandering eye. Since the woman he loves is wed and he can hardly have her publicly, his pride is wounded, I suppose, so who can blame him?"

"But you blame him."

"Indeed I do! I saw the scoundrel out riding with her on Rotten Row this morning, as did most of our friends. Did he think I wouldn't see him, discover his deception? There he was with her—a common, low woman, however fancily she tarts herself up. Skittles, I hear they call her. Skittles. No title, never been presented at court—Skittles, you know." Louisa was so furious she was stuttering. "Skittles—that bowling game where men roll balls at pins for wagers. Bending over to reset the pins to show off her breasts and bum, I hear that's how she started on her—her demimonde career!"

Abigail did not know what a demimonde career was, but she took the gist of it and knew better than to ask. "Did you confront them?" she asked.

"In public? What a wretched thought. I can't face him—any of my friends—but you."

Perhaps, Abigail thought, because she herself was a common, low woman with no title and no presentation at court. Suddenly, as much as she wanted to comfort Louisa, she was angry with her. She had a good notion to remind Louisa that she herself had often shown off her breasts to Spencer with her daringly low-cut gowns. The first day Abigail met her, she was teasing Spencer about falling and showing her "scarlet knickerbockers"—an event that probably flaunted her bum, so how dare she deride this Skittles for the same?

But Abigail was even more upset with Louisa for her weakness over a man, and one who was not hers anyway. Abigail had always thought of Louisa as proof that a woman could rule men. It was if she were one of those Greek goddesses flying high above it all at Kimbolton Castle. Abigail now saw that men really could rule her, at least one did. Louisa's pride, her control of her life, was now as ravished as had been her heart. It frightened Abigail to think that what she desired most in life might not be in her control either after all these years of fighting for the bairns against St. Kilda men—and women—who wanted nothing to do with her or her ideas.

"I knew you would understand," Louisa went on, pulling a handkerchief from the voluminous sleeve of her pelisse to dab at her eyes. "I can't let anyone else—including the villain himself, of course—know I am dismayed one whit."

"The Duchess of Manchester's credo: just do not get caught and always stay in control and above the common fray," Abigail said, her voice more bitter than she had intended. She could hear dear Curly outside, chattering away to Sarah. Louisa, of course, thought they were common and low too. Louisa had been kind to Abigail, but the wrongs she had done she was now suffering for. Abigail wanted to help her for that, but right now she felt so disappointed in Louisa—and perhaps with herself for not returning to do battle in St. Kilda yet.

"I dinna think I really do understand you," Abigail insisted. "However terrible divorce is, surely the lie you've been living is no better. Perhaps Spencer has felt so desperate he could not have you to wife that he decided to make you jealous to see if it would teach you a thing or two."

"Teach me? Such as what? To give him up *or* seek a divorce? If so, he has not succeeded! Is he mad? Does he think I could divorce the duke? It takes publicly printed charges of adultery that simply everyone would devour. It takes paying through the nose to get a divorce. Just who does he think he is?"

"He thinks he is the man you love *and* is heir to a powerful dukedom which must have at least the air of respectability and propriety about it. I take it this Skittles is not someone he could consider wedding, and it will anger his parents more than when he pursued you, so that by comparison they might look more favorably upon—"

"Fiddlesticks!" Louisa said and sank into a puff of skirts beside Abigail. "Of course, he'd never consider wedding that trollop! But," she said more quietly, "stranger things have happened, with well-connected, well-educated, monied men marrying down."

Abigail stared hard at Louisa's profile, but once again, she seemed to intend no insult, however callous her concern for Abigail's feelings. No, Louisa was so lost in her own problems she had not heard Abigail's subtle scolding and she was hardly thinking of another's marriage, perhaps unequal in the world's eyes. As ever, sadly, Louisa, Duchess of Manchester, was thinking only of herself. And so, the last flare of once golden admiration for her flickered out in Abigail, however kind Louisa had been at first when Abigail amused her. She must now leave Louisa to her own devices and reckonings, for Curly, who really needed and would heed her, awaited outside.

"Let me at least ride back home with you to make certain you are all right," Abigail said. "You'd best rest those reddish eyes and repowder your nose, if you insist on keeping your real feelings from others, including the duke and Spencer." Subdued, apparently in control now, Louisa let herself be led outside.

"May Curly ride the splash board with your footman?" Abigail asked, feeling this might be the lad's last opportunity for riding on a fancy, ducal carriage. "He's always wanted to," she added when Louisa frowned at her again.

"I suppose," she replied, her voice perfectly measured now. "Just this once, as it really isn't done—any more than are divorces if one wants to keep one's proper place," she whispered pointedly to Abigail.

When Curly heard he could ride in back, he vaulted up beside the blue and gold liveried man with a wild whoop. Louisa did not blink an eye. With not another mention of her catastrophe, she chatted to Abigail about her next soiree and how her accident-prone husband's sprained ankle was mending. Abigail squeezed her hand when they parted, as Louisa had hers so many times to encourage her. But she was glad not to go in, relieved when she and Curly were out on the street again.

"You know, my chum," she told the lad as they stopped to buy a curds and whey and ginger beer from a stand, "you and I have been walking these streets for over two years now."

"You been teaching me a lot and I been teaching you. And I was wondering if you mightn't take me with you when you go to St. Kilda and America. Like to see both, could cart your trunks or anything you and the captain want."

She was touched to the core. How much she wanted that, but she would never forgive herself if something happened to him during a war in America.

"If the captain goes off to fight, like he says," the boy plunged on, "you'd need someone to take care of you. Curly Natter could do a dev'lish good job of that."

Abigail nodded, but she could just picture what Morgan's mother and sister's family would think of her "adopting" Curly Natter. She would discuss it again with Morgan. When one was wed, great decisions must be mostly the man's, mustn't they? Sometimes she thought not, but—

"Maybe there's a war already," Curly said.

"What?"

"Those shrills hawking papers to the nobs over there—hear what they're saying?"

She stared where Curly pointed. Two lads sold the *Times* on the opposite corner. In a lull in the passing traffic she, too, heard that dreadful word "War!" as they hurried across the street.

" 'American civil war tears former colonies asunder!' " one boy screeched. " 'Southern Confederates take Union Fort Sumter! President Lincoln proclaims Union shipping blockade!' "

"See?" Curly's voice pierced her shock. "Would the captain be fighting or be blockaded already?"

"I—I dinna ken." She bought a paper, skimming it as they began to walk again, now back toward Chelsea. She had to be there in the place she had shared with Morgan. She had to tell Margaret. She had to be there if Morgan wrote, if he came, though he was not expected until next month, but now . . .

She hurried them on so quickly she soon had a stitch in her ribs. It didn't matter; she suddenly hurt everywhere inside. Worrying about Morgan at sea in peacetime had been bad enough. And late this summer, after a visit to St. Kilda, they would have been back in America together. Her thoughts in turmoil, she said nothing, heard nothing, but let the boy lead her. They cut through Ranelagh Gardens toward the house. She still read the paper: pro-Confederate Baltimore had riots when the new President Lincoln passed through en route to the Union capital of Washington.

She looked up, staring straight ahead as they prepared to cross the street. Children under the watchful eyes of their nannies rolled a hoop and flew a kite, as if there were no war in America, no bairns dying on St. Kilda. If Morgan could not come with her, she must somehow get to St. Kilda anyway. She must help the bairns; she had vowed it to herself; she had promised poor Dr. Snow as he lay dying.

"Eh," Curly's voice jolted her, "there's that bad bloke again." The lad touched her elbow; she turned to follow his narrowed gaze.

Just off to the side, in the corner of the square nearest the house, stood Edmund Drummond, under a tree, all in black, his tall-crowned top hat in hand as if he had been politely waiting to greet her. Two other men sat on a stone bench nearby, reading newspapers as Edmund strode quickly closer.

"Ye're looking a wee bit peaked, Abigail," he began. "Ye've

read the paper, I see. Indeed, I sympathize with the sad plight of yer husband's shipping firm. The bloody war will hurt my import business too."

It frightened her that he knew all about Morgan, but she did not quail. "I hope your solicitor informed you of your legal summons, Edmund. Until then, I have nothing to say to you."

"Then listen well to me, woman!" He seized her arm; she yanked free.

"Don't touch her, you slimy toad!" Curly cried.

Edmund ignored him, though he gripped his gold-headed walking stick between his hands as if to warn the lad off. Abigail put a restraining hand on Curly's shoulder. "Say your piece, Edmund, then get out of our way."

"My piece, Abigail Adair West, is that I only permitted ye to live away from me because ye dinna wed anyone else, after all the times I have asked for yer hand. But now, ye've changed all the rules."

She propelled Curly around the man and tried to hurry on, but Edmund pulled her back.

"Ye owe me, ye seducing slut!"

"No, you owe me, you wretch, for using my likeness without permission, for getting in my way—like this—all my life! Get out of—"

"Ye're mine, Abigail, and always have been! This American War will be the death of that bastard ye wed anyway, or I'd be like to make ye a widow again! But even before that, ye're mine and—"

"Get out of my way, I said!" she screamed. She hoped everyone in the gardens would come running.

Curly ducked low at Edmund to butt him like a ram. Edmund swung his stick. It cracked over the boy's head and he crumpled to the path, then tried to rise groggily. Edmund kicked at him; Abigail leapt to the lad's defense, screaming, pounding her fists on Edmund's back, grabbing for the stick he used again on the helpless lad. Suddenly, there were two other men in the fray helping Edmund, one pinning her arms behind her.

"Shall we drag the baggage off, sir?" he asked as she thrashed and kicked.

She heard other protesting screams, other footsteps. "Not now," Edmund said. "The bitch kens there will be another day of reckoning when she will be mine or no one's! And, Abigail, I'll kill the lad next time I so much as see him near ye!"

Hands released her. She threw herself over Curly's prone form. Skirts and feet surrounded her. She cradled the lad's bleeding head.

"It's her son," someone whispered.

"Fetch the peelers," someone said.

"Curly! Curly!"

The lad's eyes flickered open. "A reg'lar turk, that one. Is the blighter gone?"

"Yes. 'Tis you I have to thank for that!"

"Laws, swear there's a war here too," he said. "Oh, me—my jaw!"

She helped him sit up, her arm around his shoulders. However much of a man he fancied himself, she could not keep from hugging him as if he were a mere bairn. And, until she got Morgan back safe and sound, she thought as she dabbed at his battered face with her handkerchief, taking care of Curly would have to do.

Morgan's long-awaited letter reached Abigail on July thirtieth, though it was dated June twelfth. When hostilities began, he wrote, he had reported for duty to Wilmington, North Carolina, and was now the captain of a "runner," an iron-hulled, side wheeler he had dubbed *The Kilda*. It had low sails and stacks to hide along the misty shoreline from "cruisers." He would be sailing sometime soon, not for Bermuda as now, but through the tightening blockade clear to London, exporting cotton from his own warehouse, importing supplies—and visiting her.

Although his time in London would be short, he wrote, she should be ready to depart on a moment's notice for St. Kilda, "for the killing must be stopped there as well as here." They would take the railway to Glasgow and hire a yacht to the isle. Then, as soon as possible, they must head back to London from whence, without her, he would return to duties in the Confederacy. Now that war had begun, he would not risk taking her through the blockade to Baltimore, though he was yet considering swinging south with her to Bermuda. If she was willing, he would send her on from there with hired guards to Cuba and then to Sanibel to await his leaves or the end of the war, which he was certain would come quickly, surely before hostilities reached that far south. He had meant to surprise her about Sanibel later, but he must tell her now: to his father's land he had inherited there, he had sent men with building materials with orders for a house—a honeymoon and holiday house—to be built for them.

Also, when he was in London, he meant to briefly renew his political contacts to urge continued English neutrality and public sentiment against slavery. He was gratified to hear that Queen Victoria, under the guidance of Prime Minister Palmerston and the advice of her own Prince Albert, had issued a Proclamation of Neutrality. Still he feared English shipbuilders and cotton investors eager for quick, escalating profits would ignore the official government stand.

"And my darling wife," the lengthy letter had concluded, "however hurried I am, my thoughts are always with you. I cherish our past days on St. Kilda and in London; I plan our years ahead in London, Baltimore, and on Sanibel. On the decks of my silver ship, slipping out amid the shoals with the rising tide on a moonless night for a run, I see you just ahead of me, windblown, barefooted, luring me on—my life's figurehead guiding my vessel onward to peace, to love for us, for all. My Calpso and now my Penelope, I remain eternally your loving husband, your Ulysses, Morgan."

That next-to-last, long sentence of the letter, she thought, made the most beautiful verse she had ever heard. It would be her hearthsong linking her heart wings to his until his return.

There were two other letters, sending his love and promising his arrival, but Morgan did not arrive, even as winter did. Abigail worried, but she knew deep inside he was all right. Everyone said the transatlantic mails were slow and unsteady now. The papers declared the blockade was tightening in those first seven months of the war. Morgan was simply busy and perhaps temporarily trapped in Wilmington or Baltimore or Bermuda because of the dangers of the blockade, that was all. He would be here soon. He was well, she was certain, because she could picture him strong and sure on the deck of *The Kilda,* heading outward on the rising tide.

She was glad she had not written him of Edmund's assault on her and Curly last summer. It would have distracted him from his tasks, and she wanted his full concentration on his duty to keep him safe. Besides, Corwin had discovered that Edmund had left England again and would not return until summer, so surely by that time Morgan would have come for her and she—and Curly—would be gone. She had nursed Curly through his broken jaw, an agony for a boy who loved to chatter. Morgan would have to accept that Curly must go with them to St. Kilda and beyond. Edmund had vowed to kill him next time they met. And the lad was part of her life and family now, even as Morgan was. She would soon be losing Margaret and Janie for who knew how many years; she could not lose Curly too.

She tried to cheer others not so fortunate as she. Louisa was always glum these days as Spencer's father had insisted he leave the country until he—and his friends—forgot or forgave his "unfortunate mistake," as Louisa always referred to his blazing affair with Skittles. The Duke of Devonshire had sent his heir with a companion to view the American war, as if it were some lighthearted pastime to take one's mind off serious pursuits like an unsuitable love affair. Hearing Louisa's acceptance of that rationale, Abigail saw the gap loom even larger between her and her friend.

But it was hardly for Louisa's lovelorn plight that all England was in mourning now. Last week, on December fourteenth, typhoid fever had claimed Queen Victoria's beloved Prince Albert. People in most walks of life, including Abigail's household, wore black garments and jet jewelry. At least, for once, Louisa and her set were not sporting the white or bright plumes on their bonnets, gowns, and fans that were fast becoming the fashion rage. Still, plumes which were not so delicate were dyed black to complement mourning garb. And—as far as Abigail was concerned—to also mourn the bonny birds who died so the British might properly mourn their prince.

About town, lampposts and store windows were swagged in sable; crepe door wreaths, ebony-banded stationery and calling cards abounded. In most homes, no bright candles would light the boughs of holiday yew trees this year in the German tradition the prince had introduced. But through all that, however much Abigail sympathized with the young "Widow of Windsor"—and with her blessedly big family—Abigail held high her hopes that her own husband would soon be here.

"Mrs. West, that American sea captain who brought you the letters from Captain West last autumn is downstairs," Sarah told her the day Prince Albert was buried at Windsor Castle.

"Royce Richards? Word at last!" Abigail cried and clapped her hands. "The letter and news he brought last time were very welcome. Bring some coffee and biscuits to the parlor, won't you, Sarah?" she added as she dashed downstairs.

"Captain Richards, I am so glad to see you!" she greeted the tall, burly man. He was a bit older than Morgan, but his large size and ebullient nature reminded her of her husband. It was obvious from Captain Richards's face that the war had worn him down, as she feared it would Morgan too.

"Sad times for England today," he said gruffly as he sat on the chair across from the settee where she perched.

"The poor queen," she agreed. "Sad times for American women too. I follow the papers daily about the war. I fear 'twill worsen."

His pale eyes met her from under a thatch of sandy eyebrows. He nodded and looked down at the papers in his hand.

"Letters for me? If I canna have the man himself right now, his letters are great comfort."

"Mrs. West, I must tell you, there has been an accident. Morgan's vessel—he was chased by a Yankee man-of-war and he intentionally put his runner on a reef—a coral ledge off Hamilton Harbor, Bermuda. In October—October ninth."

"Oh."

"Yes, you see, captured runners are converted to gunboats by the Yankees, so we captains out of Wilmington vowed not to be taken. If trapped, we run the ship aground, burn her, salvage what we can, as the Yankee bastards even get a bounty for each vessel taken, the men become prisoners to be traded back eventually. Well," he said, looking up again, "Morgan was almost into port, but he was surrounded, so he boldly put her on the reef. A ship tore up like that goes down fast, but the crew of twenty generally have time to get off and be picked up, floating on bales of cotton, and the like, so—"

"Captain, you are telling me my husband has been captured by the enemy?"

"No, ma'am. Wish I was, however wild Morgan's personal

ideas he preached 'bout slavery. You see, the Yankees fired howitzers on *The Kilda* as a warning, maybe not even meaning to hit her. But they did. There was an explosion—stored kerosene, I guess. A fire, Mrs. West, a big blow, and then she sank and only 'bout half onboard were saved and their names been posted and printed."

"But you have Morgan's letters there he sent me!" she shouted and stood to reach for them. The stack of paper, bound with a bright red ribbon, felt real and sure in her hands. She saw it included newspaper articles too. "He has to be all right!"

"I'm real sorry," he said, standing too, hunching his shoulders. "I fear I made a botch of this, when I only meant to comfort, Mrs. West. Morgan—he was killed in the line of duty and—burned. They got his body though, blown into the water, I guess. His remains was shipped home to his family for burial in Baltimore over a month ago. Those are some things he wanted you to have if anything happened to him, and there's a trunk for you in the hall too. That there in your hands is articles I brought of his heroic death for the cause, letters from his family to you, his will—and a deed to some Florida land with a house for you there. After the war, I guess, there will be more money for you when his Baltimore house is sold. I'm real regretful to bring you this news, Mrs. West."

She gripped the letters in her hand, hardly hearing the last things he'd said. She stared down at them as tears as big as raindrops plopped on the paper. Her mind would go no further. She must shut this out. She tore herself in two to keep from accepting it. One part of her had heard these horrid words—burned, blown, dead, buried. But her real self must not let this be happening, this impossible, overwhelming loss of all her losses. Surely, Morgan was still at the helm of his ship, slipping out amid the rocks, sailing onward to peace, to love for us, for all, and she was there with him, windblown, barefoot, guiding him on.

Sarah came in, humming, and put the coffee tray down. The man was speaking to her; shouting, Sarah ran for Margaret. But still, this was not real. She would not let it be true, even when Margaret took her upstairs and crooned to her just as she would a blighted bairn.

15

The gap—vast it looms
Between me and those
I have loved.

The tunnel—dark it yawns
Where I must pass
Through to the dawn.

Sailing toward St. Kilda that bright day in June, Janie jumped up and down and Curly's eyes were as big as saucers. But somber-faced, Abigail and Margaret bumped shoulders at the swaying rail and watched their isle rise from the sea. The cutter yacht they had hired in Glasgow sliced neatly around the crusty, brown arm of Dun into Village Bay.

"Och, four new cottages, and our wee one still stands!" Margaret cried out, pointing. " 'Tis a bonny sight, our island home, lass."

Abigail thought at first she spoke to Janie, but Margaret's blue eyes were not on the girl. The women's gazes met, narrowed against the sweep of salt wind and bite of unshed tears.

"Here or anywhere," Abigail found her voice at last, "though we part, you will ever be my sister, Margaret. But I can never say anymore that St. Kilda is my home. How I long for such a place! Perhaps with Curly I shall be able to make one for myself, though the loss of you two dear ones and Morgan . . ." She let her voice trail off before she cried. It wouldn't do to face the powers-that-be here with a weak woman's tears in her eyes.

"And ye are my sister, no matter what they say or do here. We have come a long way, my dear, but, I ken, 'tis not quite far enough for ye."

Her hair whipping free, Abigail nodded. The long road led back to St. Kilda nearly six months after she had come to accept Morgan's death. Though he was lost forever, the bairns might still be saved. She felt hope today if not happiness.

"You will soon be with your kin," she told Margaret, "but, yes, I've a way to go yet to see it all through, here if they'll let me stay—if not, beyond."

Abigail's plan was to make a rational appeal to the new minister and Parliament—and an emotional one to the women of St. Kilda, if it came to that—to heed the warnings against the fulmar oil anointing of the infants. She also intended to offer again to fund a doctor and a school. An inheritance from Morgan, donations from Corwin—her poignant parting from the dear old man still lingered in her mind—and funds of her own from the continuing sale of Kilda art could support these works, even if she was to be sent away again after speaking her piece.

If her exile was to continue, she would take Curly to live in America on her land on that other far isle, Sanibel. Morgan had wanted her to see and have it; Edmund Drummond was growing more unpredictable and dangerous in London. At least for several years—if there were nowhere else welcoming and safe—she would make a life in what Morgan had called "frontier Florida." Though the letters from Morgan's mother and sister had been kind, she could not imagine living with them in war-torn Baltimore.

When, at last, the wind and waves sounded not so strong in their ears, Abigail heard the familiar St. Kilda concert of bird cries. "Blimey," Curly said, "never seen so many blooming birds at once! Feathers floating in the air like snow!"

"I will show you all the different kinds," Janie put in importantly and elbowed the boy to point out a diving gannet. "And maybe you can climb cliffs with the lads since you're always boasting of climbing trees."

Abigail inhaled sea wind swept with St. Kilda scents. She fancied she could smell the rich mustiness of burning peat, simmering dye pots, broiled fulmar, ripening cheese, the delicate odor of those yellow primroses decking the terraces of Oiseval. There was a rich, creamy quality of light here too, which she had not been aware of until this return. And the clouds—six shapes of them layered the wild sky right now. Despite the blindness and cruelty of the people here, her resentment was now tempered by her hard-won wisdom that people from better educated, so-called civilized places could be wrong too. How could such a world be so bonny and so brutal all at once?

The crew anchored the yacht offshore, and they all took a small boat in toward the rocky landing spot, now dotted with people. "Look, Abby," Margaret called out, "yer friends Susannah and Malcolm. There's Iain Murdoch, of course. Ye might ken, the Fergusson sisters—and, och, 'tis my father and Murdo—and mother running down waving her apron. Mother, mother, 'tis us!"

Abigail was so happy for Margaret, though the fact she had no real family to greet her made her clasp the side of the rocky boat even harder. Tidal waves of grief over Morgan's loss washed over her again, but as she had a hundred times, she fought for control and weathered it. St. Kildans with ropes and grappling hooks held the boat fast, and the four of them clambered out while the two crewmen handled the baggage. The Adairs swooped Janie into their arms, then Margaret. Susannah waved to Abigail, but did not come out on the rocks; Annie waved too, until the frowning Flora and grown Fionna pulled her away. Curly, as protective as ever, stood close to Abigail as Iain Murdoch came out to her.

"So ye've come back, Abigail Adair."

"I was absolutely compelled to do so, Mr. Murdoch. This lad is a friend of mine, Curly Natter, and my surname is West now."

"Aye. We heard ye wed the captain, among other things," he said with a stiff nod to the boy.

How ominous that sounded; Mr. Murdoch did not smile nor offer his hand. She thought of the long-ago day when Morgan, sternly welcomed by this man, had alighted on these very rocks and she had stood in the crowd awestruck, swept away by him instantly. Just then, Hamish Adair stepped forward, doffed his cap to her, and briefly took her hand.

"Thank ye for bringing our lasses back, Abigail."

"You are welcome, Father Adair, and I am very happy to see you." But that one hint of warmth waned as he moved away when they stepped onto the shingle shore. The buzzing stopped; the breeze itself seemed to still.

A stout, bewhiskered man in a tall top hat strode down from the village, his polished boots spitting stones out of his way. Those embracing dropped their arms; curious faces—even hostile ones—glazed and dulled. The man walked straight to Abigail. His narrow, pale eyes bored into hers from under his hat brim.

"Reverend MacKay," Iain Murdoch spoke up when Abigail did not blink nor budge, "this lass is Abigail Adair—ah, Mrs. West."

"Sir," she said with a slight inclination of her head.

"Mrs. Morgan, 'tis about time you returned Margaret and Jane to their family, but you are not welcome here."

Abigail's heart thudded in her throat. Whatever she had been told, she could not believe they would really cut her, cast her out, and without a chance to speak. So this was the way it was to be. This man ran roughshod here, and yet she must deal with him to achieve her ends.

"I certainly respect your feelings and authority, Reverend MacKay," she said, fighting to control her voice and hoping Curly didn't just butt the man into the water, "but I ken you will be fair and hear me out. I would like to request a brief meeting with both you and Parliament."

"Most irregular," he blustered and shook his head so hard his hairy jowls bounced. It was obvious the man was not used to anyone so much as having one's own ideas or certainly not talking back. He looked like a beached fish, gasping air for a moment. "Tomorrow then, briefly," he said, "but I dinna ken where you can stay the night ashore. Your old place is a goat-shed now, and the Adairs and no family that answers to me could rightfully take in such a—a woman."

Margaret's voice rang out clear and strong. "If good Christian charity is no longer offered on St. Kilda, I'll go back to stay on the boat the night with ye, Abigail!" The minister glared; Mairi gasped and tugged at Margaret's arm; heads turned toward them, then back to Abigail.

" 'Tis available from us," Susannah said from where she and

Malcolm had edged closer. "Abigail is nearly family to Malcolm and me, and the lad's welcome too."

"Speaking for your husband now?" Mr. MacKay said, his tone and chilling stare obviously meant to intimidate.

Susannah's lips quivered. "We are agreed," she said quietly as Malcolm nodded and stepped forward to take Abigail's satchel.

Abigail's heart swelled at these tiny kindnesses that must now be the wildest form of protest here. As ever, she grieved for the way things were—impossible—but they seemed worse than before. At least Isobel MacCrimmon was not here to darken this scene like some swooping, cawing crow.

"The lad, exactly what is he to you?" Mr. MacKay asked pointing down at the startled boy with Abigail's hand on his shoulder.

"A friend I have taken into my life. After all, sir, you well ken the Lord said 'Suffer the little children to come unto me' to set us an example. And speaking of that, I have two boxes the crew will give you of gifts for the lads and lasses of St. Kilda."

"You'll not quote scripture to me, woman!" he thundered, then turned away and strode back up the path toward the minister's manse on the ridge above. There, under the slate roof in the second-floor window, Abigail glimpsed a buxom blond woman, her round face pressed to the glass. As Abigail stared upward, the curtain fluttered back in place.

"That lass at the manse," Abigail asked Susannah later as they trudged up toward the village, "as Mr. MacKay puts it, exactly what is she to him?"

"His housekeeper," Malcolm put in hastily.

"He and the young woman—she helps him in other ways too," Susannah added, keeping her face expressionless and her eyes down as they passed the manse and church. Abigail noted that everyone seemed to shuffle now; there was no spring in their steps. She glanced up and saw the housekeeper staring down again, at closer range this time. Her face was curious but not intelligent, bonny but not kind. Their eyes met before the curtain closed this time.

"And she's not friends with anyone but Flora!" Susannah muttered and gave Abigail a little push to hurry her on by.

❦

The next day, since her summons to Parliament and the minister was for noon, Abigail roused Curly just after dawn and took him out to see the island. "If things do not go well today and they cast me out, I want to see it all once more to keep it in my heart," she told him as they climbed toward Gleann Mor. "I want to show and tell you many things, and you must help me to remember them over the years to come." His mouth full of bannock and cheese, the boy nodded.

Abigail had set out in her stocking feet as in days of old, but she was tenderfooted now and soon scurried back for shoes. She showed the lad the great glen and pointed out the Tunnel and the Gap.

"And the captain liked this place the best on the whole island!" the boy repeated her words.

"That he did, and we had our first real talk right in that stone Warrior Woman's House," she said. Fearing she would cry, she turned her back on the site where her own wee Douglas had been born. But she and Curly were close companions, and that helped to heal her heart.

They did not have time to climb Conachair, but she pointed it out and told him of the night she had run there after her grandfather died and how Morgan chased her all the way before she saw him. Then she said no more, suddenly silent.

Along the milking trail, they sat on the stone wall that had given Morgan his theory of two hostile civilizations living on St. Kilda at the same time, the theory about which he had wanted to write his book. Below them lay the village with its humped stone storage cleits, gardens, and graveyard. She found her voice again, telling Curly all about why her mother and her child were not buried within the oval fence.

"Your own son—that's why saving babies is so big to you," the boy said solemnly, "and not just 'cause of all the rest, much as they mean to you. Your own baby and your ma—I think it's better where they're laid," he declared. "Like they're not hemmed in by those walls but part of the whole pretty place."

"A very wonderful thought, me chum," she said and smiled at him through her tears.

"Dunno how you and Margaret and Janie lived here," he added under his breath. "Them—those folks make it worse than living on the parish or in prison, and in such a fine, open place like this," he concluded and swept his arm to encompass the scene.

"You ken, Curly Natter, you're a very keen, braw thinker. Though some might say you talk too much, I shall argue with them next time!"

They went back to rambling around the far end of the village where Abigail peered in the open door of her old cottage. The minister had told the truth: last winter, both rooms had been a goat shed, and no one had cleaned it out. Yet staring at it, for one moment her heart-wings took her back to the day it was well-swept and she was making cheese and had her revelation about mold growing in the bairns' bodies; she heard Morgan's voice when he came calling and Janie's earliest songs; she saw Douglas Adair standing there on their wedding night when he said to her, "My bonny Abby . . . Abby, my wife."

"Come on then," she called to Curly. "No good just standing here."

They cut off the village street and climbed the lower cliffs of Oiseval. She wanted to see again the place where she had saved her first fulmar chick. She wanted to face that very spot where her mother had been lost and where she herself had fallen in the rain, so she could put all those sad things forever behind her. On the way up, they passed a group of lads, practicing their climbing craft on the rocks. Though he kept pace with her, Curly kept looking back at their antics, fascinated by their ropes. But on the very heights, amidst the fulmar nests, Abigail found she could not share memories of this place with the boy and just sat down.

"If you'd like to walk on back and watch those lads," she told him, "I'll be down soon. I wouldna mind."

He seemed unwilling to leave her, bless his loyal soul, but at last he dashed down. She sat there, feeling the wind lift her hair and thin, narrow skirt, for she and Margaret had chosen to return in their St. Kilda gowns and leave all their London garb packed on the ship for now. As if on the wings of morning, her thoughts flew back to the promise she had made before God and herself on this very spot after she almost went over the side here: that the bairns would be saved. She had come this far—full circle—but her quest was not ended. Whatever it took, she must do everything she could to fulfill that vow.

Suddenly, she sensed she was not alone and turned, expecting to see Curly had come back. Flora Fergusson Nichol stood there, windblown and out of breath, holding a long shepherd's staff.

"Flora. I assumed you would not be speaking to the likes of me. How have you been these years?" Abigail asked as she got slowly to her feet.

"I have two live bairns and lost but the one ye harmed, if that's what ye're asking. Ye have made it so hard on my grandmother and Annie—on all us Fergussons and MacCrimmons, ye see."

"I regret that. But for the bairn you lost and I didna harm, dinna you see, the dying must be stopped? And I ken how, Flora. I swear to you it is the vile fulmar oil on—"

To Abigail's horror, Flora advanced, holding the staff out in front of her as if she would shove her over the edge. "Ye accused us all—even Annie, who ye said was once yer friend—of murdering our own bairns! Ye caused arguments, family rifts, even after ye were gone!" she screamed and swung the staff in a huge, hard arc.

Abigail ducked, grabbed for it but missed. She sat down on the ground, afraid the woman could actually throw her off balance and off the edge. But that move was a mistake: Flora thumped the staff at her, striking her shoulder. Did the demented woman mean to beat her senseless and roll her off?

Abigail clawed for stones and turf. She dodged another blow and heaved the handful in Flora's face. Flora closed her eyes, coughed, swung blindly. Abigail scrambled for the staff, but Flora backed away. Then, as if from the sky, handfuls of pebbles pelted the woman. She turned and ran, skidding down the path with the whooping Curly tearing after her. He chased her briefly, then came running back where Abigail leaned, breathless against a big boulder.

"The bloody baggage didn't hurt you, did she? Is she jingle-brained, or what? Like to kick her bum right off the cliff! Say, Abigail, what sort of folks you got here with that Drummond son-of-a-batchelor and this baggage?"

She leaned a trembling arm across the boy's sturdy shoulder. "Frightened folks, as this is a very frightening place, my lad. And what would I ever do without you?"

"Be a goner, I 'spose. 'Sides I don't like it here, 'cause those little buggers wouldn't let me even watch them, let alone climb with them, and no one would lend me a rope."

"Ropes are very important here, Curly, like having lots of coppers back in London." She heaved a deep sigh and rubbed her sore shoulder. Even if they let her stay here, it would be hard on Curly. Since Flora had been so frenzied, she feared she had torn all her ties here. All but one and that was the only Fergusson sister she dare approach. And, since she judged from the sun it was just an hour before noon, she had not much time to do what she must.

Abigail lost a few more minutes of what she feared would be her last, precious day on St. Kilda, waiting inside, looking out the window of Susannah and Malcolm's cottage for the women to return from the morning milking jaunt. When they streamed by, she pointed out to Curly which one was Annie and had him dart past her to stick a secret note in the ropes of her bucket harness. Then Abigail went out and climbed above the village and waited behind the first cleit, praying Annie would come. Though it was a warm sunny day, up here the wind howled through the holes in the cleit like a selkie's strange song.

Earlier, Curly had tried to talk Abigail out of meeting alone with "that devil baggage's sister," but Abigail had convinced him she trusted Annie, that Annie was not like Flora. Yet, she agonized, Annie was the second knee-woman in the village now, and had, of necessity, learned from and obeyed Isobel. Abigail threatened Annie's reputation, future, and family.

Her heart wrenched when she saw the boy down near the graveyard, pretending to be interested in a cluster of old stones, just to be in shouting distance if she needed him. It was then Abigail knew that, even though she had lost Morgan and might be bidding farewell to Margaret and Janie forever today, Curly was her family too—like a nephew or a beloved, adopted son. And so perhaps, like Margaret's experience returning here showed, home was where your loved ones were. Surely she could make a home for herself with Curly out there somewhere, someday.

At least a half hour passed with no Annie. Abigail's stomach knotted tighter. She feared she had misjudged the lass, perhaps from the first. How foolish and reckless she had been to think that befriending Annie, teaching her to read, and corresponding with her would earn her loyalty today. Annie dare not come, of course, even though in the note Abigail had challenged her conscience about the bairns.

"Abigail!" the voice came in the wind, so shrill Abigail was not certain she had heard it. She looked below; she peered through a gap into the dim cleit. "Abigail, up here!"

Annie gestured to her from the next cleit up the hill. Looking below and seeing only Curly staring, she motioned for him to stay away and hurried up toward her old friend, hoping Annie had not brought Flora or a shepherd's staff.

"I canna risk being seen with ye," Annie hissed.

"I understand. I wanted to say goodbye and ask—implore you to help me. Annie, if they make me leave today, in the name of God, substitute something else for the fulmar oil over the years! 'Tis in your hands—"

"They say 'tis only in God's hands, so you mustna blaspheme."

She seized Annie's upper arms in a tight grip. "If it is in God's hands, Annie, He's still expecting you to help Him save the bairns! That's why He gives us the chance to learn, like you learned to read and write. It's why He lets folks become doctors like Dr. Snow and Dr. Lister who wrote those letters here. That's—"

"That's why He gave me a friend—an inspiration—like ye!" Annie cried and hurled her head against Abigail's shoulder, embraced her, and shook with sobs.

Abigail held her close, trying to catch the garbled words. "So sorry, Abigail, that I am, so sorry and afraid we'll all be punished for what we done. I lost my own firstborn, a lass in November, and grandmother put the oil on her, while I wanted to scream, 'no, no!' And now I'm sure I'm breeding again!"

Abigail set her back and stared into her wet face. "That's why we have to stop it now! It should have been stopped years ago, before my son, before my brothers—all of them! Please, Annie, you are the bairns' last hope here, the way the new minister herds everyone about like sheep. You have to help me, help the mothers of St. Kilda!"

"Ye were so kind not to blame me for yer son's death when I—ye didna want it but I put the oil on him."

"You didna ken about it then, but now you do. If you canna stand up to the way of things—to Isobel and Parliament and that blasted new minister—"

"Abigail, 'tisn't safe to curse him!"

"—then it *will* be on your head!"

"Did ye ask to meet up here because ye kenned about my grandmother's store of the oil?"

"What?"

"The fulmar oil she keeps in this very cleit. I thought ye kenned and wanted me to destroy it, but she would just make more. She's sent me to fetch it and the birthing stool for years, but only once I saw her make the oil." She swiped at her tears and peered down around the curved side of the cleit. "That lad of yers down there," she said as she brushed by Abigail to lead her into the low doorway, "looks enough like ye and Douglas to be yer own son grown."

Abigail wondered if the gossips of St. Kilda were now spreading the rumor that Curly was hers by Morgan or another man. It evidently still seemed easier for folks here to believe lies than the truth. She stooped low to follow Annie into the cleit, again praying there could be no deceit here. But the cleit, its walls pierced by spaces between the stones was empty but for a wooden chest, an empty kettle, Isobel's birthing stool, and a low table.

Annie knelt and fumbled with the latch on the chest. She lifted the lid as Abigail bent over her. Light seeped into its depths where sat a stone bowl filled with rancid oil with a clutch of fulmar feathers in it, quills down.

" 'Tis what she stirs it with again and again, those feathers," Annie whispered. "Please dinna tell I showed you."

"But the feathers look as old as that stone bowl, and you ken how dirty and foul feathers are 'til they're washed!"

"The bowl has been passed down for years. She just draws enough oil for each birth and adds more time and again."

They both sat away from the rank scent of it now. Abigail's brain raced: Dr. Snow and Dr. Lister would have been appalled. Sepsis, fever, filth, superstition, the way of things swirled at her until she thought she would vomit.

"Now you see how there's no way I could use something else for it," Annie said. "She'd ken right away."

"Let her drink that if she thinks it's safe for bairns!" Abigail cracked out. She was tempted to pour the whole poisonous mass down the hillside, but the old woman would just stir up more with dirty feathers. It was suddenly so dark and close in here that Abigail thought she would suffocate. There had to be a way to bring all this to light without betraying poor Annie.

"I'll never forget you, my friend," Abigail told her, "but dinna ye ever forget the bairns." Abigail squeezed Annie's arm and, stooped over like an old woman, left the cleit. She strode down the hillside, hoping she was not late for the brief meeting Mr. MacKay had promised with himself and Parliament, a specially called session. She only hoped she would have the right things to say to convince everyone what they must do.

But as Abigail strode the single street, the way she had that other day so long ago when Parliament had summoned her, she saw the men gathered along the edge of the cliff before the minister's manse. Was she late and they had disbanded? But there was Mr. MacKay, in the center of the cluster, and the women were present too, off to the side. And then she saw what the minister was doing: he was ripping apart the picture and story books and lettering paper she had brought for the St. Kilda school she hoped to establish here and sailing them off the ridge where they fluttered to the shore below like flapping, dying birds.

She strode into the crowd, pushing Flora's husband Gordon back when he tried to block her way.

"Let her come, let the Jezebel see what we think of her unholy, unwomanly, scientific ways," John MacKay intoned, shaking his head, as if forced to speak obscenities.

She yearned to rip the bonny books from his grasp, but she stood her ground, stiff arms and fists tight to her sides. "Is it unholy and unwomanly to want to educate children—and to want to save their lives so they can grow to be children?" she challenged.

"You should be stoned like in the Good Book—the way you and that ruffian boy tried to stone Flora today when she went to plead with you!" MacKay roared. "Dinna think ye shall sway me with your clever, lofty ways as you did the minister before me!"

"Oh, I have no doubt your swaying, as you put it, sir, comes from another, lofty source!" she retorted, and without even looking to see if the face was there, she pointed back and upward.

Heads turned to stare up; people gasped. Mr. MacKay went sunset red and stopped tearing the books for one moment.

"This woman," he shouted, pointing at Abigail as she had at his housekeeper, "is the ultimate example of evils in the flesh being further corrupted by the world. She dares to try to change God's will! She calls the people of St. Kilda—all of you—murderers of your own bairns!"

"No, I call the foul, vile, dirty stuff that the knee-women from Isobel MacCrimmon on back have unknowingly, unfortunately put on the bairns' birth cords the murderer of the bairns. And all of you can stop this by just keeping the cord clean and using something else. I ken you think 'tis improper to speak of the private things of childbirth, but the cure is that simple. Why must St. Kildans believe they have been chosen for special punishment, unless they have been wrongly led by someone even now?"

She stared at Mr. MacKay. She was as tall as he, though his tall hat made him seem to tower over her. He blinked; his eyes darted down. He was sweating even in this bay breeze. She sensed Curly at her side; she saw Margaret back in the crowd of women, her hands clasped tightly between her breasts.

"If you will listen to none of the teachings of so-called civilization or scientific progress," Abigail plunged on, addressing all of them now, "take the leather shoes from off your feet—those of you like Mr. MacKay allowed to wear shoes in the summer. Take them off and put back on the old shoes made from solans' necks if tradition is so sacred. Rid yourself of metal garden hoes, of indigo dye, glass windows in the church, Isobel MacCrimmon's new chair she calls a birthing stool like in the old days, and all such corruptions where you have changed the way of things. You change things for your own comfort but will not change a thing for your own bairns' survival! Why, even fulmars choose to die to protect their young from death by the bonxie birds!"

"Have ye said yer piece now?" Iain Murdoch's voice rang out.

Abigail turned to face him. "Yes," she said more quietly. "Rid yourself of bad tradition and bad advisors like Parliament and this unholy holy man—even Isobel—slave drivers, it seems to me—but do not fear you will have to rid yourself of me, for I am leaving now."

"Good riddance!" Mairi Adair's voice rose above the murmurs and the loud silence from the stunned minister. Abigail spun to face the woman who had borne her beloved Douglas—and borne such hatred for her and her mother. Mairi stood next to Isobel who looked so furious she evidently could not speak.

Abigail suddenly decided to ignore Mairi. "I told you once, Mrs. MacCrimmon, that the deaths were not on your or poor Annie's head. Now that you ken the whole truth, from here on out, they are indeed."

Mairi shouted; Isobel sputtered; Flora shook her fist in the rising noise. Margaret yelled something Abigail could not decipher and disappeared, dragging Janie after her. Mr. MacKay bellowed for peace, Iain Murdoch roared for silence, all adding to the chaos. But it was Hamish Adair who jumped up on a box of books to quiet the crowd.

"Even if 'tis only perhaps the truth the lass is speaking, we must give it a try!" Hamish yelled, though he was soon shouted down.

Tears blurred Abigail's vision of the old man. He had always been her champion, hers and Douglas's, despite what others said. She held Curly's hand when he slipped it into hers. It was the sweetest moment in this terrible day, even if Hamish was not allowed to speak, nor was anyone else. Mr. MacKay, in his best brimstone voice, sent them all to their homes. There was to be no debating of God's will about the bairns' dying, not here, not in church, not in Parliament. At last, Mr. MacKay stalked off, but Hamish stayed behind; he took Abigail's other hand as he had yesterday.

"The last sermon Mr. Campbell preached before he left this place was about how no prophet is accepted in his own country, lass," he told her with a frowning glare at the minister's back. "And he meant ye and made it clear ye might be right. But the murmurings was terrible to turn some more against ye and him too. Ye ken, perhaps some of them will come round, but best depart as ye said. 'Tis not safe here for ye, nor the lad, nor for the painful truth."

"Father Adair, I can never thank you enough for all your kindly advice and comfort—to both me and my mother. And please,"—she began to cry now, though she had thought her outrage would carry her through—"tell Margaret and Janie farewell for me. We said it yesterday, in case this happened, but they—with Curly here—are my only family now. Tell them I shall write."

He nodded. "And this rope," he said, unlooping the thick coils from his stooped shoulder, "was yer Douglas's once. Margaret said yer lad here likes to climb, so let it be his."

Now tears coursed down Abigail's cheeks as Curly's eyes lit to see the big rope. He touched it tenderly, then swayed under the weight of it over his thin shoulder. Malcolm came plodding back with Abigail's satchel and stood there in the small circle of friends.

"The captain told me," Curly said, "there are real tall, thin trees reaching almost to heaven where we're going in Florida. With this, I can learn to climb them all! Can't thank you enough, sir!" Hamish nodded and swiped at his nose.

So, Abigail thought, the people of Kilda who would so much as speak to her had come down to Malcolm and Susannah, who was now cowering in her cottage; only to Hamish of the entire Adair clan that should be her kin; to Annie, perhaps, distraught and torn in two up there in Isobel's foul cleit; and, of course, to Margaret and Janie, whom she must leave. Suddenly she realized she had said it all, done her worst and her best here today. Let the minister and his "housekeeper" peer out at her and tell everyone that the sly seducer Abigail MacQueen Adair West was back again luring men. Boldly, she hugged Malcolm farewell and asked him to thank Susannah for her brave hospitality. She hugged Hamish who hugged her back hard. The men walked away. She and Curly went down to the shore, gestured for the boat, and climbed out on the rocks to wait, though Curly scrambled back to salvage some of the children's books not ruined by the rocks or water.

She stared just at Curly now; she was no longer looking back. Yet her mind rolled on, washing scenes through her brain of her mother coming here on these very rocks to her St. Kildan exile. Of other Harris brides yet to come. Of Lady Grange brought here and kept by force. Of her own sad return yesterday. Of countless sacks of feathers going out of here for stuffing and decoration to make the Louisas of the world pretty and profit the likes of Edmund Drummond. Of fulmar eggs and hatchlings without someone here to raise them, orphans like she had been, like Curly had been before she found him.

The crew helped her into the boat and the boy climbed in himself. She could not bear to look back at Village Bay, but she did not want to be seen from the glass-eyed windows of the minister's manse with her head down. So she shut her eyes but held her chin up and turned her head back toward shore when they shoved off as if she were staring up at them all in defiance to change the way of things.

But her eyes flew open when she heard the shout of the familiar voice.

Margaret and Janie scrambled out along the rocks with Mairi chasing them. Margaret tripped and went down, spilling the few garments she carried in one arm. Janie squealed and tried to help her mother up.

"Put back in! Put in!" Abigail cried to the two crewmen.

"Without someone there to help us land, the boat'll take a battering, ma'am. We'll come back for them later."

"No! They'll drag them off to spite me. We canna leave them!"

Abigail half stood to see better. The minister was running down from the manse, evidently to help Mairi. Then Hamish appeared again, tearing down to the shore, shouting something. Janie was wailing and holding her arms out toward Abigail.

"Eh," Curly cried, "how about this long rope!"

Margaret was back on her feet, urging Janie along again, further out on the rocks. Mairi scrambled after them, screaming.

"We're going with ye!" Margaret's frenzied cry rose above the wind, waves, and her mother's shouts. "Dinna leave us!"

"Curly, yes, try that rope!" Abigail ordered. "Maybe Margaret can catch it. If not, I swear I'll swim back in!"

When Curly's toss failed, a crewman managed to get the rope on the rocks. With an oar, Abigail helped the other man hold the boat from banging there as they maneuvered. But the minister, huffing hard, reached Margaret and helped Mairi pull her back. Janie screamed and flailed at him to make Curly cheer. But Hamish reached the rope and hauled the boat in closer. Abigail's oar braced the bump.

"I canna stay here, I tried, but I canna," Margaret was shouting at Mairi.

"She wilna win again, not again!" Mairi screamed.

"Your kin are not going anywhere with that vile woman!" Mr. MacKay announced and made a grab for Janie. Curly stood up in the boat as if he would fling himself on the rocks. But Abigail pulled him back, then deftly put the tip of her oar behind Mr. MacKay's knees and pushed.

The ranting man went down on his rear, then rolled off the rocks into the foaming surf. He came up sputtering, like a big, rolling seal as Margaret quickly hugged her father on the rocks above. Then, while Hamish held Mairi at arm's length, Margaret scrambled into the shifting boat. With his free arm, Hamish passed Janie to Margaret while Abigail fought to keep the hull away from the minister in the water.

For a moment, Abigail struggled about saving him at all. If she but pulled her oar in, the boat would crush him against the rocks, surge over and drown him. For the freedom of the folk, for the lives of the bairns—but this vile man had not made the worst of the way of things here. St. Kilda could rise against him, but again, they refused. This man's sins, however horrid, would not be solved by another she committed.

"Canna you walk on water, sir?" Abigail shouted down at the flailing, frenzied man. "I am sure your poor flock of sheep are expecting it!"

She kept the boat from him as Mairi railed and Hamish bent to fish him out. She sat down with a thump when Curly grabbed her skirts as the crewmen began to row out again.

"I love ye, father! Mother, forgive me, but 'tis for the best!" Margaret kept shouting back toward shore. "Farewell! Farewell!"

Abigail was half afraid the sopping, gasping minister would order St. Kildans out in the beached birlins to give chase like Yankee cruisers, but the sails of the yacht filled to pull their vessel outward bound. After tending to her little family, by the time she went up on deck to glance back at St. Kilda, all that was left of it—but forever in her heart—was a black bump on the flat gray sea.

Part 3

Sanibel
1862–1873

We skimmed before it like a bird, the coast of the island flashing by, and the view changing every minute. . . . I was greatly elated by my new command . . . and my conscience, which had smitten me hard for my desertion, was quieted by the great conquest I had made.
—ROBERT LOUIS STEVENSON,
Treasure Island

*Islands feel free despite their sea walls,
And bold love can build gates in those.
'Tis gates in ourselves we ought to fear
That isolate us when they close.*
—ABIGAIL WEST,
Sanibel diary

16

Such an exotic place and people
Surround me in this sun-swept home.
Busy, sharing, thrilled am I,
Yet, without him, alone, alone.

Set gemlike in the sparkling sea, Sanibel glittered emerald under the sun's hot stare. Abigail shaded her eyes even in the shelter of her broad-brimmed bonnet. After two months of travel, this island looked warm, welcoming, vibrant. But it seemed so wrong she should come to live in this glorious place Morgan had loved, with him gone forever and another man at her side.

"'Tis the bonniest sight," she announced to her excited little family, but it was their escort who answered.

"It is now that you will grace it with your presence, Abigail. But I hope you all keep my warnings in mind. Ladies shouldn't be living here without the protection of a man."

Curly answered for her, insisting he could take care of them. Abigail had heard such warnings from men all her life, but had hoped it would be different in this exotic, distant place. She meant to be her own master here. But she did not try to explain all that to

Lawrence Stillwell, whom she had met by chance while trying to book passage on a ship to come here. He had been a godsend since they had arrived in Havana on the last leg of their long voyage from St. Kilda that went through Liverpool, Bermuda, and Cuba. With everyone speaking Spanish in Havana, she knew they could not have managed so well without him.

Though he lived on the Florida mainland near Sanibel, he had been briefly in Havana on business. Lawrence had arranged for them to come to Florida on the blockade runner owned by his employer, Jake Summerlin. Outward bound to Cuba, the ship carried cattle grazed inland and loaded at Punta Rassa just across San Carlos Bay from Sanibel. This beef on the hoof had once helped to feed the Confederate army but now sold for even higher prices in Havana. On the inward-bound leg, Summerlin's runner imported wartime luxury goods like sugar, coffee, leather, and cloth to sell to Floridians at exhorbitant prices. During wartime, the whole operation was illegal, Lawrence had explained, and Summerlin had to be wary the small Union army contingent at nearby Ft. Myers didn't discover them.

Florida, Lawrence told them, had been virtually abandoned by the South during the war, since its myriad inlets and long shorelines were too difficult to protect. The war here had come down to sudden Union raids on blockade runners. Since Abigail had lost Morgan to the blasted Yankees that way, it did not seem fair that Mr. Summerlin and his partners were making a fortune on the war—nor that Lawrence was making his as their part-time Spanish translator and part-time Punta Rassa accountant.

When Abigail had heard Lawrence's calling, she had almost refused his offer of gentlemanly escort and free transport, but she soon realized he was nothing like Edmund Drummond. He might be a pencil pusher, as he put it, but with that pencil he also drew Florida's bonny sights, especially the birds. He had even sketched her this morning with the balmy breeze tugging at her loose hair, sitting at the prow of this small boat that now took them and their goods from Punta Rassa to Sanibel. How she wished Morgan were still at the helm of *The Kilda* so she could send him that captured moment just as he had described her in his last letter: "Windblown, luring me on, my life's figurehead." But the picture was not real life, and this man was not Morgan.

"We do appreciate your warnings, Lawrence," she told him with a small smile. "'Tis only that we mean to make a life here and fear of things that might never happen wilna help."

"No, of course not, and I admire you more than I can say even after knowing you all for such a short while."

His voice and face were so fervent that she looked away with a politely dismissive nod worthy of the Duchess of Manchester. Suddenly, Abigail realized that she carried her past friends and experiences with her yet, even in this entry to a bright, new life. As for men with that avid look, that life might include friendships, but nothing deeper.

"Look, Abigail!" Curly cried, pointing toward the dark green shoreline. "Trees that look like they're walking right out into the water on skinny legs!"

"Those are mangroves, my boy," Lawrence told him. "And those green cigars floating by on the waves are their seed pods outward bound to plant new life."

"Just like us," Abigail murmured, staring at the rippling water.

"A thousand new wonders," Margaret said.

"Wonders, yes," Lawrence murmured, his eyes still riveted on Abigail.

In his gently drawling voice—he had been reared in Savannah, far south of Baltimore, he had told them—Lawrence pointed out landmarks as the two men at the oars maneuvered them toward a clearing on the shore. Again Abigail noted that Lawrence's polite, almost shy demeanor could not hide his passion for nature's beauty, for his art—and, hopefully, that was all. His exterior seemed deceptively pallid: his skin, sun-tinged, blended with his beige, somewhat shabby garments and even with his light brown eyes, sandy hair, side whiskers, and shaggy mustache. But, his eyes gave glimpses of a soul that shone within. He had a full, expressive mouth that pursed, as if poised to talk, even when he was drawing. He cocked his head to listen; he squinted to see more clearly. Four years younger than Abigail's thirty-one, Lawrence was not tall but seemed so because he was thin and lanky. He had told them more than once, as if in apology, that it was difficult to be either a gentlemen or an artist here in frontier, war-fettered Florida.

While the oarsmen unloaded their things, they strolled a narrow, crushed-shell path away from the shore. Lawrence offered Abigail his arm. Not wanting to offend him, she took it, though she was so excited at finally being in this place Morgan had given her that she wanted to bound off ahead, alone, to see it all. But it was Curly, with his precious, coiled St. Kilda rope bouncing over his shoulder, and the giggling Janie who darted ahead; Margaret strolled behind, a proper chaperone. As if Lawrence knew he could command Abigail's attention when he gave her information about this place, his voice rolled on.

"You all will find it a short walk from your parcel of land," he told her, gesturing with his rolled sheaf of sketches, "either from this landward side of the isle on Pine Island Sound or from the Gulf of Mexico on the other side. It's a narrow but long island. There was a small town here forty or so years ago called Sanybel, a Utopian experiment of sorts in ruins now, as it just didn't make it, though they had men as well as women."

She knew the remnants of this Sanybel would be nothing like the glory of her lost Gleann Mor, but she said naught of that. "I assure you, I heard and will heed your warnings, Lawrence, subtle or otherwise."

"I don't mean to fret you. But as I was saying, don't you all wander off yonder until I can come for a visit. I explored the whole island when we were thinking of grazing cattle here, though we decided against it. You are fortunate your husband's father had government contacts to obtain the land as no one's been permitted to build since, though I told you some undesirables have been through the area for years—"

"You did indeed tell me. Seminoles during those long-ago wars, Confederate deserters, lay-bys who never registered, and escaped slaves called contrabands," she repeated his earlier lessons. "I suppose, in a way, you yourself are a bit of a lay-by, Lawrence."

She felt him stiffen. "I declare I would like to enlist, but we're doing dangerous drudgery here to aid the southern cause. Besides, before the war began, my parents insisted I come down in the employ of father's acquaintance Mr. Summerlin to—well, to toughen me up a bit. They weren't pleased to have an artist in the family— not the Savannah Stillwells, I can tell you! But, when I go back independently wealthy, my father will *have* to accept I shall have my own artist's studio and my own life!"

Deep sympathy for him seeped through her wall of wariness

for the first time. She patted his arm with her free hand. "Your talent for drawing is wonderful, and I dinna mean to insult you. I do understand and sympathize with your wanting to choose your own path despite what your family or friends say or do—despite tradition where you come from."

"You do?" he asked and stopped so fast Margaret almost bumped into them before going on behind the children. "I must tell you how very much your good wishes mean to me and vow that I shall visit you all here whenever I can get away."

"But now, I'd be so grateful," Abigail said and gently disengaged her arm from his tightening grip, "if you'd take me to the Cuban caretakers so they can show me around my new home."

Abigail was amazed by the sheer differentness of this spacious place, but she felt comforted by the simplicity of the house itself. Somehow, she had imagined a vast Baltimore brick edifice or Belgravia tallhouse or even a Kimbolton Castle. And yet, compared to a St. Kilda cottage, the one-floor pine structure was a mansion to her; Morgan must have known that when he sent the plans and workers here. He had wanted to give her a beautiful abode for their honeymoon and other happy times together. How tragic he had not seen it, but perhaps he had walked it with her in his thoughts and dreams before he died.

Now, as she walked each room, she pictured him here, so tall, even under ceilings built twelve-feet high to keep the rooms cool. She saw him with her heart-wings, dominating the broad portico called a verandah that wrapped clear around the house to shade it and snare breezes. The house was built two steps off the ground to keep crawling things out; she almost felt she could hear Morgan's footsteps reverberating when the children ran across the floor.

"This verandah is where we shall hold our school every morning before any tasks are undertaken," she told Curly and Janie with a solemn nod.

Despite the others' chattering, Abigail stood silent in the large single expanse of living and dining area. It seemed a huge parlor with pine table and chairs, a cupboard, a horsehair sofa and four wicker chairs facing a fireplace she could not imagine ever needing on a hot September day like this. Off the hall that linked the two outside doors were three bedrooms with large windows to the verandah. She managed to shuffle everyone off for a moment as she stood in the front room Morgan had obviously intended for them; it contained a large poster bed swathed in mosquito netting, a bureau, a mirror, a chair. As in the other bedrooms, curtains made from her own brightly dyed cloth stirred fitfully at the windows. And everywhere hung dried grass swishes on wall pegs to keep off insects, which evidently got in the doors or squeezed through the cheesecloth to be tacked over open windows at night. Cheesecloth, but not to make cheese in this climate, she mused. No sheep for wool, no lichens for dyes, but lots of biting bugs—so all was not perfect in this paradise after all.

She bent to pat the rosy-hued coverlet on the high mattress. She had her sunny, colorful dreamhouse at last, she thought, the one she had imagined lying abed many mornings in Lady Grange's chill, little place on St. Kilda. The man she loved had built it for her, but she would never be able to share it with him.

Quickly, so she would not cry, she went outside where Curly and Janie darted from place to place and Margaret spoke with Lawrence. María and Paulo Menéndez, the sprightly, elderly Cuban caretakers, had gone off to the small, outdoor kitchen house to prepare a meal. Other outbuildings included an enclosed privy, a one-room house for the Cubans, and a low, thatched, noisy henhouse.

"Good," Abigail announced. "We can live off those domestic birds and the fishing here and not harm a one of those wild, bonny birds we saw wading or flying."

"I can show you all their night roosting spot," Lawrence said, coming to her side again.

A brusque refusal caught in her throat. He had already offered to teach her Spanish, to draw, to sail, but she had no interest in any of that from Lawrence. She would learn Spanish from the Menéndezes, she had no talent for drawing, and Morgan—Morgan and her father had taught her how to sail, she thought.

"Since I don't have to climb trees for eggs, Abigail," Curly put in, "I can hunt white-tailed deer Mr. Stillwell told me about. He's gonna show me how to shoot when he visits us."

"Yes, I suppose so," she said and went off to examine the grove of lime, guava, mango, and orange trees again. Through the Menéndezes, Lawrence had translated that these mature trees were not planted by Morgan's men last year, but had been left here by the town of Sanybel that was no more.

"But we shall flourish in this place, we shall make a go of it!" Abigail told Margaret as the two of them walked off a ways together. "We must all work to make it home."

"That we shall, perhaps Mr. Stillwell included."

"Dinna tease, my dear," Abigail warned.

"Ye ken what they say, lass," Margaret persisted with a roll of her blue eyes. "Stillwell waters run deep."

They stiffled giggles, then Abigail turned serious again. "This will be our refuge," she vowed, "though it wilna help us forget those we yet long to help on our other far isle."

Side by side, the two of them stood warmed by the late afternoon sun, listening to the rattle of palmetto fronds and songs of birds.

After they had eaten a meal of fried chicken, hoecake with tomato gravy, bananas, and orange juice, Margaret unpacked. Abigail and Lawrence, with the children trailing, walked northwest, crossing several low shell ridges, to the roosting place. At Lawrence's insistence, they carried a small smudge pot, a kerosene-soaked pitch pine knot to light later, and swishes for mosquitos, which he said got even worse after dark. Dusk was deepening as they halted on the far side of a fresh-water pond near Pine Island Sound. Fortunately, good water was easily accessible on Sanibel from barrels sunk in the sand with cheesecloth lining or from rain runoff. In this wet season, there was even a small inland freshwater river called a slough. Abigail wondered if Morgan had remembered all that from his boyhood stay here and planned accordingly to make things easier for them. But now, as Lawrence prepared to take his leave, he shuffled through his sketches to intrude upon her musings again.

"Though the birds aren't here yet, I can't stay much longer, so let me show you all what to look for when they fly in," he said, tilting his paper to catch the last of daylight. Despite her desire to be alone, she stood awed at the strange beauty of the birds in his drawings, especially a duck-faced bird with fabulous wings, wading and feeding in a pond just like this one.

"This bird is pink, so my pencil doesn't do it justice," he explained as she recalled Morgan telling her once of such a bird, "worthy of her dyes." "A roseate spoonbill. And this one is a snowy egret in its nuptial feathers—"

She gasped aloud and bent closer. On its crest, wings, and tail, the snowy egret had delicately fringed plumes spread in the most marvelous fans. It struck her then: those were the very sort of feathers Edmund Drummond's newspaper advertisement had shown the Queen of Kilda wearing! The very ones she had seen on some of Louisa's friends' gowns and hats. And pink plumes—that gossip Lady Salisbury had flouted a pink-feathered fan at Kimbolton that time she had derided Louisa and snubbed Abigail. At least such was imported from South America and not from this refuge of Sanibel!

"Whatever is it?" Lawrence asked. "Fancy feathers—that's how these birds attract a mate. Entrancing, don't you see?" he asked.

"I've seen these plumes before—on ladies' London fashions. There's something so wrong—almost obscene—about the fact that in decking themselves to attract a mate the birds attract men who kill them for their bridal finery."

"I see what you mean. The feather trade still survives in Havana despite people's need for more than fashion in wartime. I declare, I think murdering these birds for their plumage is wrong too. I'd much rather draw than shoot them."

"You are a good man, Lawrence."

"Then I will be a welcome guest here? I—I wasn't sure."

"Of course. We shall all be pleased to see you."

"Then I leave tonight with a happy heart. But you must remember that this isn't your St. Kilda but America—the Confederate States, that is—so caution is needed."

Yet despite his final warning to her, he looked as if he would cry with joy, as if she had given him some marvelous new bird to draw. He finally left them to meet his crew down on the shore. Curly and Janie's whisperings seemed distant to her now. She stood, really alone at last after so long, in this precious place. She remembered, she mourned, she hoped.

And then, the few random sounds became a cawing cacaphony as the sky came alive with birds beating their wings to land. They sailed in, like strings of pearls against the orchid sunset sky. As night fell, the birds, ghost-white, balanced on small high branches that arched under them, perched in the mangrove, buttonwood, and coco plum trees. Egrets, ibises, herons, even gold-crested pelicans banded together in a colony against the night. They chatted with each other, shifted places, complained, cooed, then cuddled down. This was not their mating season, but they seemed to have friends to comfort them.

Swishing at mosquitos, Abigail departed to gather her dear ones close their first night on Morgan's Sanibel.

The breeze felt good on his flushed face that hot September day as his guard marched him into the office of Colonel Hill, the Union prison commander, who was reading at his desk. The prisoner's eyes darted around, then came to rest listlessly on his own hands protruding from the wrinkled shirt that was too short-armed for him. His skin looked fish-belly gray, he thought, the same hue as his clothes. Suddenly, he longed for something brightly dyed, some thing red or rose. His dulled mind groped for an image to go with the yearning, but none emerged.

His long, unkempt black beard tickled his neck when he stared down at his hands. Facial hair was a symbol of Confederate pride, especially in prison; he did remember that much. The guard behind him barked, "Attention, you lazy reb!" He jumped to a stiff stance as the commander looked up at last from his newspaper called the *Sandusky Register.*

The commander, hatless, burly and balding, shuffled through some papers on his desk, then lifted one and squinted at it. "Lt. Phillip Baldwin, first mate on the blockade runner *Kilda,* taken and burned off Bermuda, October of Sixty-one," he read. "You're from Charleston, prisoner?"

"Yes, sir."

"You can thank your lucky stars you didn't fry like your captain and half the crew. It must have been some fireworks."

"They say," the guard behind the prisoner put in, "that Lt. Baldwin here hit his head before gettin' fished out of the water and don't remember nothing, sir."

"Are we to believe that?" Colonel Hill demanded of the prisoner, his sharp voice rising. "That ruse may have kept you from intense interrogation at Fort Delaware or Fort Chase, but you're here now and you will answer any questions put to you!"

"I wish I could," the prisoner managed with a shake of his head. "My life before the war's gone too."

"You don't remember Charleston?"

"Some of it. I have a mother there, I think."

"I'm sure she's been notified. Married?"

The prisoner closed his eyes to remember, to picture someone who floated there in the red-black sea behind his eyeballs, someone trying to row to him through searing flames. That's it, he thought, tantalized by something just out of his reach again: his wife must have worn a red gown when they said goodbye, or did she have red hair?

"Damnation, is the man going to pass out on us?" the commander demanded. "I see here he remembers enough of what the rebs are fighting for to refuse to take the Oath of Allegiance like the rest of his stripe. Lock him up and keep an eye on him for later interrogation, private. I don't hold with enemy trickery and this could be one of the slipperiest! And get it through that thick head of his that those who try to escape are shot on the beach!" he shouted as he picked up his newspaper again and shook it into submission.

The guard hustled the prisoner out; he went willingly into the sun and blessed breeze, across the packed-dirt compound toward two sprawling wood and weatherboard buildings surrounded by the stockade. He knew he was on an island in Lake Erie just off a little town called Sandusky, Ohio, far away from where he had been captured. He had spent months in a hospital in Delaware, been transferred to Fort Chase in Columbus, and now was on Johnson's Island. He was proud of recalling names from the recent past, because so many memories more distant were—just gone.

Johnson's Island. Strangely, he had felt good when they had rowed him out here, even hobbled and cuffed in the boat. But, he told himself wearily, he had been first mate on a ship, they said, so perhaps it had just been that he liked the lake lapping, rocking the hull.

As he waited for the sentry to unlock the door for the guard, he stared up at the American banner, now the Union flag, blowing on a wooden pole in the center of the compound. He squinted at it to make a blur of red against the cloudy blue sky. A woman's hair blowing in the breeze as high above him as that banner . . . a woman waiting for him, beckoning to him from the cliffs of confusion . . .

He nearly jumped out of his skin when a seagull screamed from the roof of the nearby mess hall.

"Edgy bastard, ain't you?" his guard said and shoved him into the dim barracks where men were stacked three narrow bunks deep and three high like cordwood. "Now, just don't you go gettin' skittish when you're waked up sudden or gets orders shouted your way. Get up there, last row of bunks, top one."

Ignoring the curious eyes of the southern officers imprisoned here, he climbed up on the bare bunk, fell on his back, and threw an arm over his eyes. Like a whirlpool, the images spun by him again, the bird, the red hair, the heights, the water, all stirred by his strange feelings for this island.

Maybe he had lost his mind as well as his past, he thought. Phillip Baldwin of Charleston—damn, what state was that in? You must be blasted crazy to be glad to see an island that will be your prison until you can somehow get traded back or released at war's end. Of course, they said, some died here and never went home again.

The low buzz of voices flitted through his flying thoughts again, and soon he slept the sleep of the dead.

In her first six weeks on Sanibel, Abigail learned she had been wrong about two things, first, about Lawrence Stillwell. Not that he was not smitten by her; unfortunately, he was. But she had been wrong to believe he was a man who liked to have his own way. Other than his passion to be an artist and his protective desire to see no harm came to them, he was happy to let others make decisions for him. He was content to draw and do as she wished—anything, it seemed, to please her. Knowing a man like that was a heady experience in itself.

Secondly, she had been wrong to think Sanibel was only different and exotic. She had actually found her Eden on earth and thrilled to discover each new astonishment. Sunny solitudes embraced cool sanctuaries of green darkness. The heat was a blessing to a St. Kilda lass; she went barefoot as she had seldom done at home where it was tradition. She missed cliff-high views, but there were marvels aloft in the trees Curly liked to climb with his St.

Kilda rope: bright orchids flourished there; delicate, gray hair called Spanish moss swayed in the slack-skinned gumbo-limbo trees; strangler figs clinging to cypress bore delicious fruit; bees, unknown on St. Kilda, buzzed in the palmettos to provide golden treasure. The sea bestowed more bounty: rosy-throated shells whispered like sea waves and star-shaped ones seemed to have tumbled from the skies. The winds and sun lent sweet caresses. Sanibel helped heal her heart, and she fell deeply in love with it in a far different way than she had ever loved St. Kilda. Her home island had hewn the very bedrock of her being; Sanibel was God's gracious gift to the homeless.

Twirling her hoe as if it were a gentleman's fancy cane, today she walked out to her new crop of castor bean plants on a rich soil ridge at the edge of the island's interior grassy plain. Lawrence had told her the beans could be crushed to provide medicine to fight yellow fever; Abigail was only too happy to contribute to a cure, though she yet yearned to fight a far deadlier, more distant disease.

The view was good for miles from the bean patch, like standing on a sea of grass with palmetto islands called hammocks dotting it. Her 1860 Colt revolver that she had learned to shoot—both she and Curly could aim and fire bore rifles too, now—was on loan from Lawrence. The pistol bounced awkwardly at her hip in a holster embellished with Kilda Work Margaret had made for it. She wore no petticoats, and they had greatly cut down the voluminous width of several calico day gowns to wear comfortably about the island: the pressing world of crinolines and crushes at Louisa's soirees had never seemed farther away. On her head she wore a broad bonnet of palmetto fronds María had woven; fortunately, fashion was nothing here. Curly went joyously about in a pair of tattered trousers, fishing or hunting deer as today.

The crack of a distant shot assured her there would be venison at supper to break their usual fare of fish or fowl. If it was a large deer, Curly would fetch Paulo to help him bring it back. She noted how fast the castor beans were growing, sprouting just like fourteen-year-old Curly and nine-year-old Janie. How close the two children were; Janie adored Curly as if he were her elder brother and she—

A distant scream! Heart pounding, Abigail turned to squint into the sun. Waving both arms—one of which held his rifle—

shouting something she could not make out, Curly came running at her down the grassy plain. She lifted her hems and tore toward him. Surely the fact he had hit a deer would not make the lad behave so.

"Indians! Shot—help!" she made out.

Indians! Here? Shot at him! Curly could not be shot and be running like that. No one chased him. She had seen no strangers, could not believe it, for Lawrence had said this war had driven remnants of the Seminoles deep into the mainland cypress swamps.

"You're not hit?" she cried and grabbed his shoulders to swing him to her.

"Thought it was a deer, black and brown," he gasped out. "Bolted when I saw that dev'lish awful man—chased me, turned back. Shot her—a woman—didn't mean to—"

"You shot a woman! An Indian woman! Is she hurt badly?"

"Dunno."

"We have to go back and see. Maybe we can help."

"You heard what Mr. Stillwell said about Seminoles! More'n two soldiers died for every Indian that got cleared out!"

"That was years ago in an Indian war. You go on back and tell the others what happened then. I dinna shoot her, and they wilna harm a woman."

"We've gotta lay low. You can't go back there alone!"

"Then come on and show me where."

They started back; Curly was trembling. Peeking around palmettos, he led her to the spot. Slick blood stained the ground, but no one was there.

"Come on," Curly pleaded, tugging at her arm. "Least she's not dead maybe. Let's dash back and send for Mr. Stillwell and some men."

"No! They might harm the Seminoles. I told you," she insisted, head down, tracking the bloodstains across the small clearing, "Morgan always wanted to help the escaped slaves here and Seminoles too."

"Abigail," Curly protested, though his voice still shook, "Morgan's passed now, and you can't help the whole blinking world. Mr. Stillwell, Mr. Baxter-Jones, too, said I should look out for you, but you're cork-brained 'cause that Indian man looked real uppish, and . . ."

His voice faded to a squeak. Abigail looked up. Her mouth

dropped open. Fifteen feet ahead stood a tall, barefooted woman with the blackest skin and shortest, curliest hair Abigail had ever seen. Her eyes shone star-white. Her cheeks curved like scythe blades; her large features commanded attention. She wore a blue calico skirt to her ankles and a long-sleeved, loose blouse and glass beads.

"You mean to say," the woman choked out, "you want to help 'scaped slaves and Seminoles? I'm scared Taluga gonna be mad as a hornet, but I'm scareder Yo-chay gonna die of bleedin' bad 'fore he come back."

"Where is Yo-chay? Where did Taluga go?" Abigail asked, feeling she were speaking a foreign language. The woman answered neither question, but gestured to them.

"Don't go! It's a trap!" Curly cried. But in one more step Abigail could see an ebony-haired, brown-skinned woman bleeding on the ground. Thigh-high, the wound bloomed dark against her skirt; the memory of Curly's friend Moll, dying in a London gutter, flashed through Abigail's brain as she bent with the black woman over the writhing, moaning girl.

"Wouldn't let neither Taluga nor me touch her 'til he found her mother's skirt she left at camp back yonder," the woman explained.

"We have medicine at the house. We must clean out that wound or sepsis might set in," Abigail said as she lifted the girl's skirt, then tore strips from the hem of her own to staunch the blood. She wasn't sure, but it seemed the ball must still be in her. "Curly, make some sort of a sling with your rope for this lass, so the three of us can carry her back to the house."

"That boy done shot her," the woman accused.

"He mistook her for a deer," Abigail explained as she worked. "He just learned to shoot and needs more practice—and to be much more careful." Abigail turned to the woman and saw she evidently accepted that. This close to her, Abigail noted, in the curve of her right cheek, was a raised scar in the shape of an *R*. Her eyes were large, liquid brown, proud, yet afraid. She was a striking woman, one who belonged in an exotic place.

"This Taluga," Abigail asked, "is he your master?"

"No, ma'am! I 'scaped for good and the Seminoles treat me free and one a them. Taluga's my husband, and I'm Reba. This here," she said and touched her cheek, "my white master's brand when I run the first time and got took back. Can't read a lick, but it 'R' for runaway, not Reba!" she said, her voice and look defiant now. "Yo-chay's Taluga's sister and my friend, and I can't stand the sight of blood no more, so I'm beholden to your kindness."

They looked back down at Yo-chay together; blessedly, the girl had passed out as Abigail tied the cloth strips around her thigh. Her thick lashes lying sooty on her cheek; she looked as young and helpless as a child.

They lifted her carefully into Curly's makeshift sling and bore her back toward the house. They had her nearly to the steps of the verandah when a fierce-looking Indian man charged from a palmetto thicket with a shout and a flourish of his rifle—thank God, held over his head and not pointed at them.

"Dinna move, Curly," Abigail warned as the lad swung his gun up and she grabbed the barrel. When the man glared his way, Curly quickly let it wilt to his side. Margaret ran out, her eyes wide as clam shells at the sight of their visitors. She shoved Janie back inside, then stood in the door as if to protect the place.

Cruel-looking with copper skin and sleek black hair, the Seminole wore a neckerchief and a red calico shirt stuck in deerskin leggings. A bayonette blade in his belt glinted in the sun. A powder horn and bullet pouch dangled from a shoulder strap. With broad gestures, Reba spoke to him in his melodious language, calling him Taluga. He spit out a string of obvious commands, then, when Yo-chay stirred at his voice and slitted her eyes open, he bent down to extend a deerskin pouch to her. From it tumbled a skirt that looked as if it had been made from ribbons of rainbow. Despite everything, Abigail gasped at its beauty.

"See, Yo-chay, there it is! You'll get better now," Reba exulted just before Yo-chay grunted and fainted again.

"Getting that ball out and stopping her blood will make her better," Abigail insisted. "Please tell Taluga that." She took a deep breath and turned her back on the forbidding man to hurry the others up onto the verandah with their burden.

Taluga darted around to block Abigail's path with his rifle pressed across her shoulders. "*Halwuk!*" he insisted.

"He don't want her inside a whiteblood house," Reba said. "*Halwuk* mean 'it bad.' "

Abigail, staring into Taluga's black eyes, trembled at the bitterness and hatred she read there. Slowly, he lowered his rifle to his side. She knew then that, like Reba, if she didn't cower, she could do what she must, Taluga or not.

"Tell him we grieve that his sister has accidently been hurt, and we want to help," Abigail told Reba, but kept her eyes on Taluga. "Tell him we will treat her outside, but it will be *halwuk* for Yo-chay if we don't help her right now."

To her surprise, Taluga nodded. In quite clear but jerky English, he spoke to Curly. "It good you shoot bad. Taluga show you shoot good, not like whiteblood man makes birds on paper with draw stick."

A shudder shook Abigail. These people had evidently been on the island, watching them closely for weeks, and they had not even known it. With Margaret at her side and Taluga squatting to watch every move, she bent to tend to Yo-chay.

17

In wartime some folk dearly miss
New feather bonnets, sugar, coffee,
And having enslaved servants fetch
Such fashions, sweets, and niceties.

But far isle folk want other things:
A place where all are safe and free,
Peace of mind that bairns thrive,
Such absolute necessities.

Hidden in the dark depths of the palmetto copse behind the house, Abigail sat swathed in mosquito netting she had taken from her bed after everyone else retired for the night. Fully clothed, her revolver at her hip, she waited.

Wind rattled fronds around her; the occasional hawk cry of *"kir-ee, kir-ee"* kept her on edge as it no doubt did the huddled hens in the chicken house. She judged it was near midnight, but the ripe lemon moon cast shadows and made the clearing between the main house and kitchen house almost as light as day. She felt like a shrouded ghost—or St. Kildan selkie spirit in its strange skin— waiting for she knew not what. She only knew María had said some night marauder had been stealing food from the larder. Without informing the others, even Margaret, who was always tired lately, Abigail was determined to discover who and how and why.

Until this, things had gone quite smoothly for her little family the first year on Sanibel, despite the tightening blockade noose around Florida's long neck. A Union victory at Gettysburg and sieges of Vicksburg and Charleston had greatly weakened the South, but how wrong Morgan had been to believe this war would end quickly. Like her struggles to save the bairns of St. Kilda, it seemed to stretch on forever with endless battles.

Florida's imported clothing and food were nearly choked off but for risky runs by men like Jake Summerlin. That was why, María said, she had been afraid at first to tell Abigail food was disappearing. Besides, María had admitted, twisting her apron, she knew it would upset *la señora* to hear María was certain it was *los Seminoles* stealing food. Didn't *la señora* know that "*los Indios* always they take things"? So, in a way, Abigail was hiding here to prove to María that Taluga's family would not steal from those who had befriended them—especially when they weren't even on Sanibel right now! But Abigail had discovered that María, like others, believed Seminoles moved so stealthily, almost supernaturally, that they could explode from the foliage without warning, then disappear like a puff of smoke.

It wasn't that Abigail begrudged the food to someone who needed it. She pictured some desperate, escaped slave like Reba barely staying alive on pilfered victuals. Perhaps this fugitive had not heard that on the first day of the year President Lincoln had freed the slaves with the Emancipation Proclamation. Like Morgan had been once, Abigail felt so torn: she lived in the South and held it against the Union that they had destroyed Morgan's ship—and him—but she believed in the North's cause of freedom for all.

She recalled the rapture on Reba's face when she told her Lawrence's news that the slaves were free, though the Confederates refused to accept it. Reba had cried and clapped and cavorted and even made Taluga smile. How thrilled Morgan would have been. Abigail loved a country—or was this two countries now?—that could change its traditions for the better. She felt American at heart, even if she would always be St. Kildan in her soul.

On the whole, her patchwork family and friends were doing well here: the Union blockade had not reckoned on St. Kildans and Seminoles—both victims of harsh times—working together to survive and prosper. Abigail had accepted from Lawrence three cows from whose measly milk she made rather pitiful soft cheese. The Indians liked it better than the St. Kildans, and none of the adults really mourned the lack of sugar like Curly and Janie did. For sweetening they used honey and for coffee, the tiny wild coffee beans Yo-chay picked. From deerskin last winter, Margaret sewed shoes for the children's fast-growing feet, as she had the handgift of making the old traditional footwear from the necks of solan geese at home. The Seminoles had taught them to plant pumpkins, bananas, and rice and provided the delicious tail meat of the alligator they called *al-la-pa-taw*. Taluga had taught Curly to ram a ball faster and shoot straighter and to blow a poison-tipped dart through a short piece of bamboo to catch fish and rabbits for the dinner table.

But Abigail's favorite memory of her Seminole friends was the day Yo-chay and Reba gave her and Margaret the gifts of red glass beads she wore even now, fingering them nervously as she waited.

"For all you two done to help her when she got hurt," Reba had translated Yo-chay's quiet words of gratitude. "Beads real 'portant to us Seminole women, 'cause each strand mean something done real fine, like cookin', sewin', singin'."

"Oh," Abigail had said, "a sign of handgifts. 'Tis a lovely tradition, isna it, lass?" she asked Margaret who nodded and thanked Yo-chay too.

"Some women real skilled," Reba went on, "like Taluga and Yo-chay's dead mama. Hear tell she wore so many strands they weighed her down. Their mama the daughter of a *micco* chief and he was knowed for fighting whitebloods in the last Seminole War, see?"

"I do see," Abigail said. "It explains Taluga a wee bit more and 'tis why the bonny striped skirt means so much to Yo-chay."

"That's it. That patchwork skirt the last gift she got from her mama 'fore she died. They was all goin' to be sent west to Oklahoma with other Seminoles the whitebloods caught. But Taluga kilt a guard with his own bayonette blade. He freed Yo-chay and some of their kin to hide out in the big swamp waters. See, their daddy kilt by whiteblood soldiers in the last war, but I'd say their mama died from heartbreak at losin' her man and her home and people."

"I—we understand."

Reba lowered her voice, though Taluga was hunting with Curly and Yo-chay could speak almost no English. Abigail and Margaret leaned intently closer. "You right 'bout Taluga," she whispered.

"My man hate whiteblood soldiers, 'cause all they done to his kin and tribe. You lucky you got no whiteblood soldiers here, blue or gray ones, or no tellin' what Taluga do. Lucky that Mr. Stillwell not been a soldier, but Taluga still don't trust him none."

"I know that, Reba," Abigail admitted. "But Mr. Stillwell agrees you have a right to be here, and he hasna said a word to his friends about your visits."

Reba nodded. It was Reba's telling Lawrence that Taluga kept an eye on the whereabouts of the Union soldiers at Fort Myers that had made Lawrence see Taluga as helpful, though Lawrence did not trust Taluga either. Without revealing his source, Lawrence passed on Taluga's information about Fort Myers to Jake Summerlin so their covert operations on Punta Rassa could continue without Union interference. The runners of Punta Rassa and Taluga, interested in hiding his clan from soldiers on the mainland, had survival in common.

"Reba, please tell Yo-chay we treasure these beads as she treasures her rainbow skirt," Abigail spoke for her and Margaret. Anytime Taluga was so much as mentioned, Margaret was skittish, but now for some reason had gone shaky and speechless.

"Two more things she say tell you 'bout the women's beads," Reba translated the Seminole girl's melodious words again. "If'n you was real Seminole, you'd always wear the life bead strand you got when you was born, the only ones you'd be buried with—like a woman's reward for livin' life."

"A lovely idea—a woman's reward for living life," Abigail repeated, her thoughts skipping unbidden to her loves and losses. Reba had explained that Seminole babies hardly ever died young, and although both she and Yo-chay had not yet borne children, she had seen several births. She had heard only cedar leaf medicine was put on birthing cords. If only, Abigail agonized, there had been cedar trees and not fulmar oil stirred by fouled feathers on St. Kilda!

"And," Reba interrupted her thoughts, "a woman get beads for bein' wed and bearin' children too, but you don't need no beads for that, Abigail."

Abigail nodded, bit her lip, and turned her head away, even as Margaret reached out to touch her hand in silent solace. Margaret, Abigail knew, would have another strand for Janie, but Abigail Adair West would have none for a husband or children—or for saving the bairns of St. Kilda. Yet this simple, single strand and the sketches of the bonny birds Lawrence had done—to decorate the walls of the house, he had declared, nothing she had to be beholden for—were the dearest things she had received since Morgan gave her this new life on Sanibel.

Beneath her tent of netting, Abigail jolted alert. She heard soft footsteps before she saw anyone. Had she dozed and dreamed? A dark figure stood in the darker door of the kitchen house, then stepped inside.

Abigail held her breath, waiting for the person to emerge. At last, a woman, her head and upper body covered by a shawl stepped from the deep darkness. It must be an escaped slave, perhaps someone Reba had met on her mainland travels with Taluga and sent here. But no, a slip of shawl in moonglow revealed a woman's white forehead—and blond hair!

Margaret! Margaret here, stealing food in the dead of night?

Astounded, Abigail watched as Margaret walked away from the clearing and through the grove. Abigail wriggled from her netting, tripping in her haste, hopping on one foot to free herself, then scurrying not to lose her quarry. She slowed to a tiptoe walk, wanting to call out, but afraid to startle her. What could be wrong that her dearest friend kept some sort of secret from her? Margaret, unlike Abigail's mother long ago, had never sleepwalked, so something dark lurked in the shadows here.

Hardly daring to breathe, Abigail followed her sure footed friend through the grove and down the crushed shell path toward the inland shore. Up ahead, in the silence of the blowing night, she could hear the crunch, crunch of footsteps. It terrified her that she must not really know Margaret, her mainstay all these years. She felt so desolate, so alone just when she was starting to believe this place might become home.

Abigail paused now and then to be certain Margaret had not stopped and could not hear her pursuer's footfalls. She seemed to be walking clear to Pine Island Sound. When Abigail stopped again, she was certain she heard a voice on the breeze. A man's tones? She trod slowly just off the path. She stood still, her pulse pounding, straining to hear. Through high grass, around clumps of bushes, she crept closer. Ahead, moonlight and shadows striped a small sequestered clearing where stood a low lean-to half hidden by shifting foliage. Margaret sat on the ground there, her figure melded with another larger shadow, a man's indeed, for he was speaking.

"My darling, I die until I see you each night!"

"And I ye, but I dared not come before. I never ken about the Seminoles or Lawrence and canna compromise Abigail."

"I know, I know. I understand."

"Aren't ye hungry, lad? I brought some bread and meat besides the usual."

"I am only starved for the sight of you," the deep voice declared as their seated forms merged to one.

Leaning forward, peering through the leaves, Abigail stood transfixed and uncertain in her confusion. She must give them privacy; she must stay; she must not announce herself; she must demand to know all. But if she did not know her friend anymore, she certainly did not know herself. A cascade of passion crashed through her: longing for Morgan forever lost, desire for a man to hold her like that, anger at Margaret, jealousy, joy, emptiness, she did not know. Finding Louisa hidden away with her lover flashed from muted memory. Would it always be that way for her now, looking in on others while she longed for such herself, yet fought belonging to a man again? Hands pressed to her mouth, when she turned to flee, a stick cracked under her.

She heard their gasps, frenzied motions, frightened tones. Too late to flee now. She stepped from the shadows, but her voice caught in her throat. The man tried to rise, but perhaps Margaret held him back. A raised saber glinted in the glow of the moon.

" 'Tis I, lass!" Abigail choked out.

"Cal, 'tis my friend. I should have kenned that sooner or later she—Abby, I'm so sorry ye had to learn it this way."

"You dinna trust me, after all we've been through?"

"That isna it at all. Let me explain!"

Abigail shuffled closer. The man was handsome, even as distraught at he looked, hatless, blond with a straggly beard silvered in moonlight. He wore a tattered gray uniform, all silvery too. He staggered to his feet, still holding his saber, Margaret clinging to his other arm. He was tall and gaunt. He seemed some knight in moonlit-shining armor who had ridden in from old England for this dream the three of them shared.

"Abby, 'tis only—Cal, we must tell her—that my—this gentleman is a Confederate deserter who fought in the last Seminole War and we—because of Lawrence and Taluga and yer difficult position between the two of them—we couldna compromise ye nor put ye in danger—oh, lass, I yearned to tell ye so, tell ye I was in love!"

"In . . . love . . ." Abigail repeated and sank to her knees.

Margaret helped the man to sit again; only then did Abigail see his left leg was bound straight in a crude wood splint and he needed help to stand or sit. Margaret, too, sank down, holding this silver stranger's hands. Both of them told Abigail his story, their voices, like their fingers, entwined.

When he was eighteen, Calvin Dane, second son of a retired military man, had been sent to fight in the Third Seminole War from his family's cotton plantation in northern Florida near Tallahassee. His elder brother Josh would inherit the plantation; Cal inherited his father's previous career as a soldier. But he hated the hunting and capturing or killing of the Seminoles as if they were game birds. Yet he did not want to let his father down, to be less than was expected. Finally, near the end of the war in 1857, Cal was wounded and sent home. He wed his childhood sweetheart, Sally, who died of consumption a year later. When his father insisted he return to active duty when the War Between the States began, still grieving, he obeyed.

But he thought the Confederacy mistaken for insisting on states' rights over the unity of the country. Besides, after chasing, killing, and tearing Seminoles from their homes, he realized Negroes in Africa, ancestors of the slaves now working the Dane plantation, had been abused that way. He argued with his family and friends, he asked his commanding officer—an old comrade of his father—if he could be placed in a noncombative position. His petition was refused: everyone said his wife's death had unhinged him and that battle burdens had broken his manly resolve. He must sacrifice all on the altar of the great Confederate cause.

He finally snapped when he was assigned to a local Florida militia unit ordered to sweep escaped slaves, southern deserters, and ragged bands of Seminoles from Florida. He deserted and fled farther south to these offshore islands he had learned of during the Seminole War. He built a hut on Pine Island but had rowed his raft over to nearby Buck Island near Sanibel for venison last month.

There, a cottonmouth snake had surprised him; he fell over a log and broke his leg. He killed the snake but his leg—like his life, he admitted—had not set right.

"And then," Abigail prompted in the awkward silence when the two of them paused, "you found each other."

"He crawled to his raft and was trying to get across the sound when I saw him," Margaret explained. "He washed in at my feet, like that Ulysses Morgan used to tell tales of, Abigail. I helped Cal build this splint and hid him here. When I told him how ye helped others, he almost let me bring him to the house!"

"Until Miss Margaret told me about Mr. Stillwell serving the South and about that hostile Seminole brave who comes and goes, ma'am," Calvin said. "Secrecy seemed the best protection for me— all of you—if Confederate soldiers or those Seminoles came calling. I might have my ceremonial saber yet, but my guns are out of ammunition and I drew the line at my Margaret's bringing me some from your or the boy's guns."

My Margaret: that said it all, Abigail thought. Despite the fear and furtiveness in their love, her friend's face needed no moonlight to glow. Happiness for Margaret soothed Abigail's shock and pain. Besides, they had been thinking of her welfare too, though she would much rather have known about them. She liked Calvin Dane for his gentlemanly ways, for his loving Margaret, and for—like Morgan—his having suffered separations from family and friends for defending what he thought was right.

"I am very happy for you," she assured them. "But dinna you see, if we carefully explain things to Taluga—that you hated the war against the Seminoles and that you reject a soldier's life— perhaps we can patch things up so you won't have to live in fear."

"We couldna take that chance," Margaret insisted.

"Besides, Miss Abigail, the thing we haven't told you is that, for honor's sake, I intend to get to the big Union garrison at Key West to enlist to fight with the Yankees. It's important to me, the first real decision—other than asking for Miss Margaret's hand—I feel I've really made on my own."

Abigail understood that. It was not only women who must find the courage and strength to batter themselves loose from family and tradition, those things to which it was most natural to cling. Everyone must stake their claim and defend it. Morgan, Lawrence, Curly, even Douglas had done so. Lady Grange and her own mother had joined the battle; Louisa struggled with it as did Margaret and Abigail.

"But Cal's leg must get better before he enlists," Margaret insisted.

"Of course. How is it mending, sir?"

"It's healing—like my heart since I met Miss Margaret."

"Then I can only wish you both the best—and help if I can."

"Och, Abby, just knowing ye understand and forgive me is . . ." Margaret began, but her words dissolved in tears on Cal's shoulder as he held her tight.

Stiff-legged, unsure how long they had sat here, Abigail rose. "I shall leave you two alone, and Margaret and I shall make plans to add to your comfort in the morning. I think at least, lass, your Janie and Curly, too, should meet your betrothed. Oh, no, please, Mr. Dane—Cal—dinna rise on my account!"

"But it was such an honor to meet you, ma'am, though I feel I know you already with all Miss Margaret has said of you, as if you two were devoted sisters. Much obliged for your kindness and understanding," he concluded with a formal bow from where he sat.

"I could not be otherwise, having been in love when 'twas hidden and forbidden," she said, her poetic words sounding so strange. But then it had been a strange night. She had plunged into the dark to discover a theft and found there was one within her darkness too, deeper than a friend's deception. But surely there was no way to ever heal the hole in her heart Morgan had left behind.

They decided, for now, to keep Calvin Dane their secret from Lawrence, southern sympathizer that he was. María Menéndez was excited to know *Señora* Margaret had a secret suitor and she happily prepared meals for him. Janie and Curly met Cal and spent some time with him during daylight hours. The man went out of his way to win Janie over. As for Taluga, who roamed the island when he was here and seemed to be able to smell out anything amiss, they decided he would have to be carefully approached and sounded out next time the Seminoles visited. If they thought they could tell him, they would. And just when Abigail was beginning to believe that

Lawrence's avid desire to please her meant she could entrust the secret to him, his next arrival jolted that possibility from her mind.

"Abigail, you all won't believe this, but the runner just brought a letter for you clear from London!" Lawrence shouted, waving the square of parchment at her as he strode across the clearing to join her on the verandah.

Southern mail was scarcer than southern victories; Abigail had not received one letter from Corwin, though surely he had sent some. How she longed to hear how he and Louisa were doing. And if only he had some word about St. Kilda! She sank into a chair to read words already three months old:

> *20 August 1863*
>
> > *My dearest Abigail,*
>
> > *I pray this correspondence will reach you in these tenuous times. I have received your letter dated December '62 and have sent two letters to you since. If they have not been received, I tell you again how relieved I am to know that you are safely settled. But to matters at hand—*
>
> > *I must inform you news to both bless and blast your hopes that all would go well for your friends and the bairns of St. Kilda. My channels to the MacLeod laird on Harris inform me that there was considerable upheaval on St. Kilda several months after your visit.*
>
> > *To wit: Your friend Annie Gillies struck and killed her own grandmother, Isobel MacCrimmon, with some sort of ceremonial stone bowl. Being heavy with child, Mrs. Gillies was kept at the Reverend Mr. MacKay's manse while she bore and nursed her child, after which, that child—a daughter, I believe—was given to her sister, one Flora Nichol, to rear. Mrs. Gillies was sent to Glasgow for trial, pronounced guilty, and incarcerated there. As I know you would wish, I have people looking into the circumstances of this crime and this sentence.*
>
> > *And now for the only good news in this shameful sadness: the laird, perhaps at my prompting on your behalf, has sent a Harris midwife to St. Kilda to train several new ones there. Although this woman is hardly the educated doctor you have long hoped for and they yet refuse, she*

may be comparatively enlightened and, we must hope, acceptable to the St. Kildans.

I am also looking into the whereabouts of Edmund Drummond to continue the lawsuit in your behalf; however, my solicitor tells me the scoundrel is seldom in England these days, taking trips as far afield as France and South America. At least, my dear girl, you and yours are hidden safe on Sanibel.

My deepest regards to Margaret, to the irrepressible Curly, and dear Janie. Your little family, I feel, is mine too, for I claim no other.

As for London gossip, Louisa is yet at war with Lord Hartington, for, upon his return from viewing American battlefields, he established a certain "Lady Skittles" in a townhouse he visits more often than he does the salons of Manchester House or Kimbolton. Yet our duchess carries on with great public aplomb, even entertaining the young and impressionable Prince of Wales, however much Her Majesty has supposedly forbidden it. Ah, why does it seem we have trod this primrose, thorn-strewn path before?

As ever, my continued admiration and devotion,
Curwin

"Abigail, are you all right?" Lawrence asked when she sat hunched over the letter. "Not bad news?"

"What? Yes, I . . . Lawrence, please excuse me."

She went into her room and closed the door. Shaking, she sank on the bed and reread the parts of the letter about Annie. The murder scene leapt at her, for surely she herself had seen the place and weapon and, perhaps, she had incited the motive. She could imagine the two women arguing in that shadowy cleit, Annie pouring that poison oil out on the ground so it could never be used on her next bairn or others. Isobel cursing her and screaming she would make more oil. Then Annie raising the empty, traditional stone bowl and, simply, smashing the past.

Clasping her arms, wide-eyed, Abigail rocked back and forth. "I didna mean to force you to it, Annie, but it had to end. I was so harsh with you, lass, that last day, and you so frightened. Should I have done that deed for the bairns long ago?"

Suddenly, she saw Annie, staring at her from a window of the minister's manse the way that other woman had. Locked up by that dreadful Mr. MacKay, gossiped about, detested, waiting to be arrested, watching her bairn flourish on her mother's milk through the eight days. Such torment in knowing her bairn would live without the fulmar oil but be lost to her anyway, raised by Flora who had come to hate Annie for Abigail's sake. Abigail pictured Annie, taken from St. Kilda, staring back at her home and husband, leaving all she knew and loved for prison in Glasgow. Or did it warm her to ken, perhaps, with Isobel gone and a new midwife sent to replace the long line of knee-women, she must be martyred so the bairns might live?

Abigail could hear the island women now, whispering this murder too was the heritage of Abigail MacQueen Adair and her demented mother before her who had killed herself. Now, now at last, she could glimpse the black despair of her mother, destined to live without the man she adored, desolate because her two sons had died and the folks of St. Kilda were so cold and uncaring to her. She could at last realize what had happened to Glenna MacQueen; she could at last forgive her for throwing herself off the cliff into what she believed was her only escape.

Tears trembled down her cheeks until fear turned to anger. She swiped at her face and jumped up to write a letter to Corwin. Even here, so far away from Annie, whose island was a chill, lonely cell, Abigail would do what she could to help save her from such deadly despair.

The next time Taluga came to Sanibel—three months later, the longest he had been away—he brought more bad news. Union and Confederate deserters on the mainland were becoming much more numerous and reckless. They were stealing cattle grazing inland and marauding ever farther south. Hating both sides in the struggle now and out only for their own wealth, they were raiding plantations for slaves, especially helpless children. Lawrence explained these lawless deserters could get money from reselling Negro children to the other plantation owners who desperately needed workers they could control. Or the raiders were ransoming them to abolitionists who would pay anything to free a slave, especially a child.

Lawrence listened glumly; even if the blockade runners went

undiscovered by the soldiers at nearby Fort Myers, such upheaval could cause Yankee troops to be sent from the large garrison at Key West to settle the area, and thus, inadvertently discover their base.

"I hope we don't have to move," he said, his eyes on Abigail, who sat in a chair near his on the verandah with Margaret while the three Seminoles and Curly sat on the floor. "Punta Rassa's been perfect for us—and so close to you all, Abigail."

Taluga just grunted. Although he was willing to share his news with Lawrence, the Seminole never spoke directly to him, nor Lawrence to Taluga. Sometimes Taluga spoke Seminole and let Reba translate; sometimes he spoke his choppy English to Curly and let Lawrence overhear. But neither man liked nor trusted the other. For that reason, even now, Abigail and Margaret had asked everyone to keep silent about Cal until they discerned if Taluga would tolerate him at least as he did Lawrence.

"Taluga not stay here long," Taluga told Curly. "Come get yellow fever oil, go help slave children bad sick."

"What slave children are sick?" Abigail asked. "Where?"

"Need find good place hide them 'til they no sick and go to my people," Taluga said, still seemingly addressing Curly. "Deserters stole children. When they sick, deserters leave them. Taluga give food children, come here get good medicine. Taluga like kill whiteblood deserters, but they gone."

That blatant threat sucked strength from them all. Silence stretched out before Abigail spoke again. She was certain he was aiming his news at her, so why couldn't he speak directly to her?

"How many children, Taluga? I have the castor oil, but where are they?"

"Need help of Reba, Yo-chay, others go too," Taluga said and gestured in the general direction of the mainland. "Past Fort Myers on Caloosahatchee, we go around," he concluded still not looking her way.

"Taluga knows ye quite well, lass," Margaret said. "I can see ye already think you're going. Are ye daft? What if ye run into those soldiers—*deserter soldiers* Taluga would like to kill?" she asked pointedly, her voice trembling.

As if no one else had spoken, Taluga added under his breath, "Save children, learn them read."

Taluga had refused to learn to read, but some days he had listened while Abigail taught Reba right along with Curly and Janie. Yet he had indeed figured out Abigail well enough to know she could not resist helping children, especially those who were ill.

"I will go along," Abigail declared. "After all, it is my castor oil—"

"Abigail," Lawrence cut in, "I have listened to enough of this nonsense. You all surely cannot mean to go traipsing off into the— the wilds in wartime with lawless deserter bands and Union soldiers loose—and with Seminoles who—ah, who know the area as you do not—and have not asked you to go—"

"If I were ye, Lawrence," Margaret interrupted in turn, "I'd save my breath to cool my soup."

"Then I am going too, Taluga!" Lawrence addressed the Indian for the first time and rose to tower over the seated man before he too sprang to his feet. "I won't have Abigail hurt!"

Taluga swept his hand down as if to cut Lawrence off. "Abigail come, she no hurt. Tomorrow, you come too, bring guns," he concluded and stalked off, fortunately, not in the direction of Cal's little camp.

"Then 'tis settled," Abigail said, her voice shaking like Margaret's. Lawrence had not protested one thing she wanted in over a year until now. Ignoring Margaret's tragic expression and Lawrence's sputtering protests, Abigail snagged Curly's arm before he could trail after Taluga. She wanted to tell him he would be in charge here—with Cal to back him up if there were trouble—before the boy asked Taluga to go too. Curly might not be her son, but he seemed to have inherited her stubborness and fierce loyalties as if the two of them were real flesh and blood.

For two days, each carrying supplies wrapped in a blanket tied to a pine branch, Abigail and Lawrence accompanied Taluga's family northeast on the mainland through sawgrass plains and thick foliage, following the south bank of the Caloosahatchee River. They gave broad berth to stockaded Fort Myers and the few plantations along the river; Taluga did indeed know the way through all the narrow back paths. The pace he set made Abigail realize she was not half as hardy as she'd been on milking jaunts up mountains, but that had been years ago.

"Close now," Taluga said quietly, and Abigail whispered the

words back to Lawrence who brought up the rear. But then, the Indian held up his hand and they all halted, breathing hard, perspiring. *"Halwuk,"* he said. "Too quiet. Smell death on wind."

Though Abigail was glistening with sweat, a chill swept her. Her hair prickled along the nape of her neck. Lawrence came closer and cocked his rifle when Taluga did. Even slight sounds seemed deafening. To have come this far for these poor children, she thought, only to find them dead of their disease or perhaps hurt by wild animals or even more human marauders . . . but as they edged closer to the next clearing, she saw Taluga squinting upward into leafless, tattered trees. Then they all saw the carnage on the ground and stood horrified until Lawrence spoke at last.

"Those greedy plumers have been through here, but I heard they were over by Okeechobee."

"Killers, like whiteblood soldiers," Taluga said and stepped into the sad scene. He stopped to examine a torn carcass. "Scalped," he muttered.

Abigail followed, wide-eyed, afraid she would vomit at the sight. The stench was dreadful; she clamped her nostrils shut and gasped through her mouth. Masses of snowy and great egrets lay dead in discarded piles, their bloodied bodies stripped of their scalps, wing, and tail plumes. Leaves and limbs had been shot off their rookery trees to bring them down. Sticks from their nests, where instinct told them to guard their little ones, littered the ground.

Abigail swallowed back the bile that rose in her throat. Big, black vultures flapped away to circle overhead while the human intruders walked through their banquet hall. Abigail began to cry soundlessly, but she could not look away. Broken eggs and sunbaked hatchlings lay here too. If they had only come a day sooner, perhaps, as on St. Kilda, some could have been saved. Now, everywhere under their feet, like miniature beasts of carrion marched rows of black ants to and from the victims.

"The blighters, the bastards!" she choked out to Lawrence, who put his arms around her. For once, though he had done so many times and she had refused or not responded, she clung to him.

"Whitebloods!" Taluga said again and she heard him spit. "We go on, hope children not hurt. We go on!" he said and tapped Abigail's arm.

Lawrence released her reluctantly. She followed Taluga, Reba, and Yo-chay out of the devastation. Until the narrow path began again, Lawrence walked beside her, holding her arm.

We go on. Taluga's words made her angry at first but then gave her strength. Always, she thought, yes, we go on, despite people's cruelties and the world's wrongs. But she swore on her very soul that the damned plumers—all Edmund Drummond's ilk—would never touch the birds in the rookery on her sanctuary of Sanibel. For, like brave Annie sitting in that Glasgow prison, she would kill them first, just as they had these bonny birds!

Not far beyond the rookery, where Taluga had secreted them in a palmetto thicket, they found the thirteen children, once briefly liberated from slavery, now deserted to death. Before dawn the next day, they buried three and dosed the rest, hoping the castor oil would flush the poison from them. Aged approximately five to eight, the little ones clung to dark-skinned Reba, but they held out their arms to Abigail and Yo-chay too. All were soremuscled and disoriented, wracked with alternating spasms of chill and fever. When they headed back, Lawrence and Taluga carried the four heaviest children in a blanket sling between them; the women carried two each, tied to their backs by vines.

The going home was much slower, harder. Abigail's back and legs ached, her feet sank deep in sand or soil. More than once she almost lost her balance. How she longed for her old milk pail yokes to better bear the burden. But she felt strong inside, strangely fulfilled. Helping here momentarily eased the pain of her unfulfilled vow on St. Kilda and the new one she had made in the ruined bird rookery.

Finally, staggered with exhaustion the second day, they camped just back from the river before they neared Fort Myers. With Lawrence standing guard, the women tended the children while Taluga scouted ahead.

"I've always known you love children," Lawrence said when their little charges had gone to sleep on the ground. "You no doubt want a child or two of your own. Lately," he said, and captured her hand in his, "for the first time, I do too."

She almost told him she feared she could never bear her own, but she kept her silence as she gently disengaged her hand. When things were better settled, in fairness, she must tell him—and thereby give him a reason not to want her as she knew he did. But she thought again of Margaret in Cal's arms in the blowing dark of night and longed for such herself. Still, she thought as she shook her head to clear it, not with Lawrence, perhaps not with anyone again.

Her heart beat very fast and for one moment she thought that was the sound she heard. But across the stretch of grassland rode four men. Abigail had seen so few horses since England the big beasts looked gigantic. Too late to hide; the gray-clad riders saw them. The first two drew rifles from behind their saddles, the next two raised revolvers and stood in their stirrups to look around. Having no choice, Lawrence lowered his gun.

"State your names and business!" the first man, an officer, demanded as if he, a Confederate, commanded this Union-held land.

"Good southern citizens just taking some slave children back home!" Lawrence told them and came to stand next to Abigail, who kept Yo-chay behind her. Reba, curse her, stood her ground beside them too defiantly, arms akimbo, making a very large target. But Lawrence introduced himself and Abigail as if they were the only two who mattered. "So, what's amiss, sir?" he asked the officers with a stiff smile that betrayed to Abigail his enforced calm.

"We're looking for deserters on both sides who've been stirring up trouble around these parts," the officer said. "Our boys in gray need every man we can round up. We got no quarrel with loyal southern folk, but are all these pickaninnies yours?"

Abigail had never heard that word before, but she knew he was insulting her little charges. "Yes, they are," she said when Lawrence hesitated, "and I'm so glad to see you all!" She hoped her attempt at a southern drawl was not betrayed by her Scottish lilt. "You see, some of the scoundrels you gentlemen are chasing came through and stole some of my slaves and we all are just fetching them back. This slave," she went on, pointing to Reba, "is my maid and she's always rather protective of me—and you all can call me Miss Abigail if you wish."

Abigail saw Reba stiffen beside her. Surely, she would go along with this ruse.

"That's right," Lawrence said and began a rambling recital of how he was associated with the cattle runners and how they appreciated anything the Confederacy could do to protect southern interest. Yes, he told them, this lady, "Miss Abigail, the Widow West," had a house and land to work on a barrier island; he was betrothed to her, he dared to put in. Now Abigail too, like Reba, stiffened at the lies they all told to save themselves. At least the soldiers' gun barrels had been lowered now.

Two of the men dismounted; one bowed and, despite Lawrence's claim to her, gave Abigail much more of a lookover than he did the supposedly escaped and recaptured slaves. Now Lawrence's voice took on a strident tone; Reba seethed; the children waked and fussed; Yo-chay glared at them; and Abigail was torn between hope Taluga would come back and terror he would shoot any soldier he saw.

Finally, the second dismounted man asked, "this pretty little Indian gal yours too, Miz West?"

"We found her as a child," Abigail said, "and she helps when we have to nurse sick children. These are all so ill, I'd suggest you all not come closer to us if you all dinna—do not—want to catch real sick with yellow fever."

"Yellow fever?" the officer asked and stepped back from her. "Why, heard tell that can sweep a whole company of men."

"I'm sorry I've used all the medicine dosing these slaves— valuable property, you know," she tried to sound apologetic.

The two men backstepped toward their horses and remounted. Abigail realized she should have used this ploy—which was the only piece of truth they'd told—before upsetting everyone with her stories. Nor should Lawrence have said she was his betrothed!

"Be sure and steer clear of them Yankees at Fort Myers, though the place ain't much," the officer called back over his shoulder. They had no more than ridden off the opposite direction they had come than Reba turned to her, seizing Abigail's upper arms in the traditional Seminole greeting where they shook the entire person and not just the hand.

"You done real good," Reba said to Abigail's profound relief. "I'd like to brand an *R* on every one of their cheeks for rebs! You know, I'd die for sure 'fore I became anyone's slave ever again, but you'd be 'bout the best mistress there is, I bet!"

"Mistress—or fiancée," Lawrence put in with a grin and wiped sweat from his brow. Abigail put her arm around Yo-chay and smiled herself, despite her weak knees. But their brief celebration was halted when Taluga strode from the foliage, hitting his furrowed forehead with his fist.

"I wanted kill those whitebloods, but gun would call Fort Myers' men. Too many Taluga to kill at once, danger for you." He glared at Lawrence as if to demand what he would have done in such a battle. "Next whiteblood soldier Taluga see, he die!"

Such frustrated fury horrified Abigail, especially for Margaret's beloved Cal. He still walked with a pronounced, painful limp and, though she had given him some ammunition, he seemed no match for Taluga. She had to do something before all that exploded. But now, together, they had to get these children home.

18

Stand before the marriage stool
Hands, cheeks, hearts so warm.
Now live as one in weal and woe,
Whatever be the storm.

Vow to each fidelity,
Pray for sunshine all the way.
Two pasts one bright future make
On Sanibel today.

"Och, Abby, I fear I'm the first bride ever to set her wedding day by when someone *canna* come," Margaret said as Abigail buttoned the pale green silk gown up her friend's back.

"I ken, lass, and I'd love to have Yo-chay and Reba here, but they go with Taluga, so that's the way of it. 'Tis enough to ask that Lawrence abide Cal in that new Yankee uniform he's so proud of."

"Dinna my love look so braw in it? But then that man would look fine without a single stitch on his back!"

"Will you tell me about that next, lass?" Abigail teased.

They laughed as their eyes met in the bedroom mirror. Margaret, flushed and glowing, turned to face Abigail and clasped her hands. "Dearest sister," Margaret said, "this will be the first time we have really been apart in years—ever."

Abigail nodded solemnly. "I shall take good care of Janie 'til you come back."

"Ye've always been a second mother to her. Ye dinna think 'tis wrong to leave her here to go off for a bit with him?"

"We've both seen the grief that can come from separation in a marriage. I'd almost tell you to go with him into battle if you must. Besides, as soon as Cal's sent north from Key West, you will be back here with us until this terrible thing ends."

"Sometimes I think my lass would suffer more from being apart from Curly than from her own mother. But Abigail, it pains me not just to be leaving ye and Janie for a spell, but that I am so happy—this way—and ye are not."

"Of course, I am! I've never been busier with the plantation children to teach! I'm afraid they're all beginning to speak 'wi' a wee bi' of St. Kilda brogue.' "

"Ye ken what I mean. Busy is not happy, my dear, and Lawrence loves you so!"

"But I canna return those feelings, so I told him *not* to love me," Abigail declared and went to her wooden chest for the wedding gift she had made.

"Told him not to love—really, Abigail West, after all we've been through, ye dare make light of that! As if someone can harness or bridle love! Ye always said ye wanted a man who would let ye have yer way, one whose goals blended with yers. After this war ends, I think Lawrence would be content over the years to live here, or in London—even back on St. Kilda—"

"Impossible!"

"What is? Lawrence or St. Kilda? He'd be content to draw his birds—or, if ye'd wed him, give full attention to the birds and the bees, so—"

"Such fine fettle the bride is in today to tease and scold," Abigail retorted. "Thank you, my friend, for worrying about me, but I dinna mind being known as the stubborn spinster of Sanibel." She tried to keep her voice light, but they spoke of heavy things. If they didn't stop, they'd go to sobbing and be blithering bairns at the wedding. To avoid facing her own feelings about Lawrence on this special day, she stood and displayed Margaret's gift with a flourish.

"Och, Abby, a bonny St. Kilda bridal cap, starched ribbons and all!"

"You'll be able to afford your own bonnets—without feathers, mind you!—soon enough with Cal's six-hundred dollar enlistment pay, but this is special."

Abigail pinned the cap in Margaret's hair, and they admired it in the mirror. It was a windy day outside almost worthy of St. Kilda; how pretty the ribbons would bounce in the breeze, Abigail thought proudly. It was pieced together from selvage cuttings from the last of her London gowns. But for using a wedding stool for the bridal couple to kneel on today, other St. Kilda marriage traditions seemed out of place here—except for the hearthsong she would sing. Now, with a last hug, the two went out onto the verandah to face the tiny, expectant congregation.

Lawrence stood smiling in his Sunday best, turning his top hat in his hands, ready to give the bride away to a nervous, handsome bridegroom. Cal was finally getting about without a cane; he had insisted he be able to walk freely at Margaret's side before they wed. Janie handed her mother a bouquet of pink swamp azaleas and kissed her cheek. Then the grinning, scrubbed Curly gave Janie his arm and escorted her grandly to their wicker chairs of honor. Standing behind them, María and Paulo Menéndez beamed as if they were proud parents. Sitting on woven mats, their backs against the house, sat the children, squirming with anticipation of the wedding feast to come. Mr. Morrison, the somewhat seedy-looking Methodist lay minister Lawrence had paid to come over from Punta Rassa, cleared his throat and began with "Dearly beloved, we all are gathered here ..."

Abigail and Lawrence stood with the bridal couple, facing slightly inward on either side. His pale brown eyes fixed on hers; the wind winnowed her hair against her flushed cheeks. More than once, Lawrence had hinted he wanted to ask for her hand. This morning, he had whispered, "If you all but say the word, the next special day could be ours." But, blessedly, he had not pushed nor demanded. Unlike other men she had known, he had always let her set the pace and make the major decisions.

She appreciated that, and yet, as passionately as Lawrence looked at her now, she still did not feel as she had with Morgan. Even with Douglas in her youth, there had been that burning need to belong to him, although then his flame consumed her entire life; with Morgan a conflagration had roared in her, despite their disagreements. Yes, as Margaret had said, she had once thought she wanted a man she could rule, but now she knew that wasn't it at all. She needed a man with strength that struck against and kindled her own. That must be what would make sparks fly again. And yet, with Lawrence, there could be calm, comfort, companionship, and perhaps—her wildest hope, though she was getting on in years for it—children. Not a marriage of convenience, but one of confidence for years to come.

She wondered if Lawrence knew her blushes were for such wayward thoughts at this solemn moment. She was grateful he had helped arrange this hasty ceremony as soon as Taluga left this time, so the Seminole would not catch them wedding Margaret to Cal. As tensions increased on the mainland, Taluga had been gone a great deal so they did not have to worry about his finding Cal here. His vows to kill whiteblood soldiers still terrified her and Margaret.

Just after the exchanging of the vows, when her time came to sing, Abigail finally turned away from Lawrence's intense perusal to face her little audience. She began the soaring notes of the old St. Kilda wedding hearthsong, so far away from its home. She had re-written the last stanza, though, as befitted new traditions in sunny Sanibel.

But she screamed her last high note as Taluga exploded from the distant shadows of the grove. For one moment, she thought her fears had caused a vision, but he was a living nightmare! He halted near the verandah, taking everything in. Reba and Yo-chay were not with him. The warrior frowned, then pointed his rifle right at Cal and Margaret. His revolver and bayonette blade glinted in his belt. None of them had guns.

Margaret shrieked; Lawrence shouted "No!" Curly did too as he and Janie rose from their chairs. Margaret pulled Janie to her as Cal thrust them behind him and drew his ceremonial sabre. María Menéndez began to wail. The minister cowered behind Lawrence. Wide-eyed, the little children did not budge from their place on the floor. Before Lawrence could stop her, Abigail stepped in front of the newly married couple and held up both hands as if to ward off Taluga's anger, hatred—and bullet.

"Taluga, dinna shoot!"

Holding the rifle steady, Taluga lifted his head from the sight to scan the area, evidently for other blue-clad soldiers. He came closer, still not looking at her. He edged around the corner of the verandah to take aim at the men as if Abigail and Margaret were not even there.

"Taluga," Abigail said, "this man is Calvin Dane, a good whiteblood, a friend to us all. He just joined the Yankee army last week. We have invited him here. He comes to marry—take for a wife—Margaret." Her voice broke. It was obvious Taluga was here to deal only with the men and with his gun still raised. She had to make him listen to her!

"Whiteblood soldier *halwuk,*" Taluga muttered.

"You know that isna true of all whiteblood men," she dared to argue. "Not of Lawrence, and Curly has been to you like—like a whiteblood son."

That got Taluga's eye off his gun sight again, though he was close enough it didn't matter now. From there, with both his guns, he could shoot them all to pieces point-blank. Abigail's legs were shaking, but she shuffled in front of the gun barrel again. Her eyes jumped to the bayonette in his belt; she was certain it was the very one Reba had said he used to kill a white soldier to escape. She fingered her Seminole beads, hoping that would mean something to him. They were all afraid to move, but Cal pushed her slightly away. When Curly stepped forward, Abigail yanked him back, gripping his arm so hard he stood at attention like the grown men.

Cal spoke before she could again. "As Miss Abigail says, I have just joined the Union army at Fort Myers, Taluga, but I told them not a word of you or your people coming through these parts. I am a southern deserter who had been living on Pine Island and then here for a short time. I want to fight against those who believe in slavery—slavery of Negroes like your wife or the Seminoles."

Abigail carefully shifted her weight to stand on his foot. If he went on to give his entire tale of fighting in the Seminole Wars, Taluga would kill him for certain. Then, one child Taluga and Lawrence had carried back scooted closer to grin and wiggle fingers at Taluga as if this was some sort of game. One of the younger ones crawled closer, just under the potential line of fire.

"Sit still, all you children! No one moves!" Abigail commanded. "You may watch from over there what your good, brave Seminole friend decides to do."

Taluga's eyes slammed into hers at last. His bronze brow crashed over his slitted stare, but she glimpsed something there besides hatred before they shut her out again. She had seen that disdainful look from men in the St. Kilda Parliament, from London doctors, Edmund Drummond, others. Her stomach flopped over; now Taluga would shoot Cal, Lawrence, perhaps her too to show he was master of this world.

"This new whiteblood here long time, Abi-gail? Knows too much," Taluga muttered.

"He is just like you in that way, Taluga. You were here and cleverly watched us long before we met you, though you meant us no harm. And I wouldna like to take a bloody, blasted bullet out of anyone here today the way we took that one out of Yo-chay together."

"*Halwuk*," Taluga said and spit on the verandah steps. "No time for women's talk. Law-rence, Taluga came tell you deserters attack Punta Rassa cattle. Trouble there. Want no soldiers like this man here. He maybe get shot, tell him!"

Abigail gasped, as Taluga moved to pull the trigger of his rifle, but he yanked the barrel straight up into the air before it blasted. "Come now, Law rence!" Taluga threw back over his shoulder and sprinted for the path to the sound.

Lawrence pulled Abigail hard to him and kissed her on the mouth when it was Cal and Margaret who should kiss so. Abigail felt so staggered by everything, she held tightly to him.

"However bold you are, you still need me in all sorts of ways," he whispered to her, his voice ragged as if he'd run miles. "I will be back with an important question for you, no matter what's happening over there." He dashed inside to fetch his gun and loped after Taluga toward the shore. The minister ran too, his coattails bobbing.

But for María's continued sniffling, the rest of them stood silent, close together, just breathing. Even the little ones had not budged since Abigail's stern scolding. Curly spoke at last.

"No wonder Taluga's name means wet crow! Now don't he just shake his feathers sometimes! Abigail, can I go with them to help?"

"No! I mean, we need your protection here as Cal and Margaret will be leaving soon."

They heard the crackle of distant shots. Margaret, held tight in Cal's arms, smiled tearily at Abigail over his shoulder.

" 'Tis a wedding day we shalna forget, Mrs. Dane," Abigail told her and turned to tend to the children. Utter relief made her want to cry, but she blinked back the tears. Yet they matted her eyelashes and flew when she blinked. She admitted to herself that she cried not only in gratitude and joy, but in the anticipation of hearing Lawrence's question for her when he returned. Perhaps, just perhaps, she had borne the burdens of going it alone without a man too long.

"Look at these lily-livered, ragtag and bobtail rebs, will you, boys?" Colonel Hall's shrill voice rang out over the decimated ranks of assembled prisoners surrounded by armed guards in the stockade yard. "Not even enough backbone in the lot of 'em to measure up to you boys, even in a little baseball match!"

"I'd like to see," the prisoner next to Phillip Baldwin whispered out of the side of his mouth, "those damned Yankees strike a ball or run a base after living on rats this spring and shivering through the fuel famine! Thunderation!"

It had been a horrible year with many prisoners lost to disease; now they faced another grueling winter. Both sides had halted prisoner exchanges when the North insisted captured Negro soldiers be treated as prisoners of war just like white soldiers. Knowing they would waste away here until the cessation of hostilities—which now, for certain, meant a brutal Southern defeat—had been the final blow on broken spirits for most of these Johnson Island prisoners. Yet now, the early September sun felt good on their backs and bare heads and they breathed in the cool, fresh breeze from the lake.

"Hill just likes to see us ground under his boot, even if it's supposedly a game," Phillip muttered. "I'm as listless and hollow-bellied as the rest of you, but I say let's take them and win!"

"Wha's 'at back there?" the fat guard standing next to the commander said and ambled into the ranks, scratching his chin stubble. "We got us a man or two here thinks he can crack a little ball with a stick?"

"I would rather crack that one's head wide open," another soft, well-cultured southern voice whispered from the back row, "but I'm willing to try for the glory of poor Dixie!"

"For Dixie!" became their whispered motto as the nine strongest of them stepped forward to accept Colonel Hill's challenge. The commander climbed to his elevated seat on a wooden platform where he could view the playing field as if he were a battlefield general. Within the stockade there was not much space, and the small, hard leather ball was often blasted out onto the beach; the guards never let the prisoners go for it there, though they were expected to retrieve any ball either side put up on the flat roofs. Suddenly, in the chance to battle the Yankees again, even in this new game called baseball the northerners liked to play, pride and power poured back into the prisoner's limbs.

Though the Confederate officers played valiantly, the match went against them from the first. Colonel Hill adjudicated any disputes his way, and the Yankees had a fine hurler. His pitches made striker after striker dead. Phillip hated the way the camp commander controlled this game: the idea of the godlike overseer pronouncing reb after reb "dead" at the bag made bitter bile rise in his throat.

His final turn to be the striker came when they had three men on bags, though that had happened six of their seven other turns up and they had often been pronounced dead. The count was ten Yankee runs to their six. Standing ready, he gritted his teeth; he tried to ignore the continuous cutting remarks of the behind who caught each missed ball just in back of the striker.

"That ball sank just like your ship, right reb?" the bastard goaded as the ball smacked into his hand. Phillip would not have been a bit surprised if Colonel Hall promoted men on Johnson's Island by the brutality of their insults as well as their tactics. He swung at the next hurl but caught only air. "Missed that one the way you did the whole damned war just rotting away here, Johnny reb. We're gonna beat you chicken-hearted Confederates into the dust today, just the way our troops beat—"

Phillip turned to curse the man—or batter him with the stick—he wasn't sure which. He only knew something in him had snapped, and he didn't care if the armed guards along the stockade shot him or not. He should have died with the others on the ship. He had tried futilely to recall his past. Without that, he was not really a person, less than most of these men who had lost their freedom but not their entire being . . .

But he spun at the wrong time. The next ball, no doubt hurled high intentionally, glanced off his temple. It hurt like hell; he shook his head to clear it of the ringing sound, then rubbed it dazedly. And got angrier than ever.

"Not 'sposed to hit it with that wooden head of yours, numb-skull!" someone shouted and the Yankees roared with laughter.

Gripping the stick, he faced the hurler. "Hurl the last damned one then!"

"Let's just see if I can put it in that big reb mouth of yours!" the Yankee said and threw another hard, high pitch.

Phillip ducked, swung, and cracked the ball. He ran on stiff legs, his long beard flying; the men ahead of him on bags took off. Caught by lake wind, the ball soared so high they all ran home safe before it came down with a thud on the top of the farthest wooden barracks.

"Beyond bounds!" Colonel Hill shouted again and again against the deafening cheers of the prisoners. Everyone knew that was not beyond bounds if the Yankees hit it there. "Wind took the ball! No runs count and get that blockhead up to fetch it down!" the commander screamed until he was red-faced.

Muttering aloud, cursing silently, a gun in his back, Phillip was prodded toward the barracks, then boosted up by two other prisoners to retrieve the ball. Standing on the flat roof, overlooking the beach and blue Lake Erie with free sky and clouds above and beyond, he paused, not picking up the ball. That hit would have tied the match for the prisoners and given them a chance to win. But suddenly, none of that, not even the real war mattered as he stood, gazing down from the heights, his head throbbing, his heart hurting. And he remembered.

A woman on the cliffs overlooking the sea . . . sailing the sea with her. Red-haired Abigail in glorious Gleann Mor. His beloved, beautiful, brave Abigail. On St. Kilda, so many had turned against her, yet she had gone boldly on. He had asked her to wed him on a London rooftop where they pretended that they were back on St. Kilda, free, together. His wife Abigail: he saw her now, windblown, barefoot, smiling, calling him back to her, even as his ship went down in flames.

"Hey, reb, that crack on the head make it worse?" someone shouted.

"Phillip, what do you see up there?" his friend Jason Amory's familiar but distant voice demanded.

His face transfigured, tears blurring the sweep of scene, the prisoner turned to face the men below. "I see my wife! I see my past! I see who I am!"

The enemy gaped and glared; his comrades dared to whoop and cheer. They might, Morgan West thought, have lost this unfair game, they might have lost the cruel war, but victory was his!

Memories like new knowledge came pouring back to stagger him. With a past, he could now have a future. Once the war was over, he must find Abigail. Would they let him write her in London to tell her he was alive? Had she been told he was dead and Phillip Baldwin alive? His first mate's height and coloring was—had been—much the same as his. Mistaken identity and switched bodies in that inferno—that must have been what happened.

And if Abigail thought he were dead all this time—blue blazes, it must be over three years!—might she not have gone on with her life—with another man perhaps? Who could not love Abigail? But surely, surely, she would be his, waiting for him when he saw her in the flesh and not only in his head and heart!

Near dawn on a chill February morn, Abigail dreamed of Morgan. The same vision had haunted her over the years since he had been gone: he was wounded, adrift at sea. She rowed closer, trying to reach him, to save him, to pull him into the boat and her arms. But huge waves ripped him away into blackness, as the boom, boom of sea and guns—

"Abigail! Wake up!"

She sat bolt upright in bed, her heart thundering. Fully dressed, Curly stood in the open doorway of her room, barely illumined by thin dawn. The next boom, though distant, shuddered the furniture. She was on her feet with a cloak around her before the next blast resounded.

"Another Yankee attack on Punta Rassa?" she asked, as she jammed her feet into her shoes. "Lawrence was afraid all that shooting at those deserters they beat off last autumn would tip off Fort Myers that they were there."

"Fort Myers must have sent for some cannon! I already been to look. A big sidewheeler gunboat and at least eight smaller ships shooting at Punta Rassa. Too bad Lawrence just came back because they'll never beat off that firepower! At least their runner went right back out, so it won't get caught."

They ran to the shore where she saw all Curly said was true. The Union navy in force had finally found the blockade runners of Punta Rassa. Smoke spit from the barrels of guns on the largest ship. Puffs of clouds erupted where the cattle pens and offices and barracks stood; seconds after each belch, the retort resounded, echoing across the bay.

Abigail clasped her hands together, terrified for Lawrence and his fellow workers. How ironic he had just returned from nearly four months away, only to be caught by this. She had not even seen him yet, but he had sent over a note that he had returned and would come calling today so that they could make plans. For during these last four months, Lawrence Stillwell had been her betrothed, even though she realized too late she had made a mistake to accept his proposal. Swept away, she had been, by the passions of Margaret and Cal's wedding day. But she had planned to tell Lawrence she could not wed him when he arrived.

He had been in Havana making extensive contingency arrangements in case some such catastrophe as this attack occurred. They had corresponded warmly, but she had come to realize she was relieved to have him away. She thought it unfair to refuse him via the sporadic mails as if she were too cowardly to face him. But she planned to tell him personally that she must belatedly refuse him. Or might this deadly barrage take him before she had that chance? Then, too, if he escaped with all lost there, could she be so cruel to refuse him now?

"Curly, let's go back to the house. If they're not up, we've got to rouse everyone and practice where we will hide if those Yankees come over here. They might find out we were friends with Lawrence, or be foraging for food."

"Reba's too big with that baby to practice hiding anywhere!"

"Reba is wily at hiding, so she'll manage, but 'tis the children I fear for. Come on!"

They spent most of the morning teaching the little ones to play "Hide and No Speak," instead of their usual game. Paulo and Curly pretended to be soldiers seeking them; even if there was a mosquito or snake, no one moved, no one whispered. Abigail forced herself to hold school in the afternoon while Curly kept a distant watch on the action over at Punta Rassa.

Evidently, Curly reported, the attackers had been victorious: the Yankees had anchored close to shore for several hours, burned the buildings, then sailed away. Still, Abigail's stomach twisted in knots. Had the Yankees killed Lawrence as they had Morgan? Had they really left the area?

The hours dragged on. She spent time with Reba and Yo-chay in Margaret's room where Abigail had insisted they would be more comfortable for now. When Reba's labor pains began, she said, there would be time to move outside for the birth as Taluga wanted. Reba was so heavy with this first child that Taluga had brought her here, since he was moving about more on the mainland. Reba, too, feared for her man; the gunfire today had made her cross and fretful. Yo-chay had helped the children with their hiding games, but now did not move from Reba's side.

Abigail paced the verandah around and around, her revolver at her hip, her rifle at the ready. At least, she tried to assure herself, Margaret was safe. She was still in Key West with Cal who had been assigned a secretarial job there, because "he writes in a graceful hand, and, after all, he will never really walk gracefully again," as Margaret's last letter put it. Perhaps Cal and Margaret knew of this raid and were fearful of the danger to Lawrence and the citizens of Sanibel. Since Janie was thriving on the island, Abigail had agreed Margaret should stay with Cal. Now her responsibility for the lass and all her charges hung heavy in her heart with the war so close across the narrow stretch of water.

She longed to cross it to see if anyone needed help at Punta Rassa. But with all that firepower, the cattle runners must be captured or worse, and the Yankees might have left guards behind.

Poor, dear, gentle Lawrence; well, perhaps wherever he was, he felt he had something to live for when the war was over. Still, she still felt that she could not wed him. And she must tell him so, tell him she had been wrong, that she was sorry, no matter if she hurt him. Wedding a man she could never love when her heart was yet with one lost had been the great mistake of her mother's life and had driven her to desperate measures. Her daughter would not make the same dire error. Honesty was best in the long run; she had seen that on their mainland journey to save the children. Besides, her first two husbands had died tragic, violent deaths. Suddenly superstitious, she agonized that Lawrence might suffer that same fate. Had such tragedy engulfed him today?

After the sun set, Abigail let Curly climb back in the big cypress tree on the beach. He made himself a sling with his rope where he could continue to act as a lookout for boats approaching from the sound. Although the Gulf shore was also long and difficult to cover, Paulo had camped over there tonight.

Near midnight, Abigail jolted from her uneasy watch at her bedroom window. She had heard the warning curlew cry she had taught Curly, the same Douglas had used to call her years ago to their secret meeting place on Mullach Sgar.

Terrified of an invasion, she met Curly in the hall. "A boat all right," he gasped out, "but just two men—and Lawrence is one of them. I heard his voice."

"Why dinna you say so straightaway?"

She ran down the path, heedless of the dark. She was nearly to the beach when she too heard the voices, then saw Lawrence. She was so relieved he was in one piece she hugged him and the bundle in his arms.

"My darling!" he cried.

"Thank the Lord you're all right! I feared for all of you!"

"A few killed and captured, but Summerlin and many of the boys fled inland, and I got off in a small sailboat to Pine Island. Spent the day at Cal's old camp there he built on a high hammock. This bundle is all my worldly goods, I'm afraid, but my money's safe in Havana."

She noted the bedraggled man with him was Mr. Morrison, the lay minister who had married Margaret and Cal last fall. "Sir, I am glad to offer you our hospitality here," she told him. "Besides, Reba's child is due and we shall have a proper christening!"

"We can't stay, my love," Lawrence told her and turned her up the path toward the house, while his companion trailed behind. "Too dangerous for you in case the enemy combs the area. But I had to see you first—we've been apart so much and when we part now," he whispered and leaned close to her, "we could be one."

"What?"

"Morrison married Margaret and Cal in haste. If you're willing, he can marry us now. I will not ask you to flee to Havana with me, for it's a long, dangerous journey and you have responsibilities here. But after we are man and wife—after this one night we shall share together now—I will leave these things with you all for safe-keeping and flee. But I will come back to you! You and my art, Abigail—you are everything to me, one and the same, the beauty of life itself!"

After that speech, she did not argue now. Trembling at what she must do, she fed the men before they washed in a tub of rain-water behind the house. After Curly went back to his watch, she sat in the big, empty parlor with Lawrence. She could hear Yo-chay's gentle voice crooning to Reba in the bedroom. Almost time for a new life to begin, but time now for some things to end, Abigail thought. Pain churned inside her to have to hurt Lawrence. She thought of just putting him off again—saying she would wed him after the war perhaps, but that would be unworthy of her and un-just to him.

"Lawrence," she began, letting him take her hand, holding off the caresses he tried to initiate when the minister went to lie down in Curly's room, "I dreamed of Morgan again, and realized it is wrong of me to let you believe I could love—"

"I expect your hand and but hope for your love, Abigail. My love is enough for both of us right now. Yours will come later."

"But we have known each other for over two years. I canna take that risk for you."

"For me? I cannot believe you all tell me this today, after all I've been through! It's been the worst day of my life!"

"I would say it has been one of the best, Lawrence. You are alive and well, a fine artist still with healthy hands and eyes, and you said your money is safe in Havana. Then so is your future."

"I have no future without you! I loved you at first sight!"

" 'Tis a curse as well as a blessing. But of course, you have a future. I've been through losses far greater, so I know. But you have a right to be angry with me since I dinna decide sooner. I admire you deeply, Lawrence, but that wilna do for a marriage of hearts—of bodies, perhaps, of minds, but—"

"I am not one of your students to lecture, my love. Just wed me and whatever happens, you can claim my fortune in Havana. That way, you all can help more children here after the war, carry on against the plume hunters or even make another visit to insist on better birthing practices back in Scotland! I don't mean to try to buy your love, but be reasonable."

"Lawrence, I have some money of my own. And another man once tried to buy my hand, the one who kills the birds. So I tell you I *am* being reasonable. I am so sorry to hurt you, but you will be better off without a woman who loves elsewhere more and—"

"You still love your dead husband? I've waited patiently for you to forget him! Are you demented?"

"Dinna say that to me! I only mean you will be better off without a woman who loves distant bairns and local birds more than she does you." She thought that would be the final blow, but she was wrong. He shook his head; he argued on.

"But I know all that, Abigail! I am not like the others you've told me of. I shall help you all with those causes, be at your side, let you have your way with things!"

"It would be wrong and foolish of you to want to stay unless we were wed, Lawrence. I've come to see the hard way that a sound marriage cannot be based on either partner letting the other have his or her way. It must be a mutual helping of each other. After the war, you must pursue your art—and a woman who can love you and give you the children you long for."

"I am certain we can have children, Ab—"

"No!" she cried and rose. "Lawrence, I am wrong for you and that's the way of it."

"You mean it the other way around," he accused. "You think I'm wrong for you."

"That too. You are welcome to stay here, of course, and—"

"Another of your charity cases, Abigail?"

"I do not look at any of my guests nor charges that way."

"No, I realize that. It's just the way you are, curse it. I'm just—I'm devastated by it all today." His shoulder slumped; his hands drooped between his knees; for once, he gazed at the floor and not at her. She stood silent. At last he said quietly, "I'd best rouse the minister I bribed to come to marry us and be off sailing south. I have a long, long way to go."

"I'll pack you food and blankets. The nights have been so cold."

His head snapped up. "Ah, yes, my Abigail, kill me with kindness and the damned truth. My pack of things—keep them for me, because I will be back for them at least." His voice broke on a stifled sob. "There are some things there for you. You will, I hope, at least, take those from me."

She too cried when black night swallowed his white sail, but she did not waver in her decision. Until dawn, while she was not with Reba, she sat on the verandah, very sure she had done the right thing. But she was equally sure she had said farewell to the last man she would ever consider wedding and her last desperate chance to have her own child.

Swollen-eyed at first light, Abigail went to her room and looked through the things Lawrence had left her. A packet of letters addressed to her which she was not certain she would ever read now; many beautiful sketches of the egrets of her rookery, just as they looked now, coming into this years' nuptial finery.

Here was a letter, evidently from his father, who he longed to please but who he must defy in the battle for his future; and several northern newspapers—even a copy of the London *Times* he must have gotten through Havana.

She skimmed it eagerly for news of England: the Prince of Wales and his new Danish Princess Alexandra had been entertained at Manchester House in "an extravaganza orchestrated by the illustrious Duchess of Manchester." The royal pair evidently led quite a gay life while the reclusive, widowed queen disdained London for rural Windsor and Scottish Balmoral.

"Still grieving in self-exile, just like the Queen of Kilda," Abigail whispered and turned the page.

American war news included President Lincoln's reelection between the fall of Atlanta last September and Savannah's fall in December. There was a sad article on the disgraceful harshness of prisoner of war camps, both Union and Confederate. Illness had claimed many men on both sides in the camps as well as on the battlefields. Andersonville in Georgia was dubbed a death camp; in Fort Delaware, seven hundred men washed in a muddy moat from which was drawn water for soup; at a camp for southern officers called Johnson's Island in Ohio, a devastating hurricane had killed several prisoners in late September.

"Thank God the hurricanes Lawrence used to warn of havena

touched us here," she murmured, and went on to find that advertisements for ladies' "suitings" included plumed hats with "French" aigrettes of all kinds.

She slapped the pages shut and stood to stretch. All that prison news—even the advertisements—reminded her of dying birds and bairns and poor Annie in her prison cell. Corwin had written that the Harris midwife's different practices were only accepted by some St. Kildans. Surely, Abigail thought, when they recalled her words of warning about the fulmar oil and saw which bairns now lived and died, they would break with that dread tradition. At least, at Abigail's urging, Corwin's solicitors had appealed to the Glasgow courts with a mitigating-circumstances petition for Annie's crime, but she would evidently need to serve years of her sentence before the plea could even be heard.

"Abi-gail," Yo-chay's voice floated through the door. "Reba— it time."

The two of them helped Reba outside onto the verandah to a soft pallet they had prepared days ago. "I swear, all that there shootin' 'nough to scare a child from comin' into this world, even if his father a full-blooded Seminole and likes a good fight!" Reba panted out.

"You just remember this child's mother is a full-blooded free American," Abigail told her. "I thought you might like to know that Lawrence told me the Union troops aboard the gunboat which attacked Punta Rassa from Key West were colored infantry troops. You'd best tell that man of yours no shooting of American soldiers or he might hit your own people! And no more calling them whiteblood soldiers anymore either," she teased.

"Mm," Reba grunted as a labor pain crunched the breath from her as hard as she pressed Yo-chay's hand. When she got her air again, she said, "You best tell Taluga yourself, as he listenin' to you better'n me these days. But ain't that fine 'bout colored soldiers fightin' for the land that freed them? Wouldn't mind that for my son, but 'spose he'll be all Seminole—ah!"

"Breathe easy now, just relax," Abigail crooned while Yo-chay sang a chant. Later, Abigail hummed along too. It was a far site better, she thought, than tying mothers down and kneading babies from the womb who would come in their own good time.

"You not sad 'bout not weddin' Mr. Lawrence, Abigail?" Reba asked during a lull.

"Thank you for thinking of my feelings at such a time, my friend. No, just relieved for having done what was right." She thought of Morgan's Charlotte, who surely had loved him to distraction, but he had disappointed her. So sad that Abigail Adair and Morgan West seemed fated to be together only until fate forever tore them apart.

The long night stretched on as Reba labored to bring forth a child. It was not Taluga's expected son but a lusty-lunged lass with such pale skin compared to her happy mother.

"You go 'head tell Taluga when he come he gotta girl child," Reba managed to tease Abigail. She smiled wearily as she stroked her new daughter's satin cheek with her finger. "See, my little gal got no brand on her face!" she declared proudly before she drifted off in exhausted sleep.

Abigail and Yo-chay cut the umbilical cord and rubbed paste made from cedar leaf to heal it. Abigail said a silent prayer of gratitude that there were no eight days of fear to face here in this land. Again, in tending another woman's child, she found, strangely, it helped to heal her and did not make her jealous or joyless. Humming the old St. Kilda cradle song, she cuddled the little mite in her arms, her finger grasped tight in a tiny fist.

19

The stone-hewn past can crush us,
But I shall not allow it.
Today I start to break and strike
And sculpt a new tomorrow.

Just after the baby birds had flown their rookery that year, Curly got stung so badly by a nest of fire ants that Abigail feared for his life. His legs and arms were a mass of red, oozing pinpoints. With Janie often sitting by his side singing to him, Abigail tended him day and night as she had when Edmund Drummond had brutally beaten him four years ago. But the lad's sturdy body and brash spirit brought him back.

Making Curly promise to stay in bed just one more day, though the late April weather was warm, Abigail took her little charges on a long-delayed beach walk along the gulf. They collected shells with which she created a new game to explain how money and banks worked. "Money is not good for itself, but only for the good things it does to help us and other people," she told them. And then she happened to glance down the beach and saw two men emerge from the thicket. One had a gun.

"And now," she announced to her little brood without pointing out the men, "we are going to change games to 'Hide and No Speak.' Everyone into the high grass and be quiet, no matter what happens!"

Without suspecting anything, the younger ones scrambled to obey; the oldest two, nine-year-old Sam and seven-year-old Betty who helped oversee the group, frowned down the beach at the men before they ducked into the thick, blowing sea oats.

The strangers, both in civilian clothes, did not seem to be leaving despite their small sailboat waiting on the shore. Unfortunately, they had seen her too and strode this way, their feet spitting sand. And, as they came and she shaded her eyes against the glare even under her bonnet, she gasped.

It could not be! One of the men had a paper and pencil in his hand, but it was not Lawrence. He carried a rifle; the other man did not. Quickly, she drew her pistol from its holster in the folds of her skirt and hid it along her hip. Her heart boomed like the breakers to see it was—it could not be, but it was—Edmund Drummond!

This was too much to be coincidence: he must have come looking for her. But for the children, she would have fled. She bit her lower lip so hard she tasted blood. Taluga and his family were on the mainland, Paulo was fishing on the other side of the island, Curly weak in bed. She felt mired in the sand; her index finger curled around the trigger. Shakily she walked to meet them to get more distance from the children's hiding place.

" 'Tis been a long time, dear Abigail!" Edmund called out with counterfeit jauntiness. "I was going to find yer house for a taste of yer warm hospitality," he dared with a mocking bow, "but thought I'd scout for rookeries first. 'Tis a big one I found, and I regret I missed the pretty plume show there this year."

He looked much the same if not as grandly garbed as he had been in London. She wondered if the scribbling on the paper he hastily pocketed estimated how many birds he could massacre here. She found her voice at last, but it trembled.

"Thank God, the nestlings have flown and their parents are not in plumage now, or I'm sure you'd kill them to the last chick to fill your dirty coffers!"

"Ooh, I'd hoped we could strike a bargain on my harvesting the rookery next year, but I detect an unfriendly tone, lass." He chuckled, a strangled sound. His eyes raked her. "Canna we let bygones be bygones? Now the war's over, I'll be branching out and 'twould profit us both grandly. We're destined and always have been, my dear. Isna she a wild beauty just waiting to be tamed, like I told ye, Murphy?" he threw back over his shoulder to the other man.

For the first time, Abigail's eyes darted to the burly stranger. The lout nodded and winked at her, then licked his lips. Abigail's stomach turned over in fear and revulsion.

"To tell true, lass," Edmund said and shuffled slightly closer, cradling his rifle in his arms, "I believe my London solicitor bribed someone who knew where ye were—or came upon some lost letters sent to that rich, old man you bilked 'til you tired of him and found the lusty Captain West—ah, that's right, my deepest condolences upon the sad occasion of yer second widowhood are in order."

"Get off this island and do not return!"

"The place is hardly yers. I rather fancy it. It shall be mine next plumage season, now that the rookeries along the Caloosahatchee and near Okeechobee need a rest to rebuild."

"You did that? I should have known, you damned murderer!"

"Ah, such heathen talk from a churched St. Kilda lass! No, I'm just wily and willful, Abigail, wily and willful like yerself—we both have our stubborn whims. And well-heeled for our lowly beginnings, aren't we, lass?"

His eyes darted behind her. "Ye ken," he said with a grin that flaunted his crooked teeth, "I saw yer wee darkies. I warrant ye've spent a fortune to free them all or been hiding them when they escaped. Never could resist guttersnipes whatever country, whatever color, could ye? Got one I could use for a fetch-it lad on my ship? Ye see, I even have my own ship now, just like the poor, departed captain ye wed, if that was the allure. Come with me, Ab—"

She stepped back and lifted her pistol straight-armed at his chest. "I said get off this island, but put your gun down first!"

She saw she had surprised him. His mouth dropped open; his nostrils flared; his eyes widened.

"Ooh, always up to new tricks, Abigail." His goading voice wavered now, but she was relieved to see him slowly lower his gun to lay it gently on the sand. But before she could blink, he slung a quick handful of it up at her.

She closed her eyes too late. She jumped back and fired. She

heard a scream—hers. Hard hands pushed her down on the sand.
A man's big body slammed her breath from her. She struggled,
writhing, scratching. Another gunshot. She fought free and sat
up, scooting sideways in the sand like a crab.

Her eyes streamed tears; she tried to blink the grit from them.
The big man lay near her, swearing, holding his leg. It was he who
had jumped at her. But Edmund too was down, clutching his ankle.
And—his rifle smoking, dressed only in his underdrawers and out
of breath—Curly stood just beyond them with Sam panting at his
side. The lad must have run for Curly the moment she told them to
hide; she was grateful he had not obeyed this time. Now the boy
scrambled for Edmund's flung rifle and her pistol. He gave them
both to Curly. Slowly, Abigail got to her feet.

Seeing he was beaten and Curly did not fire again, Edmund
stood, stumbled, and tried to drag his wounded friend down the
beach. He limped; his ankle wound trailed blood. But how, Abigail
thought, could Curly have shot both men without reloading?

Now Curly loudly cocked her pistol, pointing it toward the
men. Hatred distorted the boy's fine features. He lifted the pistol so
deliberately and steadily toward Edmund, she gasped.

"Wait," she cried and ran to him. "We canna just kill the
blackguard the way he does the poor birds. I wilna have you in
prison like Annie!"

"Your bullet hit Drummond and there's plenty more for him in
your revolver," Curly countered. But he handed her the pistol and
reloaded his rifle.

Abigail kept her gun on them. "Edmund, I and others shall
guard this island from your greedy slaughter. Set foot here again
and face a war! And next time my bullet will be in your black heart
and not your short legs, you little, little man!"

His face contorted in agony. Falling to his knees in a futile attempt to drag his friend away, he did not respond. He only loosed
the big man's arm, despite his pleas, and stumbled on toward the
boat alone.

"Curly, hold the gun on them. Here, curse you!" she cried to
Edmund and put her pistol in its holster. With Sam's help, she
slowly yanked and tugged Edmund's man bit by bit toward their
beached boat. Moaning, Edmund limped more slowly every step behind them.

She dumped the man on the sand and peered into the boat: another rifle and a big box clearly marked AMMUNITION. She clambered in before Edmund reached them. Because she could not lift the box, she tossed handfuls of cartridges and flasks of powder up on the sand, then climbed out with the gun. Panting, sweating, Edmund fell into the boat and fumbled with the sails. She and Curly propped the other man up, then rolled him in over the gunwales. Abigail lifted the rifle and spoke, like Taluga did at his most menacing, from behind the gunsight.

"We've many weapons here, Edmund, and now two more with bullets and powder. If a lad and a woman can do this, you blighter, think what will happen if you set foot here again! If I havena seen the last of you, I swear you will have seen the last of life next time you dare come here after me, my friends, or my birds!"

Despite his physical agony, Edmund leveled such a malevolent glare at her, she began to tremble again. She could have shot him; she almost wanted to. Yet Annie in that distant cell stopped her. Maybe, with the way Edmund looked now, he would not make it back to his ship to return again. She squinted to scan the horizon for the silhouette of a vessel, but it must be anchored at some other nearby isle they meant to rape.

Curly put his rifle down, shoved the boat's prow off the sand, then turned it outward. Only then, standing knee-deep in the surf, did he scream at Edmund every Soho curse he'd ever known. Through the tirade as the wind took the boat out, Abigail stood in the sand, stunned.

It seemed, unlike any of Sanibel's other visitors, even the savage, exotic ones, that Edmund Drummond had violated her sanctuary here. She prayed it would be the last time she ever laid eyes on him or put a bullet in anyone. The big war between the states had ended last month with a long siege, the South ravaged, the bitter surrender at Appomattox, and President Lincoln's murder. She could only hope her bloody little war with Edmund would not end so horribly.

Although the war was over, Abigail still felt herself and Sanibel were under siege. From April to August of 1865, Edmund did not come back; she did not even know if he was alive. But she and the others planned for his ultimate return. It might not be until the birds came into their plumes next winter, but she would not be caught off guard again.

And so, through sending Paulo to the mainland with letters offering to pay for guards, she hired four mainland lay-bys who had been cattlemen at Punta Rassa before the blockade runners made them move their operations elsewhere and who became legitimate traders after the war. Taluga came and went, but vowed he would help protect the Sanibel birds during plumage season. Lawrence had left Cuba for Savannah to survey the war ruination there and help finance his family's rebuilding—and to inform them he would become a professional artist. Abigail wrote him of Edmund's visit when she sent him his letters; he wrote back that he would return next winter to protect the egrets he had drawn so lovingly.

Lawrence's friendly letter warmed her heart as did those of Corwin and even Louisa now that the mails were back to normal. A mail boat stopped by en route from Key West to Tampa once a month. But the best news of all was that Corwin's solicitor reported the infant death rate on St. Kilda had dropped by half. Still, all that was not enough. Nor, she feared, was the watch on Sanibel enough to keep out that devil Drummond and his demons. She longed to cast off the past, but she must defeat him first.

On the morning of August eleventh, a muggy, strength-sapping day, a heavy fog engulfed the island, making everything seem distant and dreamy. Over a listless breakfast Abigail shared with Curly and Janie on the verandah, she fell to daydreaming about the fog pouring off the summit of St. Kilda's Conachair that first night Morgan had kissed her like a lover.

"We're gonna nab old Greedy Guts, I know we are!" Curly's exuberant voice jolted her from her bittersweet musings.

"All those traps we laid will get him!" Janie piped up.

Abigail smiled at their bright faces. Sometimes the two of them reminded her so of herself and Douglas in their early years, young and innocently happy each day just for the fact they breathed the same island air. And here, there was no family feud to separate them, no Mairi Adair with her inflated slights and imagined sins to keep them apart, and—

"Miz West!" a man's voice bellowed from the fog before Pat, one of her hired guards, emerged. "Can't see worth beans offshore with floating patches of this stuff, but Ed and I hear stationary voices not far out in the gulf."

Abigail leapt up so fast her chair scraped, then toppled. "A ship! Curly, get your rifle. Janie, help the children hide."

"But Aunt Abigail, it could be any ship," Janie protested quietly. "Maybe the navy is bringing mother and my new father back! They said he's to be mustered out soon!"

"Go on, lass. I'll send for you right away if 'tis them," she insisted and pushed Janie toward the house where the children slept in removable pallets on the parlor floor.

Abigail grabbed two rifles—one was Edmund's—and strapped on her belt with cartridge pouch and powder flask. The only thing she did not like about her new country was that it seemed to breed the need for guns. Still, it was a land with freedom and beauty worth fighting for, so she meant to do just that.

She and Curly ran with Pat down to the long gulf beach where another guard named Ed awaited. "Oh, no," she cried when Ed pointed and she glimpsed the spectral bulk of a vessel through shifting fog. "'Tis the very spot the blighter put in last May."

"Listen!" Pat whispered. "I hear oars splashing. Danged if we won't see a hair of 'em 'til they're ashore if this don't lift quick!"

"Remember," Abigail said quietly, "we want to take them prisoner. But if we must, we shoot. They're after us, not the rookery right now, for those feathers molting from the backs of our birds are a far cry from pretty plumes!"

They hid behind big leaves of the seagrape trees and waited, leaning forward, getting a bead on the sounds, praying the mist would lift again so they could see to fire if they must. But the fog seemed to thicken. Creak, splash, creak, splash came closer on the whisper of the low-tide waves. A man's voice, and another.

Abigail knew that Lawrence or anyone from Punta Rassa would have anchored in the sound, not the gulf. It must be Edmund and his brigands in that ship he had spoken of, hoping to take them unaware, off-season, fog-shrouded. She gripped her gun, shivering, straining to catch Edmund's high-pitched brogue. But the man she heard spoke low and not Scottish at all . . .

She jerked upright. Chills raced along her spine. Her stomach cartwheeled. That day in Corwin's tallhouse she had heard that distant, distinctive voice behind the door—the voice in her dreams calling to her. No, she was losing her reason, losing control, waiting to face Edmund again. The past was gone.

But again, she heard that very voice, a bold American voice, a man who sounded like Morgan. Mere happenstance, she scolded herself. Her ears, her heart were playing tricks on her.

The prow of the ghost ship crunched sand. Men leapt out. The fog floated just high enough she could see feet and legs. She meant to keep her gun up, but she was trembling too hard. With it hanging in her hands, before the others could stop her, she walked out of their cover. She heard curses and clicks behind her as the guards cocked their guns to cover her. Curly scrambled out to try to pull her back.

"Who is it?" she cried into the mist when she meant to hold her silence. But that voice— she had to know she wasn't like her mother—demented, clinging to a man lost forever, to a past that could devour her.

"Abigail? Abigail!"

She dropped her rifle. A tall, dark-haired, clean-shaven man stepped from the fog but ten feet from her. He was too thin and hollow-cheeked and pale, she had never seen his whole face, but his burning brown eyes on her—

"It—canna be!"

"Another man died, and I wrote to England to you and Corwin, but he wrote back you'd come here. My mother could not believe it at first either. Oh, Abigail . . ."

Curly's restraining hand fell from her arm. She ran to Morgan, slipping, crying, arms outstretched. His embrace came hard around her. She feared she was dreaming, but the feel of him, that scent of sea and leather were so real. She clung to him. She tried to say his name, tried to tell the others her husband had come back from the war, from the grave, but nothing came out. Only her eyes shouted tears of shock and joy.

"Captain Morgan, dev'lish fine to see you!" Curly cried.

Morgan was shaking as hard as she. Other voices swirled around; some cheered; nothing else but holding to him mattered.

"My boy!" Morgan said finally, and she felt him shift his weight to reach out to Curly while she kept her face pressed tight against his neck. Morgan's voice broke; he was crying too. "I see you took good care of Abigail for me!"

"Everybody said to, but I did it 'cause I love her too!"

"Love her too," Morgan repeated, and lifted Abigail's wet face to his. For the first time she gazed at him to see the pain mingled with exultation in his eyes. But she could erase the pain; they had forever together now. Surely nothing else would go wrong for them again. In that glorious moment, Edmund Drummond did not exist; no bairns or birds died, no one was alone or sad.

"You are still my wife—mine alone?" he asked with a narrow glance at her guards.

"Even when—I thought that you were dead—there could be no one else."

"Then I am home. Boys," he addressed the gaggle of gawking sailors who appeared from the mist, "give Captain Amory my best regards and toss my gear ashore. I'll be in touch with him about our dealings when—" his voice broke again "—when I have been home a while."

Despite his thinness and trembling, he swept her up into his arms, still wiry strong. "I know where the house is despite this fog," he whispered to her as he began to walk away from everyone. "I know where our room is though I've seen it only in my dreams. Abigail, I didn't know who I was for years, remembered nothing, and now I have myself back and you too! We were starving in the prison camp and a hurricane came that killed some of my comrades . . ." He stopped and buried his face in her hair to speak in a mere whisper. "I just want to be alone with you now—quiet and alone."

His long strides crunched deep in the sand and then the shell path toward the house. But in the clearing, Janie saw him coming and squealed; the little ones ran from their hiding places to cluster around them when Janie realized who he was and called his name. The lass cried and clung to him. The little ones who had only heard of him jumped up and down and yelled.

"Quiet and alone?" Abigail spoke at last from her vantage point in his arms above the fray.

"I should have known," he said, amazed, and put her down. He knelt amid the children to give Janie a better hug. But he looked up at Abigail again, grinning while tears coursed down his pale face. "I should have known, wherever there is Abigail, there is love—and tumult."

"Oh, my big, braw lad," she said, reaching over Janie to embrace him again, "I have so much to tell you and so much to hear."

Still, they managed to be quiet and alone, that night and the next, talking, sharing, learning each other again. In the heat of the next afternoon, while the children took a rest in the shade of the verandah—when Abigail usually read them a story from the books salvaged from the cliffs of St. Kilda—Morgan had Janie read the tale today and took Abigail fishing. They carried a bottle of water, a bamboo pole, and two rifles.

"But I havena fished since you took me out in Village Bay," she told him with a laugh. "Curly and Paulo always do it."

"Not anymore," he told her.

She welcomed his changing things to suit his desires as well as hers. What had been *her* life was fast becoming *theirs*. After Morgan had been told what to do so long in prison—and had done precious little—tasks of simple organization and a multitude of choices confounded him. What to eat, what to wear, what to do next loomed large decisions, she could tell. But she was careful not to take over. St. Kilda had not really taught him patience as he had once claimed, but evidently prison had done so. Ah, thank the Good Lord, they had long days ahead to learn to work together now. He had vague plans to reestablish a shipping firm with a friend from prison, but that, too, would come in its time. Today, despite the other island citizens, he was hers, and this was the Sanibel honeymoon he had promised her so long ago.

She held his hand tightly, her eyes on him, even when she stumbled on the path. She felt afraid to blink: he might disappear. She fought falling asleep at night: she feared she dreamed this all. But she was coming to accept that he was real. Even in their most intimate moments, though at first he seemed a stranger to her house and body, she adored him.

And he looked so different thinner and beardless; she was coming to realize that, even within, he was not quite the same man she had known and loved before. He seemed warier but wiser and stronger, not so quick to judge others, not so authoritarian, more forgiving. Still, he was willing to fight for what he believed and was adamant they must stand up to Edmund Drummond. Perhaps, she thought, though he did not say so, the patriotic prison beard he had shaved off was one attempt to shed his wartime past. But he would always carry it with him, even though he had not known who he was for so long. He said he felt the war was worth the cost, for the nation was reunited and the slaves were free—as the two of them were now. But the cost of his inner battles, as much as his outer ones, had changed him, even, she supposed, as her own over the years had changed her.

Today they walked a long way down the gulf shore, admiring little things beyond themselves for the first time since he'd returned. They watched a V-formation of gold-crested pelicans fly overhead and dolphins frolic just beyond the surf. They laughed at the male fiddler crabs waving their larger claw in a come-hither gesture to lure females into their burrows.

"Ah," Morgan teased her, the first time he had been anything but serious with her, "a crab after my own heart."

She sat watching in the shade of seagrape trees while he dug the big gray bugs called sand fleas from the edge of the waves, baited the hook with them, threw the line out, and stuck the bamboo pole in the sand. But he ignored the line the moment it was in the water; his eyes were hotter than the August sun on her as he sat down beside her in the mottled shade.

"With your light skin, I suppose you've never taken a sunbath," he said, as he peeled his shirt off, "but I need to. I'm still prison gray."

"You look fine to me, more than fine," she told him with a tremulous smile and ran her hand down his warm skin, shoulder to elbow.

"I tell you what," he murmured. "We're secluded here even if someone should come along. Why don't you take your gown off, and I'll shade you if the sun gets hotter through the leaves."

" 'Tis such a kindly offer, what lady could resist?" she replied and stretched lazily, blushing hot at his gaze and not the sun. "Then, too, the beach breeze keeps the mosquitos off, so I guess I dinna mind."

"And since their nap keeps the thousands of Sanibel children off . . ."

"And Curly's with the guards . . ."

"And that Seminole warrior friend of yours is still away . . ."

"But my love," she said as she helped him pull her gown over her head, "María still believes Taluga can just materialize from the foliage at will."

"Then he's going to be very shocked," Morgan muttered as he skimmed his trousers off. They both laughed, perhaps intoxicated with the time to tease, yet then they both fell solemnly silent again.

They lay in each others arms, gazing deep into each other's eyes, mesmerized by the depths there. The rhythmic roll of waves on the sand just beyond their leafy cave lulled them.

"Calypso and Ulysses back together on her new enchanted isle," she whispered, tracing his lips with her fingertip.

"Ulysses and Penelope, his faithful wife," he said and kissed her fingers, then, wetly, the palm of her hand.

She had told him all about Lawrence, even that he said he would be back to help protect the rookery. "I pity the poor man, loving then losing you," Morgan had said. "But at last, I can settle everything with that damned Drummond nemesis of yours if he dares to return!"

But now, she wanted nothing to intrude upon their closeness, this world of wonder they built between them at the merest glance or whisper or touch.

"I remember on our wedding night in London," he said, brushing back her tumbled tresses, "I told you I longed to love you under the sun in broad daylight instead of in the weak glimmer of that lamp."

"Yes. It was cold and wintry that night. Louisa and Dr. Snow pulled us apart."

"But not for long. And nothing can part us now, not after the war, all we've been through. And, finally, my wedding wish comes true. Besides," he added and grinned boyishly, "this sun peeking through will burn your beautiful skin if I don't shade you with my body and tend to each lovely stretch of curve and valley . . ."

He hovered over her as she lay naked on her back upon their garments. He stroked and kissed her, first her mouth and temples, her cheeks, earlobes, her throat and shoulders, her breasts. She murmured and arched her back and bit her lower lip in the sheer pleasure of each sparkling sensation. He caressed her hips and thighs with his free hand until their breath came faster than the pounding waves.

She entwined her long legs around his, gasping at each delight, exploring him anew in return. She nibbled his salty skin, and whispered endearments in his ear, tempting him until their tongues dueled breathlessly in the sweet shade of their mouths. He was indeed her shelter from the sun, she thought, her protection in this world—and she was his. She embraced and drew him to her. Merging lips, loins, lives, they shared lover's love again, at last.

Sunday, February 11, 1866, began a happy day. Morgan had been home half a year, and they celebrated with family and friends. In the clearing, Abigail and Morgan presided over a long plank table overflowing with food. Cal and Margaret had been back since autumn; sawhorses and planking from their home being built across the clearing made the table. Taluga and his family were here for the plumage season as promised, though only Reba, big with her second child, chose to sit at the table holding her daughter, Cho-fee. Taluga and Yo-chay sat companionably eating on the verandah. The children—the ten young ones overseen by their idols Janie and Curly—were on their best behavior up and down the table.

Lawrence, who had returned as promised, sat with the hired men, who ate in shifts at the foot of the table, one at a time. He kept sketching the scene even while he ate, as he had recently undertaken to improve his drawings of people and not only do birds as had Audubon, an artist he told them had visited Florida some thirty years ago.

"Do you all know," he had told them, "Audubon used to shoot more fowl than he drew before he finally decided that the two things might not be compatible?"

Lawrence and Morgan had made an awkward peace with each other; perhaps, Abigail thought, in comparison to Edmund's obsession with her over the years, quiet, gentle Lawrence seemed no threat.

Jason Amory, Morgan's new business partner for setting up shipping runs between the reconstructed southern states and England sat on her other side. Morgan and Jason, another former blockading captain, had been friends in prison, although Jason had first thought his comrade was named Phillip Baldwin. Abigail liked Jason very much and intended to visit Baltimore and England with them when they rebuilt ties there instead of just shipping to Bermuda as they did now. And, Morgan said, he would put himself in charge of the Florida warehouses to be home as much as possible when she did not sail with him. They were determined not to be separated; somehow, she thought, they would make this all work.

Margaret and Abigail shared a quick smile across the noisy table. Margaret was six months into a pregnancy; Abigail was very happy for her. As Morgan had said once, even without a child, their marriage would be enough for them over the years to come. Abigail breathed deeply and blinked back tears of joy at the noisy, busy scene. What a perfect day this was!

But when Tom, one of the guards, arrived early for his turn at the table, she immediately sensed something was wrong. He strode straight to Morgan. She was pleased how quickly the men had learned to look to him for leadership. She didn't even mind that Taluga always addressed Morgan first before he spoke to her. It was a victory that the Seminole spoke and listened to her at all!

Now she heard every word Tom whispered: "Cap'n, a ship off the nor'east gulf shore, with four boats rowing in with armed men."

"How many total?"

"Least thirty-two."

"They must believe that power will out even in a daylight assault," Morgan muttered. "But, blue blazes, I'll be glad to see the bastards clearly than have them here at night."

"'Spose they're thinkin' the same, cap'n."

Morgan took Abigail's hand and pulled her up to stand beside him. "It seems our unwanted visitors have arrived at last!" he announced. Silence descended with a final *ding* of pewter on china.

"You might ken," Abigail said, "the infidels would dare to try to ruin the Lord's day of rest along with everything else."

"Everyone to battle assignments," Morgan announced, "and no one stirs until the warning shot."

The children were divided into groups overseen by Margaret, Janie, Reba, and Yo-chay and hidden deep in the brush toward the old ruins of Sanybel. The ten adults took rifles, some carried pistols too, and went to their foliage-cloaked posts. Curly quickly scaled the tallest cedar tree near the rookery where the snowy and great egrets innocently preened their nuptial feathers and hatched and fed their young.

"I canna believe he came back," Abigail muttered when,

crouched beside Morgan, she spotted Edmund through the telescope from far down the beach. "He's limping as bad as Cal, but
'tis Edmund. God forgive me, I was hoping he was dead."

"He will be if he shoots so much as one more bird. But I think
we're ready for them."

Abigail and Curly's original protective plans had been en-
hanced by Morgan, Cal, and then Taluga. While Edmund led the
plumers into the interior of the island, leaving two men to guard
each boat, Abigail and Morgan scrambled to their separate positions. The Sanibel citizens waited, barely breathing, hoping their
prey would not string out too far along the path. It was a new one,
helpfully cut through the brush toward the rookery; there was another well-marked one from the inland shore in case the invaders
had come that way. Along these paths were traps to turn the hunters into the hunted, but the defenders had to let the plumers into
the target area near the rookery before they attacked.

At Morgan's general signal, Cal and two guards would fire on
the boat guards with so many guns they hoped they would panic
and flee. But now, all awaited Morgan's shot.

In her assigned place, the last bastion before the rookery, Abigail huddled in the palmetto thicket where she could oversee the
birds, see Curly overhead, and see Taluga's hiding place in a thicket
by the pond. If the plumers broke through the barriers, they would
meet a barrage of bullets from the three of them. The hungry *yelp-
yelp* cry of the earliest born nestlings, could, unfortunately, lead the
hunters here, though the new path eventually took them to a dead-
end. Still, Edmund might remember the way and cut off from it.

Abigail heard Curly's curlew cry warn Morgan that the invaders were in place. Morgan's gun banged; she could picture what was
happening now, all at once. Cords across their way, hidden under
leaves and shells, were yanked tight, ankle-high, to trip them.
Nooses and snares based on St. Kilda birding skills fell from the
trees. Tents of mosquito netting, carefully hung above the path and
edged with Curly's long, heavy rope, dropped on the men. And
within the netting and ropes were clumps of sandburs, sharp
sawgrass, and underfoot, nests of fire ants. If anyone escaped or cut
free of the massive trap, guards were stationed nearby with bamboo
poles to blow poison-fish darts at them that would surely stupefy a
man.

Abigail gripped her rifle as sporadic gunfire and shouts drifted to her. Their plan to catch and incapacitate most of the invaders so the rest could be captured must be working. But she saw four men had cut through to the rookery. Surely, with most of the others trapped behind them, they would simply double back and flee to their boats—which, hopefully, would not be there. The tragic thing was, the plumers they caught would not be prosecuted by authorities because they were not breaking man's law, only, Abigail was certain, God's laws. But since He was not here to punish the blackguards, she and her friends would do it for Him!

But then she clearly saw the first man. "Edmund!" she whispered. Aiming for his legs, she cocked her gun. He had his up as if he would dare to shoot down the birds when he must know his cause here was doomed. Defiant, devious to the end, she thought, and braced her back against a palmetto trunk to fire. But overhead, Curly's gun clattered to the ground. He must have slipped; he swung free beneath the foliage, trying to right himself, a perfect target like the birds. Edmund spun quickly; he lifted his gun, not at the birds, but at Curly. Abigail sighted again. She thought she must have screamed when she fired, but in that instant, Taluga leapt from the foliage with a bloodcurdling cry. Edmund's men aimed at Taluga; Edmund fired first, then Abigail and Taluga.

Birds exploded noisily into the sky, flapping, cawing. To Abigail's dazed view, Taluga seemed to fly too, straight at Edmund and his men, screaming, scattering them, swinging his spent rifle. A steel bayonette blade flashed. Another unearthly cry, another. All this in a tiny second before Abigail tore her eyes up to Curly to see he swung there in his own sling, safe, his eyes wide as hers.

All four men lay prone by the pond as the birds, still protesting, settled slowly back on branches. Quickly reloading, clasping her pistol, Abigail advanced on the pond. Edmund lay facedown in the water with a big red bloom between his shoulder blades. His maimed hand was stretched out toward his gun. Taluga squatted over the other three men, turning them facedown.

"*Halwuk* whitebloods," he said and spat on the ground.

"Did I—did I shoot this one?" she asked, pointing at Edmund.

"That their chief? Taluga kill him for you, Abi-gail. Women no good killing. These others dead too."

Four men that quickly with but one shot? She did not argue

that Morgan's orders had been only to capture these men if possible. For Taluga, it had not been possible. She was only perversely grateful that his long pent-up anger at the whitebloods had not come against Morgan, Cal, or Lawrence. He had finally exploded against those who obviously would have been as happy to massacre people as birds if they thought it could turn them a pretty penny. And, after all, the men had guns on Taluga when he charged them.

Morgan ran from the thicket toward her. "I heard a shot and I don't know if Drummond's among the ones we have, so . . ." he said, then saw Taluga leaning over the four men on the ground.

"Taluga saved me and Curly," Abigail said. "They were going to shoot Taluga too. That's Edmund."

Morgan knelt and turned him faceup; Abigail looked only at Taluga's impassive countenance as the Indian stood.

"Finally, I see him face to face and he's dead," Morgan muttered. "But he brought it on himself. It's the fate he had planned for the birds and maybe all of us. I'd say that lead ball went into him from quite a distance and straight through, so it wasn't Curly from up there. Who got him?"

Abigail glanced up. The boy had righted himself and was coming slowly down the tree. Then *she* must have shot Edmund, she thought, for Curly did not fire and Taluga was so close.

"Taluga shoot him," the Seminole said. "Quick, fast. Abi-gail's bullet in tree over there, shake it, make birds fly."

Over Morgan's bent head, the Seminole's black eyes challenged Abigail to silence. Morgan turned Edmund facedown again. "He doesn't deserve to look up at the birds or the sky. Come on, Curly," he called to the boy, "we can use another gun to herd these plumers out onto the beach so we can send them off. Without their leader, we can always hope they won't return."

"Fashion plumes are so lucrative I'm afraid there will be other hunters," Abigail said hugging herself to stop her trembling. "But not here. And they will be stopped all over Florida legally instead of with traps and bullets next time, if I can help it!"

"Then, in the long run, they are doomed," Morgan said and embraced her. "Sweetheart, I'll be right back."

"I'm fine. I'll go tell the women and children all went—went well."

"Come on, Curly," Morgan said, "and we'll send someone

back to bury these trespassers who tried to kill a woman and a boy and met Seminole justice. Now, Taluga, all the wars are over and there will be *no more killing.*"

Morgan's eyes locked with the Seminole's. Taluga nodded stiffly before Morgan put his arm around Curly's shoulders and turned away. Taluga started to follow them, then spun back to Abigail again.

"Taluga long time killer inside here," he said and thumped his chest with his fist. "Abi-gail always healer in her heart," he added, his voice cracking on the last word. Swiftly, silently the leaves swallowed him.

Abigail looked down at Edmund again. In death, he seemed to have shrunk even smaller. She had feared him, hated him, been taken in by him again and again before she learned he was not to be trusted. Then finally, whatever Taluga said, she had killed Edmund before he could kill Curly or her birds.

No more killing, Morgan's final words echoed in her brain.

Good riddance that you're dead! she meant to spit out at Edmund, but no sound would come. After all, even with the bastard finally gone for good, the long nightmare of St. Kilda killing its own bairns could not end until not one died of infant tetanus. "No more killing!" she repeated Morgan's words instead of cursing Edmund.

Shaking so hard with mingled relief and anger that her teeth began to chatter, Abigail trudged away from the complaining cries of the birds.

20

'Tis the time to give to others,
Sharing the best we can be,
Talents, tenderness, and time,
Precious things once given me.

—JANIE NATTER
CHRISTMAS, 1872

Smiling with pride, sitting on her bed in a splash of afternoon sun, Abigail wrote in the new leather-bound diary Morgan had given her for Christmas. She copied Janie's hearthsong into it, the dearest gift the lass could have given her. After the first four lines, the song included verses dedicated to individual family members, listing things for which she was grateful.

Curly, Janie's husband, of course, headed her list. She had written and sung a verse to their year-old daughter Margaret Abigail Natter; verses for her two much younger half-siblings, Mary and Joshua Dane; ones to her mother and step-father; and a verse to her sad, silent Aunt Annie Gillies, who had come to live on Sanibel after ten years in a Glasgow prison. Although Corwin's lawyers' petition had finally freed Annie, she was not welcome on St. Kilda, even by her husband, Gavin. So she had come, another outcast, to her sisters-in-law Abigail and Margaret.

Janie had written and sung verses for Morgan, even old María and Paulo. But the best, in Abigail's opinion, had been the one to her, "my other mother, for what a lucky lass am I to have the best of both."

Having Curly and Janie with her over the years, Abigail mused as she closed the rich-smelling book, was *almost* like having her own children. Indeed, *almost* was a massive, ponderous word. Because the number of infant deaths on St. Kilda had dwindled to *almost* nothing and she had turned her energies to the struggle to save the Florida rookeries from extinction—a task which *almost* overwhelmed her in the storm of fervent feather fashion—she still knew *almost* was a huge word.

Shouts drifted in the window from the baseball match Morgan had organized in the recently enlarged clearing; Curly and Janie's new home had joined the other two houses there. Josh and Cal, Morgan's partners in the shipping firm, and Curly, the junior partner, had joined the fun outside. Morgan's mother, his sister Priscilla, her husband William, and their two children were here for a two-month visit from Baltimore, so they were either in the game or cheering everyone on. Though it was noisy outside, this was the first quiet time to herself Abigail had managed in days.

Even their latest guest, the staid Dr. Oscar Leighton, a famous Harvard ornithologist and author, here at Abigail's invitation, had been tugged along to play, probably so Morgan could pry more information from him about how to get his nearly finished book on warring civilizations published. The elderly scholar reminded her of dear Corwin, who had died last year of the lung disease that had plagued him since his rescue on St. Kilda. He had left her the half of his fortune it did not take to endow his museum. With their new wealth she and Morgan had funded a school for orphans in London, built up their shipping business, and sent a schoolteacher and doctor to St. Kilda, though, evidently few islanders heeded their advice.

Screams urging on a base runner pulled her from her thoughts again. How excited everyone sounded. She could pick out the voices of some of the children rescued from yellow fever eight years ago, who still lived on Sanibel. Abigail had tried but failed to trace their parents after the war. Only Sam, who was the overseer of the Key West warehouse, and Betty, who had wed Taluga's cousin and lived with the unconquered Seminoles deep in the mainland cypress swamps, had left the island. Ah, Abigail thought, if she did not feel so tired—and as if yesterday's big Christmas dinner still sat heavily in her—she would *almost* go outside and cheer everyone on.

She walked through the sprawling house they had increased by four rooms since Morgan's return. She fussed over her Christmas gifts from Curly: brightly hued tree orchids, fresh plucked figs, a big crock filled with honey. Though a grown man, he still loved to climb trees with his rope and harvest things from the heights, like any good St. Kilda cragsman. She supposed some would say these rooms were cluttered now, but Abigail only thought they were homey.

Homey. Yes, finally, she had a real home, she thought, for she had learned the hard way that home was security. It was the place you could be with those you loved, both family and friends. That knowledge was no doubt one of the things she had been searching for all along. St. Kilda was her homeland but not her home; England had been a necessary school for her, but had not captured her heart. Nor had St. Kilda at first, because she, as her mother had said once, had not suffered enough to recognize it for what it was.

"The way of things for women can be accepted—or defied— only with suffering." Yes, those were Glorious Glenna MacQueen's very words her daughter still treasured deep inside her. And then, as if to prove that was ever newly true, no matter what small victories a woman won in her life battles, Abigail saw Annie, in the corner of the parlor by the empty hearth, just sitting and staring as usual. For Annie, this blessed place of Abigail's was hardly home.

"Do you want to walk out with me, lass?" Abigail asked. "We dinna need to watch the fun if you'd rather stroll the shore." Unfortunately, the effect of all the children and happiness on Annie had seemed to sink her deeper in her private darkness. Her husband not only did not want her back but refused to join her in America; Mr. MacKay had decreed that Flora could keep Annie's daughter, who no doubt by now, knew no other mother anyway.

Annie just shrugged, then shook her head. Her gloom blew cold toward Abigail, who had tried everything to comfort her. The lass was willing to work with her hands but only at menial, mindless tasks helping old María; she would have nothing to do with the children, especially Janie's bairn. Abigail steeled herself to sit with her and try to draw her out again, but then she heard Margaret's anxious voice calling her from outside amid all the shouts and cheers. Instinct after all their years together had Abigail up and out the door by the time Margaret reached the verandah.

"Abby, 'tis a letter just came by mail boat from Key West, a letter from my mother!"

"At last!"

"'Tis by some else's hand, of course," Margaret went on, shaking as she opened the stiff envelope. "To think she's finally going to answer all those letters I wrote her. Maybe she forgives me, misses me. Oh, this is writ by the schoolteacher, Mr. Forbes, you sent there. And the thing is, my dear, she's included a wee note for ye at the bottom!"

"For me? I—read it to me, will you then?" Abigail asked as she saw Annie come to the door. But she merely stood on the other side, as if encased in the filmy shroud of cheesecloth nailed there.

Margaret began to read the entire letter aloud. Mairi Adair sent her love to her daughter and granddaughter—and Margaret's husband and wee ones. Mairi included news of Margaret's younger brothers and their families. Both lads had lost bairns to the eight-day sickness. The green sickness had plagued Mairi sore every spring and greatly weakened her. Hamish was hale and hearty, still busy at tasks. There was promise that Flora Nichol's eldest lad would become the next great cragsman of the isle, though, of course, Mairi noted, not as braw nor skilled as their own Douglas had once been.

"No, no one could be that," Abigail whispered. She saw Annie now pressed her nose to the screen at word of her sister Flora.

"Och, Abby, read me the rest," Margaret said and thrust the letter at her. "I'm going to cry like a bairn."

Abigail held it gingerly. Before she began to read, Morgan came up the steps, his damp, bronze forehead creased with worry. "Not more bad news from Tallahassee?" he asked.

"No, the illustrious elected politicians of our state are still not listening about the slaughtering of birds any more than they are in Washington," Abigail declared, "but they will!"

"'Tis from my mother," Margaret told him, swiping at her eyes with her sleeve. "Go on, lass."

" 'And I would have these final words for Abigail, whom you

have always chosen over me,' " Abigail began to read. Her voice, so strong at the mention of the feather trade, now trembled. She felt her stomach roll. She almost could not bear to face again the bitterness from Mairi that raked up the worst of the past. But she read on.

" 'Tell her, my daughter, that as I face the final—the final days of my life—' "

"That canna be!" Margaret insisted. "She said naught of such earlier, nary a word."

" 'Tell her,' " Abigail read, " 'that I realize I have blamed her for some things for which she was not guilty. And that I see now, despite her waywardness, she was trying to save the bairns. We were wrong to cast her out. 'Twas indeed the evil oil of the knee-women that killed our bairns and made us bitter against life—and against Abigail's daring to demand change, a young woman and poor Glenna's lass at that.' " Abigail paused to clear her throat before she read on.

" 'I have told the few foolish women who cling to the old ways to heed the doctor sent here, to heed the warnings of the Harris midwife the laird sent years ago—and heed the words of Abigail herself, no matter what Mr. MacKay still says of her. So, please tell Abigail, my Margaret, that your father at my bidding carved a bonny driftwood cross and put it on her mother's grave. I hope our blessed Savior in heaven will forgive me my blindness and biting tongue. Please ask the savior of the bairns, your friend Abigail, to forgive me too."

The words blurred before her; her voice shuddered to a sob. Morgan embraced her, then Margaret did. Abigail felt a huge weight lift from her chest. All these years of fearing for the bairns and their families, of desperately desiring to give her own bairn's death some meaning, of mourning that Mairi hated her as she had her mother before her—it was all over now.

"Another war won, but at great cost," Abigail said and lifted her eyes over Morgan's shoulder to see Annie no longer stood in the door. She whispered to the others she must go to her; she gave Margaret her letter and went inside. The lass stood, staring down into the empty hearth as she had earlier.

"All you've done—your sacrifices—are now vindicated too, Annie," Abigail told her, walking closer.

"Even my living child will never be mine." Annie spoke so quietly that Abigail had to strain to catch the words.

"Then you and I will love other children and manage together to—"

Annie whirled to her. Though Abigail rejoiced to see finally some emotion from her, blame and bitterness distorted the woman's fine features.

"Abigail Adair West, always seeing the best, always having all the answers," Annie taunted. "Well, why not? Ye have yer man and yer child!"

"Curly is not really mine. He only— "

"*Yer* child!" She accusingly pointed at Abigail's middle. "Are ye blind? Yer breeding! Dinna ye ken one of St. Kilda's murdering midwives would be able to spot it if ye canna! It's fine Mairi Adair forgave ye, for I never shall, with all this family warmth ye torment me with! Ye had best just let me rot in prison, for I deserved it—and this is worse!"

She spun away, dashed down the hall, and slammed her door.

Abigail stood frozen to the floor before the hearth, her heart pounding, her brain clinging to some of those frenzied words.

Her? Breeding? With child at age forty-two after all the years of loving with Morgan? Annie must be wrong, of course, and yet, what of the exhaustion lately, the feeling off her food? The lack of flux was nothing, but could it be?

She pressed her hands gently to her belly. Barely a slight swelling yet, but, could it be? On the very day she felt the bairns of St. Kilda would now live, could this be?

Should she tell Morgan yet, tell Margaret? After so many hopes blasted before, after all their prayers and the way they never even dared to whisper their wish for a child anymore, after all the bairns and nestlings she had tended over the years—could this be?

She grasped the mantel to steady herself as Morgan and Margaret came in. Suddenly, somehow, she knew that it was true, God's great gift to her for facing life, grander than any Seminole set of life beads. Even Annie's grief did not pierce her now—not yet.

"Are ye sure ye're all right, lass?" Margaret asked.

"Never better," Abigail declared, turning to face them. Her lower lip quivered; tears stung her eyes, but her voice was strong.

"There has never been a better day. Now sit, both of you, as I have a secret to share before we tell Morgan's family and the others."

"The sky over the gulf looks like pea soup," Morgan reported glumly as he came in the house five months later and bent to kiss Abigail before heading for the ship's barometer he kept on the wall.

"I knew there was a bad blow coming two days ago," Abigail told him, fanning herself even harder with her palmetto fan. "The birds always fly closer together when a storm's approaching, and Curly says the fish aren't biting. I will actually welcome the cooler air, as I'm not only eating for two but sweating for two!"

Her best reckoning was that she was six to eight weeks from bearing the child, but she wasn't really sure. Still, her and Margaret's calculations—for Annie refused to so much as comment on anything to do with delivering bairns these days—might be off the time of conception because of her erratic monthlies. They only knew she was not yet as big as she or Margaret had ever been when they delivered before. The ultimate heaviness which portended imminent birth was not with her yet.

"Dropping like a brick," Morgan said, staring at the barometer gauge, then tapping it to see if the needle jumped. "Taluga always says when the sawgrass blooms, head to high ground. I actually think this may be a bad one, And," he went on and came over to pull another chair close to hers to capture her hands in his, "with living through that Ohio hurricane during the war—"

"A hurricane here? Surely not!"

"If it is, it won't be the wind or rain that wreaks havoc as much as the storm surge of rising water that comes with it. And we can't take any chances having you trapped here in that condition."

"Or any of us in any condition. But after seeing all the worst storms here these eleven years, I canna believe it could be really bad. The beach sand gets moved around, a few trees bend or snap—"

"Don't argue with a sea captain and hurricane survivor on this, Abigail. We're going to lash down what we can and head for the mainland to sit this out. One of the plantations along the Caloosahatchee will take us in if we make it that far before all hell breaks loose. I'll tell Curly and Janie to take their brood, the other children, and go now. Meanwhile, I don't want you doing anything more strenuous than packing a few clothes and having María get us some food and water to last several days!"

Abigail sat rigid in her chair as he banged out the front door. For one moment she had wanted to tell him she would do whatever she thought was needed. She'd been through many a violent blow on St. Kilda to beat anything she'd seen here. Why, if the water rose as he was implying, there were many things she must care for before they fled!

But she knew he ordered her about because there was danger and he wanted to protect her. So she rose to obey, though her panicked mind raced over things she must do. She told the sullen Annie, staring out the window in her room, that they were going to flee the island and to go out and help María pack some food. Then she gathered clothing for Morgan, Annie, and herself in three bundles made from sheets. But in one, wrapped in oilcloth, she secreted Morgan's now completed manuscript and, in the other, the old diary she had kept since her youth and her latest correspondence with key state senators about making the feather trade unlawful.

She was relieved that Margaret, Cal, and their two youngest children were in Key West for the week. At least they were safe, unless the storm hit there too. She walked through the house, putting breakable things on the top of higher, heavier furniture. With ropes made from her twisted yarn, she lashed wooden pieces to door jams, hoping they would not float around. And then she felt the strangest, twisting pain low in her belly and leaned against the wall until it passed.

Surely, that could not be the bairn, not so soon! She slid down onto the floor where she was, breathing heavily, her heart thudding. She had been doing too much, not heeding Morgan's advice. She had simply twisted a muscle reaching and bending, that was all. But another grinding pain swept her, low in the back. And suddenly, just as the pelting rain began outside, she found herself sitting in a pool of her own water.

"Oh, no!" she cried. It was too early for this bairn. Could she flee the island if this child intended to be born? She rose on shaking legs and started for her bedroom. She heard the door bang and turned, expecting to see Morgan or Annie. Curly stood there, dripping wet, his blond curls plastered flat to his head.

"Morgan says Janie and I are to take the larger sailboat and get all ten children across to the mainland," he shouted to her. He came across the room in big strides, his shoes sloshing water. "We're loaded, but I had to say goodbye. Don't worry, Abigail, things will be fine here."

She knew if he realized she had begun labor, it would delay him. He might not even leave her, her braw protector all the years she was without Morgan. She kept her back to him so he would not see her wet skirt. She hugged him back hard when he put his arms around her. He was so tall and broadshouldered, her lanky, little London street lad.

"Hurry now," she said. "Take good care of them, and we'll see you soon." She managed a wave when he looked back at the door and then was gone. He passed Annie, coming in, carrying a sack of food. Leaning against the wall for support again, Abigail braced herself against the next onslaught. This one was not so bad, she told herself, though she slid to the floor again.

Annie put the sack down and dashed over, the fastest Abigail had seen her move in years. "Yer not having pangs, Abigail?"

"My water broke and much too early. Will you help me?"

"I'll clean you up, but you canna mean to help bring the child. I told ye I'd ne'er touch a birthing again. Margaret should be here like she said. I'll go fetch Janie back—"

"No!" Abigail said and grabbed Annie's skirt. "Let them go before the storm gets worse. You're a midwife, Annie, and I trust and need you."

Annie backed away, snatching her skirt from Abigail's grasp just as Morgan came in. He saw only Annie until he came closer.

"Blue blazes, Abigail!" he cried and bent to lift her.

" 'Tis the child. Oh, Morgan, I dinna do much, not enough to bring it early!" she insisted as he carried her into their room with Annie following behind.

"Dinna blame her, captain," Annie said. "Ye remember, Abigail, when bad blows came at home, lasses oft went into the throes early."

"That's it," Abigail said as Morgan put her in the chair and Annie bent to her trunk for fresh clothes. "Annie, remember, I even thought once a bairn coming early could be related to the sickness, but our records showed it only meant they sometimes had lungs too small to breathe or cry. They might die from that," her voice trembled now, "but that wasna the sickness."

"This is all we need!" Morgan muttered, a frown etching his worry lines deeper. "Dropping air pressure bringing a hurricane and an early baby. And, damn it, with Margaret and Janie gone. And I sent María and Paulo with Curly!"

"But," Abigail said and grasped Annie's wrist as she helped her change her garments, "I have a friend, an enlightened midwife right here."

"No!" Morgan said the same moment Annie shook her head. "After everything—how Annie feels—I can deliver the child, Abigail. She—with what happened with your first, she doesn't need to help here."

"He's right, lass, I shouldna and couldna," Annie insisted. "I as good as killed yer son, and I'll not turn a hand to being part of an early birth and have—"

"Stop it, both of you!" Abigail shouted. "If this bairn's ready to be born, that's the way of it. All of us together—the child will be all right. After everything, it has to be!"

Annie's face was still as stubborn as Morgan's was determined when the three of them left the house for the sailboat on the inland shore. Though it was midafternoon, it looked dark as night. Rain slanted needlelike from the northwest. Morgan helped Abigail walk and ended up carrying her; Annie bent like an old woman, toting food and the packs. Even before they made the beach, Abigail knew this was no ordinary storm: already the rain tasted of salt water as if the entire brew of sky and sea were churning.

Pine Island Sound, usually so placid, looked frenzied. Breakers crashed; wind howled. But Morgan was a good sailor, she tried to buck herself up. And she had faced rough seas before, even that day they rescued Corwin and Parker, the day she became the Heroine of the North, the Queen of Kilda. Now, she wanted none of those things, only for this child to be born safely and for her dear ones to survive the storm. Morgan lay her on the floor of the boat and covered her to her chin with the extra sail.

"Until we make land, Annie will have to tend you," he shouted. "I know sometimes it takes hours to bring a child. At least the wind is with us!"

Annie bent over her as they cast off, but soon had to bail. Abigail lay, tilting in the listing craft, jarred at each smack of wave as they made for the mainland. The voyage seemed endless; even Abigail was soon soaked. But she kept her eyes tightly shut to keep salt water out, to concentrate on feeling what was within her instead of without. She tried to send a silent message to her beloved unborn bairn: you will be all right . . . I will let no harm come to you.

But she could not believe this nightmare was real. Soon she would wake in her bed next to Morgan. She would turn to him in the steady calm of his strong arms; she would cradle her child in her embrace, this wee one she had yearned for so long who wanted to be with them so badly it came early.

The next pain made her thrash and rear up, even as tossed as she was. Annie pressed her shoulders down, saying something in the shriek of storm and pain. Abigail felt the child shift lower, pressing against her when she must keep it until they reached the safety of the land. All bairns came in their own good time, but this one seemed determined to come at the very worst time. And she would not lose it! She would not! Not ever again!

"The tide's gone way out!" Morgan's shout pierced her panic. "Pine Island's bigger than usual. That must mean a surge is coming. I'm going to put in here. We might not make the mainland, we'll have to put in here . . ."

Her thoughts roared through her like the wind. Pine Island. But that was another barrier island, she thought, though an inner one. Barrier islands were notoriously dangerous in a hurricane, Lawrence had told her that once, dear Lawrence, a famous artist now, wed only to his work. But, if this was a hurricane, would not they be caught in the storm surge here too? Or would her dear Sanibel shelter them, sacrifice itself to take the brunt of the storm? That is what poor Annie had done to save the bairns of Kilda . . . sacrifice . . . it was what she had done too, to live away and detested all those years in other storms.

And then Taluga's words Morgan had repeated earlier today came to her: the Seminoles headed for high ground in a severe storm. She recalled that when Cal lived on Pine Island, his camp was built on a palmetto hammock, and Lawrence had fled there when the Union navy attacked Punta Rassa. She had never seen it, but Curly had told her where it was, standing above the low, grassy plain like a small, high island.

"Morgan, I know where there is high land here—a palmetto hammock."

"Where?" he cried and she told him as best she could. He tied the boat with anchor ropes to the two biggest trees he could find, giving it enough slack to ride the onslaught. Bent against the roaring blackness and stinging water, Annie and Morgan, holding Abigail between them, stumbled inland for what seemed hours, all huddling on their knees when a spasm wracked her. They waded through wild rivulets of rain, slogged through soft sand while water rose higher and higher as if chasing them. Finally, they lay her on the open, leeward slant of the hammock, for taking shelter under the creaking, thrashing trees in Cal's old camp was too dangerous. Under screaming skies, Morgan bent over her to try to break the whip of wind. Annie knelt, her blond, wet hair streaming, holding her hand as salt water lapped nearly at their feet. They could go a bit higher, but not without danger from falling trees.

"This bairn's coming, lass," Abigail cried in a slight lull. "You must help me, help Morgan!"

"I said I canna. I killed yer first! I killed other bairns and then my grandmother! I can see the look on her face when I raised that stone bowl, Abigail! Murderers canna bring life!"

"And I killed Edmund, but it was because he was going to murder Curly and the birds! Yes, Morgan, 'tis I shot him no matter what Taluga said! Annie, you only struck Isobel to save the bairns! And now I want you to help me save mine!"

As the pains crowded closer, Abigail was not sure what Annie or Morgan said or did. She felt broken, bearing down to bring the child; through agonizing moments, with Morgan's desperate voice in her ear, she prayed this early child would live. Why must it always be this way for her, to live in blasts and battles with people howling at her, beating her down like this? But Morgan's hands were strong on her. His voice muted the shrieking sounds, some of which must be her own. And then she knew that Annie was helping too.

After an eternity of black noise, it went strangely, suddenly silent all around Abigail.

"The eye of the storm," she heard Morgan say to Annie.

"When I went through a hurricane in prison, the aftermath of the eye was worse than the rest."

"Someday," Annie said, "will ye tell me how it was for ye in prison?"

"Yes—of course, if you want."

"I sometimes fear the memories will never leave me, but perhaps, I can bury them with new ones . . ."

Later, Abigail opened her eyes and stared straight up at a clear blue sky. "Is it over?" she asked.

Morgan and Annie looked surprised she had spoken. She must have slept; perhaps she had fainted.

"Not quite yet, for ye either," Annie told her as a piercing pain pounded her again.

And then, even with sun warming them through a high hole in the clouds like a giant eye staring down, Abigail pushed all the pain away. And when she opened her eyes again, Annie held in her hands a wee, wet, limp lass, a reddish-gold–haired bairn.

Morgan looked awed; Annie cried and smiled at the same time. The child did not move.

"Is she all right?" Abigail demanded. "Is she breathing?"

And then, as if waiting for her mother's voice, the bairn flailed her little legs and opened her mouth and wailed.

"Aye, she's all right, and ye will be too!" Annie promised and handed Abigail the hastily wrapped bairn while she cared for the rest.

"Tiny, that she is, but she's going to live!" Abigail vowed, while Morgan huddled close.

"She's going to flourish despite adversity, like her mother!" he declared, but tears still ran down his cheeks to mingle with the crusted salt water there.

When the other side of the storm came through from the opposite direction, the sea surge rose and roiled again. Now that some of the trees were down overhead, they moved to higher ground, then to the other side of the hammock to blunt the battering wind. Morgan and Annie sheltered Abigail who in turn made a safe haven for the child. The bairn slept through the next two hours of screaming fury and gave them all courage. Perhaps, Abigail thought, next to being born, a full-fledged hurricane was nothing.

Day blurred with night. Finally, the storm stopped and all was silence again.

"Can we go home now?" Abigail asked, emerging from the sleep of exhaustion she had fallen into after nursing the child.

"If there's a home left to go to," Morgan said and stood and stretched from his huddled position. "At last, the water's going down fast."

He shaded his eyes to survey the ruin of this area; Abigail saw him shudder, obviously to think what awaited them on Sanibel farther out in the gulf.

"The three of you—your family," Annie said and warmed Abigail with the glow of her smile, "surely if ye're all together, anywhere can be home."

"I canna thank you enough for delivering my child, my dear," Abigail told her, then whispered, "even though Morgan helped too. The bairn's middle name is Annie, Morgan and I decided weeks ago, should she be a lass. Glenna Annie, and, just like I've been to Margaret's Janie, you will be a second mother to her."

"A godmother, a *ghosti*, like on St. Kilda?" Annie asked.

"Not exactly, for we make our own traditions here in America. Not her *ghosti*, but her other mother until you find a man and have a bairn of your own. Life goes on, Annie, so 'tis best to face it boldly. Margaret and I can tell you, that we can."

The wind picked up again, a bit of fitful rain still fell when they set foot on the ravaged beach of Sanibel. Drowned deer studded the scoured shore; porpoise swam where there was land before. Morgan carried Abigail and Annie carried the child up what had once been the shell path toward the clearing. Curly and Janie and the others were not back yet, but they had farther to come.

Ropes of sodden beach sand were strewn across the clearing and the gardens. The scent of broken leaves and flowers lay heavy and damp, even when the rain and wind finally stopped. Palm fronds that had not been torn away shivered in shreds. Trees were snapped off, twisted, or bent like matchsticks crushed under a giant's shoe. Abigail recognized a piece of Margaret's wedding dress flapping like a flag in a tree, but did not point it out. Morgan put her down, and she took the baby from Annie; they all just stood and stared.

The outbuildings were gone but for the chicken coop with a few squawking hens caught sideways high in one of the remaining trees. Furniture from Curly's house, closest to the gulf, haphazardly littered the yard. The walls of the main house still stood, but the added rooms were atilt off their foundations. The verandah steps were stuck in a tree. The entire roof was ripped away. Even the chimney had collapsed into a pile of rubble. A tree trunk like a battering ram had smashed through the front door. The grove looked ravaged; crops were washed away from gardens. Water had flowed through like a river, four feet deep, shifting things, dropping things, drowning things, leaving a thin coating of crusty salt everywhere, including in the house when they peeked inside.

"If that sea salt's leached into the soil," Morgan said, sounding utterly exhausted, "we'll have to plow down to get some good from it."

"We will," Abigail declared. "And when we rebuild the house, perhaps we can add a schoolroom. Our Glenna as well as Janie and Margaret's brood will be needing it on days where 'tis too windy or rainy on the verandah. I want them to go to London and St. Kilda with us next year too, but when they're not traveling, they'll have to get their lessons here."

Even when Curly and Janie brought the others back, after the initial glad greetings and joyous surprise of the newborn bairn, they all stood in silent awe, feeling stunned, insignificant, afraid.

"At least," Curly said with false bravado, "it's blown those dev'lish biting bugs clear to Soho!" For once, no one laughed.

He climbed the tree to rescue the hens; María and Janie fixed a meager meal they ate sitting on the hard, damp verandah floor. Still, they spoke little. Abigail noted that only Annie managed a smile as she rocked her little namesake in her arms after Abigail nursed her.

But then, overhead as the sun set beyond their makeshift camp, they heard the familiar sounds of the rookery birds coming home to roost. On Morgan's arm, holding her daughter, Abigail stood, looking upward into the fading sky.

"Thank God, they survived," she said. "I thought they got

blown to bits or wouldna return since Curly says the rookery trees are devastated."

"Maybe they don't know it yet and will leave," Morgan said.

"No. My braw, bonny birds will stick it out. They know we have much work to do to make it a safe home for them here, but they are not afraid."

Morgan shook his head in wonderment at her words, but he held her close.

As ever, the birds came sailing in, strings of lights against the darkening night, flying farther apart now as if to assure the mere humans below that the storm was over. Apparently exhausted, complaining, they wheeled looking for their traditional trees. When they didn't find them, they settled on the few ragged ones just beyond the clearing, closer to the house. On new territory, they bickered, preened, shook their tattered feathers, some in pairs or groups and some alone. But all together.

" 'Black night may be,' " Abigail whispered the old St. Kilda hearthsong to Morgan and her bairn, " 'but here are we, outward bound and ready for the dawn.' "

AUTHOR'S NOTE

St. Kilda was evacuated by the British government in 1930 when life there became too arduous for the remaining thirty-six inhabitants. The St. Kildans had been exempted from the 1869 Act of Preservation of Sea Birds so that they could continue to harvest fowl in their traditional way, but the lure of the mainland and harsh times defeated this unique culture.

Today, few people visit the island unless they are volunteer work crews to keep up the cleits and cottages, staff of the British Army St. Kilda radar station, or ornithologists with special permission. However, in 1986, UNESCO named St. Kilda a World Heritage site, added to a list of such eminent places as Stonehenge, the Taj Mahal, the Pyramids, and the Grand Canyon, where thousands visit yearly. Perhaps someday, regular tourists trips can be arranged to St. Kilda. Or, as the Victorian invasion of St. Kilda in this story suggests, St. Kilda might best be left untouched by masses of tourists, a far isles shrine to other people and times.

Although unable to do on-site research there, I have tried to keep my story true to St. Kildan events and traditions as recorded in books and articles. I was able to visit a Hebridean black house at the Highland Village Museum in Iona, Nova Scotia. Unfortunately, the sad things about St. Kilda are often worse than I have portrayed them. The 1861 Census records that only two islanders could speak English (they spoke Gaelic), and only two could sign their names. The first schoolmaster actually arrived there in 1884, some years later than in my story. And the island's rampant infant tetanus was only eradicated in the 1890s after a long battle between mainland medical experts and the island's powerful knee-women. As late as 1877, a visiting nurse was told, "If it is God's will that babies should die, nothing you can do will save them." (From Francis Thompson's book, *St. Kilda and Other Hebridean Outliers*, 1931.) Besides his dictatorial governing of the island, the minister John MacKay was infamous for his "uncrowned queen" (his housekeeper) and for throwing books off the cliff which were donated for the island's children.

In the London section of the story, the slum called the rookery actually existed. I based the Victorians' adulation of Abigail as "Virtue Victorious" on the true story of an 1838 sea rescue by a Farne Isles young woman named Grace Darling. The Victorians lionized Miss Darling, ignoring the fact her lighthouse keeper father had been at the helm of the rescue boat. The Duke and Duchess of Manchester are historic figures, as is Skittles. The indomitable Louisa, after being Lord Hartington's mistress for some thirty years, was widowed and finally wed him. As he was then Eighth Duke of Devonshire, Louisa became known as the Double Duchess. Although Queen Victoria was heard to tell her heir that the duchess was "not a fit companion for you," the Prince and Princess of Wales remained her close friends.

I must note that, for the sake of simplicity and effect, I have changed or omitted several minor facts. The name St. Kilda actually designates the grouping of several islands and stone stacks; the main island that contains Village Bay and Gleann Mor is often called Hirta. At Kimbolton Castle, Pelligrini's painted Greek goddesses adorn the ceiling above the grand staircase instead of the ballroom. On Punta Rassa during the Civil War, Jake Summerlin had a partner named James McKay and their blockade runner was called the *Scottish Chief,* but I thought two men with the name MacKay/McKay and a boat with a Scottish name in Florida would be confusing.

The ravaging of the plume bird rookeries is all too true. After the Civil War, feather prices continued to climb, and in 1886 the plume industry employed 83,000 people in the United States. It was not until several men were murdered guarding the rookeries that conservationists got protective legislation passed. Even then, the birds were saved more by the passing of that fashion fad than by hunters and plumers obeying the law.

I am very grateful to my friend Marnie McCall, Audubon member and docent at the Corkscrew Swamp Bird Sanctuary, Naples, Florida, for help in finding facts on the plume trade. The National Audubon Society has a booklet entitled *Outrage to Action: The Story of the National Audubon Society,* which explains the entire anti–plume trade battle. Also, I would like to note that there is now a Wildlife Refuge, administered by the Department of the Interior, near the site of Abigail's fictional rookery on Sanibel.

Johnson's Island can be visited today, just off Sandusky, Ohio, in Lake Erie. It is marked only by a cemetery of Confederate dead, a monument, and two signs describing the prison. I found additional information on that place from Edmund DeWitt Patterson's diary *Yankee Rebel,* an eyewitness account of terrible times. Colonel Hill was an actual figure; the hurricane there—like the 1873 hurricane on Sanibel—really happened.

I would like to give special thanks for support and advice to my editor, Hilary Ross, and her assistant, Danielle Perez; publicists, Jennifer Marcus and Tina Salerno; my enthusiastic agent and avid birder, Meg Ruley, who encouraged me as I wrote this story; and, of course, as ever, to my husband, Don Harper, who does double duty as business manager and proofreader, who also copes with a writer who is often mentally mired in the past.

I am also grateful to people who assisted me with my Florida research: the docents at the Sanibel Island Historical Museum; the Heritage Day Living History staff at the Collier County Museum; and Gary Bryant, an historic-arms gunsmith, at Firearms Unlimited, Naples, Florida. If there are any mistakes in research for the story, they are mine and not those of these people who generously shared their expertise.

—KAREN HARPER